MURDER WEARS
A HIDDEN FACE

Books by Rosemary Simpson

WHAT THE DEAD LEAVE BEHIND

LIES THAT COMFORT AND BETRAY

LET THE DEAD KEEP THEIR SECRETS

DEATH BRINGS A SHADOW

DEATH, DIAMONDS, AND DECEPTION

THE DEAD CRY JUSTICE

DEATH AT THE FALLS

MURDER WEARS A HIDDEN FACE

Published by Kensington Publishing Corp.

MURDER WEARS A HIDDEN FACE

ROSEMARY SIMPSON

KENSINGTON
PUBLISHING CORP.

www.kensingtonbooks.com

KENSINGTON BOOKS are published by

Kensington Publishing Corp.
119 West 40th Street
New York, NY 10018

All Kensington titles, imprints and distributed lines are available at special quantity discounts for bulk purchases for sales promotion, premiums, fund-raising, educational or institutional use. Special book excerpts or customized printings can also be created to fit specific needs. For details, write or phone the office of the Kensington Special Sales Manager: Kensington Publishing Corp., 119 West 40th Street, New York, NY, 10018. Attn. Special Sales Department. Phone: 1-800-221-2647.

K with book logo Reg. US Pat. & TM Off.

Library of Congress Card Catalogue Number: 2023941650

ISBN: 978-1-4967-4106-6
First Kensington Hardcover Edition: December 2023

ISBN: 978-1-4967-4109-7 (ebook)

10 9 8 7 6 5 4 3 2 1

Printed in the United States of America

Be it enacted by the Senate and House of Representatives of the United States of America in Congress assembled . . . That the importation into the United States of women for the purposes of prostitution is hereby forbidden.

Page Act, March 3, 1875
Signed into law by President Ulysses S. Grant

Be it enacted by the Senate and House of Representatives of the United States of America in Congress assembled . . . That from and after the expiration of ninety days next after the passage of this act, and until the expiration of ten years next after the passage of this act, the coming of Chinese laborers to the United States be . . . suspended; and during such suspension it shall not be lawful for any Chinese laborer to come, or having so come after the expiration of said ninety days to remain within the United States.

That hereafter no State court or court of the United States shall admit Chinese to citizenship; and all laws in conflict with this act are hereby repealed.

Chinese Exclusion Act, May 6, 1882
Signed into law by President Chester A. Arthur

CHAPTER 1

Ten years after the Metropolitan Museum of Art moved into its new building at Fifth Avenue and Eighty-second Street, a wealthy widower bequeathed his trove of Chinese artifacts dating back to the Ming Dynasty that ruled China during the early European Middle Ages. Each item had been painstakingly and expensively acquired over years of dedicated collecting.

To celebrate the donation, Luigi Palma di Cesnola, the Met's first and current director, announced a special exhibition of the exquisite porcelains, rare jades, cloisonné enamels, and intricately embroidered silks, timing the event to coincide with the appointment of a new cultural attaché to the Chinese embassy in Washington, D.C. Westernized by years of residence in London, Lord Peng Tha Mah, arriving in New York City in February 1891, agreed that his wife, son, and two daughters would also grace the opening ceremonies with their presence.

Invitations had gone out to the museum's board of trustees and patrons, all of whom figured prominently in New York society, though not every benefactor could be counted among Mrs. Astor's Four Hundred. The event would open with a reception in the glass-roofed gallery where the collection was on display, followed by luncheon for a select group of the museum's deepest pocketed and most influential sponsors. Catered by Delmonico's, the menu was a masterpiece of dishes made famous by the celebrated restaurant, a gastronomic triumph designed to eclipse anything London or Washington had to offer. Nothing to equal di Cesnola's extravaganza had ever been mounted at the museum.

Security was adequate, though not as tight as the Pinkerton National Detective Agency would have provided. Geoffrey Hunter counted only a handful of uniformed gallery attendants stationed at key points in the exhibition hall, regular museum employees by their demeanor. The fit of their jackets told him that none of them was armed.

"Not the way you would have done it," Prudence MacKenzie commented, pale gray eyes following her partner's scan of the room.

"I haven't been a Pinkerton in charge of something like this in years," he reminded her. "But you're right. The director seems to have cut budgetary corners exactly where he shouldn't have. Very careless for a man who understands firsthand how tempting artifact theft is. Every archaeological dig I've ever heard of is bedeviled by looters and forgers. He should know better."

"Delmonico's is expensive," Prudence murmured, drifting from Geoffrey's side toward a display of brilliantly colored silks. The exhibit was stunning, but she couldn't help wondering if the wide-sleeved robes wouldn't be uncomfortably heavy and unwieldy. Ladies' corsets and her own fashionable Worth gown were difficult enough to maneuver in, but they didn't appear to be nearly as cumbersome. Still, she supposed women the world over got used to whatever idiocy fashion dictated. By the display explanations she was reading, it seemed that Chinese noblemen burdened themselves with robes that were even more ostentatious and elaborate than those of their spouses and concubines.

"They take your breath away, don't they?" Josiah Gregory's vest was a match for anything he was admiring in the glass cases around the room's walls. Its vividly colored embroidered peacocks had caught more than one admiring male eye. Josiah's suits might be a gentlemanly black, his shirts blindingly white, but his vests had always been a feast of extravagant showmanship.

He hadn't asked how Miss Prudence had wangled him a ticket to the reception. It was enough to remember that her late father, Judge Thomas Pickering MacKenzie, had been a prominent member of the Met's board of trustees and a generous patron of the city's arts. She might have scandalized society by eschewing a suitable marriage to pursue a career in law and detection, but the MacKenzie family name guaranteed that no one would exclude her, including the redoubtable Caroline Astor.

Josiah's admiration for his employer was nearly boundless. It was matched only by his loyalty to her partner, the Southern-born plantation owner's son who had abandoned his heritage and established himself in the North. Any day now, Josiah hoped, their on-again, off-again, undeclared courtship would blossom into the passionate wooing he'd thought it should have been from the beginning. He was losing patience with the elaborate dance that appeared to be going nowhere but around in circles. He stroked the silk threads of his vest as he contemplated what a Hunter-MacKenzie marriage might look like.

Prudence smiled at her secretary, thinking how much Josiah resembled the peacocks on his vest, proud birds whose tails could swirl open to reveal hidden depths of color and the startling pattern of unsuspected eyes.

Being surrounded by the wealth, beauty, and artistic glory of a foreign culture was a soothing invitation to set aside the complexities and raw ugliness of the investigative work she and Geoffrey routinely took on. They were between active cases at the moment, though, as Josiah had reminded her that morning, there were several possibilities simmering. Hunter and MacKenzie, Investigative Law, had the distinction of being able to pick and choose its clientele. Lately, now that Prudence had been admitted to the bar, she'd leaned toward considering inquiries that promised intriguing legal components, but she'd yet to step inside a courtroom. Women's progress toward greater equality was slow and faltering. Men fought it at every opportunity.

She thought there must be several hundred guests in the gallery and the two smaller adjoining rooms where display cases featured exquisite enamels and glazed ceramics. Most of the attendees knew one another, New York society being both closed to outsiders and tribal in its makeup. The museum's patrons murmured polite greetings as they glided slowly and gracefully to the whisper of the ladies' skirts and the occasional tap of a gentleman's walking stick. Not unlike dancers in a sequence of well-orchestrated quadrilles.

"Geoffrey, look," Prudence said, directing his attention toward a tall, familiar-looking figure just entering the gallery. A slender young woman clung to his arm as if in need of support. "Isn't that Warren Lowry?"

"You're right. I thought he and Bettina were in Switzerland."

At the end of May, nearly nine months ago, Geoffrey and Prudence had seen Lowry and his fragile sister off on a journey that would take them to a sanitorium near Geneva where damaged minds were said to be healed through a new and controversial treatment known as the talking cure. Bettina had been the victim of a cruel kidnapping and two years of unspeakably evil abuse. Whether she would ever recover had been unknown, but Lowry, who had joined the New York City Police Department as a detective in hopes of finding her, had refused to admit defeat.

As if he felt Prudence's gaze, Warren Lowry turned from the display case of jade earrings and necklaces that had attracted his sister's attention. His eyes swept the room in the measured, searching scan familiar to every good investigator. It touched briefly on the flamboyantly vested Josiah, lingered for a moment to assess Geoffrey, then settled on Prudence. He smiled and dipped his head in a greeting that was scrupulously polite and impersonal, yet also intensely private. Intimate, as though no one else were in the exhibition hall but they two.

He touched Bettina's elbow lightly, spoke quietly to her, then folded her arm into his and steered her across the broad expanse of the gallery. She walked with the slow, deliberate steps of someone newly restored to health, head tilted downward to avoid the inspection of curious onlookers. Her experience, though never trumpeted in the city's newspapers, had been widely hinted at in the discreet gossip that kept society informed of its members' indiscretions and peccadillos. A sudden departure for Europe was always grist for the scandal mill.

"I don't think you've met the other member of our firm. This is Josiah Gregory," Prudence said, introducing him.

An awkward silence followed the initial greetings. Bettina didn't raise her eyes from their contemplation of the floor. Geoffrey and Lowry exchanged the briefest of handshakes.

Josiah assessed the situation with one keen glance; he was familiar with Bettina's abduction and eventual rescue from the reports Geoffrey and Prudence had filed. Prudence's account of how she came to seek Warren Lowry's help when Geoffrey was still recovering from near-fatal bullet wounds had been less detailed, but Josiah had long experience reading between the lines of the documents that landed on his desk.

Lowry had been one of New York City's most eligible bachelors before his sister's disappearance and his own withdrawal from society to devote all his energies to finding her. The months spent in the Swiss mountains had burnished his skin with a skier's tan and brightened the silver streaks in his blond hair. He was still wealthy, unmarried, and as handsome as the devil. Josiah suspected that the latent attraction between the ex-detective and Miss Prudence would spark back into life unless Mr. Hunter did something to tamp it down. Right away.

He stepped back from the foursome, the better to listen and observe.

"We met Lord Peng and his family aboard ship," Lowry said. "Lady Peng and her elder daughter seldom left their cabin, but Bettina struck up an acquaintance with the younger girl. Peng Mei Sha. The Chinese introduce themselves with the family name first, then the given name," he explained. "It emphasizes one of the essential facets of their culture, an intense loyalty and responsibility to blood kin that is quite remarkable."

"How wonderful for you, Bettina," Prudence said. "Atlantic crossings can be dreary without an agreeable companion to help while away the time. And the voyage can be uncomfortable in January and February when the seas are rough and the winds high."

"Mei Sha is a few years older than I am," Bettina said, finally raising her head to look at Prudence. "She went to an English boarding school for a while, but also had a governess. Her English is impeccable." She paused for a moment, as if deciding what else she should reveal about her Chinese friend. "Her brother is even more westernized. He studied engineering at the Royal Naval College in Portsmouth. Peng Fa Cho. His English friends called him Johnny. Mei wrote her name as May when she was at school. That's short for Mary, but she's not a Christian." Bettina fell silent, her eyes drifting downward again.

"I assume you'll be attending the luncheon," Lowry said. He patted Bettina's arm softly, as if to congratulate her on having contributed to the conversation.

"We will," Prudence answered. She'd hesitated about accepting the invitation, but now was glad she had.

"And how goes the investigation business?" Lowry turned

from Prudence to Geoffrey. "I'm not sure I ever thanked you properly for what you did for Bettina. Without your ex-Pinks, we might not have succeeded in freeing her."

"We're on hiatus at the moment," Geoffrey said, not adding that they had more prospective clients than time to take on all their cases. He was watching Lowry with the concentration of one man absorbed in figuring out another. He had no proof of it, but he was certain in his own mind that Bettina's brother had deliberately burned down the mansion where his sister had been held captive, assuring that the guilty parties sheltering in the basement would not escape. Lowry had never expressed remorse or regret for killing them.

"Something worthy of your talents is bound to come along."

Prudence had been contemplating attending law school or sitting for the bar without formal study when Lowry and Bettina sailed for Europe. It was a step Lowry had encouraged her to take, yet so far, he'd steered the conversation away from anything personal.

"I think they're coming now," Josiah said, interrupting the faltering exchange.

General Luigi Palma di Cesnola was a portly man in his late fifties, distinguished by the military bearing he'd never abandoned and a pair of distinctively thick white mustaches. He'd been a subject of controversy ever since his appointment as director of the museum, but he'd survived accusations of tampering with the Cypriot artifacts he'd excavated and subsequently sold to the Met, multiple complaints to the board of trustees, and a suit for libel. He insisted on being addressed as General, even though the commission to brigadier at the end of the war had been sidetracked by Lincoln's assassination. In his own mind, di Cesnola would always be a distinguished American war hero awarded the Medal of Honor. He could do no wrong, no matter what others thought. Few people found him easy to get along with.

Flanking di Cesnola were two museum guards who fanned

out to clear a path through the throng of guests as Lord Peng and his party made their appearance. China's cultural attaché was as splendidly dressed as any of the mannequins in the exhibit, enveloped from head to foot in emerald-green silk and sunrise-yellow satin. Like di Cesnola, Lord Peng wore a set of swooping mustaches, but his were paired with a long, wispy, triangular shaped beard. He carried a fan and stepped lightly in embroidered satin shoes soled in a thick layer of soft leather, wide sleeves like wings greeting the spectators who were spellbound at the sight of such magnificence.

Behind him marched his son, Peng Fa Cho, a young man in his twenties, also clad in the traditional robes of the Chinese nobility, but whose expression of lively curiosity signaled that this member of the family was at ease in the Western world, curious to explore its possibilities and eager to understand its inhabitants.

Following the son processed the women, Lady Peng first, then her daughters.

Every female in the room stared at Lady Peng's feet, tiny appendages shod in sharply pointed, high-heeled embroidered red satin. A shoe not quite four inches long. Those who had read about the odd Chinese custom of breaking and binding their women's feet expected her to mince, totter, shuffle, or hobble, but the attaché's wife glided across the floor with fluid grace. The eldest daughter also approached on tiny feet with unnaturally high arches, but the younger girl wore shoes that would have fit any of her Western counterparts. No one knew why.

General di Cesnola guided Lord Peng and his entourage through the exhibition, smiling, nodding, pointing out the highlights of the collection. Lord Peng was reputed to speak excellent English, but he had chosen to be accompanied today by a translator who murmured softly in Chinese, then conveyed the attaché's words loudly enough to be heard by most of those standing closest to the distinguished visitor. The translator's English was accurate, though so heavily accented it brought frowns of concentration to the foreheads of his listeners.

Prudence, standing beside Bettina, caught Mei Sha's glance in their direction, Bettina's answering smile, and the quick flick of her friend's finger. No expression marred the stillness of the Chinese girl's features, but Bettina gave a barely audible chuckle.

"The family is staying at the Fifth Avenue Hotel," she said. "I was able to get a note delivered to their suite as soon as I found out Warren and I had been invited to the luncheon. They're leaving for Washington tomorrow or the next day, but her father has promised that I'll be welcome to visit once they're settled."

"That will be wonderful," Prudence agreed.

"She doesn't know," Bettina whispered. "About what happened to me. And she's too polite to ask why my face looks the way it does."

"It's hardly noticeable," Prudence lied. Bettina's eyebrows and eyelashes had been plucked by her abductors, doll-like arcs tattooed on. Her skin had been artificially whitened, cheeks and lips died a bright crimson. Months of treatment in the Swiss clinic had included removing or lightening the cosmetic enhancements that had turned a once lovely face into a distorted facsimile of natural beauty. "Perhaps with the passage of time . . ."

"The doctors were very kind, but they didn't try to hide the truth from me. It *will* get better, but I'll never be exactly as I was before."

Prudence thought Geoffrey was about to reassure Bettina that he found her nearly perfect, but then he stiffened and took a step forward, eyes fixed on what appeared to be an unplanned interruption. She saw his hand stray toward where he usually wore a concealed holster. Not today.

A thin man dressed in dark blue trousers, frogged jacket, and round cap was making his way through the mix of Chinese guests, museum officials, and members of the board of trustees. They parted to let him pass, he, in turn, bowing and begging their forgiveness and indulgence for disturbing their important selves. Something consequential, an urgent message, to impart to the Lord Peng. It couldn't wait.

He brushed past Lady Peng and her daughters, kept several feet away from the son, then, as he reached Lord Peng's side, pulled a wide-bladed knife from his sleeve. A stray beam of sunlight through the arched glass roof caught the steel and flashed like lightning. But soundless.

The knife disappeared into the folds of Lord Peng's emerald-and-yellow gown, spouting gouts of bright red blood as the assassin plunged it into the attaché's body. The arm in the dark blue jacket rose and fell, striking again and again, the sun glaring off the blade with every blow. Without a word or cry, Lord Peng crumpled to the floor, blood pooling across his chest and onto the back-and-white tiles.

For a moment no one moved except the spectators who were too far away to see what was happening.

Then a shrill scream pierced the hush, Lord Peng's daughters wailed, and the dead man's two bodyguards leaped toward their master, guns drawn and pointed at the figure streaking toward the far archway where the gallery opened onto the museum's foyer. Cloakroom, ticket booth, a pair of heavy wooden doors opening onto Central Park and Fifth Avenue.

They shouted something in Chinese, but no one understood what they were yelling, so no one got out of their way, no one crouched to avoid a bullet. The bodyguards ran through the crowd of guests, shoving and pushing aside New York City's most distinguished citizens. Within moments they'd disappeared from sight.

In the appalled silence, the gunshots echoing in the high-ceilinged foyer at the Fifth Avenue entrance were as rapid and loud as the clacking wheels of the city's elevated trains. The bodyguards emptied their pistols, the bullets thwacking into walls and ricocheting off the marble floor.

Like Geoffrey, General di Cesnola had instinctively reached for a gun he was not wearing, then shouted orders at the museum attendants who were also unarmed. Lacking training to act as guards and confused by the director's contradictory commands, they milled about uncertainly, succeeding only in further alarming the crowd. The Chinese physician who had traveled with Lord Peng and was also on his way to the embassy in Washington fell to his knees beside the attaché's body, deft hands checking pulse points where he was already certain he would find no throb of life.

When General di Cesnola touched him on the shoulder, the doctor shook his head and closed the eyes that stared upward but saw nothing.

Geoffrey and Warren Lowry exchanged looks.

They moved together toward Lord Peng's family, reaching them just as Lady Peng gathered her daughters into her outstretched arms.

Peng Fa Cho stepped forward, his face contorted with shock, anger, and grief.

"Mr. Lowry?" he asked, looking from Warren to Geoffrey and back again. "Who would do this? Did someone order my father's death?"

"We'll find out," Lowry promised, ignoring the fact that he was no longer a member of the New York City Police Department's Detective Bureau. Hadn't been for the past nine months. "I promise you. We'll find him, whoever he is."

Lowry turned to Prudence and Geoffrey.

"You've blood on your skirt," he said matter-of-factly, pointing to the faint spray of red across the hem of Prudence's pale gray dress. "As a favor to me, will you take the case?"

CHAPTER 2

Director di Cesnola sent one museum attendant running outside to find a beat cop, another to telephone Mulberry Street Police Headquarters. The reporters assigned to cover the opening of the exhibition took out their pads and pencils, scribbling notes and elbowing their way through the crowd to ask questions and get a better look at the blood-soaked corpse. One of them, who freelanced as a sketch artist, had nearly finished a preliminary drawing when the Chinese bodyguards returned with their emptied revolvers.

There wasn't time to wait for the police to arrive.

Leaving Prudence to see to Bettina and the attaché's youngest daughter, while the son comforted his mother and other sister, Geoffrey and Lowry reached the museum's lobby area before the huge central doors had swung shut behind the man sent to locate a beat cop. A dusting of fresh snow had covered the ground overnight, but the morning's foot traffic had churned it into icy, muddy slush. Street sweepers who usually mounded horse dung into steaming piles in the roadway were brushing the walkways clean.

With a nod to signal agreement, Lowry turned into Central

Park, and Geoffrey struck off across Fifth Avenue where rows of brownstones were interspersed between the mansions, apartment houses, and luxurious hotels that had sprung up when lower Fifth no longer had room for expansion.

It had been years since either of them had done basic foot reconnaissance, but lessons well learned are never forgotten. There was no telling in which direction the man in the blue jacket and trousers had run, so the two most likely possibilities had to be explored. Few pedestrians strode the sidewalks opposite Central Park and the museum, but here and there servants swept front steps and areaways, polished brass doorknobs, and walked pampered pets. Someone running for his life would be noticed, even if he slowed to a walk after leaving the museum's immediate area. Especially if he still clutched a bloody knife in his hand.

Three blocks into his search, Geoffrey knew the man hadn't run in that direction. No one had seen him, and the description he gave raised eyebrows. There were no Chinese living in this part of the city, no Chinese servants employed by hotels or householders. He was usually only a few sentences into his description before the individual he was questioning shook his head and walked away.

His last stop before turning back was at the small and very select apartment hotel where he'd briefly considered renting rooms before deciding on the far grander Fifth Avenue Hotel. The Vienna Arts catered to an older, more settled crowd of wealthy New Yorkers than those who frequented the larger hotels, the plush lobby so silent you could hear the swish of its ferns whenever the front door opened. The doorman pocketed Geoffrey's generous tip and assured him that no one who shouldn't be there had come by.

It had been a long shot, but even the least likely gambles sometimes paid off. He took a moment to catch his breath and drink a whiskey at the bar, wondering if Prudence had managed to question any of the Peng family despite the shock of what they had witnessed. Then he pushed through the beveled glass doors and turned south on Fifth Avenue, hoping Lowry had had better luck than he.

Warren had hoped to pick up traces of heavy footsteps in the lightly snow-covered grass or along the muddied gravel paths, but he found no sign that anyone had made a swift getaway through the park. He stopped frequently, asking everyone out for a constitutional or walking a dog whether he had seen anyone matching the description that grew less and less detailed the more often he repeated it. No one had. It was as if the man in the dark trousers and jacket had willed himself to disappear into thin air. Still carrying a bloody knife, because although Lowry kept a sharp eye out for all the places where the weapon might have been tossed, there was no trace of it. No drops of blood that might have fallen to the ground as it sailed through the air toward a trash can or thicket of brambles.

As he made his way back to the museum, Lowry tried to picture the killer's back as he'd disappeared into the throng of guests crowding the exhibit hall. Had he worn a queue? Had a long pigtail trailed down his spine, swaying from side to side as he ran? He couldn't remember. He'd gleaned a bit of Chinese history during the long hours crossing the Atlantic, but not enough to have more than a superficial understanding of why Chinese men grew and braided their hair while shaving the front of their heads. Something to do with manifesting subservience to the Manchu dynasty that ruled the country. He'd have to find a book about Chinese culture. He certainly couldn't ask Fa Cho to explain it again.

"The police have arrived," Geoffrey announced when they met at the carriageway that delivered important visitors to the museum's front entrance.

Two hansom cabs and a morgue wagon blocked the road, a line of uniformed officers had formed a cordon across the building's steps, and a growing clump of curiosity seekers was drifting toward the building from Fifth Avenue. It wasn't often that this somewhat staid section of the city saw the type of violence that brought out the long arm of the law.

It took some arguing and one of the policemen recognizing Lowry from his days on the force, but eventually the senior officer on duty conceded that they might indeed have run out of the museum in pursuit of the culprit and should therefore be allowed to go back in. The detective in charge would insist on questioning them; they were witnesses. Money changed hands, as it always did in New York when anything needed to be done.

The morgue attendants had placed Lord Peng's body on a stretcher. They'd covered it with a canvas cloth, secured by loops of rope. No one had mopped the floor. The dead man's blood had begun to coagulate on the cold marble, a pool of bright red gradually turning darker around the edges.

Looming over the deceased was Detective Steven Phelan from Mulberry Street Police Headquarters. Beside him, taking notes as General di Cesnola recounted what had happened, stood Phelan's partner, Pat Corcoran. Neither policeman paid attention to the mutterings of the crowd of spectators, most of whom had asked more than once when they would be permitted to leave. Two uniformed officers worked at ticking off names on separate pages of a guest list provided by di Cesnola's secretary.

"I don't see any of Lord Peng's family," Lowry remarked as he and Geoffrey assessed the situation from the vantage point of the Fifth Avenue side of the gallery.

"I imagine Prudence had them taken to one of the private parlors where the board of trustees meets," Geoffrey said. "Bettina also."

"I won't worry about her, then," Lowry said. He lowered his voice. "Have you worked with Phelan?"

"Our paths have crossed. I wouldn't go so far as to say we more than tolerate each other. Why do you ask?"

"He had a reputation when I was at headquarters. Once he caught hold of a suspect, he never let him go. Guilty or innocent, it made no difference if Phelan had you in his sights."

"He's a tough cop, and I suspect he cuts corners whenever he can. Maybe jumps to conclusions before all the evidence is in. But he does his job. Most of the time."

They'd worked their way from the Fifth Avenue entrance to the display cases in front of which Lord Peng had been struck down. Phelan hadn't turned around at their approach, but Corcoran caught sight of them and nudged his partner.

"There they are," di Cesnola said, waving them forward. "Did you find him?"

"Lowry took the park, and I went up Fifth Avenue," Geoffrey told Phelan, moving close enough to keep the reporters from making out what he was saying. "Nobody on the avenue saw anything and Lowry didn't so much as find a decent footprint in the park."

"Dog walkers and old men out for a constitutional," Lowry said.

"Did you get a look at him when he attacked?" Phelan asked. "Or when he was working his way through the crowd?"

"Short, though maybe of average height for a Chinese person," Geoffrey said. "Loose dark blue pants and wide-sleeved jacket. A round hat on his head."

"He drew the knife out of his left sleeve," Lowry added.

"So he was right-handed?" Phelan asked.

Lowry paused before answering. "That's what I saw." He glanced down at the pool of blood at his feet. "It happened so quickly. Lord Peng never had a chance to defend himself."

"I understand you knew the deceased," Phelan said.

"We met on the boat coming over from Southampton," Lowry explained. "My sister and his younger daughter hit it off from the first day. The son is very westernized and plays a mean hand of whist. Lord Peng was polite and good company, but closemouthed the way diplomats are trained to be. I don't know what precipitated his reassignment from London to Washington. Apparently, the opening of the exhibition had been planned some time ago to coincide with his arrival in New York."

Pat Corcoran's pencil moved rapidly across his notebook as he recorded Lowry's statement. He was an affable young fellow, recently married, with a gift for getting odd bits of useful information out of witnesses who were usually hostile to or afraid of the police. There had been general relief at headquarters when he'd been partnered with the short-tempered and notoriously difficult Steven Phelan. The Irish cops said the phlegmatic Corcoran had the patience of a saint and opened a betting book on whether he carried a rosary in his pants pocket.

"The bodyguards don't speak much English," Phelan said, nodding toward the two men who had followed the assassin from the gallery and shot up the foyer as he fled onto Fifth Avenue. "We confiscated their weapons. Webleys. Bought in London. If I understood what they were trying to tell us, they're relatively new to the job. Assigned to guard Lord Peng a few months before his orders came to leave London and report to Washington."

"Any special reason why?" Geoffrey asked.

"I couldn't get that out of them," Phelan said.

"Fa Cho might be able to tell us," Lowry suggested.

It was beneath Phelan's dignity to ask either Lowry or Geoffrey Hunter if either of them had had a professional association with the dead man that might interfere with the police investigation. He didn't like the superior attitude of many Pinks and ex-Pinks, and he'd never reconciled Lowry's easy purchase of his detective rank with the long, costly haul he himself had had to make up the department ladder. He might have to secure justice for rich men, but he didn't have to like them.

"Shall I talk to this Fa Cho?" Corcoran asked. "The son," he clarified when Phelan looked puzzled.

"I'll introduce you," Lowry offered.

"I'll ask the questions," Phelan said. He gave instructions to one of the uniformed officers and authorized the removal of the body to the Bellevue morgue. "Tell some of your people to clean up this mess," he told Director di Cesnola, pointing to the floor. "Names and addresses of everyone on your guest list who actually turned up."

A museum attendant led Phelan, Corcoran, Lowry, and Geoffrey from the gallery to the small, private trustees' parlor on the other side of the building.

As soon as they were out of sight, di Cesnola ordered the champagne for the reception uncorked. Waiters from the museum's private dining room circulated through the crowd, balancing trays of crystal glasses. Tempers that had been about to flare cooled as the wine flowed and platters of hors d'oeuvres intended for the trustees' banquet made their appearance. Di Cesnola made sure the policemen who had been tasked with control of the gathering had all the champagne they could wish for. And no, the museum kitchens didn't stock beer.

Hardly anyone noticed the small squad of cleaners who mopped up Lord Peng's blood and laid down a fresh coat of clean-smelling wax. One of them stood guard for the few minutes it took for the polish to dry. When he moved away, the crowd drifted over the spot as though it had never been stained by anything other than what they'd carried in on the soles of their shoes.

By the time the waiters had begun to refill the champagne glasses, speculation about the foreigner's death in the gallery had nearly ceased. Conversation turned to the upcoming Third Patriarchs' Ball, an exclusive annual event that officially ended the social season, scheduled this year to be held Monday night at Delmonico's. Two days later, Ash Wednesday would mark the beginning of Lent, not that anyone was planning to deny himself anything, but one did pay lip service to the liturgical calendar. Many of the guests would be embarking for Europe, not to return until it was time to go to Newport. Wardrobes had to be fitted, art bought, prospective grooms hunted down for daughters whose debutante year had receded into the distant past. There was always something to do, dinners to be planned, gossip to be exchanged. It was a shame about the Chinese diplomat, but really, what difference did the death of one foreigner make in the busy world of high society?

Couple by couple, the gallery emptied until no one remained except the museum custodians and the uniformed officers finishing up the champagne. Several of them burped and remarked for the second time that they would have preferred beer—but at least the bubbly was free.

The trustees' parlor was empty except for a single housekeeper who was pulling closed the room's dark green velvet drapes when Detective Phelan opened the door.

A flood of angry red surged across his cheeks, then spread to his ears. He clenched and unclenched his fingers as if his next move would be to reach out for someone's neck. But there was no one to grab, no one to bellow at except the housekeeper.

"Where are they?" he demanded. "Where did they go?"

Maura Kennedy shook the drape she was holding to settle its folds, not the least bit perturbed by Phelan's irate tone of voice or mottled face. Her late father, current husband, and three sons all had ferocious tempers. She knew very well who he meant, but he had to pay for the discourtesy of shouting at her.

"And who would that be?" she asked, flicking a cloth over an immaculately dust-free table.

"Perhaps you heard about the unfortunate event that took place in the gallery?" Lowry said politely while Phelan raged soundlessly beside him. "Miss MacKenzie brought the unfortunate man's family here for a bit of privacy."

"Lovely lady, Miss MacKenzie," Maura said. "All she'd let me bring them was some tea. *If it wasn't too much of a bother.* Lovely lady. And the young miss, too, the one with the scars on her face. Lovely ladies, both of them."

"Yes, but where are they now?" Phelan demanded. He pushed past Lowry and glared at the housekeeper, who tucked the dustcloth in the pocket of her apron and stared silently back at him as if she hadn't understood the question.

"I wonder if Miss MacKenzie thought they'd be better off back at their hotel," Geoffrey suggested. He'd seen Irish servants outwait and outwit their employers before now. Phelan, an Irishman himself, should have known better than to antagonize a stubborn countrywoman.

"That's it," Maura told him, liking the look of the man and the smile he lavished on her. "Miss MacKenzie had her carriage brought round. It was a squeeze, but they managed. It near broke my heart to see the Chinese lady and the two daughters holding back their tears the way they did. And the son, too. Very polite, all of them." The young man had slipped her more than he should have, for the tea, but the police didn't need to know that.

"They're staying at the Fifth Avenue Hotel," Lowry said, nodding his thanks to Maura Kennedy and pressing a decent coin into her hand.

Corcoran put away his notebook and pencil.

"Give your statements to one of the officers in the gallery," Phelan snarled at Geoffrey and Lowry. He neither needed nor wanted them at his heels. It was bad enough to have Corcoran trailing him everywhere he went, but at least his partner could be put to good use.

He stomped from the room, slamming the door behind him for good measure.

"Would you gentlemen like to be shown the back door?" Maura Kennedy asked. She had a sparkle in her eye, a dimple showing in her wrinkled cheek, and a lock of red and gray hair hanging flirtatiously out from beneath her cap.

"I can think of nothing better," Geoffrey said.

"You can get a hansom cab down the block."

This time it was a folded bill Lowry tucked between Maura's work-worn fingers.

CHAPTER 3

Josiah arrived at the Fifth Avenue Hotel fifteen minutes before Detectives Phelan and Corcoran. He'd left the museum at a dead run, collaring one of Danny Dennis's street boys on the corner of Fifth Avenue and Eighty- second Street and sending him off to bring back the cabbie and his enormous white horse. Danny and Mr. Washington could weave their way faster through downtown traffic than any other hansom cab in the city. They made it to the Hunter and MacKenzie office near Trinity Church and then to the hotel in record time.

"Shall I wait?" Danny asked as Josiah climbed out of the cab, briefcase clutched under one arm.

"I don't see Miss Prudence's carriage," Josiah said. "I suppose you'd better, just in case."

He disappeared into the hotel as Danny directed Mr. Washington toward the rank of hansoms waiting for passengers. He'd attach a feed bag to Mr. Washington's muzzle, light his pipe, and catch up on the gossip that went with the job. Drivers sat high up and behind their clients, who invariably forgot that their voices carried through cracks around the trapdoor in the cab's roof. People sometimes marveled at the speed with which a tidbit of intimate information appeared in *Town Topics*. Nobody remembered the faceless hansom cab operator who'd overheard every word they said.

Josiah made his way quickly through the hotel's marble-floored lobby, reminding himself as he went that Miss Prudence had emphasized the importance of speed when she sent him back to the office. The hotel's lobby, bar, and dining rooms might be thronged with important political and financial figures, but there was no time to linger among the country's movers and shakers. Mostly Republicans, since the Fifth Avenue was well-known as that party's special watering hole. Two now-deceased presidents had frequented its suites and meeting rooms, moguls from Jay Gould to Commodore Vanderbilt had talked business there, and the Prince of Wales had graced it with his presence. It was still the most famous hotel in the city.

The suite occupied by the Pengs was on the second floor, so no need to wait for the elevator. Josiah presented himself a little out of breath, but in time to time to lay out the contract that made Hunter and MacKenzie both the legal and the investigatory representative of the Peng family. Miss Prudence signed the document, as did the young man she was calling Johnny, although that seemed a strange name for the son of a deceased Chinese diplomat. Josiah witnessed the agreement, giving one copy to the client and keeping another for the files.

He was fastening the buckles on his briefcase when a pounding on the door announced the arrival of the police.

On Prudence's warning that New York City detectives were probably not far behind them, Peng Fa Cho had changed from his ceremonial Chinese robes into a bespoke London suit and asked his lawyer to call him Johnny. He looked the personification of an aristocratic visitor, and his perfect English boasted the unmistakable accent of the British upper class. He wasn't taking any chances; he'd had enough run-ins with constabulary in England to know that foreigners were always regarded with suspicion. Native dress was welcomed at Victoria's court when it emphasized the power and extent of the empire, but to the ordinary citizen it remained strange and not quite right. Threatening. There was no reason to believe things would be any different in New York City.

He held a furiously whispered conversation with his mother, whose facial features stiffened into immobility though her eyes blazed fury. She bowed politely in Prudence's direction, then shepherded her two daughters and Bettina Lowry from the suite's main parlor, leaving slightly ajar the door behind which she stationed herself to listen to whatever was about to be said. Lady Peng was used to being excluded from important discussions about her own and her children's lives, but over the years she'd grown adept at behind-the-scenes manipulation.

There had been no time for Prudence to do more than make a quick assessment of the Peng women based on their reaction to Lord Peng's violent death. There had been a scream when the knife flashed, and Lady Peng had sheltered her daughters in her arms, but had it been from anguished grief or fear that they would be next? No tears had been shed. No one had flung herself despairingly toward the body. Except for the initial shock, all three of the Peng women had remained composed. Recovering so quickly that Prudence wondered whether the distress could have been feigned. What did behavior like that mean?

"It's best that your police have no contact with my lady mother and sisters," Johnny Peng explained as he folded and put away the contract he had signed with both Chinese characters and his English language signature. "They saw nothing, and I won't have them insulted and upset by questions to which they do not have answers. I'm sure Warren will not want Bettina bothered either."

It was on the tip of Prudence's tongue to suggest that Lady Peng was the most controlled witness to a violent murder she had ever encountered, but her new client was still too much of an enigma to chance offending him. She'd hold back, at least until she had the opportunity to question Warren Lowry about the impressions he'd formed during the transatlantic crossing. She and Geoffrey, she corrected herself. She and Geoffrey would pick Lowry's brain together.

"Arrangements can be made to ensure they aren't interrogated." It was Prudence's subtle way of telling him that payoffs were as much a way of life in New York as anywhere else in the world. She wouldn't risk extending the bribe herself, since as only the second woman admitted to the state bar, everything she said and did was subject to intense scrutiny from obdurate men who insisted that the inferior female sex had no place in the professions. But she knew instinctively that Johnny Peng or someone from the Chinese embassy would manage it.

She shook her head at Josiah's raised eyebrows. He'd handled under-the-table arrangements for her in the past, and he was good at it. Not this time, she signaled. Better that the bribe come from an outside source.

When Phelan's knock echoed through the suite, Josiah took out his stenographer's notepad and pencil, slid his briefcase out of sight behind a drape, and stepped back discreetly from the area in which Prudence and Johnny Peng sat. He'd seen the two detectives bending over the body in the gallery and reported back to Miss Prudence that Mulberry Street had assigned Steven Phelan to the case and that Pat Corcoran had accompanied his partner to the museum. Phelan had long ago made it clear that he didn't relish having to deal with Hunter and MacKenzie on any of the investigations that came his way, but other than sidestep whenever possible, there wasn't anything Prudence or Geoffrey could do to avoid him. Phelan was one of the department's senior detectives. If a case was deemed important or tricky, it had his name written all over it.

"Now then, Mr. Peng," Steven Phelan began, standing wide-legged and intimidating before the dead man's son and the annoying socialite-turned-sleuth he'd hoped not to have to encounter again. "I understand you were only a few feet away from your father when he was struck down. That makes you a primary witness to the crime."

Johnny Peng glanced at Prudence, remaining silent as she had instructed him. He would answer direct questions but volunteer nothing. It was the standard advice lawyers gave their clients—rarely followed by the garrulous and the guilty.

"Start at the beginning, from when you and the others entered the gallery. What did you see? What did you hear?"

Prudence nodded permission for him to speak.

"The collection was displayed on the gallery walls and in rows of glass cabinets."

Johnny paused and closed his eyes, as if visualizing the moment he and his family had first glimpsed the splendor of the Met's exhibition. He had few memories of the gilded halls of his childhood home in China, nothing more than vague impressions of frightening jade dragons and far-off figures garbed in glittering silk robes. He thought he must have been presented to some great lord at one time, or perhaps it was just his own important family's palace that he recalled. His father had been set on westernizing him during their years in London. He suspected that powerful people back in China disagreed with Lord Peng's decision.

"We formed a procession," he continued. "My father and General di Cesnola at the head. I followed, and then behind me came my mother and my two sisters." Like actors slowly and majestically entering a stage. "Behind them and then fanning out to the sides were the museum trustees and important guests."

"Where were Lord Peng's bodyguards?" Phelan interrupted.

"I'm not sure. We'd gotten so used to their always being nearby that I don't think any of the family paid much attention to them. My father insisted they wear western clothing when we were out in public. He said it was so they would be less noticeable to the crowds who came to gawk at us."

Prudence made the smallest of throat-clearing noises. Johnny Peng stopped talking.

"When did you spot the man with the knife?" Phelan asked. He shot a warning glare at Prudence. *Don't interfere again if you know what's good for you.*

She ignored him, kept her eyes on her client.

"I'd turned to pay a compliment to General di Cesnola about the way the exhibition was mounted. My father had instructed me to speak English while we were in the museum. He preferred that the director and the others not realize or forget that he also understood what they were saying. I'm not sure why. Then I noticed what I thought was a servant making his way toward us, and I remember thinking that was very odd. It seemed like only a few seconds before he pulled a knife from his sleeve. I saw it flash. Blood flew everywhere. My father reached out to me, trying to clutch at my arm. Then he fell to the floor. The man disappeared."

"Who was he? Did you recognize him?" Phelan asked.

Corcoran's pencil sped across his notebook as he recorded Peng's testimony. Word for word. Or as close to that as he could manage.

"All I saw was dark blue trousers and jacket. A Chinese face beneath a small round hat. No embroidery on it. His arm reaching up, plunging down. I never looked at his features."

"But you'd know him if you saw him again?"

Johnny looked at Prudence. She nodded.

"I'm not sure I would," he said.

"You're not about to tell me all Chinese look the same to you," Phelan growled. He turned toward Corcoran, expecting to hear a chortle of amusement at his witticism. Pat kept his head down and his pencil busy.

"That's enough," Prudence snapped. "My client has told you all he knows. I think it's time to allow him some privacy in which to mourn the loss of his father." She rose to her feet, motioning Josiah to her side, glancing for a moment at his notebook, nodding approval at what she saw. Phelan didn't have to know that her secretary's shorthand was as incomprehensible as a child's scribbling.

"I'm not done yet," Phelan blustered.

"I think you are," Prudence insisted. "Unless you arrest my client. Which I think you'll agree would be a monumental mistake. One that would incur the wrath of the powers that be, something I'm sure you don't want to experience."

Phelan's run-ins with Inspector Thomas Byrnes, head of the police department's detective branch, had been well publicized by the penny press. Byrnes had invented what he called the third degree, ritualized viciousness during questioning that produced results and earned him a well-deserved reputation for cold-bloodedness. When the ambitious Phelan followed too closely on his heels, Byrnes warned him off and threatened a demotion in rank if he stepped too far out of line.

Corcoran muttered something that sounded like *time to go*, closed his notebook, and dropped the pencil he'd been writing with into a jacket pocket. Like many subordinates to short-tempered men, he'd learned early on when it was advisable to step back and how to avoid an outburst that would bring down regrettable consequences on both their heads.

"You haven't heard the last from me," Phelan said, heeding Corcoran's warning without looking at the man.

He wasn't about to touch a respectful finger to his hat for a Chinese foreigner, but it wasn't wise to antagonize the late Judge MacKenzie's daughter too much. She had influential friends everywhere in the city. It was what money and family bought you, and he bitterly resented that power of such magnitude would never come his way.

It was a sketchy salute, but adequate. All he could manage without grinding his teeth.

Prudence smiled when the door closed behind the two detectives. They'd be back, but she and her client would once again be ready for them.

*   *   *

"Is Bettina all right?" Lowry asked.

He and Geoffrey had stood aside as Phelan and Corcoran left the Pengs' suite. Geoffrey had flashed a frigid smile, but Warren hadn't bothered.

"She's in the small parlor with my mother and sisters," Johnny reassured him. Lord Peng had reserved two connecting suites for the family, ensuring that the ladies would have a private withdrawing space whenever needed.

"I appreciate your keeping Detective Phelan away from her. Bettina's doctors have persuaded me that she is largely cured, but Phelan can be too rough in his ways for any lady to have to endure."

"What did he want to know?" Geoffrey asked.

"The usual," Prudence replied. "What we saw. Could we identify the assailant? Where were the bodyguards?" She repeated what Johnny had told the detectives, adding that Phelan had promised to return. "He said we hadn't seen the last of him. Or words to that effect."

"Where *were* the bodyguards?" Based on years of experience, Geoffrey knew that hired guns were sometimes the weakest link in anyone's chain of protection. Especially if they weren't being paid enough. "Did the Chinese government supply them or were they private contractors?"

"My father believed they reported on him to Premier Li Hung Chang. He didn't trust them. We never spoke of anything but the most mundane daily matters whenever they were within hearing distance."

"But he believed they would keep him safe?" Warren asked.

"As long as those were Li Hung Chang's orders," Johnny Peng said. "They were trained in firearms and martial arts. I used to watch them from an upstairs window in the London embassy when they practiced in the courtyard. They're very good at what they do."

"And the western clothes?"

"That was my father's idea. He felt it made them less obtrusive."

"Johnny, did you have bodyguards when you attended the Royal Naval College in Portsmouth?" Prudence asked.

"I wasn't considered important enough. There had been other Chinese students there before me, so I wasn't even an anomaly."

"What about to protect your mother and sisters?"

"They never left the embassy without an entourage. I'm sure bodyguards were part of the retinue. Except for Mei Sha at boarding school. My father gave her extraordinary freedom for a girl."

"Let's get back to the two bodyguards who were at the museum today," Geoffrey urged. "Where are they now?"

"One of them will remain with my father's body until it's prepared for the return voyage to China," Johnny said. "The other, Chen Gang Lei, informed the embassy in Washington of what happened today. He's awaiting orders."

"So neither of them returned to the hotel?"

"Chen is here."

"I saw him at the end of the corridor when I arrived," Josiah volunteered. "I think he's keeping watch over who comes and goes from the suite."

"Do either of them speak English?" Lowry asked.

"They pretend not to, but Premier Li wouldn't have sent non-English-speaking security people to London. They're as much spies as they are bodyguards."

"Johnny, I know Detective Phelan asked if you recognized the man who killed your father," Prudence said as evenly as she could. "We have to know if Lord Peng had enemies."

"Political or personal," Geoffrey added.

A stubborn, tight-mouthed expression settled over Johnny Peng's face.

"We have to know," Prudence urged.

"My father was greatly respected," Johnny finally said, "a man to whom personal honor was sacred. He had no enemies because he would never have done anything to bring dishonor on the Peng family." He stood. "Perhaps we can continue this tomorrow?"

The faint click of a door being softly closed told Prudence that someone who didn't want her presence known had been listening to their conversation. Had she also overheard the questions Steven Phelan had asked?

She glanced at Geoffrey, who moved his head so slightly that if she hadn't been looking for the gesture, Prudence would have missed it.

CHAPTER 4

"Johnny Peng is hiding something," Prudence said.

"I agree." Geoffrey sipped the thick black New Orleans-style coffee Josiah brewed only for him, ignoring the plate of German pastries the secretary believed were a necessary part of every Hunter and MacKenzie discussion.

They had seen Warren and his sister into the carriage that would return them to the Lowry mansion on Fifth Avenue, then taken Danny Dennis's hansom to their office where Josiah joined them, pastry box and special-edition afternoon papers filling his arms.

The headlines screamed MURDER! CHINESE DIPLOMAT KNIFED AT THE MET! and as many variations on the theme as an enterprising editor could invent. Prudence glanced at the most outrageous of them, then settled in to read the front pages of the *Times* and the *Herald*.

Geoffrey had set himself the task of creating a list of ex-Pinkertons in New York who might have contacts in the immigrant neighborhoods around Mott Street, especially the area referred to as Chinatown. He'd come up with three names.

"See what we've got in the files on these men." He handed the meager list to Josiah.

It was a given in investigatory work that the sooner a criminal's trail could be picked up and followed, the better the chance of apprehending the perpetrator. Witnesses provided descriptions, snitches supplied names, even empty rented rooms held clues to where the offender might go to ground.

Prudence and Geoffrey had cultivated a wide network of casual informants, but few from the cluster of city streets whose inhabitants were mainly Chinese, a population considered insular, linguistically inaccessible, and tethered to their homeland by unbreakable family ties. Mostly unable to marry and create a family life in America because the immigration of Chinese women was even more severely restricted than that of men, the people called Celestials by some newspapers remained a culture apart and largely alien.

"Did you see the look on Johnny's face when you asked if Lord Peng had enemies?" Geoffrey remarked.

Prudence had set aside the *Times* and was frowning at the *Herald*. "The papers don't seem to know any more about him than we do. There's background on Peng's time in London, but nothing that would indicate he made adversaries who would follow him to the States." She folded the *Herald* into a compact square, the Lord Peng story uppermost.

"Nothing stays buried forever," Geoffrey said. "Especially if it involves money, politics, or passion." History and the gossip sheets should certainly have disabused people of thinking they could hide or escape from what they were ashamed or afraid to admit having done.

"Have you found anyone who can provide us with a contact?" Prudence asked when Josiah returned carrying a disappointingly thin file folder.

"The three names you gave me were originally supplied by Amos Lang," Josiah said. "Two of them are confirmed ex-

Pinks. The first has an in with the Irish gangs around Mulberry Street, and the second with the Italians. Born in Italy, speaks the language fluently. Not useful in this particular case."

"What about the third man?" Prudence asked.

"Not much information except his name. Matthew Lamb. Lang wrote that he's a Yale graduate, recently arrived in the city. Vague, but interesting. No mention of him having worked for the Pinkerton Agency."

"Amos must have had some reason for recommending him."

"I agree," Geoffrey said.

"Can we contact Amos for more details?" Prudence asked.

"He's out of town," Josiah said. "Stopped by the office some weeks back to let us know he wouldn't be available for a while but didn't say where he was going or how long he'd be gone." Josiah had known better than to ask the ferret who he was working for. Amos picked and chose his jobs depending on mood and how much money he needed. Once he signed on, he was indefatigable, and he never quit until a case was closed, but he was independent minded and uncommunicative about his personal life.

"Send Lamb a telegram," Geoffrey instructed. He waited until Josiah had removed the coffee tray and closed the door behind him. "What do we do about Warren Lowry?"

The question caught Prudence off guard. She felt a warm flush on her cheeks and a tingling sensation at the nape of her neck.

"The contract Johnny Peng signed is with Hunter and MacKenzie," Geoffrey continued. "Not Hunter, MacKenzie, and Lowry."

"I doubt Warren expects to take an active part in the investigation. He'll want to spend as much time as possible with Bettina. The Swiss doctors may have done all they could for her, but I think she's far from well. And it's not as though Warren needs the work."

The Lowry family had been among the wealthiest in the city

for generations. Warren had inherited the bulk of the fortune, but Bettina was also an heiress. Her heartbroken father had inserted a clause into his will. *In the event my beloved daughter is found and returned to us alive.* She was, in theory, a catch on the marriage market. Except that something terrible had happened to her, though no one in society knew quite what. Money and threats had ensured that her secret would be kept.

"Lowry was a detective during the years Bettina was missing. He was one of New York City's best," Geoffrey reminded her. "He'll want to take charge of this investigation. That can't be allowed to happen."

"I don't imagine Bettina can be left on her own very much," Prudence reiterated.

"She has a nurse," Geoffrey said. "And a lady's maid. Which leaves Warren free to pursue his own interests."

"Still . . ."

"You're making excuses for him, Prudence."

She was. If she were truthful with herself, she had to admit that things would go a lot more smoothly without Warren Lowry's help. And constant presence. But she'd worked alongside him in the case that involved his sister, and she knew he was not the type to back away from a challenge. He'd assured Johnny Peng that they'd find Lord Peng's murderer. It might have been a promise made on the spur of the moment, but that didn't really matter. Once Lowry gave his word, nothing and no one could prevent him from keeping it.

"We'll have to talk," she admitted reluctantly.

The two men needed to talk. Like it or not, Prudence would have to be part of the conversation.

"He's here," Josiah announced, stepping into Geoffrey's office and closing the door behind him.

"Who's here? There's no one on my appointment calendar."

"I sent the telegram asking him to come by as soon as possible," Josiah explained. "And he did."

"The Yale man Amos Lang recommended?"

"Matthew Lamb. That's the one."

"Ask Miss Prudence to join me. Then show him in."

Josiah hesitated, one hand resting on the doorknob as if he'd forgotten something.

"Josiah?"

"Nothing, sir. I'll let Miss MacKenzie know." He hesitated again, this time turning toward Geoffrey as if to explain something. Then he shrugged his shoulders and left.

Five minutes later Prudence appeared in the doorway, behind her a slender man wearing a dark suit.

"Geoffrey, this is Matthew Lamb," she announced, leading the visitor into the office. "Mr. Lamb, my partner, Geoffrey Hunter." She sank into one of the leather chairs positioned in front of the desk for clients, lips tilted in the beginning of a smile. Or a laugh. Depending on Geoffrey's reaction.

Matthew Lamb extended his hand, gave a brief nod, then raised his head to look directly at the man who had summoned him.

He was Chinese.

Geoffrey had had years of practice in not revealing what he was thinking. Now he looked at Prudence, caught the hint of her amused smile, and gestured Matthew Lamb toward the other visitor's chair.

"We got your name from Amos Lang," Geoffrey began, getting right to the point. "But he didn't tell us very much about your background and experience."

"I'd like to hear what the assignment is first," Lamb said.

His English was unaccented.

"You may have seen the headlines in the afternoon papers," Prudence said. "The newly appointed Chinese cultural delegate was killed this morning at the Met."

"I read about it. Peng Tha Mah. Lord Peng."

"He was stabbed to death by a man who got away before

most of the attendees in the gallery realized what had happened."

"You were there?"

"We were." Geoffrey liked an operative who drew logical conclusions from even the scantiest information supplied him. "And we've been retained by Lord Peng's son to find his father's assassin."

"Who you have to assume has disappeared into the bowels of what the newspapers call Chinatown."

"Correct." Geoffrey was curious to see how far this unproven investigator would take the speculation.

"Where you presume someone is hiding him."

"Possibly."

"There aren't many Europeans in that part of the city. Occasional tourists, of course. None of them unaccompanied by a guide."

"No one in our agency speaks Chinese."

"The Empire of China is home to a host of languages, Mr. Hunter. Most of the Chinese in America are from the southeastern region where Cantonese is spoken. I'm also proficient in Mandarin."

"Amos said you went to Yale," Prudence remarked.

"My father was one of the first Chinese brought to this country by missionaries for a western education. He graduated from Yale. I followed in his footsteps."

They waited, Prudence studying Matthew Lamb's face, Geoffrey watching to see if the young man would begin to swing a leg or twitch his fingers nervously.

He did neither. Nor did he volunteer any more information about himself.

"Have you had any investigative training?" Geoffrey finally asked. "I'm thinking of what the Pinkertons provide for all of their operatives."

"I was never a Pinkerton. Nor a policeman," Lamb said.

"What I am is someone who learned a long time ago how to stay alive in a country that has never really wanted me. I know when to ask questions, when to stay silent. I can follow someone without his suspecting I'm behind him. And I practice the ancient Chinese art of *gongfu*." He paused. "Would you like a demonstration?"

"That won't be necessary," Geoffrey said, confident now that they'd found their man.

Matthew Lamb turned to Prudence. "You are quite right in what you are thinking, Miss MacKenzie. My mother is not Chinese. She's the daughter of the missionary who sponsored my father. And my name is not spelled like the offspring of a sheep. It's Lam. *L-A-M*. It means *forest* in Cantonese."

"Mr. Forest. I'm delighted that you'll be working with us." Prudence held out her hand.

His handshake was firm, the skin cool and dry. This was obviously a young man who was afraid of nothing.

Out of deference to their latest hire, Josiah served tea as the afternoon wore on and early-February darkness fell. He lit the fire in Geoffrey's office, pulled the drapes, and turned up the gas lights.

"Do you know who chose today as the date for the exhibition's opening?" Matthew Lam asked.

"We were told that it was timed to coincide with Lord Peng's arrival from England," Prudence said. "General di Cesnola considered it a great social coup to have the new cultural attaché there to launch the showing."

"Was Shen Woon in attendance?"

Prudence turned to Geoffrey, who shrugged his shoulders.

"Shen Woon is the Chinese consul who lives and has offices on West Ninth Street. Near Washington Square Park." Matthew sipped his tea.

"I'm sure I would have realized there had to be a Chinese consul in New York if I'd thought about it," Geoffrey said.

"But I didn't. Di Cesnola made introductions before we went into the gallery. I don't recall that name."

"Neither do I," Prudence said. "I wonder if Lord Peng was planning to pay a formal call on Mr. Shen and that's why he wasn't there. Something to do with presenting credentials?"

"Or a not very subtle message that Lord Peng was falling out of favor with Premier Li Hung Chang, and that this assignment to Washington was a last opportunity to redeem himself," Lam said.

"The bodyguards," Geoffrey commented. "Johnny Peng told us his father believed they were sent to spy on him."

"Very possibly," Lam concurred. "Things can change very quickly in China. An important official one day can have his head separated from his body the next. With little or no warning."

"Are you saying this was an execution?"

"I doubt it. Lord Peng would be allowed to return to China or recalled. Several weeks or months might pass before the sword fell. Sometimes, in return for acceptance of his fate, a man is allowed to make provisions for some members of his family, but they usually share his disgrace."

"Would Shen Woon be a party to what happened?" Prudence asked.

"Again, I think it unlikely. But he might spread the word that no one in Chinatown is to help the police locate the killer. That would give him time to receive instructions from Peking. From what you've told me, and what I read in the papers this afternoon, I think there's a much simpler explanation. We just don't know what it is."

"The only thing I can imagine is a personal vendetta," Prudence said.

"A crime of honor."

"A revenge killing?" Geoffrey asked.

"Some killings are permitted, even encouraged, when a family's honor must be satisfied."

"Why did you want to know who had chosen the date for the opening of the exhibition?" Prudence asked, returning to Matthew's first question.

"Do you know what Sunday is?"

"February eighth," Prudence answered. "For the Four Hundred it's the day before the Third Patriarchs' Ball and the end of the social season."

"And for the population of Chinatown, it's an even bigger event. The first day of the celebration of the Lunar New Year, when it's traditional to pay ceremonial calls and offer sacrifices to the ancestors. All the storefronts will be decorated in red to signify luck and happiness, restaurants will serve festive dinners, special foods will be sold from barrows. Imagine drums and fireworks, parades, dragon and lion dances in the streets. Crowds everywhere, the noise so loud you can't hear yourself think."

"The perfect setting for someone who wants to disappear," Geoffrey said. "How long do the celebrations last?"

"In China the festivities can go on for weeks, but I don't think the men of New York's Chinatown can give up more than two or three days of work. Life is hard down on Mott Street. They're packed like canned fish into tiny rooms where cots are stacked to the ceiling and there's barely room to walk between the beds."

"Survival. Every immigrant group goes through it." Prudence had heard some of the horror stories, seen the pictures Jacob Riis took in the slums. Compassion for those less fortunate than she was one of the qualities that made her a good investigator. And, she hoped, would inspire the arguments she longed to give in a courtroom. Someday.

"I'll disappear down there myself," Matthew said. "Tomorrow. Everyone will be so busy with preparations that a new face won't be noticed."

"You don't look entirely Chinese," Prudence ventured.

Matthew's straight hair was black and his skin a medium olive tone, but his eyes were lighter than might be expected and his features had what to Prudence looked like traces of a craggy-faced New England ship captain. Which is what one of his missionary grandfather's ancestors might well have been.

He laughed. "There are as many ethnic groups in China as there are different languages. Westerners don't see that. They lump us all together and think we look alike. We don't, not to one another. Trust me, I'll fit in better there than I do uptown, or I ever did in Connecticut."

There were housekeeping details to settle, and arrangements to be made. Matthew would spend the night in Danny Dennis's stable, where a host of street urchins would wander in to gape at him. The boys were smart, daring, and fast on their feet. For however long Matthew remained in Chinatown, they would be his only means of getting in touch. They'd run messages, keep him in sight, and let Danny know his whereabouts. If he got into trouble, Danny's boys might be his sole hope of rescue.

For added security and in case anyone should overhear them, the boys would call him *Forest*.

It had been Prudence's suggestion.

CHAPTER 5

Huang Ma Tu boarded the early train from Washington, D.C. the morning after the telegram arrived at the embassy.

Lord Peng assassinated. Urgently need instructions.

Huang had been raised in one of the orphanages run by American missionaries, spoke fluent English, and was comfortable in western dress. Which made him the ambassador's overworked and underappreciated dogsbody, a position he often resented but was powerless to refuse.

He'd warned the ambassador that once the New York newspapers sensationalized Lord Peng's murder, even Chinatown's elaborate preparations for the New Year's celebration would not distract them from delving into the dead man's past. The Washington press was already clamoring for an interview.

The ambassador telegrammed the New York consul to make himself unavailable for comment, then withdrew into his private quarters at the embassy on Dupont Circle and ordered that neither the telephone nor the front door were to be answered. A press release announced that although the nation's capital did not contain a Chinatown to rival the festivities of New York or San Francisco, the empire's representative would scrupulously observe its more solemn rituals in uninterrupted privacy.

In the meantime, he dispatched Huang to America's largest city while he awaited overnight and next day instructions from Peking, where the advent of a telegraphy system had made swift communications possible between major cities of the empire. It might take time to decide on a strategy in any given crisis with the West, but once a decision had been reached, it was implemented with a speed the ancestors could not have imagined.

When Huang arrived at Grand Central Depot, newsboys were no longer shouting the attaché's murder on the city's street corners. By a stupendous piece of coincidental good luck, Lord Peng's death had become yesterday's news. London was reporting that the Prince of Wales might be called to testify in open court about his involvement in the titillating baccarat scandal that had fascinated society on both sides of the Atlantic for weeks now. The Peng story hadn't disappeared entirely, but Huang noted with relief that it was no longer a major front-page headline. The British royal family's peccadillos upstaged a foreigner with an unpronounceable name every time.

He had his instructions. Unless he received orders to the contrary, Huang's mission in New York City was to ensure they were carried out to the letter.

Until their departure for China, which was to take place immediately after orders from Peking reached Washington, Lord Peng's family should remain at the Fifth Avenue Hotel. It was the most exclusive in the city and could therefore be depended upon to keep newspaper reporters from its premises. When the time came for Lady Peng and her children to begin their homeward journey, the departure should be unannounced and discreetly effected. Neither the ambassador nor his emissary expected anything but dignified obedience.

There was also the matter of the disposition of Lord Peng's remains.

* * *

Huang Ma Tu bowed, then averted his eyes, shocked and dismayed to find two Americans, one of them a woman, drinking tea in the parlor of the late diplomat's suite. He waited politely for the young Lord Peng to rid himself of the interlopers.

He did not.

Three pairs of eyes fastened themselves dispassionately on the messenger from Washington. A sheen of sweat broke out on his forehead.

Peng Fa Cho nodded permission to speak.

"The ambassador sends his condolences, and regrets that he is unable to honor the late Lord Peng with his presence," Huang pronounced in his most formal Cantonese. The stratagem was intended to exclude the foreigners, but they continued to stare at him in a disconcertingly familiar way. As though they understood what he had said. Which he knew they did not.

Peng Fa Cho accepted the ritual expression of sympathy with a perfunctory nod. His eyes were dry and showed no signs of the grief befitting a devoted son who had just lost his father. Most disturbing of all, he wasn't dressed in the elaborate mourning robes tradition demanded, but in a bespoke suit that Huang recognized as the product of one of London's finest Savile Row tailors.

"I regret that Mr. Warren Lowry, an esteemed acquaintance whose companionship brightened an otherwise dreary ocean voyage, is unable to be with us this morning." The new head of the Peng family pointedly made the introductions in English. "However, I am honored to present Mr. Geoffrey Hunter, a renowned American detective who has agreed to undertake a private investigation of my father's death." He nodded in Prudence's direction. "Miss MacKenzie is an esteemed member of the legal profession."

It wasn't quite the introduction Prudence would have preferred, but it was better than some others she'd experienced since embarking on her unladylike career. She smiled a welcome as Geoffrey stood and stepped forward to shake hands with the new arrival.

Huang remained where he was, hands at his sides, eyes fixed on Peng Fa Cho as though he were the only other person in the room. How do you tell a man in front of witnesses that his world is about to be shattered?

After a few moments of uncomfortable silence, the tall American sat down.

There was nothing Huang could do that would make what he had to say more palatable or easier to bear. After a sleepless night, the ambassador had for once been both forceful and intractable, certain that Peking would agree with his preliminary decisions. He would not lower himself or his government to beg a favor from the American secretary of state whose dislike and disdain for the Chinese people was a matter of record. Cooperation between nations required mutual respect. The United States had heaped disgrace on its Chinese residents and insulted those who sought to cross its borders. Cold compliance with laws that could not be changed at least preserved the appearance of honor.

The Peng family would return to China without Lord Peng's remains.

"It is unfortunate that Lord Peng had not yet assumed the post to which he was appointed," Huang began, softening the statement with every subtle nuance the Cantonese language had to offer.

"We will speak English," Fa Cho directed.

The three pairs of eyes continued to study Huang intently.

"As you may know, Lord Peng surrendered his diplomatic credentials when he left the London delegation," Huang said, acquiescing to the inevitable, switching smoothly to English. "Until he presented his new brief in Washington he could be considered, according to the American government, a private citizen, although his diplomatic status would have been reinstated as soon as he reached Washington." The situation was much more complicated than that, but he couldn't expect Peng Fa Cho to understand the nuances that Lord Peng would have grasped immediately. The son had been trained in engineering, not diplomacy. Huang glanced toward the Americans, who had straightened in their seats and were ignoring their teacups. He had the odd feeling that they, unlike Fa Cho, knew what was coming next.

"Is there a point to this information?" Fa Cho said. He had never in his life been less than a privileged member of a noble family, welcomed and fawned over wherever he or they went. He, too, glanced at the Americans, who seemed preternaturally alert.

"The ambassador would remind you that Lord Peng and everyone traveling with him became subject to the laws of this country as soon as they landed. His unfortunate death prevented him from securing the diplomatic status normally granted to accredited representatives of a foreign government. And their families." He'd mentioned the importance of diplomatic status twice, but Peng Fa Cho still didn't seem to grasp the significance of what Huang was trying to make clear.

The American woman took a notebook from her reticule, scribbled something across one of its pages, and showed it to the man sitting next to her. Concern settled onto their faces as they waited for Fa Cho to understand the consequences of his late father's temporary lack of protected status.

Comprehension began to dawn, but slowly, reluctantly. The situation at which Huang was hinting was so demeaning as to be impossible to accept.

"My father would not wish to lie anywhere but with his ancestors," Peng Fa Cho said. "I'm depending on the ambassador to arrange things with the American government."

"That will not be possible," Huang said. "If I could be permitted to explain?"

* * *

The words Prudence had scribbled into her notebook were *Chinese Exclusion Act.*

The Exclusion Act had been controversial and devasting to the population of Chinese already living and working in the United States. In New York City its passage in 1882 amid the rise of anti-Chinese violence in California had led to an explosive growth of the population in the Five Points area of Mott, Pell, and Doyers Streets. The *Times* had dubbed the area Chinatown.

Though neither Prudence nor Geoffrey had been approached for legal or investigatory services from any of the residents of Chinatown, both were aware of the onerous restrictions the Exclusion Act placed on its largely male population. The Page Law of 1875 had already banned Chinese women from entering the United States. The Exclusion Act barred all Chinese laborers from the country and required that exempt individuals, even diplomats and their staffs, have their status certified by the Chinese government. Chinese were no longer allowed to become citizens, and a Chinese national who left on business or to visit family in China was rarely permitted to return. The act was due to expire in 1892, but already there was legislation being drafted to extend its prohibitions indefinitely.

"We have evolved special arrangements to return the bones of our deceased to the country of their ancestors," Huang began. "They may sound unusual or unacceptable to you at first, but they allow honor to be satisfied and the law to be obeyed."

He accepted the cup of tea Prudence poured and handed him, making eye contact as his training in western customs had taught him to do. He was certain the ambassador would order Peng Fa Cho to sever the connection he had made with these Americans, but he was a past master at adapting to confusing or regrettable circumstances. Especially when they were destined to be temporary.

He wasn't as westernized as Matthew Lam, Prudence thought, *but probably far more so than the ambassador he represents.* It was also obvious that Huang knew more than either she or Geoffrey about how his countrymen survived in the hostile world to which they had immigrated.

They'd debated how much to tell the client they always referred to as Johnny Peng about the operative they were sending into Chinatown. In the end, they'd decided to remain intentionally vague. There was no telling who in the Peng household and entourage might be in the pay of the Chinese government. The only thing certain, as the dead man had suspected, was that Peking had planted someone—or several someones—to report on Lord Peng's activities. No country trusted its own representatives enough to give them an entirely free hand, but some were more suspicious and restrictive than others.

It was already obvious that Detective Steven Phelan did not welcome their interest in the affair of the murdered foreigner. Cooperation and the sharing of information obtained by the New York City Police Department was not to be expected. In this case, perhaps more so than any other they'd investigated, Hunter and MacKenzie were very much on their own. Another hiccup they deemed prudent not to disclose to their client.

Huang's arrival had been unexpected, but perhaps they could turn it to their advantage. If nothing else, he could act as a bridge to the absent consul. With Matthew Lam working from the street level, that would give them more access to the community than they had originally hoped for.

In Prudence's opinion, there was still one important person missing from the conversation.

"Perhaps we should ask Lady Peng to join us," she suggested, catching an abruptly stifled demur from the ambassador's messenger. "I am certain she has concerns about what the loss of their father will mean for her daughters."

Johnny Peng looked perplexed, as if the idea of consulting his mother had never occurred to him. Even among New York's most influential families, sons were often on little more than a distant footing with the women who had given birth to them. Wives shed tears when their husbands died but secretly welcomed the freedom of widowhood. Prudence knew very little about how Chinese families structured their relationships, but if Johnny Peng's apparent absence of deep personal sorrow was any indication, it might be that there were more similarities than differences. The only way to find out was to force the issue.

Huang's features smoothed themselves into unreadability.

Geoffrey nodded brisk agreement.

"From the legal point of view," he said, lending the weight of his masculinity to Prudence's proposal, "it would be wise for Lady Peng to be made aware of how matters stand. I assume that after so many years in London, she speaks English?"

"Queen Victoria found my accent charming," a warm, cultured female voice announced from the far side of the parlor where no one had noticed that a door stood open. "Or so she said."

Lady Peng, not overly tall for a woman, slender, beautifully garbed in a flowing blue silk embroidered robe and intricate headdress, drifted lightly across the room, her tiny feet in small silk shoes seeming barely to touch the carpet. She carried an ivory fan in long, tapered fingers, the other hand hidden in a voluminous sleeve. Behind her, posed in the doorway but not entering the parlor, the two daughters watched and listened. They drew back out of sight when their brother waved them from the threshold.

Something in the room's atmosphere underwent a subtle shift as soon as Lady Peng established herself beside Prudence on one of the suite's Louis XV sofas. She had no real power, as men understood it, but her beauty and grace were such that she drew all eyes. Her presence could not be ignored. Certainly not by the ambassador's envoy and her own son.

"You were about to tell us of the special ways in which our

people are returned to the country of their ancestors." Lady Peng snapped open her fan but left it lying in her lap. "Before my late husband can find peace, his murder must be avenged. There can be no disagreement on that point."

Lady Peng did not wait for Huang to react or signal agreement with her statement. "As my son has told you, we have engaged the services of Mr. Hunter and Mr. Lowry, whom you haven't met, to find the man who killed Lord Peng." She paused for a moment, then added. "Miss MacKenzie, also. We are aware that the police may not consider the killing of a foreigner worthy of serious investigation. For that reason, we believe that hiring private inquiry agents will hasten the resolution of the case. This is true in many countries where criminal elements thrive. We observed this during our years in London."

She was evading what Prudence knew to be the most pressing subject needing to be discussed—how the legal provisions of the Exclusion Act would dictate the widow's immediate future and that of her children. Finding Lord Peng's killer could be done without his family's continued presence in New York City. Even if the police department eventually sidelined an unsuccessful investigation, Hunter and MacKenzie would not.

Could it be that Lady Peng was better versed in American attitudes toward the Chinese than her son? Was she playing for time? Angling to remain ensconced in the Fifth Avenue Hotel until her husband's murderer could be found, tried, and executed? If so, Prudence was beginning to suspect that more lay behind her maneuvering than the lady was willing to admit openly. Josiah had hurriedly put together a compact briefing on what could be expected when a Chinese diplomat serving abroad died. He'd leaned heavily on the few articles that had run in the *New York Times,* with whose archives he was intimately familiar. The resulting report had been grim.

"The ambassador has urged me to arrange for Lord Peng's funeral and burial here in New York City," Huang said, refusing to be distracted by talk of policemen and investigators. "It is established procedure to inter our countrymen's remains for a period of five to seven years, at the end of which time the bones are contained within a suitable urn and returned to the family in China." He recited the ritual as though expecting it to be accepted without discussion or argument. There were Chinese cemeteries in the western United States where burials were deliberately shallow to make eventual exhumation easier.

Shocked silence greeted Huang's blunt description. He waited a moment, then broached the topic which the ambassador had insisted was just as important as what to do with Lord Peng's body.

"Arrangements are being made for your swift return to the Celestial Empire," he said. Since he was speaking English, he chose the designation foreigners often used. He forbore from mentioning what he suspected awaited them. Confiscation of Lord Peng's wealth and estates, possibly the execution of his son since the father was no longer available to punish.

Diplomats served the empire at their peril, Josiah had discovered. Few of them survived opprobrium once their missions were over. Attitudes toward the West changed as swiftly as the tides. The current prime minister, who directed the empire's foreign policy at the direction of the Empress Dowager Cixi, was known for his quick temper and summary dismissal of officials who had not followed his contradictory commands to the letter. Rumors had begun to circulate about some of Lord Peng's actions and attitudes during his time in London.

If Johnny Peng and his family agreed to leave the United States as quickly as Huang expected, the contract he had signed with Prudence and Geoffrey might be rendered null and void. A case could be made that as an alien without the right to establish residency in the country he had never had the legal ability to enter into a binding agreement in the first place.

"It will take time to make suitable arrangements," Johnny Peng said. "The funeral must be commensurate with my father's rank, and a suitable cemetery plot and marker will have to be arranged. With the New Year's celebrations about to begin, this may take longer than you anticipate. I'm sure the ambassador will agree that a reasonable delay is unavoidable."

Lady Peng flicked open her fan, clearly a dismissal.

Huang Ma Tu bowed himself from the suite.

"You may have to work more quickly than you had planned," Johnny Peng said as Prudence and Geoffrey prepared to take their leave as well.

"How long can you delay?" Prudence asked.

"Indefinitely. We will appear to cooperate in every way with the ambassador's instructions and whatever orders come from Peking. That should slow things down considerably."

Lady Peng smiled a wondrously gentle expression that made Prudence shiver.

She'd seen socialites display that steely determination so often that she almost felt sorry for Huang Ma Tu. He had no idea what kind of opposition he would have to overcome.

If he could.

They compared notes until first Prudence and then Geoffrey fell silent, staring out the sides of Danny Dennis's hansom cab as it carried them back to the office where Josiah waited for them.

They had both agreed that the world into which the investigation would take them was unlike anything they had explored in the past. Chinatown might exist only a short hansom cab ride away from where they lived and worked, but its denizens, their language, and their way of life were as foreign and unknown as the country from which they came. The diplomats in Washington might think the exclusion laws they passed controlled the existing Chinese population, but Prudence sensed that their authority was flouted as often as possible.

Prudence had never set foot inside the area of Lower Manhattan called Chinatown, but she had no qualms about conjecturing what she would find there. It wouldn't be exactly like Five Points where the Quaker Refuge for the Sick Poor was located, but she imagined the streets would be as crowded and the residents probably just as impoverished. When she glanced at Geoffrey and saw his smile, she knew he shared her burgeoning curiosity. Not only for the challenge of the crime they would delve into, but also for the new world that was about to open to them.

If the lawmakers and bureaucrats in Washington, D.C., didn't get in their way.

CHAPTER 6

Matthew Lam surfaced in Chinatown wearing the same dark blue trousers and jacket that nearly every other male on the street sported. Broad-brimmed black hat, traditional white-cotton lined slippers, and a small, battered suitcase. He had no queue, but he had a story to explain its loss, one he'd heard years ago from an illegal who'd made his way into the States via the porous Canadian border. It had the ring of truth about it because it was, or had been, factual. He doubted that successful smugglers had changed many of their methods in the intervening years except to increase their prices.

He threaded through the crowds on Mott Street, stepping off the sidewalk and onto the cobblestones when necessary, careful to avoid any jostled contact that could be misinterpreted as contention or challenge. His aim was to disappear into the population, but to do so he had to find a safe hideaway into which he could retreat and assess his surroundings without drawing attention to himself. Anonymity was safety.

The noise was deafening. Drum bands had gathered on every corner, furiously outpracticing one another in preparation for tomorrow's parade. Merchants cursed and shouted directions to the employees stringing red lanterns and gold dragons above their shops, delivery wagons piled high with supplies and embroidered robes trundled their deliveries, and the opium parlors readied themselves for a clientele eager to spend a year's savings on one day's oblivion. The heavy smell of cooking was everywhere, mingling with clouds of cheap tobacco smoke, whorls of incense, and the ever-present stench of human waste from backyard privies.

Pell and Doyers Streets were shorter and narrower than Mott, but just as crowded. Shops occupied the ground floor of all the buildings, their doors opened wide to entice passing customers. Fresh produce spilled out onto the sidewalk and racks of cooked meats hung in the open air. Bundles and burlap bags of dried herbs and spices gave off the remembered marketplace scents of faraway China. And everywhere the sound of loud voices bargaining, arguing, boasting, and striking deals. Chinatown was alive with the vigorous daily business of survival and the extra animation of the New Year's celebrations to come.

ROOM TO LET signs were few. Chinatown was overcrowded, many of its inhabitants claiming only a single bed in a room shared with perhaps a dozen other men. Washbasin at the end of the hall if the building had running water. Most did not, their tenants making do with an outdoor pump. None of the structures was more than five stories tall; there were no elevators in this part of the city. Information could be picked up in the congested sleeping quarters, but there was also nighttime danger. Which was why men slept with whatever they valued shoved under a pillow alongside their knives.

Matthew was about to give up and retrace his steps onto Mott Street when the flash of a white placard being placed in the flamboyantly decorated window of the Golden Dragon Noodle Palace caught his eye. He ducked inside the restaurant, plucking the sign from the window before anyone else on the street had time to register its message. ROOM. HIRE.

Moving carefully through a maze of tables, Matthew made

his way toward a podium behind which sat an elderly gentleman wearing the traditional long robe known as *changpao,*
topped by a short jacket. From beneath a round black hat
trailed a queue that reached his waist, and although the light in
the restaurant was dim, a pair of darkly smoked glasses hid his
eyes. Brush in hand, he seemed to have paused in his writing to
follow Matthew's progress.

Waiters in black pants, white dress shirts, and black bow ties
wiped and set tables, their heads turning just a fraction from
their work as the stranger brushed past them. The chopping
and chatter of the cooks and vegetable boys readying for the
day's first serving grew quieter. Matthew could hear his footsteps on the wooden floor, sense the anticipation that settled
over the room. Surely the approach of a man seeking an advertised job didn't always attract this degree of attention.

It had to be because of the suitcase he carried. That and a face
no one recognized marked him as a newcomer. From where?
And how had he managed it? If he'd been a paper son, someone
would have had to arrange the documents; someone would
have been paid to attest that he was their son, brother, nephew,
cousin. It didn't always work, but often enough so the ruse was
worth trying despite the cost. Often the only way a desperate
immigrant could make his way past the laws and the anti-
Chinese prejudices was by giving up his precious family name
for a false identity under which he would labor for the rest of
his life. Somehow, the community always knew. There were
few secrets when men were packed so tightly together and
clinging to life was each day's greatest ambition. He could hear
the whisperings, see the quick negative movements of heads
and hands. Nobody had heard even a rumor that another paper
son was expected.

Placing the white placard on the nearest table, Matthew bowed
respectfully, concentrating on keeping his movements fluid and
measured. Straightening, he kept his gaze just below the smoked
glasses. Unlike many older men, the restaurant's owner, as

Matthew presumed him to be, was clean shaven. Lips pressed into a thin line, eyes hidden, he seemed to be assessing the new arrival from the toes of his shoes to the hat atop his short hair. A grunt signaled that the scrutiny had been completed and Matthew was free to speak.

But he didn't dare. From the age of ten, Matthew had been raised by his American mother and missionary grandparents on a stony New England farm after his father had traveled back to China and disappeared. He spoke Cantonese without the English accent and cadence that marred so many foreigners' speech, but his knowledge of the niceties of Chinese culture and the appropriate honorifics that were an important part of daily courtesy was limited and uncertain. He'd learned what he could from a lone fellow Chinese student at Yale, but their exchanges had been in English as often as not. If he was to succeed in the mission he had set himself, as well as the task Hunter and MacKenzie had hired him to do, he could not afford to make a mistake.

So he remained silent, head bowed, until his eyes chanced on a menu where English was printed alongside the Chinese characters. He'd lucked into one of the restaurants where guides were paid to bring parties of tourists.

"I'm inquiring about the position you have advertised, honorable sir," he said in English, careful to imitate the accent his Yale friend had labored so hard to eradicate from his speech. "And also the room. Perhaps they go together?"

"Your English is very good," the restaurant owner, whose name was Zhu Ling, said in Cantonese. He gestured toward the suitcase.

"I have waited tables before," Matthew replied. "In Vancouver." It was a chance he had to take, hinting at the route some Chinese were taking to get from the West Coast of America to the East where they hoped to find better working and living conditions than in the virulently anti-Chinese atmosphere of California. If asked, he would claim he did not know the names of those who had helped him make the illegal entry from Canada into New York State.

Each time Zhu asked a question, Matthew replied either in Cantonese or English, sometimes mixing the two in a single reply. In the rapt quiet around him, he could sense the envious concentration of waiters who wrestled daily with the language of the foreigners they served. Battling through the confusing mix of words whose tongue-twisting pronunciation nearly defeated them was exhausting and sometimes humiliating, especially when diners raised their voices in the mistaken belief that shouting made English more comprehensible.

Finally, when Matthew felt himself wrung dry with the effort to be more than he was, Zhu nodded in satisfaction. Gestured to a waiter about Matthew's own age and ordered him to take the new hire to the tiny upstairs room that was part of the compensation for his labors and to find him a pair of black trousers, a white shirt, and a black bow tie. "You start right away," Zhu said, dipping his brush into the pot of ink on the podium, dismissing both young men.

The waiter neither bowed nor offered to take Matthew's suitcase as he led the way through the kitchen to a narrow staircase at the back of the building. It was a clear signal that Matthew's language skills and immediate hiring fresh off the street could be a disadvantage rather than a plus. He would have to work twice as hard as anyone else to prove himself, to overcome the jealousy his English skills were bound to generate. No one liked to be upstaged by someone who made a struggle seem easy.

It had taken some doing, but Josiah managed to persuade Prosper Grevillot, head chef of Delmonico's outside catering division, to grant Geoffrey Hunter twenty minutes out of his overbooked and impossibly busy day. The interview would take place in the tiny, cramped office out of which flowed the most famous menus in America's world of fine dining. Some of

New York City's legendary hostesses had been heard to de-
clare that they couldn't imagine a successful culinary season
without Delmonico's. They meant the restaurant, of course,
but Charles Delmonico's reluctant sortie into private catering
beyond the premises of his dining rooms had proved immensely popular and lucrative.

Since Delmonico's had been hired to cater the luncheon intended to celebrate the opening of the Chinese exhibition at the
Met, Prudence had theorized that it wasn't unreasonable to
suppose that one or more of the staff might have noticed the
presence in their midst of an otherwise unidentified Chinese
worker. Organized chaos was how she'd described the behind-
the-scenes preparations of every successful society event of
which she'd been a part. She'd been able to conjure up for her
partner the unpacking of the restaurant's wicker baskets, the
setting of its exquisitely laid tables, and the final assembling of
the Delmonico's specialty dishes ordered by General di Cesnola.

"Anyone could have wandered through that pandemonium
without attracting more than a preoccupied glance," she promised. "I'm speculating, of course, but if our killer did make his
way into the museum through the kitchen area, the Delmonico's people would have presumed that he belonged to the staff
of the banquet's honored guest."

It made sense. So did sending Geoffrey to ask the questions.
Women were as scarce in exclusive restaurant kitchens as they
were in the professions at whose gateways Prudence was
knocking—detection and law. Until attitudes changed, Prudence and Geoffrey had agreed, albeit reluctantly, that for the
sake of efficiency, she would handle delicate situations with
women clients, and he would confront the men.

Chef Grevillot's kingdom was run largely in French, as were
many other kitchens where the chef de cuisine had been trained
in Paris. Everyone from the sous-chefs to the dishwashers was
dressed in immaculate white, but only Grevillot was permitted

to grow the distinctive handlebar mustache and chin hair of the Van Dyke goatee. Like many chefs, he was portly without being obese, possessing eyes that roved constantly and remarked everything. No one escaped his reprimands, but, as Geoffrey observed from the doorway, these were delivered without sarcasm or a caustic sting.

"Monsieur Grevillot, I thank you for agreeing to see me," he began in his New Orleans French.

"It isn't often that a Delmonico's luncheon is interrupted by murder," Grevillot answered, in English, blue eyes sparking. "Cancelled, of course. Nothing else would do, under the circumstances."

It was on the tip of Geoffrey's tongue to ask what had happened to the magnificent dishes intended to prove to the newly arrived Chinese cultural attaché that New York was more than a match for London's finest restaurants. Surely, they hadn't been carted back to the kitchens and served up to the Delmonico's restaurant clientele. But neither could he picture lobster thermidor, steak Delmonico, and Baked Alaska scraped from serving platters into garbage cans for the alleyway denizens to scrabble through.

"We shall have some privacy back here," Grevillot promised, ushering Geoffrey through the kitchen, past a wall of storage pantries, and into a doorless room so narrow that the men had to turn sideways to enter it. The desk at which Grevillot sat was scarred, the wood blotched with rings made by hot pans and wet bottles. Instead of a chair, he perched on a backless stool that rubbed against the wall. Geoffrey's seat was only slightly better.

"I don't have much time," Grevillot said, shuffling through a stack of handwritten menus and what looked like lists of ingredients, bills, and delivery invoices.

"There are only two ways Lord Peng's murderer could have gotten into the museum," Geoffrey began. "We know he didn't come through the main entrance because greeters were stationed there to welcome the guests and answer any questions they might have had. As part of the security precautions invitations were checked against a master list. The exhibition wasn't scheduled to be open to the public until several hours after the reception and banquet had ended." He paused. "Which means he had to have entered the only other way possible, by the kitchen and back delivery doors where your people were unloading their wagons."

"There was a guard there."

"One. He unlocked the doors, waited until you, your cooks, and servers arrived, then rejoined the other museum attendants in the main hall."

"You've spoken to him?"

Geoffrey nodded. "And so have the police. There's no reason to doubt his story."

"The police asked for a list of everyone from Delmonico's," Grevillot said. "I myself handed it to Detective Phelan."

"Do you have a copy?"

"Of course. We keep track of when and where and for how long each of our employees works. Most of them are paid by the hour or the day." He handed Geoffrey a neatly written set of names. "We were twenty-five at the museum yesterday, including the men who loaded and drove the wagons."

"So many?"

"Half of them were waiters. One for every five guests seated at the table. Sixty diners, twelve waiters. One headwaiter at either end of the room to oversee the service. The waiters who served at table were also to have served the champagne in the exhibition hall before the dinner began."

"I'll have to speak to all of them," Geoffrey said.

"Most will have gone directly from the wagons into the reception and banquet rooms," Grevillot explained. "Only the drivers, the cooks, and the dishwashers would have stayed in or near the kitchen area where your killer presumably slipped past them."

"Would any of them have challenged someone who obviously wasn't part of the crew?"

"I doubt it. Everyone knew that the guests of honor were Chinese, and it was expected they would be traveling with an entourage of servants and attendants. My people might have been curious, but they were far too busy to stop and stare even for a moment, let alone the time it would have taken to ask questions. No. If anyone did remark him, it would have been nothing more than a fleeting impression. You have my permission to interview all the personnel on that list, but I doubt you'll learn anything from it."

An hour and a half later, Geoffrey was tempted to agree with Monsieur Grevillot. Most of the Delmonico's catering staff were in and out of the stuffy little office in the time it took to ask one or two questions and tick a name off the list. *Did you see anyone who was not previously known to you enter the museum through the kitchen? Specifically, did you see or notice anyone of Chinese origin wearing dark blue trousers, a dark blue jacket, and a round black hat—and whose hair was braided into a long queue hanging down his back?*

After a while the questions no longer had to be asked. One by one the catering staff paused in the doorway, declared they had seen no one they didn't already know, and especially not a Chinese, and if that was all could they go now?

It came as a surprise when a thin, rabbity-faced dishwasher with crooked teeth volunteered that not only had he seen a Chinese wearing those dark trousers, coat, hat, and the long braid swinging across his back, but he'd actually spoken to him.

"What did you say?" Geoffrey asked.

"I said I guessed he'd just got off the boat," the dishwasher replied.

"And what did he say back?"

"Nothing. He just stared at me like he didn't understand a

word, then shook his head, and ran past me inside to the kitchen. The thing was, when I looked for him, he wasn't there."

"Can you describe him?"

"I already did, didn't I?"

"Young? Old? Tall? Short? Fat? Skinny?"

"I'd say about ten years older than me, and I'm seventeen.
Only, he didn't look like he had much of a beard. About my
height, skinny like you said. If he weren't Chinese, I'd think he
was kinda good-looking."

"Is that what you told the police?"

"The police never asked me nothing."

"Nothing?"

The dishwasher shook his head. "Nope. The first I heard
anyone was interested in what I saw was when Chef Grevillot
told us you were gonna be asking questions and we had to answer 'em. I got pots to scrub. Can I go now?"

"One more thing. Did it look to you like he was alone in the
alleyway? Did you see any other Chinese person out there? In
the driveway or close by in the park? Think hard before you
answer."

"I don't have to think hard. He was alone. I'm sure of it. Can
I go now?"

Not until he'd repeated everything he'd already said. Every
description, every impression. Finally, when he was satisfied
the young man had nothing to add, Geoffrey sent him back to
his sink.

On his way to the office to share what he'd learned with
Prudence, he arranged with Danny Dennis to send a messenger
boy into Chinatown as soon as Matthew Lam's whereabouts
could be verified. The description he'd gotten from the dishwasher was far from perfect, but at least it was a place to start.

CHAPTER 7

Geoffrey had left for Delmonico's and Prudence was reading an article from Monday's *Times* about crowds of curiosity seekers who had turned up on Mott Street a week early for the Chinese New Year.

"This just arrived by private messenger," Josiah announced as he hurried into her office, waving a white envelope bearing the return address of the Fifth Avenue Hotel. "He's waiting for an answer."

"Close the door." Prudence slit open the envelope and extracted a piece of hotel stationery, reading quickly and then handing it to Josiah. "What do you make of this?"

"Lady Peng is thanking you for the invitation to take her for a carriage ride in Central Park." Josiah frowned. "Did you?"

"No. When Geoffrey and I left the suite, Lady Peng and her son were deep in a discussion of funeral plans. They were also intending to ignore or circumvent instructions brought by the ambassador's envoy from Washington, but they didn't seem to think that would present problems. This carriage ride in Central Park has a note of panic about it."

"Something's happened," Josiah said.

"She thanks me for wearing western mourning appropriate to her widowed state." Prudence frowned. "Lady Peng and I are about the same height. In veils and black weeds, it would be difficult to tell us apart." She tapped her fountain pen against her front teeth, thinking through the answer she was about to pen. "As soon as the messenger is out of the office, place a telephone call to my house. I'll instruct Cameron to have Colleen pack up my mourning gear. Kincaid can bring it in the carriage, I'll change here, and then go straight on to the hotel."

"Shall I try to reach Mr. Hunter?"

"Don't bother. It's important that he question the Delmonico's staff before they have a chance to decide not to cooperate. I'll handle whatever is troubling Lady Peng and tell him about it later."

Lady Peng donned a black silk Worth gown she'd last put on for a private visit with Queen Victoria, who had never left off mourning after the death of her beloved Prince Albert in mid-December 1861. Two layers of gossamer black veiling had been pinned across the brim of her hat, covering her face and falling well beneath her shoulders. Black-gloved hands carried a black reticule. She was the very picture of a well-bred society woman observing the death of a beloved spouse.

That was the plan.

"I don't know any more than that we're going to Central Park," Prudence told her coachman, James Kincaid. "I've apparently persuaded Lady Peng that she needs to take a drive for the sake of her health."

Both Josiah and Kincaid had played significant roles in past cases. They weren't formally trained operatives, but they considered themselves members of the investigative team. Neither would presume to say it in words, but each had privately vowed that Miss Prudence's life was safe in his hands.

"Is that so, miss?"

"It doesn't matter. Something has happened that she believes requires secrecy. Probably concealment from her servants, and definitely from the bodyguards assigned to protect Lord Peng."

"They didn't do a very good job of that." Kincaid helped Prudence into the carriage where a footman had arranged hot bricks wrapped in a piece of wool to warm her feet.

"The last I heard, one of them was to remain with Lord Peng's body while the other kept watch in the hotel corridor. That was yesterday."

"Just one bodyguard then." Kincaid knew himself to be more than capable of dealing with a single adversary, should it come to that. With Miss Prudence, you never knew what talents you'd be called upon to exercise.

In the end, though, she went up to the Peng suite by herself, leaving him and the carriage to wait for her at the Fifth Avenue entrance to the hotel.

When she emerged, accompanied by another woman in mourning, he was hard-pressed to tell them apart. Both wore wide-brimmed hats swathed in black veiling and the latest Parisian garb for the fashionable widow. As the hotel doorman ushered the ladies toward the carriage, Kincaid decided that being unable to distinguish between them was probably the point.

"Johnny has gone to ask for the consul's help," Lady Peng said as soon as the carriage moved up Fifth Avenue. "Huang Ma Tu left Washington before Peking replied to the ambassador's telegram. He came back to the hotel this afternoon with final instructions. The premier has decided our fate and there is no way to escape it."

"You'd better tell me," Prudence said.

"We're to leave New York by private railway car as soon as one can be reserved. It could be as early as Tuesday or Wednesday."

"Three or four days. I don't see how that's possible."

"Arrangements are already being made," Lady Peng said. "Two more bodyguards will arrive from Washington to escort us across the country to San Francisco. We'll board ship as soon as we arrive there."

"That's kidnapping," Prudence exclaimed. "There are laws against forcible abduction."

"Huang assured us that American jurisprudence won't be any protection," Lady Peng said.

"I don't understand why your government is so intent on speed. Surely that's not how things are done in China when someone as important as Lord Peng dies."

"We celebrate death with long and elaborate rituals," Lady Peng said. "China is entering the modern age, but we are bringing with us everything from the past that gives meaning and beauty to our lives."

It sounded like a sentiment composed for release to the press, as though Lady Peng was responding automatically to an anticipated question. Prudence had to bring her back to the now, to the personal.

"How long have you been away?" she asked.

"Mei Sha was barely three years old when we arrived in London." She still sounded distracted, but a measure of warmth had crept into Lady Peng's voice.

"Is that why her feet weren't bound?"

"It's a long story. Perhaps one day I'll tell you." Lady Peng opened her reticule and took out a small white envelope and a yellow Western Union telegram. "This is why I sent for you. A bouquet of flowers was delivered to the suite just after Johnny left." Lady Peng opened the envelope and handed Prudence a calling card. "This came with it."

Condolences on the demise of Lord Peng, it read in English. There was no signature.

"What are these?" Prudence asked, pointing to beautifully inked Chinese characters encircling the message like a wreath.

"Can he hear?" Lady Peng asked, tipping her head toward where Kincaid sat high up at the front of the carriage.

"No. It's just the hansom cabs that have a trapdoor in their ceilings," Prudence said.

"What you're looking at are the characters for *little brother* and *needle*. They've been worked into a decorative border to disguise the meaning, but I knew immediately what I was looking at."

Prudence waited. Better not to ask the obvious question. Not yet.

"Just before a bellboy brought the flowers, I went into my bedroom to lie down for a while." She handed Prudence the Western Union flimsy. The original message had been inked out and another handwritten in barely visible pencil. *Central Park this afternoon. Use a private carriage. Western mourning. Burn this.*

"Where did you find it?"

"Under my pillow. Miss MacKenzie, no one else has been in my room except my maid."

"Do you trust her? How long has she been with you?"

"Her family has served mine for generations."

"Only someone who is literate in Chinese would understand the meaning of the characters on the card," Prudence said. "But the directions you were to follow were written in English, as was the expression of sympathy for your loss."

"As you see, I didn't follow all the directions. I didn't burn the telegram paper or the card."

"Has anyone else seen them?"

"I took the card and its envelope out of the bouquet myself. As soon as I'd read it, I put them in my reticule, along with what was under the pillow. The reticule hasn't been out of my sight, even while my maid was helping me dress."

"Someone was in your bedroom. How many waiters served lunch? I assume you ate in your suite?"

"We did. My son, my daughters, and I. There were two waiters, and a boy to roll the cart. While they were there, I sent our staff to eat in the servants' dining room downstairs."

"All of them?"

"It gave us a chance to talk together as a family without being overheard."

"Because the hotel's waiters wouldn't understand Chinese?"

Lady Peng nodded.

"And presumably your personal servants wouldn't understand the messages written in English."

"They are not literate," Lady Peng said. "In either language."

"If I'm to be of any assistance, you mustn't hold back any piece of information, no matter how unimportant you think it may be."

"My son and I believe he will be executed, in place of Lord Peng. His life for his father's."

The widow neither bowed her head nor reached beneath her veil to press a handkerchief to her eyes. Even at the museum, while they sheltered in the trustees' parlor, Lady Peng had remained stoic and emotionless after witnessing the stabbing. No tears.

"That's not all, Lady Peng. You're keeping something from me."

"I can't be certain."

"Then why did you send for me? Why arrange this absurd carriage ride?"

"You must wait." Lady Peng's gloved hand twitched aside the leather curtain hiding the carriage's occupants from passersby. She leaned forward as Kincaid made the turn off Fifth Avenue into the park, gentling the horses to a walk, waiting for instructions.

"Tell your coachman to drive slowly," Lady Peng said.

"Where to?" Central Park was a maze of intersecting roadways.

"I'll know when to tell him to stop."

She refused to answer any more of Prudence's questions.

There were few carriages in Central Park and fewer pedestrians taking constitutionals or exercising their pets. Early February was cold in New York City, colder than usual that Saturday because a snowstorm blowing toward Albany was lowering downstate temperatures as well.

The hot bricks beneath the women's feet were the only source of warmth in the carriage, but Lady Peng seemed unaffected by the frigid air she was allowing to sweep past the leather curtain. As the carriage rolled sedately northward along East Drive, Prudence's companion continued to stare out the window.

Searching for something. Or someone.

It was almost dusk when the Egyptian obelisk known as Cleopatra's Needle came into view.

"There's a Cleopatra's Needle in London," Lady Peng said. "On the Victoria Embankment." Her breathing grew rapid, and the leather curtain trembled in her hand. "Tell your driver to stop," she ordered Prudence.

Before the carriage came to a halt, Lady Peng had flung open the door and stepped down onto the dirt roadway. For several long minutes she stood as straight and unmoving as the obelisk itself, then with both hands she lifted the veil from her face.

A man appeared from behind the obelisk, descending the grassy slope toward Lady Peng. Her tiny feet had begun to walk slowly in his direction, as though reluctantly pulled along by a magnetic force too powerful to resist.

He stepped onto the roadway before she could begin to climb the hill, reaching out with both arms. Slowly, she placed her hands in his and bowed her head.

From where she sat inside the carriage, Prudence heard a strangled cry that sounded like a sob.

* * *

"We've known each other since before I married," Lady Peng began.

The man she had come to meet sat beside her in the carriage, both of them facing Prudence, who had also lifted her veil. There was something distinctly familiar about him, though she couldn't decide exactly what it was. He was handsome and dignified, his hair cut short in the western way, wearing clothes that would have gone unremarked in any of the city's most exclusive men's clubs. Eyes that looked black rather than brown, skin a shade darker than Lady Peng's, beardless. Wide shouldered, as though the muscles beneath the expertly tailored overcoat were those of a laborer rather than a gentleman of leisure. A mass of contradictions, Prudence decided. It was the same first impression she'd had of Geoffrey. Power and danger concealed by a façade of gentility and good manners.

"The late Lord Peng was my elder brother. I read of his death in the newspaper." He held one of Lady Peng's hands firmly in his own. "She will not return to China. We will not be separated for a second time."

Lady Peng's beautiful oval face was set in the stubborn lines of a woman who knows that a last and only hope of happiness lay within her grasp—if only she had the strength to seize it despite seemingly insurmountable obstacles.

Matthew Lam began his first shift in the Golden Dragon Noodle Palace restaurant with that day's evening meal. The restaurant opened at four in the afternoon for early diners, but waiters reported to the kitchen at three-thirty, dressed in the obligatory black pants, white shirt, and black bow tie. If a man passed inspection, he was given a bowl of noodles and a clean white apron to tie around his waist. If a tie was crooked or a white shirt stained, the offending waiter worked hungry. But everybody worked.

And everybody smoked. Out back in the alley where feral cats and dogs prowled, knocking down overflowing trash cans and snatching whatever they could before being chased away. Matthew had been raised in a household where smoking was frowned upon, but he'd learned to appreciate the vice at Yale.

When a ragged street urchin appeared in the alley, running barefoot toward a duck carcass dropped and then abandoned by one of the dogs, Matthew surged after him, to the encouraging cheers and catcalls of his fellow smokers. He collared the boy, gave him a good shake, sent him sprawling, then joined in the jeers as the child grabbed for the duck and made his getaway.

But not before Matthew had whispered in his ear. Danny Dennis would pass along the report. Matthew was no longer alone in Chinatown. Someone would know what he was doing and where to find him. It wasn't much, but if things went badly wrong, it was his only link to a rescue.

The dining room filled up slowly as parties of well-dressed men, some in traditional robes, others in western garb, gradually made their way to the seats many of them occupied every evening. The regulars knew to avoid certain tables, though they were not marked in any way. Waiters steered newcomers and a few tourists toward booths and tables near the large windows overlooking the street. See and be seen.

Not so the serious men speaking in low tones as they sipped their tea, nearly lost in the shadows as far away from the windows as it was possible to get. The same waiters who had served them last night served them again today, knowing in advance each client's preferences, whispering discreetly the names of the special dishes over which chefs had been laboring for hours.

Matthew, because of his English skills, was given the tables reserved for tourists, and the owner noted that even on his first night, he did well there, suggesting dishes that had been created to cater to western tastes, such as chop suey, unknown in

China but beloved by Americans. He smiled and flattered the diners who expressed a desire to try something a little more daring than the mélange of odds and ends an enterprising Chinese cook had dreamed up in the goldfield towns of California. The tips Matthew's customers left were substantial, their comments to the restaurant's owner appreciative of the waiter at whom they didn't have to shout to make themselves understood.

By the end of the evening, when the tourists had gone home and the older waiters were flagging, Matthew was drafted to the tables in the shadows, where plates of sweet buns, pots of tea, and carafes of hot rice wine were regularly replenished. A fug of smoke hung over these tables, three of them, at one of which four determined drinkers were playing an intense game of Liar's Dice. The rattle of five dice inside each man's cup drowned out conversation, and perhaps that was intentional. When there was a lull in the shaking, talk at the other tables stopped abruptly, not to begin again until the cracking of the dice resumed.

It was too soon for Matthew to linger by the tables. He was unknown, and therefore not to be trusted. He removed dirty plates and empty teapots, replaced them with fresh buns and steaming oolong, moved as quickly and smoothly away from the tables as he had approached them. Voices lowered when he was close enough to overhear, just enough to warn him that he must not appear interested in what was being discussed.

He used his eyes instead, under the pretext of scanning the tables for what needed attention. One man, neither old nor young, but some indefinable age in between, had arrived a full hour later than all the others. Clean-shaven, his hair cut in the western style, he was dressed in a richly embroidered, wide-sleeved robe and a black silk cap, the type of ceremonial clothing many would be wearing as the New Year was celebrated for the next two days. Matthew wondered if this man, with the elaborate garments and aloof bearing of someone rich or important, could be one of the consul's staff. He couldn't stay close long enough to catch his name and didn't dare ask any of the other waiters. But he memorized the features of the man's face and the sound of his voice.

When Matthew went into the alley to smoke his last cigarette of the working day with the cooks and other waiters, three or four street boys had clustered around the most recently filled garbage can, the one holding the remnants of tonight's dinners. Their fingers moved with the lightning speed of expert pickers. Recognizable bits of meat, fish, fowl, and vegetables disappeared into their mouths, grains of rice fell over their tattered coats, sauce dribbled down their chins, and strands of noodles hung from their teeth. They ran as soon as the restaurant's back door opened, but not before one of them winked in Matthew's direction.

Message delivered.

CHAPTER 8

Lady Peng planned their escape for just before midnight, when the hotel corridors would be empty, the very young and the very old guests asleep in their beds, while revelers of all ages had not begun to return from their night out.

It was simple and, she hoped, flawless, the details worked out with Younger Brother and Prudence as the carriage rolled through and then out of Central Park.

"The name I am known by in America is Wei Fu Jian." Younger Brother had shrugged dismissively. "That was what was written on the papers I was given. It was safer to keep it than to argue or demand a correction. Many of us became other people when we crossed the sea."

Kincaid had reined in the horses for a few moments before making the turn onto busy Fifth Avenue. Wei Fu Jian slipped out of the carriage and into the shrubbery as smoothly as a snake, unnoticed by anyone who might have followed them. Kincaid had kept a close eye out as he drove, confident that no vehicle took an interest in them after they'd pulled away from the Fifth Avenue Hotel. But, as Prudence had often reminded him, a really good operative was never noticed until it was too late.

Lady Peng entered the hotel slowly and alone, making sure she was recognized by anyone who might be asked later if it was indeed she who had returned from the park. She lifted the heavy veiling that hid her face and spoke briefly to the doorman, to one of the bellhops, to the clerk on duty at the main desk, and to the elevator operator who saw her enter the family's suite and also noted the presence of a bodyguard in the hallway. Poor foreign lady. So quiet and polite.

Dinner was ordered up from the kitchen, trays brought to the corridor guard and the family's personal servants, Saturday being the busiest night of the week in the hotel's bars and dining rooms. The waiters who served the Peng family reported to colleagues that little was said as they ate, either in English or Chinese. They seemed exhausted and as though what had happened at the museum on Friday morning had just begun to seem real and not a terrible nightmare. The son tipped them extravagantly well, perhaps not knowing the value of the coins and bills he pressed into their hands. No one told him it was far too much.

"We'll take the stairs up one flight, to Mr. Hunter's apartment," Lady Peng whispered to her children. "Don't put on shoes."

"Barefoot and in our nightclothes?" An Bao, the eldest daughter, protested.

"Miss MacKenzie is meeting us there. She'll have new clothes for us. We don't want there to be a description of what we might be wearing."

"What about the bodyguard?" Johnny asked.

"I'm giving Amah two bottles of rice wine to share among the staff. A gift to celebrate the beginning of the new year." Lady Peng took a small brown apothecary's bottle from one of the pockets of her embroidered robe. "This is chloral hydrate. I brought it with us from London in case anyone got seasick on the boat and needed it to sleep. I'll instruct Amah to put two or three drops in the bottom of each cup. Not enough to make anyone suspicious when they're questioned, but sufficient to lull them into what will seem a natural sleep for servants who have worked hard during the day and are not used to consuming wine in the evening."

"Is Amah coming with us?" Mei Sha asked. She'd been put into Amah's arms minutes after birth. The woman she and everyone else in the family called *Amah* was the only nurse she had ever known.

"No," Lady Peng said.

"But she's aware we're going into hiding?"

"I have not told her that in so many words. Nor will I."

"She'll know," Mei Sha said. "As soon as you tell her to put the drops in the wine cups, she'll realize what's happening. It will break her heart to be left behind."

"It can't be helped," Lady Peng said.

"Would going back to China be so bad?" An Bao asked. She had forgotten the years of unbearable pain when her feet were bound at the age of four. By the time her father accepted the position in London, the damage to her broken arches and folded-over toes could not be undone. The binding had continued. When her feet were crushed, so was her spirit.

"It would mean your brother's death," her mother said.

"By beheading," Johnny confirmed. "It's considered a quick and honorable death for someone of our rank." He took a deep breath. "But it's not one I can accept for the good of the family. I don't believe I have to die because my father can no longer be executed. I won't submit to that kind of reasoning."

"You're all to go to bed as if you want nothing more than a full night's sleep. You're exhausted and you mourn your father. I'll come for you when it's time to go. Take nothing with you. Nothing."

Lady Peng had already emptied the ivory inlaid box, rarely

unlocked, that contained the most valuable of the western jewels she had acquired during the London years. Huang Ma Tu would pry it open and guess that she had managed to get away with a small fortune in precious stones, but the maid who dressed her would be unable to swear to the box's contents. When it came time to sell a piece, it would fetch a better price for being untraceable.

Tonight wasn't the first time Lady Peng had contemplated escaping the marriage that had bound her as tightly as the bandages used to break the bones of her feet. Until now, the certainty that Peng would take revenge on her daughters had dissuaded her. She had thought of her son and the girls as the bars on her prison. Now they had become fellow escapees.

By nine o'clock Prudence had returned to the hotel, dining with Geoffrey at a table in the restaurant where their presence together was sure to be noted and reported in one of the gossip columns. *Oysters on the half shell, terrapin soup, filet of beef en Macédoine, asperges.* Every delicious bite stuck in her throat, washed down with a tiny sip of wine that never quite emptied her glass because it was immediately followed by a swallow of water. She couldn't afford a light head with the plans that had been made. Success depended on each step being carried out with secrecy and precision.

She and Geoffrey smiled at each other, chatting inconsequentially of nothing at all while their eyes spoke volumes. Two maids' uniforms and a housekeeper's black bombazine dress waited upstairs in Geoffrey's suite, carried into the hotel in prominently labeled boxes from a stylish men's haberdashery. Colleen had provided the clothing, Josiah the cardboard containers. A room service waiter's suit had disappeared from a bin where soiled uniforms were piled before being sent out for cleaning. Slightly wrinkled though not badly stained, it would transform handsome Johnny Peng into a staff member unworthy of notice. Lady Peng would be the most difficult one to disguise, but padding her girth from slender to stout should prove effective.

"Mei Sha spent more than two years in an English boarding school," Prudence reminded Geoffrey. "There's no better training for learning to sneak through hallways and escape from behind high walls. Or so I'm told by friends who were lucky enough to have the experience."

"While you had to master French and sketching from governesses." Geoffrey could not imagine his smart, daring, and determined partner obediently conjugating irregular verbs and creating pen-and-ink drawings of cut flowers. His own years in a Yankee boarding school after the war had been nearly as valuable as his Pinkerton training. He often wondered why the masters hadn't realized that the stricter the rules, the more cunning, devious, and adept the boys became at flouting them with impunity.

They lingered over coffee until most of their fellow diners had finished and left, some of them stopping by to greet Prudence, exchange a few words, and be introduced to the man all society had heard of, but not everyone had met. The scandalous Southerner who had persuaded Judge MacKenzie's daughter to take up a profession wholly foreign to her upbringing. Two professions, if the recent gossip could be trusted. Investigator and lawyer. Shockingly brazen, if such a word could be applied to someone whose maternal Knickerbocker ancestors were no doubt turning in their graves.

Prudence thought the situation highly amusing.

"It's time," Geoffrey said, when the faraway chime of a longcase clock announced that it was an hour before midnight. He followed Prudence into the lobby and saw her into the carriage waiting outside. Kincaid would drive around the block to a largely forgotten delivery entrance that hadn't been used since kitchen renovations had created a much larger space infinitely easier for heavily laden wagons and porters to negotiate. It had become one of Geoffrey's favorite passages in and out of the hotel, secured by a key he wore on his watch chain. He'd had a new lock installed one dark night by an ex-Pink who'd taken up the trade after ending a far more dangerous career as a wartime spy. To the casual eye, nothing had changed.

"I didn't see anyone leaving the hotel by the back door into the alley," Prudence said as she slipped past Geoffrey and into the empty storage space from which a narrow, uncarpeted staircase rose into the darkness.

"It will probably be another half hour before the kitchen staff is let go," he answered, securing the door behind her. "There's a skeleton housekeeping crew on duty, but if we've timed this right, our clients should be able to blend into the exodus of kitchen workers without questions being asked."

"All anyone will be thinking about is getting home as soon as possible," Prudence agreed. Once, during her regular volunteer hours at the Quaker Refuge for the Sick Poor, she'd been asked to take over food preparation duties for a worker who'd fallen ill. For the first time in her life, she'd stood at a wooden table chopping vegetables until her arms ached and she could hardly hold the knife. And then she'd washed a sinkful of greasy dishes. The experience had given new meaning to the word *fatigue*.

The back stairs into the guest premises above were steep and slippery with unswept dust.

"Careful," Geoffrey cautioned, staying as close behind her as he could manage.

When they reached the floor on which he'd had an apartment ever since taking up permanent residence in New York City, he put one finger to his lips, unlocked the door, and peered into the carpeted corridor where the gaslights had been turned down low. Beckoning to Prudence to follow him, he led the way to the rooms where Josiah waited.

"Do you have keys to every door in the hotel?" Prudence asked as soon as they were safely inside, and Josiah had helped her off with her coat.

"Not every door," Geoffrey said. "Only the ones I need." His broad smile told her that he could pick a lock as easily as he could insert a key.

"Danny Dennis is waiting on Twenty-third Street," Prudence said. "He's driving an unmarked carriage and not using Mr. Washington tonight." The huge white horse with distinctively large teeth was easily recognizable even on a faintly gaslit road.

"Twenty minutes," Josiah announced, consulting the solid gold pocket watch whose chain and fob looped across a vest only slightly less extravagantly embroidered than the one he'd worn to the museum. He stationed himself at the door, one hand resting lightly on the knob. He wouldn't wait for a knock. As soon as he heard the whisper of bare feet on the hall carpet, the door would open just wide enough to admit the Pengs. One by one. He'd already dimmed the foyer gaslights so they wouldn't shine into the hall. He thought he'd planned for every contingency, but his fingers trembled nonetheless.

The minutes passed with agonizing slowness. Geoffrey stared out the parlor window overlooking Fifth Avenue, paced, peered out the window again. Prudence sat, fingering the small bottle of laudanum she'd begged from her housekeeper, just in case one of the Peng women needed calming. She doubted anything would unnerve Lady Peng, but Mei Sha might be too primed for adventure, and she didn't know the eldest daughter at all. She'd shown the bottle to Geoffrey who had reached to take it from her, then pulled back his hand. *Are you sure?* he seemed to ask. She was. Not for anything in the world would she hold that uncapped bottle to her lips. That way lay the path to unredeemable addiction, a course down which she'd taken the first deadly steps before pulling herself back into religiously maintained abstinence. Laudanum had its uses. But not for Prudence.

Lady Peng swept into the apartment as softly as a zephyr. She'd washed every trace of expensive perfume from her skin and made sure her daughters did the same. The only instruction she hadn't followed was the injunction to go barefoot. Not even for this life-saving escape would she bare her bound feet to strangers' eyes. She and An Bao wore soft white cotton socks that were as silent as skin.

Prudence led the women into Geoffrey's bedroom where the maids' uniforms and the housekeeper's dress lay on the bed. For each of them there was also a tidy pile of western underclothes, including a chemise, a whalebone corset, petticoats, and stockings. Sturdy leather boots, too, though Prudence had had to guess at the sizes, and for Lady Peng and her eldest daughter, there were men's handkerchiefs to stuff into the toes.

Mei Sha giggled when she saw the disguises. The servants' clothing wasn't too different from the dark wool boarding school uniform she'd once worn. With Prudence assisting Lady Peng and Mei Sha helping her sister, it took barely fifteen minutes to shed their Chinese nightclothes, don the western dresses, and restyle their hair in demure buns. Heavy winter coats further camouflaged their slender frames, and Prudence wound woolen scarves around their necks and chins, leaving only a narrow space beneath the concealing hats that might give them away. It couldn't be helped. If they kept their heads bowed, eyes on the ground, there was a very good chance they'd get away with it.

Prudence would be leading them out the unused storage room door into the alleyway, ready to spring into action if they were challenged. All they had to do was get around the corner to Twenty-third Street and climb into the carriage that would be waiting there. Danny Dennis knew what to do and where to go.

Johnny Peng looked so much like a room service waiter on his way home after a long day that Prudence kept her fingers crossed no one would open a suite door and demand late-night service. Like the women, he wore a disguising hat, woolen scarf, and gloves. Josiah fussed at his creation when Johnny momentarily pulled down the scarf to beam a huge smile at his mother and sisters. For a man whose neck was literally on the line, he seemed cocksure and unconcerned.

"I'll wait for you here," Geoffrey said as he opened the suite door and checked the corridor. Reluctantly, because he never liked ceding the action to anyone else, he'd agreed not to chance being seen with the runaways. He was too tall and too familiar to hotel staff and fellow guests to be mistaken for anyone but who he was. He'd run a great enough risk already tonight going down to let Prudence in. But there was no possibility of talking his way out of being caught smuggling four Chinese nationals out of the hotel.

With Prudence leading the way, the Pengs tiptoed into the corridor and down the servants' staircase, boots in hand to be put on when they reached the bottom. Johnny supported his mother while Mei Sha held her sister's arm and urged her to go slowly, to be sure each small bound foot was firmly in place before taking another step. Geoffrey had lit a gas lantern and left it at the bottom of the stairs. The flame was flickering wildly, with just enough fuel left to allow them to see the laces of the boots that didn't quite fit anyone, but still had to be worn.

"Are you ready?" Prudence whispered, blowing out the lantern. She could hear voices and footsteps outside and knew that the kitchen workers must be leaving. The plan was to follow along behind them to the end of the alley, make the turn onto Twenty-third Street, and disappear into Danny Dennis's carriage. Once she'd seen them safely off, Prudence would return to Geoffrey's suite, then leave through the Fifth Avenue entrance with Josiah as her escort. Not the most decorous of exits, but there was little likelihood a reporter for one of the scandal sheets would be lurking in the lobby.

A handful of twittering kitchen maids walked directly in front of them, five or six bellboys and dishwashers bracketing the group, teasing and laughing and trying unsuccessfully to persuade the girls to stop at a tavern for a drink or two. The maids weren't having it.

Prudence and the Pengs nearly caught up with them at the end of the alley, but the girls broke off from their would-be admirers and set a determined pace for home. Staying together for safety, glancing around to make sure no one was following them as they disappeared down the street. The young men were gone nearly as quickly, arguing about which drinking establishment they would grace with their presence and who would stand the first round.

"Now," Prudence urged as they made the turn. Twenty-third Street lay empty and dark before them, Danny Dennis's carriage the only vehicle in the road. He'd lit the side lanterns but turned the flames down low.

The tap of their boots on the pavement resonated like whiplashes in the quiet night, punctuated by the sharp intake of nervous, desperate breaths.

"We're almost there," Prudence murmured. She saw Danny turn his head and raise his whip in salute. He wouldn't leave his perch to help them into the carriage, but as soon as the door was latched shut, they'd be off.

Johnny helped his mother in first. Lady Peng reached out for An Bao, who was having difficulty climbing the vehicle's single narrow step. She made it, but not without a cry that echoed off the near side of the hotel. Mei Sha was next, as nimble as a rabbit. Johnny paused to clasp Prudence's hand and whisper his thanks.

A ground-floor window flew open behind them, and a man's voice called out.

Without thinking, Prudence clambered into the carriage, keeping hold of Johnny's hand and pulling him in after her. The door slammed shut and Danny's whip flicked above the backs of his horses.

Prudence was on her way to Chinatown.

CHAPTER 9

The Lunar New Year celebrations were to begin at one A.M. with fireworks, drums, and every brass band that could make itself heard over the din. Delivery wagons had been removed from Chinatown's narrow streets and the day's manure shoveled and brushed from underfoot. Lanterns and candles glowed in every window and the corner gaslights burned brightly to dispel the darkness. Men who would work hard all their lives bathed and donned clean clothes, yearned for the families so many thousands of miles away, and prepared to honor the ancestors with the special dishes that were all the more delicious for being so seldom tasted.

Matthew Lam stepped out of the Golden Dragon Noodle Palace onto crooked Doyers Street, nearly knocked off balance by the press of the crowd moving toward where most of the fireworks would be set off. The kitchen and restaurant had been cleaned and readied for the next shift in record time, waiters and cooks given an hour off to join the celebration, the restaurant itself locked tight. Matthew had been the last man out, Zhu Ling's warning that anyone who did not return on time would lose his job and his bed hissed in his ear as the lock snicked closed behind him. The next two days would be the restaurant's busiest of the year; lazy or absent workers would not be tolerated. Did he understand? He did.

When Doyers Street dead-ended into Pell Street, the crowd surged west, toward the noisier and larger throng assembling on Mott Street. Nobody noticed that one of their number slipped off toward the other end of Pell. Matthew had a goal, a purpose, and very little time to accomplish it.

The man whose table he'd served after the English-speaking tourists left the restaurant lived at the lower end of Pell Street in a red brick building that housed both his business and his home. Every window was fronted by a metal balcony whose filigreed ornamentation had been created by a master craftsman, one of many who had worked for Wei Fu Jian over the years. Carpenters, plasterers, furniture makers, seamstresses, carvers of ivory—he demanded beauty and paid good money for it.

The potboy whose tongue Matthew had loosened with rice wine eagerly shared the little he knew about Wei Fu Jian, doubtless a paper identity. Hardly anyone who came to America did so under the family names he had borne in China. Matthew had nodded sagely, acknowledging without words that he, too, now lived under an alias someone else had chosen for him.

There were rumors that Wei was creating an organization to rival the benevolent associations of San Francisco, a society of brothers who would look out for one another, help when aid was needed, find work and housing, offer protection. Not for free. Nothing was free. You paid a membership fee, swore an oath of loyalty. Was Matthew familiar with how things were done in San Francisco?

He admitted that he was, then helped the potboy up the stairs to his miserably overcrowded room. Saw to it that he washed, dressed, and gulped down several cups of hot tea. Handed him into the care of another young kitchen worker and forgot about the two of them as soon as they disappeared into the crowd.

A man like Wei Fu Jian, if what the potboy had told him was reliable, knew everything that went on in Chinatown. If there was a hired assassin in hiding, one of Wei's informants would have discovered his whereabouts, who he worked for, and the name of the man he had killed. Information was power.

Wei's home and business were as the potboy had described, perhaps more impressive for what he hadn't said. The building had the look of a fortress to anyone with eyes to assess strength and vulnerability before architectural elegance.

He'd return in daylight, but from where he stood, across the street in the shadows just beyond a pool of gaslight, Matthew judged that someone had given a great deal of thought to protecting his personal privacy and the secrets that made for a successful business in this part of the world. The windows behind the decorative balconies of what he assumed were living quarters and offices were barred, and from the looks of them, securely set in their frames. Rolling security gates covered the shop door and the display windows on either side. Through the bars he glimpsed a well-stocked compendium of carved furniture, decorative porcelains, tea sets, and beautifully illustrated silk wall hangings. Everything to beguile a customer with time to dawdle and the cash to buy.

The potboy had said that Wei was considered Chinatown's foremost importer of items from the Celestial Empire, and so it appeared on the surface. Matthew was certain that another, darker world existed beneath the façade presented to the public, one that was illegal, dangerous, and immensely profitable. That's how fortunes were made and kept in this country, how the unwelcome Chinese profited and protected themselves, how graft-ridden local police were able to indulge the appetites their public payroll salaries couldn't afford. He would remain where he was, a waiter in the Golden Dragon Noodle Palace, but Matthew would take the risk of drawing notice to himself when he placed a bowl of noodles or a teapot in front of Wei Fu Jian. He would deliberately set himself up to be recruited and do his best to make sure it was sooner rather than later.

He moved into the shadows, waiting for a glimmer of candle or lantern light to reveal the presence of master or servants moving from room to room, but shades or curtains had been tightly drawn over every window. He assumed that like most important residents of Chinatown, Wei had allowed his people time to attend the opening fireworks but had prudently remained off the streets himself. He would pay his New Year respects to the consul tomorrow, host an elaborate banquet, refurbish the ancestral altar that lay somewhere in the depths of the house, and enjoy the public holiday festivities from afar. Whether Wei was harboring a contract killer in one of the buildings he owned was a question that could not be answered tonight.

The borders of the triangular stretch of streets known as Chinatown were as well defined as every other neighborhood in New York City. Newcomers might not understand that every ethnic group and every financial stratum existed within rigidly defined demarcations, but New Yorkers, even recently arrived immigrants, recognized the nuances and largely abided by them. Life was simpler if you knew your place and remained within its confines.

It took a little more than thirty minutes for Danny Dennis to make the drive from the Fifth Avenue Hotel to the corner of Pell Street and Bowery, where the carriage was to be met and its occupants escorted into safe hiding. For much of the way, he kept to the shadows of the Third Avenue El, the horses' hooves muffled by thick canvas wrappings. There was no reason to think they might be followed, but Danny believed in taking all possible precautions. Silencing a horse's hooves was a trick he had learned years ago in Dublin, before a single spot of care-lessness had landed him a stretch in Kilmainham Gaol, a place he never recalled without a shudder and clenched teeth.

He pulled the horses up in the darkness where Pell dead-ended into Bowery, acutely aware that someone had extin-guished the gas streetlight marking the corner. Good. That meant the plan was still in place, though he couldn't spot the men who should be waiting in the darkness.

The carriage door eased open, and he heard the rustle of skirts and the soft brush of feet meeting the ground. He'd caught only a glimpse of the three ladies and young man Miss Prudence had shepherded around the corner from the hotel, but he wondered if it had been wise to dress them in western clothing tonight. Most of the tourists curious about the Lunar New Year celebrations would be smart enough to confine their excursions to daylight hours, but there were bound to be young adventurers from outside Chinatown daring the crowds.

For the moment this street corner in Chinatown was quiet except for the echoing thunder of drums, the blare of brass bands, and the roar of the restless crowd on Mott Street.

"Do you see them?" Prudence whispered from where she was standing in the street below Danny's seat atop the carriage. One hand clung to the vehicle's large front wheel while she stretched onto tiptoes.

"Nothing," he answered.

"We're on time," she said. "I'm sure of it."

"They'll be here, Miss Prudence. They've already darkened the streetlamp, so they're ready for us."

Minutes passed. The Pengs huddled together in silence, heads turned toward the noise filtering down Pell from Mott Street.

Mei Sha slipped away from her mother's side. "Shall I go look?" she asked Prudence quietly. "My friends and I used to sneak out of boarding school all the time. We never got caught."

The faint gleam of white teeth told Prudence that the girl who had befriended Warren's damaged sister was smiling conspiratorially.

"This isn't a boarding school lark." Whatever else happened, Mei Sha couldn't be allowed to think tonight's escape was anything but deadly serious.

Mei took a couple of quick steps away from Prudence's side, stopped by her brother's strong arm. A furious hiss of whispered Chinese told Prudence she wasn't the only one afraid the girl would put herself and the rest of them in jeopardy.

"We can't wait too long," Danny said, peering up Pell, turning to stare behind and in front of them. Despite his earlier reassurance to Prudence, he was beginning to wonder if something *had* gone wrong, if he shouldn't take his passengers back to the Fifth Avenue Hotel where they could sneak inside without anyone knowing they'd ever been gone.

Bowery stretched empty in both directions.

Matthew had taken a first few cautious steps out of the shadows when he heard the jingle of harness and the creak of carriage wheels at the end of Pell Street where it ended at Bowery. He drew back, uneasy at being seen to be the only occupant of the street on a night when its residents were elsewhere. It would look suspicious, his lurking in an area of glass-windowed storefronts and buildings that weren't tenements.

The carriage pulled to a halt. A party of four or five people spilled out onto the sidewalk. He could make out their forms, hear the swish of women's skirts. Whoever they were, they wore western clothing; there was no mistaking wool for the fine whisper of silk and thick soled boots for soft leather shoes with cotton uppers. They seemed to be waiting for someone, whispering among themselves and shifting nervously from foot to foot as the minutes dragged by.

Something about the shape of the coachman's plumed hat looked familiar. Matthew thought he had seen him in the driver's seat of a hansom cab parked at the curb outside the building that housed the offices of Hunter and MacKenzie. He remembered Amos Lang telling him about an Irishman who drove a huge white horse and commandeered an army of street urchins, not unlike Sherlock Holmes's Baker Street Irregulars. If that was Danny Dennis at the end of the street, what was he doing in Chinatown at this time of night?

A woman detached herself from the group and walked to the carriage, half climbing one of the front wheels to talk to the driver. He had no logical reason to believe it was Prudence MacKenzie, but Matthew was suddenly very sure it could be no one else.

Hugging the storefronts and avoiding the lamplight, he started down the street, thankful the buildings were packed so closely together there were no alleyways between them. No dark passageways in which an assailant could hide. The sidewalk had been swept clean earlier in the evening. There was nothing to trip over, nothing to make noise beneath his feet as he picked up the pace. Nothing except . . . someone huddled in a doorway, body doubled over too awkwardly to be folded comfortably in sleep. Two men, propped on either side of the recessed entrance to a butcher's shop. Silent. Unmoving.

A trickle of dark liquid had spilled out of the doorway and gelled on the sidewalk.

He knew without dipping his finger in it that the fluid was blood, and the men were dead. Knifed and dragged out of sight.

A shadow moved, coalesced into the shape of a man wearing loose trousers and flowing jacket, a close-fitting silk hat on his head, a long queue like a whip down his back as he raced toward the carriage. One hand raised high above his head, steel blade catching a flicker of gaslight.

"Miss Prudence!" Matthew shouted as loudly as he could, feet pounding a loud tattoo as he ran. "Miss Prudence!"

He saw the woman at the carriage wheel hauled up by the coachman, legs kicking in empty air before her feet found a purchase. Heard her yell something to the people with her, saw them rush toward the carriage's open passenger door, scramble to climb inside. Even with the training he'd received on the Yale track team, Matthew knew he wouldn't make it to the bottom of the street in time to tackle the assailant with the knife.

He heard the crack of a whip, the howl of a man whose arm had been lashed, the clatter of a knife falling to the road. A shot. Another. The hammering of desperate feet running away, down Bowery toward Five Points. Too far a lead to catch him before he disappeared into the surging night life of the city's filthiest and most unsafe neighborhood. Matthew slowed down, trotting toward the carriage, chest heaving, throat raw.

Behind him, in the handsomely built brick building he'd been watching, a lantern appeared in an upstairs window, another in the window beside it. There was no electricity in this part of the city, but within moments the building came alive with light. Then noise as the front door opened and half a dozen men poured out, running toward Matthew, toward the carriage where one of its passengers had fallen to the ground and lay still.

Danny Dennis raised his whip, but Prudence pulled at his arm to lower it. She shoved the gun she'd just fired below his driver's seat, whispered a few quick words of explanation, then hitched up her skirts and climbed down to the street.

"She's all right," Johnny Peng said, cradling his older sister in his arms. "Frightened and knocked down when the man you shot at collided with her. But he'd dropped the knife before he could use it and then he ran for his life."

"I missed him in the dark," Prudence said. She'd been shooting more to frighten than to kill, but now she wondered if that had been a good choice. Geoffrey had told her more than once that you didn't carry a gun unless you meant to use it the way it was intended. To take a life. She had yet to make her first kill.

She didn't understand a word of what was being whispered around her, but she recognized Matthew Lam in the glow of a lantern that had appeared from nowhere. Bent over at the waist, hands pushing against his thighs, he wheezed like a spent racehorse before straightening to take deep breaths, brushing away hands that reached out to steady him.

"They're dead," the man Lady Peng had called Younger Brother told Prudence in his not-quite-perfect English. "The men I sent to meet you were knifed, their bodies hidden in a doorway. Who knew you were coming?" Anger hardened his voice.

"No one," Prudence answered. She turned to Johnny Peng, who had relinquished his sister to the arms of his mother. "Johnny?"

"Amah put chloral hydrate in everyone's rice wine," he said. "Exactly as we'd planned. No one else could have known we were leaving."

"Someone did," Prudence insisted. It was useless to deny that a leak had occurred. When she and Geoffrey had worked out all the final details of the flight from the hotel it had seemed a foolproof scheme. But something had obviously gone wrong. Failure was a bitter pill to swallow but gulp it down she must.

"It's time to leave, miss," Danny Dennis said from far above them. He'd lit the carriage's side lanterns but kept the flames low. "Horses don't like the smell of blood."

Prudence could hear metal shoes shifting on the cobblestones and the shake of harness. The bodies of the dead men had been loaded into a barrow and were being wheeled across the street toward the open door of the large brick house. Someone lit incense sticks to disguise the faint whiff of spilled blood hanging in the air. She glimpsed figures moving swiftly in and out of darkness and lamplight and realized that Wei Fu Jian had unleashed a small army into the emptiness of this end of Pell Street.

Lady Peng and her elder daughter were being helped away, half carried over the rough surface as their tiny feet fumbled for purchase. Mei Sha fairly skipped alongside them, clearly enjoying the unexpected end to their escapade, one arm held tightly by her brother. He turned and caught Prudence's eye, nodded his head briefly, then said something to his younger sister. Her steps slowed, but Prudence suspected it was only in token obedience.

Wei Fu Jian and Matthew Lam lingered beside the carriage as one by one the lanterns and the light they cast receded.

"I have to be back at the restaurant when it reopens," Matthew said when Prudence joined them.

"Go," she urged. "You've done good work tonight."

"He's new at this," Wei judged as Matthew took off at a trot for Doyers Street. "But you're right. He'll do well for himself."

"The man with the knife . . ." Prudence began.

"He dropped it, but Johnny said he saw him pick it up with the uninjured arm before he fled," Wei interrupted. "My men will find him. And deal with him."

"Lady Peng and her family are my responsibility," Prudence argued.

"I think you're mistaken about that." Wei touched her elbow, a prelude to assisting her into the carriage.

"I'm not going anywhere," Prudence said firmly, shrugging him off, stepping closer to where Danny Dennis waited for instructions.

"Tell Mr. Hunter what's happened, and that I've gone with the Pengs," she said. "He'll know what to do."

Without waiting for Wei to agree, she strode off, pausing only long enough to see Danny Dennis turn the carriage and disappear down Bowery, leaving her alone in Chinatown.

CHAPTER 10

"Two hours!" Geoffrey raged. "Two hours without a word about what was going on!" He'd scuffed an angry trail across the parlor carpeting in his suite and refused to drink the calming tea Josiah had ordered from room service. "What got into her, Danny? Why did she think she had to stay in Chinatown? What the hell was she doing there in the first place? That wasn't the plan!"

"It happened too fast. There wasn't time to think before she acted." Danny used the voice that soothed horses and carriage dogs.

"Twice?" Anger had given way to sarcasm.

"There was a beat cop on Fifth Avenue," Danny explained. "When the hotel window went up and whoever was in that room started calling out, I think she was afraid the cop would come around the corner, see the carriage waiting there, and want to know what was going on. She couldn't let that happen."

"A beat cop on Fifth Avenue in the middle of the night?"

Danny shrugged. A business like the Fifth Avenue Hotel could arrange just about anything with the local precinct if the cash payment was large enough. And relatively discreet.

"I can almost understand that decision," Geoffrey said, a shade less irate as Danny's explanations began to register with his innate sense of logic. "But why wasn't there a street boy nearby? And what could have prompted her to think that remaining in Chinatown was necessary?"

"I didn't think we'd need the boys," Danny confessed. A handful of his ragged band of street urchins slept in the stable with Mr. Washington and a five-month-old puppy named Flower, dog and urchins huddled together under blankets spread on heaped-up straw. Early February was a particularly vexious time for children who lived on the streets. Rarely dry and warm after the first snowfall, they weakened as winter coughs they hadn't managed to throw off grew worse. They died of consumption and just about anything else you could name before spring reached the alleyways.

Geoffrey seemed to sense what Danny had not said. "You're right. There wasn't any reason for them to be out tonight." He'd never known personal poverty, but he'd seen enough of it in the war-ravaged South where his estranged family still lived, in undercover Pinkerton assignments, and in the rat-infested and disease-ridden immigrant neighborhoods of the city in which he'd chosen to live. The street orphans Danny employed and looked out for were irreplaceable when it came to passing along information and following unsuspecting wrongdoers, but although it was part of their code never to admit weakness, the truth was that many of them fell into sleep at night with something less than an even chance of waking up. If he'd been in Danny's shoes when a plan was a sure thing, Geoffrey thought that he, too, might have given the boys some time off.

It was harder to curb his anger at Prudence's ill-considered choices. She'd acted impulsively on more than one occasion, and every escape from precarious circumstances seemed to fuel her willingness to take chances that would have given a more experienced operative pause. He had begun to wonder if the devil-may-care exploits were deliberate provocation, if Prudence was goading him into laying down the law about what she was and was not allowed to do. Which would be disastrous, leading to a monumental fight that neither of them could hope to win. The stakes were too high. Each of them would walk away with wounds that might never heal.

"It's too late and too risky to attempt to retrieve her tonight," Geoffrey said. "We can't afford to lay down a trail to where the Pengs are hiding. Their absence will be discovered as soon as servants bring them morning tea."

"Which isn't too many hours away," Danny agreed.

"I think it's time I brought Warren Lowry back onto the scene. He may know someone down at the Sixth Precinct who can keep an eye out for us."

"Before you do that, there's more you need to know." Danny had held off until now because Geoffrey's outburst at Prudence's having gone into Chinatown was nothing to the explosion to be expected when he learned the rest of the story.

"What else?"

"There wasn't anyone at the meeting place when we got to the corner of Pell and Bowery," Danny began. "We didn't worry at first, because the streetlamp had been doused. We figured they were waiting in the shadows until they could be certain we were the right carriage."

"Go on."

"Pell was deserted. Everyone had gone up to Mott Street for the fireworks."

"All right."

"Miss Prudence and the Pengs got out of the carriage. You could have heard a pin drop except that off in the distance was the sound of a crowd. After we'd been there for a few minutes, I told Miss Prudence it wasn't a good idea to stay much longer. I got antsy, Mr. Hunter, but I couldn't for the life of me tell you why. Maybe because it felt like the night I got picked up and sent to Kilmainham Gaol. The same sense that something had gone wrong."

"Then what happened?"

"A man came roaring out of the dark with a knife in his hand, raised up high like he meant business. I'd swear he was headed for Johnny Peng. Straight as an arrow. The women were together, off to one side, and Miss Prudence was standing at the front of the carriage, but young Peng was out in the open, all alone."

"Is Johnny alive?"

"Not a scratch on him. I used my whip and thought for a minute I'd managed to break the fellow's arm. No such luck. He dropped the knife, then grabbed it up before getting away down Bowery. There wasn't any way to stop him. Not with the ladies to protect."

Geoffrey cursed—round, ripe syllables that not even Danny had heard before.

"We had a couple of seconds warning because that young Chinese man you hired to go undercover yelled out Miss Prudence's name and ran like the devil down the street toward us. I don't like to think what might have happened if he hadn't."

"What was he doing there?"

"Staking out Wei Fu Jian's building. He didn't know what the connection was, only that he'd seen him at the restaurant and decided he was important enough to learn more about him. Not to worry, though. Lam went back to the restaurant in time not to get fired. Wei was taking the Pengs in, as arranged, when Miss Prudence got her back up. Said she wasn't leaving without them because their welfare was her responsibility. Words to that effect. So off she went. The last I saw she was disappearing through the door of that brick building. She looked very pleased with herself."

Wei Fu Jian's home was on the topmost two floors of the building that also housed his business and some of the men who worked for him. Like most of Chinatown's structures, it was narrow, five windows wide, with one locked door opening directly onto a staircase that led to the living quarters, bypassing the storefront, the business offices on the second floor, and the warren of small sleeping rooms on the third.

Prudence heard the thud of an iron bar across the street level entrance after they had begun climbing the stairs, but it wasn't until they'd reached the third floor that she realized there was access to the stairway from every story. Two of the men who had guarded their retreat from the carriage disappeared through a narrow door that fitted framelessly into the wall. You had to know what you were looking for to find it. She'd lost track of the rest of Wei Fu Jian's crew, but then she remembered the wheelbarrow with two bodies piled inside. Best not to think about where they were being taken.

The parlor into which they were shown was the most opulently furnished room Prudence had ever seen, though the style was unlike anything to be found on Fifth Avenue. The wooden furniture was carved, cushioned, highly polished, inlaid with gold dragons or hand painted in multicolored floral designs. Deeply piled rugs covered the floors, tall porcelain vases stood in every corner, and elaborate screens created private alcoves. Small tables were scattered throughout, shuttered lanterns hung from the coffered ceiling, and pots of incense perfumed the air. It was luxury that Mrs. Astor might have envied if it hadn't been so unlike the European palaces the Four Hundred had become obsessed with duplicating.

"You'll be safe here," Wei said in English. "There will be men guarding the street door from the outside and from within. Your privacy will not be invaded, but you need not fear that anyone who means harm will be able to reach you."

"The man with the knife," Johnny Peng said. "He meant to kill me, as I have to suppose he killed my father. If it hadn't been for the coachman and his whip, he might have succeeded."

"Tell me," Wei ordered.

"Danny Dennis works for us," Prudence said, interrupting Johnny Peng so smoothly that he hardly noticed he'd been edged out of the conversation. "He's used the whip to good effect before when things turned desperate. It's possible the assailant's arm was injured badly enough that he won't be able to use it for a while. He may seek treatment."

"He'll be identified if he does."

"Danny will tell my partner where we are and what happened."

"Is that wise? You were never supposed to know exactly where Lady Peng and her family were hidden."

"It's too late for that."

"The streets will be crowded with people celebrating the New Year tomorrow. I'm not sure I can get you out of Chinatown without your being seen. We can't risk it," Wei said.

"I agree. I'll stay for as long as necessary. At least until the celebrations are over and the revelers have gone home to nurse their sick heads."

"I'm honored that you choose to be my guest." Wei bowed, then turned his attention to Lady Peng and her daughters.

He spoke to them courteously but without the show of feeling he'd demonstrated in the carriage in Central Park. Prudence had felt sparks fly between him and Lady Peng at that meeting, though each had pulled back as soon as they realized how much they had given away. He had said he was Lord Peng's younger brother, and that Lady Peng would not go back to China. *We will not be separated for a second time.*

They were speaking Chinese, Lady Peng and the man she had called Younger Brother. Not to exclude Prudence, she decided, but because it was more comfortable, more familiar, more reassuring than English.

Prudence stepped away to give them an illusion of solitude, but really to assess from a distance how each of them felt about the other. Johnny and the girls were puzzled, but also intrigued. Lady Peng had assumed the mask of gracious indifference that must have served her well at Victoria's Court. But Wei was clearly frustrated that his careful plotting had been foiled, that an attempt had been made on Lady Peng's son, and that a gray-eyed American female detective had been thrust into his private and hitherto impregnable retreat.

Prudence sensed old secrets, painstakingly hidden for many years.

"As it happens, I do know someone at the Sixth Precinct," Warren Lowry said, inviting Geoffrey to make himself comfortable in the library of the Fifth Avenue mansion that had been closed up during the months he and Bettina had lived in Switzerland and traveled on the Continent.

"It's early in the day, I know," Geoffrey apologized, "but I want to get Prudence out of Chinatown as soon as possible." He'd walked the short distance from his hotel to the Lowry family residence immediately after breakfast, while Fifth Avenue was still virtually deserted, before the Sunday family carriage rides to fashionable churches began.

Lowry had been surprised to find him on his doorstep, but like any detective who'd spent years investigating crime, he was accustomed to odd hours and sudden twists of action in the case he was working. He'd listened attentively to Geoffrey's explanation of how a man identified as Lord Peng's younger brother had seemingly taken over arranging the family's future. Danny Dennis's role in the escape into Chinatown. It wasn't the only time a case had been thrown off track by circumstances no one could have predicted.

For the first time since they had left New York nearly a year ago, Lowry had begun to feel the bits and pieces of his life coalescing again. Bettina was safe and cared for, tended by the nurse who had traveled with them from Switzerland. If her recovery progressed as smoothly as the sanitorium's doctors hoped it would, he could get on with the professional life he had voluntarily set aside for her sake.

But he knew himself to be a third wheel in the Peng inquiry, a case that had come his way only because of a chance encounter with Johnny Peng aboard ship. He'd asked Prudence and Geoffrey Hunter to take it on as a personal favor to him, and they'd agreed, probably expecting him to be not much more than a shadowy presence in the investigation. Backing off whenever Bettina needed him. He guessed that Prudence's partner would pull every trick of the trade to keep him away from her, but he needed a Sixth Precinct contact. You played the cards you were dealt.

"You may not be able to manage a rescue right away," he told Geoffrey.

"How so?"

"I remember from my days with the police department that every street down there was impassable while the New Year celebrations were going on." Lowry paused for a moment, thinking. "Except for the area immediately around the consul's home. They kept that open so the carriages of important people could call on him to pay their respects."

"So another carriage won't be noticed in the crush," Geoffrey said. "The consul's home is on West Ninth Street. That's north of Washington Square, nowhere near the center of Chinatown." He waited a moment. "Danny Dennis told me."

"I'm sure Danny has a plan," Lowry said.

"He shouldn't have let Prudence get away from him, and he knows it. He's proposing that if Wei Fu Jian calls on Shen Woon, as etiquette demands, all he has to do is get Prudence out of the house on Pell Street without attracting attention. Once Wei's brougham reaches Ninth Street and enters the line of carriages waiting there, Danny will pull up next to him."

"She steps out of one vehicle into the other, with no one the wiser. Very nice," Lowry said. "Very neat."

"Who's your man at the Sixth Precinct?" Geoffrey asked, returning to his original question.

"His name is Alfred Hanrahan."

"Irish?"

"Mostly. Enough so no one asks if he's anything else."

"What does that mean?"

"Hanrahan may be the only cop down there who requested the assignment. The Sixth has a reputation for being rough duty."

"Rough duty can be profitable," Geoffrey said. Policemen in some areas of the city shook down both the criminals they were supposed to arrest and the citizens they were allegedly protecting. A man could and often did pocket more than his salary. It took skill, persistence, and sometimes the rough side of his nightstick, but the graft was well worth what he paid to join the force and rise through the ranks. "We need to know everything Hanrahan can find out for us about Wei Fu Jian, starting with how long he's been in Chinatown. How he got there, who sponsored him, the status of his papers."

"I'll send word," Lowry promised. "I did Hanrahan a favor once. He owes me."

"Good. Danny's waiting for the go-ahead. I'll let him know he can send one of his street runners to where the Pengs are hiding. Whether she wants to leave or not, we're taking Prudence out of there."

"You're sure about this?"

Geoffrey didn't answer. It was none of Lowry's business what Prudence wanted, and especially none of his business what she and Geoffrey might have to say to one another about it.

CHAPTER 11

Prudence didn't sleep well despite the comfortable bed in one of Wei Fu Jian's luxurious guestrooms. She tossed and turned, lighting, blowing out, and then relighting the candle on the bedside table. With nothing to read, she couldn't distract herself from the day's disturbing incidents. They played behind her closed eyes as though she were flipping through a sheaf of photographs, drawing her inexorably back to confusing reality when what she needed was some peaceful oblivion.

Finally, after hours of fitful dozing interspersed with restless wakefulness, she plumped the pillows behind her back and turned her mind to unraveling the complexities of what she knew about the Pengs. She was convinced that somewhere in the knot of secrets that was their family history lay a clue to the assassin's identity and the explanation for Lady Peng's apparent indifference to her husband's death.

She started by considering the person about whom she knew the least—Elder Sister, as the family often called her—whose name, Prudence remembered, was An Bao. She of the bound feet, exquisite porcelain skin, luminous dark eyes, and impeccably correct manners. Prudence tried to remember what An

Bao's voice sounded like and found she could only recall a few times in the past two days when she had spoken. Odd, because her younger sister, Mei Sha, sometimes chattered like a magpie, interested in everything and everyone, spouting opinions she didn't think to keep to herself. Elder Sister was twenty or more years of age, well educated, but not the product of years spent at an English boarding school. Perhaps that accounted for her silence and the self-effacing way she walked and held herself, as though her sole function in a room was to grace it with her uncommunicative presence.

As far as Prudence could judge, An Bao had not objected to the precipitous flight from the Fifth Avenue Hotel. She'd donned the maid's uniform without protest, stuffed handkerchiefs into the normal-sized ladies' walking boots that didn't fit her deformed feet, and followed her mother's instructions to the letter. There was danger in what they had done, so she must have wanted it enough to risk the certainty of punishment if they were caught. There had been no mention of a future husband in the offing, so perhaps an arranged marriage hadn't yet been contracted. Women of her rank did not choose their own spouses, did not expect any voice in selecting the man with whom they would spend the rest of their lives and whose children they would bear.

Elder Sister was as much of an enigma as some of the New York debutantes Prudence knew, the ones whose faces never revealed a conroversial thought or opinion, whose expensive clothing always reflected the latest Parisian trend, and whose sole preoccupation in life was to make the right marriage. It was the world into which Prudence had been born, but which she'd roundly rejected. Whether An Bao was content in the Chinese version of that universe or harbored rebellious thoughts was another of the mysteries keeping Prudence awake.

She thought she understood Mei Sha better, because she saw something of herself in the youngest Peng child. Prudence had never been to boarding or any other kind of school, but she'd delighted in confounding and successfully disobeying the governesses who had passed through her life. She'd learned outward restraint, but inwardly the young Prudence had seethed and bubbled with rebellion. As did Mei Sha. Unbound feet. Boarding school hijinks. Writing her name as *May* to imitate her English acquaintances. The quick shipboard friendship with Bettina Lowry. They all suggested to Prudence that Mei Sha might dread returning to China as much as the brother for whom Lady Peng claimed it meant certain execution.

Mei Sha, or May, as she'd told Prudence to call her, spoke perfect English, her accent that of the privileged British aristocracy. If all you heard was her voice, you would never guess she was anything but the daughter of a titled nobleman of Victoria's court. Yet as far as Prudence knew, she hadn't resisted leaving England, hadn't objected to her father's new posting in America and what it meant for her personal life. Prudence thought she might be seventeen or eighteen, old enough to be married off, young enough to want to choose her own life and not accept that it wasn't possible for someone of her background.

Life for Mei in Washington, D.C., would have meant virtual imprisonment in whichever mansion the Chinese government rented for Lord Peng. There would have been no more schooling, no opportunity to socialize with American girls or the daughters of other foreign diplomats living in the capital. Prudence could envision both An Bao and Mei Sha at their mother's side throughout long, boring days. Doing whatever it was women of their rank were condemned to do in order to make the hours pass. Needlework. Flower arranging. Composing letters. Sipping cup after cup of tea. It made her shudder to think how narrowly she had escaped such a fate.

There was something about Mei Sha that bore watching. She was too alert to everything going on around her, too aware of the world of adventure that had beckoned during her time in boarding school. If anyone in the family were to inadvertently betray their whereabouts, it was likely to be the youngest daughter.

On the surface, Johnny was the most transparent of the Pengs. Likable, intelligent, enthusiastic, athletic. Handsome. The perfect son of a cultural attaché. Proficient in languages, especially English, charming to the ladies, hardworking and obedient to his father, respectful of his mother. He'd studied engineering, which meant that at some point he must have been destined to be one of China's new men, leading the country into competition with the West. Then, with his father's murder, his life had foundered. If he and his lady mother were reading the signs correctly, Johnny's future was the blade of a sword slicing through his neck.

But if he remained in the United States? He would have to live the rest of his life underground. Change his name. Disappear. Could he go back to England? Would Victoria's royal court welcome him? Would her majesty's government protect him?

The more she thought about each of Lord Peng's children, the less sanguine she became.

And then there was Lady Peng.

When Prudence blew out the candle for the last time, she dreamed of a flaming dragon with the inscrutable face of a beautiful woman.

"I was three years old when we left China," Mei Sha said. She'd eaten nearly as much at breakfast as her brother, defiantly putting two steamed buns on her plate despite her mother's frown. "The only country I've ever known is England." She twitched aside a curtain covering one of the parlor windows overlooking Pell Street. "What's going on down there is as foreign to me as it must be to you, Miss Prudence."

"Careful," Prudence cautioned. "We don't want to be seen if anyone looks up." She tugged the curtain from between Mei's fingers and let it fall back into place.

"They're all enjoying themselves too much to bother."

"This is a rich man's house," Prudence reminded her. "People are always curious about wealthy, powerful men."

"Wei Fu Jian is our uncle. My mother sometimes calls him Younger Brother," Mei said. "We didn't even know he existed."

"Your father never spoke of him?"

"My father seldom talked to any of us about anything."

"He must have been a very busy man."

"He could smoke his pipe and play *xiangqi* against himself for hours. We were never permitted to interrupt or make a sound once the board was set up. *Xiangqi* is Chinese chess," Mei explained.

"A game of strategy," Prudence said.

"When Johnny got older, our father made him learn to play. He beat the palms of his hands with a bamboo rod whenever my brother lost. Which was almost always. Sometimes the welts were so swollen that Johnny couldn't bend his fingers. Amah bathed his hands in ice water and rubbed a healing cream into them."

"Amah?"

"She was our nurse when we were babies. She's always taken care of us. We wouldn't have been able to get out of the hotel suite without her."

"Yet she didn't come with you?"

"She'll find us," Mei Sha predicted.

"I'm sorry you lost your father," Prudence said after a moment or two of silence. "I know what it's like when a parent dies."

"Only Elder Sister wept. An Bao. It sounds strange to call her Elder Sister when I speak English," Mei said. "Johnny isn't sorry. He's honor bound to avenge him, so he'll do his duty, but he won't miss him. Neither will I."

"Your mother?"

Mei Sha shook her head. "My father had concubines in China.

He visited them when he reported in person to the empress, but as far as I know my brother is the only son. Does that shock you?"

"I'm not sure," Prudence said. It wasn't uncommon for wealthy men to have mistresses, but to speak so casually and openly of them was something she'd never encountered before.

Neither Prudence nor Mei Sha had heard Lady Peng enter the room.

"My husband was very much like the Prince of Wales," she said with a touch of asperity to her normally even tone of voice. "He never met a woman he didn't want to bed. Edward prefers his mistresses and casual conquests be married. Lord Peng didn't make any such distinctions so long as the woman was available."

"I beg your pardon, Lady Peng. I didn't mean to intrude." There was a great deal more Prudence wanted to learn about the late attaché, but she knew from experience that it was best to feign an apology followed by a show of indifference toward the subject under discussion. The combination often unleashed a flood of confidences.

Lady Peng spoke quietly to her daughter in Chinese. Mei Sha stiffened, then bowed and left the room.

Stalked from the room is how Prudence later described it to Geoffrey.

"My youngest daughter has yet to acquire the virtue of discretion," Lady Peng said, smiling to soften the criticism. "It's best not to encourage her."

"She's a very intelligent young lady."

"So she proved to be in that school to which we sent her. We may be suffering the consequences for many years to come. Did she tell you to call her May?"

"I'm trying to understand," Prudence said.

"Are we that strange to you?"

"The orders to return to China came so quickly from your government. And the decision not to obey was equally swift."

"It's very simple, Miss MacKenzie. I don't want to have to witness my son's execution."

"Surely Lord Peng was aware he had enemies when he left London."

"Every powerful man has enemies. He took precautions."

"What did he expect?"

"Not what happened. That should be obvious. My late husband anticipated something more subtle, a move against him that he could counter with a stratagem of his own. I wasn't privy to his innermost thoughts, but I lived with him long enough to be able to predict what he was likely to do. He believed the danger would come when we reached Washington, and that it would be delivered through diplomatic channels. Perhaps a demotion in rank. He did not foresee naked violence."

"You're certain the government wanted him dead? It wasn't a personal vendetta?"

"Isn't that what my son has hired you to find out?"

"We have so little information," Prudence began. "So few leads to follow."

"Now I'm not understanding you," Lady Peng said.

"Normally, when we begin an investigation, we interview everyone who knew or had contact with the victim. We dig into his personal life. His business affairs. We uncover what he tried to hide, the secrets he didn't want anyone to know. Including his family. We follow threads that lead us to suspects. We learn everything we can about each dubious individual. It's a laborious process, but one that seldom fails. Most murder victims are killed by people they know. Rarely by a stranger."

"Please don't question my daughters unless I'm present," Lady Peng ordered. "I would say the same for Johnny, but as he's a man, I can't expect him to abide by all my wishes."

Strange that she called her son by the name his English friends had given him.

Prudence wondered if she'd made a mistake explaining so forthrightly how inquiry agents worked. She'd put Lady Peng on her guard, warned her that the personal questions she found objectionable would not go away, would be asked again and again until they were answered. Truthfully. Fully.

If Lady Peng chose obstructive silence or lies, there were other ways of getting at the facts.

It was left up to Josiah to spirit the Pengs' nightclothes out of the hotel, a task far easier than smuggling in the maids' uniforms and housekeeper's dress. He only needed two of the haberdashery boxes, and because he was compulsively neat, he folded the ladies' nightgowns and Johnny's bulkier nightshirt as neatly as though they were newly ordered items being readied for delivery. Mr. Hunter was used to his ways, but Josiah was glad, nonetheless, that his employer had gone to the Lowry mansion, leaving Josiah alone to set things right in the apartment suite before the hotel housekeeping staff appeared. The secretary never liked being watched while he straightened up.

He thought housekeeping had arrived early when he heard a rapid tattoo on the door, but everything incriminating was out of sight, so he supposed he might as well let the maid in. She'd only come back if he didn't.

A very short, very broad elderly lady pushed past him and kicked the door closed behind her. She was wearing baggy pants and a long jacket with frogged closings and wide sleeves. Her black hair was gray streaked and pulled back from her face in a tight bun nestled at the base of her head. She was, he intuited, Chinese. The language in which she was scolding him certainly wasn't English. She clutched a brown medicine bottle in one hand, thrusting it at him as she marched farther into the parlor.

Chloral hydrate.

"Amah?" Mei Sha had begged her mother to allow someone by that name to come with them. Lady Peng had refused.

"I put them to sleep," the Chinese lady said. Her English was labored but comprehensible. "They know it this morning, so I leave."

"Knockout drops?" There was a trace of admiration in Josiah's voice. He'd done many odd things for Hunter and MacKenzie, but so far he hadn't actually rendered anyone unconscious. He wondered how many drops you administered to induce sleep rather than death.

"They gone?"

"Last night. Within an hour of leaving their suite they were safely on the way."

"That true?"

He nodded, not sure how much he should reveal. What on earth would Mr. Hunter do with Amah when he returned? She couldn't very well remain in the hotel, not if the other servants knew what she'd done. The police would want to question her, and while he thought admiringly that she might prove a match for them, he didn't see any point subjecting her or them to the ordeal.

"Would you care for some tea?" he asked, then suddenly realized he didn't dare telephone room service.

"Tea, yes."

"Sorry. No tea after all. We can't have you found by one of the waiters, can we?"

A key turned in the lock.

Amah looked around frantically, then grabbed the cane that Geoffrey sometimes used and more often left leaning against a piece of furniture. Brandishing it over her head she spread her legs wide and sank into a crouch.

Muttering a long string of what Josiah assumed were Chinese threats and curses.

Geoffrey closed the door behind him, then paused for a moment in the foyer, taking in the scene. "Ah," he said. "I see you've been busy, Josiah."

What was there to say?

Geoffrey walked directly to Amah, bowed politely to her, and gently extracted the cane from her hand.

"I assume I'm meeting Amah. We've heard about your cleverness putting the servants to sleep with knockout drops. I must congratulate you on a job well done."

He bowed again, and this time Amah returned the courtesy.

It seemed they understood one another.

CHAPTER 12

Wei Fu Jian stationed six of his men on the sidewalk at the outside door to his personal quarters. The moment they heard the click of the lock opening, each of them unfurled a colorful umbrella so that a silk and oil paper canopy rose between the building and the carriage waiting in the street. No one looking down from a neighboring building or walking by saw two figures enter the vehicle, one dressed in the formal robes donned for special occasions, and the other clad in western dress. One male, one female.

The umbrellas came down, the horses stomped their hooves, and the carriage moved off, its destination the home of the Chinese consul on West Ninth Street.

Prudence had had no part in concocting the scheme to smuggle her out of Chinatown. One of Danny's street urchins had memorized the instructions. Albeit transfixed by the red and gold splendor of the store and the luxury of the proprietor's private office, he managed to repeat them verbatim to Wei. There were very few children in the Chinese population, just as there were almost no Chinese women. Anti-Chinese legislation had seen to that. Wei had tipped Danny's messenger generously, slightly envious that he hadn't a comparable pool of fleet-footed youngsters at his beck and call.

He'd given Prudence no choice when she protested that she preferred to remain with the Pengs whom she stubbornly insisted on calling her clients.

"You are no longer bound to them," he'd informed her. "Their safety is now my concern."

"I'll have to hear it from Johnny's own lips," Prudence had argued, knowing that using the English nickname was likely to infuriate the man she sometimes called Younger Brother in her own mind. It made him seem less formidable.

"Fa Cho is not the head of this family. He does not make decisions."

"He hired my firm and signed a contract with us, a valid legal document in the state of New York." She was on shaky ground here because it wasn't at all certain that Johnny Peng's signature was worth the ink it had taken to write it. She had banked on the fact that Wei Fu Jian would assume she knew what she was talking about.

He hadn't given her the satisfaction of a decent war of words. It was beneath his dignity to quarrel with a woman. She'd waited alone in the parlor, no member of the Peng family to keep her company, until two of the guards ushered her down the stairs and into the carriage.

Where she sat in silence as the brougham rolled slowly through the crowds thronging the streets.

Wei said not a word, and when she turned to speak to him snapped open a fan that effectively blocked his face from view.

Disgusted at being treated like a nonentity, annoyed that she'd had no say in this plan to spirit her out of Chinatown, Prudence folded her arms and stewed.

Warren Lowry insisted on going with Geoffrey to Chinatown.

"Hanrahan might be doing crowd control outside the consul's house," he argued. "I can have a few words with him."

"That's not part of the plan," Geoffrey said. "We don't get out of the carriage. Prudence is the only one who moves, and she does it without attracting attention. As soon as we have her, Danny whips up the horses and we're gone."

Lowry shrugged, but didn't give in. The carriage Danny would be driving was large enough to seat the three of them without crowding. He'd be at the Fifth Avenue Hotel in plenty of time.

And he'd come armed.

Amah wouldn't be left behind either. She marched down the main hotel staircase as if the Pengs had not gone missing, as if her lady mistress was sending her out into the city on an urgent errand. As if she weren't following Geoffrey at a decent distance, watching to see which carriage he got into.

No one noticed an old servant woman. No one paid the slightest attention to where she went or what she did. Amah turned a beaming, self-satisfied smile on Geoffrey, and settled in beside Warren Lowry for the ride to Chinatown. In the pocket of her trousers, she'd hidden the bottle of chloral hydrate. There was no telling when she might need it again.

The carriages lined up outside consul Shen Woon's home stretched for several blocks along Ninth Street, each of them cleaned and polished to show respect, some decorated in red for luck, gold for prosperity and good fortune.

The shades were drawn on Wei Fu Jian's vehicle. One bodyguard rode beside the driver and two others stood perched behind the passenger compartment. It wasn't unusual for him to appear in public with attendants in tow, but there was something about their marked alertness that drew curious glances. The carriage took its place at the end of the column, which was a bit strange. Wei never waited, wherever he went. Minutes passed. Elaborately gowned men entered the consul's residence, made their obeisances, and returned to the celebrations in Chinatown. The procession moved slowly up the street, exuding patience, dignity, and pride. Daily life in America might be hard and precarious, but there was comfort and honor in preserving old ways, old customs.

Danny Dennis's carriage pulled alongside Wei's brougham and stopped. The bodyguards leaped from their stations and opened a door in each carriage, their bodies shielding the figures who moved quickly from one into the other. Before anyone who might be watching realized what had happened, Danny's horses had moved off again, picking up speed as they passed alongside and then beyond the column. Moments later the carriage was out of sight.

Lowry slid his revolver back into the shoulder holster from which he'd loosened it. His bright blue eyes crinkled at the corners as he smiled at Prudence, and he risked presumption by leaning forward across the space that separated them to whisper, "Well done!"

Geoffrey said nothing.

Prudence settled back in the seat, appraising the two very different men. One dark, silent, and coldly angry. The other, all smiles and warm welcome.

"In case either of you is interested," she began, "the Pengs made it to safety, but that's the only thing that happened according to plan." She paused for a moment. "I presume that elderly woman who nearly knocked me off my feet between the carriages is the amah who administered the chloral hydrate on Lady Peng's orders?"

"She showed up at the suite while I was out this morning," Geoffrey said stiffly, glancing at Lowry. "Josiah was there getting rid of anything incriminating. She insisted on being allowed to join the Pengs. There was no way to stop her."

"I find it's rarely possible to interfere with what old ladies are determined to accomplish," Lowry said. "Nannies and housekeepers are the worst of the lot." Again he smiled, white teeth against skin tanned on the ski slopes of Switzerland. He was obviously thinking of the women who had raised and nurtured him.

"Mei Sha and her sister will be glad she's joined them," Prudence said. "My impression is that Lady Peng shows very little emotion to anyone. She doesn't want to see her son executed, but love or grief was never mentioned. I did find out there's at least one concubine in China, but no additional sons."

"You might have been killed," Geoffrey barked. "If Danny hadn't used his whip, if the assailant hadn't been so single-mindedly focused on Johnny Peng . . ."

"It happened so quickly . . ." Prudence began.

"That's exactly why the attack on Lord Peng was successful. It came out of nowhere and was over before anyone realized what was happening," Geoffrey said.

"What else could she have done?" Lowry asked. His voice was measured, his question reasonable.

"I would never have been able to explain to the policeman stationed outside the hotel what I was doing without an escort on the side street at midnight," Prudence argued. "Warren is right. I had no choice. I had to get into the carriage and Danny had to drive all of us to Chinatown as fast as he could." She stared challengingly at Geoffrey. "You would have done the same in my place. Don't deny it."

She felt his eyes on her, boring into her skin as they moved across her face and down her body.

"I wasn't hurt," she said. "What happened was unforeseen, unexpected, and yes, violent. But I dealt with it the way you trained me to do, Geoffrey. And I've come through without injury to anything but my pride." She was explaining and apologizing, two things she had promised herself she would not do.

She reached out a gloved hand to touch the man sitting next to her, eyes seeking his from behind the veil Wei had insisted she wear. A wave of emotion so strong she was powerless against it overcame every other feeling. It was as though she had slipped from her body into his, as though for the first time she saw herself the way she appeared to him, resolute and brave, but fragile. For the briefest moment, she understood his need to protect her. She had shared that fervor when he lay on the floor of a railway car, bleeding to death in her arms.

When the immediate danger had passed, when she'd been confident he would live, she'd fought against the passion, naming it the enemy of her independence. But perhaps she'd been wrong. Perhaps there was nothing to fear but her own uncertainties. She felt his fingers close around hers and she lifted one hand to raise the veil that separated them.

Then she remembered they were not alone in the dimness of the carriage. Warren Lowry sat opposite, a very large intrusion whose presence could not be wished away. Enough of what Prudence's governesses had drilled into her remained so that she reluctantly withdrew her hand from Geoffrey's. The length of her arm remained pressed lightly against his, but the temperature of her body cooled. She was once again in control, though slightly curious about what might have happened, what might have been said, had not an observant third party been present.

Society's small talk, as it was designed to do, came to her rescue.

"The Patriarchs' Ball is tomorrow night," she said, remembering the invitation that sat on her mantelpiece, a much sought-after summons to the last major event of the social season, one it had been unthinkable to refuse. People who didn't receive the so-called ticket, printed on heavy stock with the guest's name handwritten above that of the patriarch who had invited him or her, frequently fled the city on some fabricated excuse for their urgent departure. Better to be gone than known to have been excluded.

Warren Lowry looked puzzled, but Geoffrey understood immediately.

"The best way to ensure that no one suspects a link between

us and the Pengs' disappearance is to appear at Delmonico's as if unaware of anything untoward," he said. "Even after their flight is discovered, Danny's role in the escape is unlikely to be suspected. Impossible to prove even if Detective Phelan were smart enough to ask the right questions."

"They are still our clients, despite what Wei Fu Jian might think," Prudence asserted.

"They are," Geoffrey agreed.

"We promised to find Lord Peng's murderer," Prudence continued.

"I dragged you into this," Lowry interrupted. "No one will hold it against you if you decide to withdraw."

"Hunter and MacKenzie doesn't go back on their word," Geoffrey said.

"We never have," Prudence agreed.

"Nor have I," Lowry reminded them.

Wei Fu Jian had ordered food from the Golden Dragon Noodle Palace before he left Pell Street with Prudence in tow. He'd known Zhu Ling for years, ever since he himself had arrived in Chinatown looking for work and a new life. Like Matthew Lam, Wei had been given a job as a waiter, not because he had any previous experience in eateries of any kind, but because Zhu read something in his eyes and the way he carried himself. Within a very few years, Wei had more than fulfilled that early promise, rising quickly to a position of power and prestige that owed much to Zhu's support.

The restaurant owner's ambition was an odd one. He didn't seek advancement for himself, but for the promising young men who showed up at his door needing only a slight push to send them on their way. Zhu may have been the only one to understand that as his protégés gained stature in Chinatown, he also profited. Each of them owed him a debt which they were honor bound to discharge. Zhu build around himself a cordon of physical protection and financial security that was the envy

of everyone who observed its extent and permanence. Since he
wasn't greedy in the way of most men, and he was content with
a modest way of life, hardly anyone harbored animosity toward him.

Matthew Lam was one of the brightest prospects to come his
way in a long time. Clever, talented on many levels, a hard
worker whose eyes missed nothing and whose ears heard and
understood everything. Wei Fu Jian favored him, which was a
good sign and an invitation. When Wei's order was brought to
the restaurant, Zhu plucked Matthew from among the most
practiced young waiters and named him his assistant. There
was no question of delegating service; Zhu himself would see
that nothing was wanting, and perfection realized.

It wasn't until they had arrived at the brick house on Pell
Street that Zhu realized how very unlike other dinners this
one would be. His most important client had only just returned from paying his respects to Shen Woon. He was still
wearing the embroidered robes of a formal caller, but he ordered that the special dishes he had commanded were to be
served to his honored guests immediately, while still at the
peak of their flavor.

Honored guests. Never before, to Zhu's knowledge, had
Wei entertained anywhere but in the public setting of a restaurant. For guests who were not family members to be welcomed
into the private rooms of a man's home was a rare honor, one
that inevitably incited curiosity.

The honored guests were Chinese, with the pale skin and
delicately molded features of generations of aristocratic breed-
ing, but as they entered the dining room and took their places
around the lacquered table while Wei briefly excused himself,
they spoke English to one another. Zhu did not understand
what they said, but Matthew Lam did. He thought it a very as-
tute thing to do, since it was obvious that Wei's servants and
bodyguards were far from adept in the language.

Last night, after Matthew had come roaring out of the darkness to warn the Pengs and frighten off the assailant, Wei had given orders that no one but Matthew had heard. He was to remain at Zhu Ling's restaurant but keep his ears open and report the whereabouts of any new arrival who might have knowledge of or been involved in the death of Lord Peng and the assault on his son. There was no question of refusing. That simply, that quickly, Matthew was recruited into what would later become one of the most feared tongs in Chinatown. His allegiance had to remain secret for the time being. Did he understand?

He had understood all too well. Wei Fu Jian had marked him. No cleanser on earth could wipe away the stain. He wondered whether Miss MacKenzie and Mr. Hunter would comprehend the significance of what he had had no choice but to agree to.

Lady Peng was the most beautiful woman Zhu had ever seen, her daughters nearly so. When she smiled at him and complimented him on the excellence of the dishes he had prepared for them, Zhu's heart nearly burst through his gown. He was old and a man of distinction in Chinatown, but Lady Peng's casual attention made him feel like a young man again. A young lover on the verge of the greatest happiness of his life. He contrived to serve her and the daughters seated on either side, leaving Wei and the man he learned was the lady's son to the waiter he had chosen to accompany him. Whom he knew spoke English and could therefore tell him the details of the conversation he had not understood.

Once Wei rejoined his guests, clad in finer though lighter-weight robes, English was abandoned in favor of Cantonese. Zhu learned more than he wished to know about the host's guests. Dangerous knowledge for which someone would pay him generously. If he had a death wish. Betrayal would cost him his life. When he was able to exchange glances with Matthew Lam, he saw that the young waiter had reached the same conclusion.

"You will say nothing of what you have seen here," Wei told

him at the end of the meal, counting shiny American coins into Zhu's outstretched hand.

The restaurant owner bowed his dutiful acquiescence. Not a word would pass his lips.

Matthew Lam caught Mei Sha's eye as he removed a dish of Eight Treasure Rice Pudding from the table. The serving spoon brushed his thumb and rattled against the bone china.

She smiled. *Clumsy*, she mouthed. Smiled again.

He felt the blood rise to his ears and knew she had recognized him from last night. He'd thought it too dark for him to be remembered, but the Peng daughter looking so intently at him as she waited for a silent reply did not resemble the few shy Chinese girls he had met. This female was brightly alert, alive with curiosity, unafraid to put herself forward.

Wei touched the girl lightly on the shoulder.

"Come, niece," he said, a shade louder than necessary.

Matthew knew he was meant to hear and be warned.

CHAPTER 13

"Jack Astor is getting married next week in Philadelphia," Prudence said, rattling the pages of the newspaper she was reading. "Tuesday, to be precise."

"That means the Four Hundred will all be out of town," Josiah remarked. "It's the end of the season after tonight's Patriarchs' Ball, so it hardly matters." He ran a small feather duster over the surface of his spotlessly clean desk, readying for the day. "Will you be going, Miss Prudence?" As if he weren't holding his breath for her answer.

"Definitely not to Philadelphia," she said, loudly enough for Geoffrey to hear through the open door of his office. "Not while we're working a case as unusual as the Peng murder." She thought she heard a noise somewhere between a scoff and a chuckle. "The Astors are furnishing a private train for two hundred guests, so not everybody will be gone."

He couldn't quite figure out how to ask if his employer had been one of the exclusive two hundred, so Josiah studied his feather duster.

It amazed him that Prudence MacKenzie treated the invitations that came her way as though they were of no more social importance than a casual stroll along the Fifth Avenue stores of the Ladies' Mile. He knew for a fact that New York society was a hotbed of ambition, jealousy, and cupidity. Those who were in had to play by Mrs. Astor's rules in order to remain so, while those on the outside coped with exclusion and the dread probability of never breaking through the barriers erected to keep them out.

The wedding of John Jacob Astor IV and Miss Ava Lowle Willing was as much an arranged joining together of two enormously wealthy and influential families as any European royal marriage. Josiah would have to content himself with reading about the twenty-five-year-old groom and his twenty-two-year-old bride in the *Times* and *Town Topics*. Even when she did attend major social events of the season, his employer rarely paid close attention to the details of decoration, menu, and guest lists; he had to glean these from the society columns.

"It's given me an idea though," Prudence said, putting down the paper, drifting toward Geoffrey's office.

"What's that?" Geoffrey asked. Gentleman to the core, he rose to his feet as Prudence approached his desk.

"We're definitely going to Delmonico's tonight," she began. "You haven't changed your mind?" Geoffrey had as little patience for and interest in the doings of high society as she.

"No. I still think it's a good way to pick up any gossip about the Pengs. No one needs to know we have inside information about their disappearance. In fact, I'm beginning to doubt it's public knowledge yet."

"Detective Phelan hasn't contacted you?"

"Not a word."

"The Pengs have been gone from the Fifth Avenue Hotel for twenty-four hours."

"My guess is that the Chinese government is making its own arrangements behind the scenes," Geoffrey said. "They'd just as soon not attract any attention until they've figured out where the family has gone into hiding and who helped them."

"The hotel is bound to report them missing soon." Prudence ticked off the most obvious reasons. "No maid or waiter has been inside the suite for almost a day and a half. People like the Pengs are used to having their meals served, their beds made, and towels replaced. There's bound to be gossip downstairs."

"Lord Peng's staff have been given their instructions by the bodyguards and the man the ambassador sent up from Washington. They'll be too frightened of the consequences to do anything but obey."

"So as far as the public is concerned, the Pengs have retreated into their hotel suite to mourn the death of the head of the family. And requested that they not be disturbed. No visitors."

"Two detectives in the New York City Police Department may be the only people in the city to know that Lady Peng and her son have hired a private inquiry firm to look into the death," Geoffrey said.

"The police won't be in a hurry to confirm that story if a reporter broaches it. Phelan especially won't want any implication that he and his colleagues can't solve the case."

"So that leaves us in the shadows. A very desirable place to be in this instance."

"Which brings me to the idea I had," Prudence said.

"Explain?"

"There are two prongs to this case. Agreed?"

"One—Find Lord Peng's killer, and two—ensure that Johnny Peng doesn't get deported to China to have his head detached from his body."

"Exactly. If we accept the fact that the murderer is blending into the Chinatown population, then Matthew Lam is our best chance at finding him. Or Wei Fu Jian. We leave Matthew alone and hope for the best. For the time being anyway.

"Younger Brother's house is probably the safest place for

the family to be right now. Whoever he is, Wei seems to command a small army of armed men. They're more than bodyguards. And his association with Lady Peng is not that of your typical brother-in-law. If he thinks she's in danger, he'll have every man he can spare out on the streets."

Josiah had gotten up from his desk and inched his way toward Geoffrey's office, stenography pad and pencil in hand. He knew they'd want notes, even if neither of them had thought to ask.

"Which brings us to how we keep our government from loading Johnny onto a ship outward bound from San Francisco harbor."

"I'm listening," Geoffrey said.

So was Josiah.

"William Whitney and his wife will be at the ball tonight. So will Senator Hiscock."

"Whitney is a Bourbon Democrat and Hiscock's a Republican who doesn't stand a chance of being reelected," Geoffrey said.

"Ward McAllister and Flora Whitney are leading the procession into supper."

"Not Mrs. Astor?"

"I've heard whispers that the queen bee is slowing down. She's sixty years old. And she's distracted right now by Jack's wedding. She has four daughters, but only one son. Flora Whitney is only ten years younger than Mrs. Astor, but I have it on good authority that she's one of the she-wolves nipping at Lina's heels."

"Where do you get this kind of information, Prudence?" Geoffrey asked, eyes twinkling at the delight of his normally very serious partner revealing herself to be just as enthralled by titillating gossip as the next woman.

Josiah was spellbound. Miss Prudence had called Mrs. Astor *Lina*.

"William Whitney is the important one," Prudence said, ignoring Geoffrey's question. "Someone has to distract his wife long enough for me to make my case."

"Won't she be dancing with McAllister?"

"He flits like a blood-sucking mosquito from one socialite to another," Prudence said. "I'm going to need a little time."

"So I'm to be the victim laid on Flora Whitney's altar?"

"You may not want to admit it, but you *are* one of the city's most eligible bachelors. Every debutante's eye will be on you whirling Flora across the dance floor. Believe me, she'll want to be the envy of all the younger women."

"How many dances?"

"One. That should be enough. You don't want to make a boor of yourself by ignoring the rules of etiquette. Just make sure it's a long one."

"Definitely not a boor." It was all Geoffrey could do not to tell Prudence that in this moment she resembled her aunt, the dowager Viscountess Rotherton, so closely that the thought of it made him shudder.

"William Whitney was Grover Cleveland's Secretary of the Navy," Prudence continued, nodding at Josiah, laying out the plan she hoped Geoffrey would agree to. "He was very good at it if you can believe what was in the papers. Nearly single-handedly rebuilt the way the Navy Department is organized and run, not to mention commissioning a small fleet of steel cruisers and gunboats. The only thing standing in his way of completing the job was Cleveland's not getting reelected. Though rumor has it he plans to run again in ninety-two."

"Whitney?"

"Grover Cleveland. Whitney's a close friend, and he'll be involved with the election campaign, but I think Flora wants to be in New York City when Lina Astor falls. William seems to have retired from active government service. He's deeply into private investments in real estate development, street railways, and thoroughbred horse racing. His personal ambitions no longer lie in Washington."

"You've lost me," Geoffrey said.

"I had to give you the background," Prudence explained. "The point I'm going to make is that Johnny Peng is as westernized as a Chinese can be, and, like Whitney, he's a navy man. Do you remember that Warren told us Johnny studied at the Royal Naval College in Portsmouth? That makes him a sailor as well as an engineer. I'm going to appeal to Whitney's naval experience and the loyalty one mariner owes another. If anyone can slip Johnny Peng through the Washington bureaucracy and get him a special license to remain in the United States, it's William Collins Whitney."

"And if he takes up Johnny's cause, he'll have to include Lady Peng and her two daughters."

"Anything else would be unthinkable."

Josiah nearly dropped his stenographer's pad and pencil. He'd almost thrown out his hands in wild applause. Leave it to Miss Prudence!

Geoffrey said nothing for a few moments, running the scheme over in his head, searching for flaws. He didn't think the Pengs stood much of a chance fighting extradition in a U.S. court. Their only hope of remaining in America was by the kind of backroom deal that experienced Washington politicians made every day of their terms.

"That just might work," he said. "The new Secretary of the Navy is building on what was accomplished during Cleveland's term, so even though he's a Republican, he and Whitney ought to have a good off-the-record relationship."

"Benjamin F. Tracy," Prudence said. She'd done her homework. "He's even more of a high seas navy man than Whitney. Johnny's training at the Royal Naval College is the best credential anyone could earn. It won't hurt to hint that someone like Johnny Peng is the kind of new American a burgeoning fleet will need."

"Don't push it too far," Geoffrey warned. "The Chinese Exclusion Act is still very popular."

"I'll keep Senator Hiscock in reserve in case Whitney isn't as receptive as I'm hoping he'll be. He could decide that sponsoring a Chinese would be bad for business," Prudence said. "Hiscock has always been someone who never quite made it into the inner circle, but he is one of the United States senators from New York. He has influence while he's in office, and if we have to, we can use him. In a pinch."

She cocked her head slightly to one side, looking up at Geoffrey from pale gray eyes half hidden behind lowered lids and soft lashes.

"I give up," he said, raising his hands in surrender.

"Good. I like a man who accepts defeat gracefully," Prudence said. "I think I'll wear the pale yellow silk Worth ballgown that Aunt Gillian thought was too daring for Queen Victoria's court. It should be just right for the last Patriarchs' Ball of the season. Don't you think?"

Josiah couldn't have agreed more.

Matthew wasn't sure where he stood. Zhu Ling expected him to serve Monday lunch in the restaurant, but the slightly less iron-handed way he spoke to his most recent hire hinted that he also knew Wei Fu Jian had laid claim to the new waiter's time and loyalty. The threads and layers of power in Chinatown were complex and challenging to navigate successfully. It was sometimes called *changing faces* when a man had to choose between two masters. In Sichuan opera performers donned and discarded masks with lightning-fast speed, obscuring the risks of deception with style.

In Matthew's case, he was already serving three masters: Hunter and MacKenzie, the owner of the Golden Dragon Noodle Palace, and Wei Fu Jian. But there was a fourth, known only to Matthew himself, though he'd be hard-pressed to explain the why of it. He was a creature caught between two cultures, knowing his mother's world far better than his father's, but compelled to make peace with the two warring sides of himself. Perhaps only another such as he would understand the conflict, but he knew no one else who claimed one Chinese and one American parent. He'd been called *mongrel* so often he'd lost count.

For the moment, and until he was given other orders, his task was to ferret out any newcomer to Pell, Doyers, and Mott Streets who might have had a reason to kill Lord Peng. Whether the individual was a paid assassin or exacting a personal vengeance was immaterial until he'd been delivered into the hands of the man who would judge him. By right that could only be Johnny Peng, whose father had been the victim. No Chinese law would condemn him for demanding whatever price would satisfy honor. The son alone had the right to torture until the truth was known or, if such was his will, to execute and leave the offenses of the past in the shadows where some might say they belonged.

Matthew began by using Monday's morning hours to drift slowly along the streets and sidewalks that were thronged with tired celebrants of the Lunar New Year. Men stumbling homeward to catch a few hours of sleep before the fireworks woke them for a second night of revelry. Men moving slowly under the rice wine and opium haze that dulled the pain of living far from homeland and family, the deep sadness of siring neither sons nor daughters, the fear of never being able to rejoin their ancestors.

He studied the passing faces, looking for the confusion of someone new to Chinatown's streets, the desperation of a man searching for a hiding place, the frequent backward glances to assure himself he was not being followed. A professional killer for hire would not betray himself, but an ordinary man who had committed an extraordinary act of honorable vengeance was likely to be suffering the aftershock of having succeeded.

Despite his wealth and phalanx of bodyguards, Lord Peng was dead, and if Matthew's suspicions were correct, the bloodied knife that had done the deed was still concealed somewhere on the killer's person.

He searched for an hour, drank a small cup of hot tea from a street vendor, walked for another hour. It was all the time he could spare before having to present himself at the restaurant, where there would be tables to check and the clean white shirt, bow tie, and black pants to don before Zhu opened the doors. Most of Chinatown's inhabitants were from China's southeastern provinces; Matthew recognized them by their speech and facial features. He remembered the stories his father had told of the village in which he had been born and the small city in whose Presbyterian mission he had grown to adolescence. Orphaned. Alone in the world. Also in southeast China.

At the end of the two hours he'd allotted himself, Matthew was no further along in his quest than he'd been at the beginning. Except to begin to question the logic of what he was doing. He hadn't seen a single Chinese who didn't seem at home and at ease in the crowded streets, who didn't appear to know exactly where he was going and how to get there. The only outsiders were small groups of tourists following behind guides like goslings after a goose. The sightseers seemed to find everything in Chinatown intriguing, strange, and amusing, staring at shopkeepers as though they were a different species of human, commenting in loud English they obviously didn't expect anyone to understand. Or perhaps they did, and simply didn't care.

Matthew had visited the Central Park Zoo. He thought the crowds in front of the animal cages and the visitors to Mott Street had a great deal in common.

Matthew stood at the entrance to the Golden Dragon Noodle Palace as Zhu unlocked the door. He bowed and welcomed the tourist diners in broadly accented English, remembering to mispronounce his *l*'s and *r*'s. He smiled warmly, ushering them to tables next to the large windows where they could view the activity in the street. Handed them menus, recommended the chop suey that every Chinese knew had been invented in California for American palates.

He'd half expected to see Wei Fu Jian at his usual table, then realized that as long as the Peng family was in hiding in the brick house on Pell Street, he was unlikely to leave them. Matthew had sensed something between the beautiful, widowed Lady Pell and the man she'd addressed once as Younger Brother, quickly correcting herself, using thereafter the name he'd probably assumed on coming to America. A paper son? A contract laborer? Someone in Chinatown might know who Wei had been before he'd arrived, what his family name had been in China. It might hold the key to why he'd stepped forward when the Peng family needed rescuing.

No one made the journey to New York City from wherever he'd been without a guide, whether it was a smuggler who worked the eastern Canadian border or a series of handoffs from the docks of a port of arrival to a contract job for which the laborer was paid a pittance. Everything cost money. What you couldn't pay in cash you worked off—for years, sometimes most of a lifetime.

Traffickers were notoriously edgy, implacably set against negotiation, indifferent to the human plights of their cargo. They seldom worked alone, paying protection cuts up the line, often living as close to the edge as the people they transported. One mistake, and your career was over. Your life forfeit if your carelessness threatened to disrupt or reveal the workings of the chain.

But a smuggler was always open to putting more money in his pocket. And if a new customer demanded proof of success before handing over a fistful of hard-earned cash for a relative still on the West Coast or in faraway China, he might just pick up the name of another contact or a satisfied customer. Greed, more than anything else, made cautious men foolhardy.

Matthew would start with Zhu Ling. He'd ask one question. And if Zhu believed he was doing a favor for one of Wei Fu Jian's recruits, Matthew could walk away with a name that would eventually lead him to the man he was hunting. A risky and uncertain step, but the only one he felt would set him in the right direction.

CHAPTER 14

"I can't breathe," Prudence complained, one hand placed delicately on Geoffrey's arm as they walked the red carpet into Delmonico's shortly before midnight. "I told Colleen not to lace me so tightly, but either I've been eating too many tea cakes lately or the blasted dress has shrunk."

"You look beautiful," Geoffrey said. "Language." Prudence's aristocratic aunt could swear like a sailor when so inclined. This was the second time in a single day that his partner had reminded him of Lady Rotherton. He wasn't sure how he felt about it.

"You're insufferable when you want to be," Prudence chided, smiling radiantly at no one in particular as they paused at the entrance to the restaurant's scarlet room, where the pre-supper dancing was well under way. Towering palms, exotic potted plants, and bowers of hothouse flowers lined the walls, their fragrances warring with the ladies' French perfumes and the gentlemen's Macassar oil. "The Archduke Joseph's Royal Hungarian Band again," she commented. "You'd think twice this season would have been enough."

Geoffrey bent solicitously toward her, lifting one gloved

hand to his lips. "Stop complaining. You're working tonight," he whispered. "Shall we dance?"

It was a waltz, Prudence's favorite, and she melted into Geoffrey's arms without further comment. They'd danced together before, but each time was as exciting as though it were the first. She'd accepted that there was something between them that attracted, titillated, and pleasured her, but Prudence had grown determinedly wary of the legal commitment of marriage and its financial and social consequences.

After years of struggling to believe in herself and fighting for independence, she could not bear the thought of surrendering to the subservience of the marital state. Neither was she inclined to throw off all the traces of acceptable behavior and indulge in what she knew her father would have condemned as licentiousness. People did it, even icons of high society, but Prudence was certain Geoffrey wouldn't bend that far. The woman always suffered greater opprobrium than the man.

She breathed as soft a sigh as she could manage, but the tightening of his arm around her waist told her he'd felt the whisper of her breath. They'd come close so many times, and always it was Prudence who pulled back, Geoffrey whose dark, disappointed eyes neither pressured nor judged. Lately she'd begun to wonder if he'd once pushed too hard and lost someone very dear to him, if he'd vowed never to make that mistake again. There were questions she had long ago decided she would not ask; a mark of the growing trust between them would be the depth and extent of unsought confidences. But for the moment, and until the music ended, she was content to enjoy the nearness.

Ward McAllister did indeed lead the procession into the dining room below the floor where the dancing took place, Flora Whitney on his arm. Four hundred guests were accommodated at magnificently laid tables: white linen cloths ironed to perfection; heavy silverware gleaming in the candlelight; crystal glasses sparkling; oysters, canvasback duck, foie gras, English pheasants among the gustatory delights served on Delmonico's distinctive china. Precious jewels flashed like shooting stars as the ladies turned their heads, raised and lowered arms and hands. The gentlemen, an army of expensive black and white, touched heavy napkins to beards and mustaches between courses, pretended to listen to what their dinner partners were saying, and noted who was here and who wasn't, who with a quick glance and nod seemed to be arranging a private conversation. Society was business and business was society.

Prudence located William Whitney as soon as she was ushered to her table, deciding that she could easily make her way in his direction as soon as the supper ended and the cotillion began in the large ballroom. Every eye would be on the season's debutantes, making their final formal appearances in carefully chosen and much rehearsed quadrilles. Which of them had managed to snare the supreme prize of a wealthy fiancé from a family of impeccable lineage? And which deflated young beauties would pin their hopes on the Newport season or go abroad with their families to await an embarrassing second try at the marriage market?

With gossip traveling through the crowd at a speed unmatched by any conveyance, and Geoffrey on the dance floor with Flora Whitney, Prudence thought she would have no difficulty drawing aside the former Secretary of the Navy. If she remembered correctly, there was a small alcove near one of the velvet-draped windows that would do nicely. Quiet, private, yet in full public view so as not to excite speculation.

It was even easier than Prudence had thought it would be. Her late father had known everyone of importance in New York City and the nation's capital, and all of them had respected the judge's powerful integrity. His reach had extended well beyond the bench he'd occupied for half his lifetime; his own and his beloved wife's families were bastions of old New

York Knickerbocker lineage. No one and nothing, including recently acquired fortunes, could influence the staid Dutch descendants of the city's original settlers. Unless and until they chose to intermingle and then intermarry.

So when Prudence greeted William Whitney with a shy, sweet smile, he smiled in return and bent to kiss her softly on the cheek, as befitted an old friend of the family. As a young man, he'd once been in love with her beautiful mother, and he'd shared many a cigar and snifter of brandy with her father. Old New York City was changing, too rapidly for some, but William Whitney and Judge Thomas Pickering MacKenzie had controlled it for as long as they could. Whitney, now that he was no longer serving the chief executive in Washington, D.C., was poised to reclaim his hold on the city's financial growth and development wars. Building construction, street transportation, racetracks—mention any of the rapidly expanding enterprises and you would find Whitney's name attached.

"Might we step aside for a few moments?" Prudence asked, hinting at a topic too delicate for public conversation. She pictured her father's face in the place of Whitney's and hoped her imagination would lend a daughterly cast to her own facial features.

"Of course, my dear." Whitney glanced around, spotted the alcove toward which Prudence had been leading him, and promptly stepped into its shadowy privacy. "Now, what seems to be the trouble?"

It was a phrase so often used by her father that Prudence immediately felt reassured. The judge had said more than once that his most important talent was to be a problem solver. William Whitney, successful in business and politics, was cut from the same cloth.

"Did you read the *Times* story about the death of Lord Peng at the Met?" Prudence began. Whitney and his wife were generous supporters of the museum but hadn't attended the reception that welcomed the attaché to New York and opened the exhibition of rare Chinese artifacts and textiles. Their absence from so important a cultural event was unusual.

"I did read the article," Whitney said. "And for once I was glad Mrs. Whitney and I had chosen to remain at home that day. She was indisposed." It was an explanation he would have offered only to family or close friends. One did not publicly acknowledge a lady's illness.

"I'm so sorry," Prudence said. Someone had told her that Flora Whitney suffered from a weak heart and had intermittent attacks of frailty and fatigue. Yet she was dancing tonight with Geoffrey as though in perfect health. "It was probably to the good that Mrs. Whitney wasn't there to witness the stabbing. It was unlike anything I've ever seen. Drops of blood flying everywhere."

"According to the papers, the assassin got away," Whitney said.

"No one thought he was anything but one of Lord Peng's servants or bodyguards when he was making his way through the crowd," Prudence explained. "Then, after he'd done what he came to do, he disappeared out onto Fifth Avenue. Geoffrey and Warren Lowry chased after him, but he moved so quickly there was no catching him. And no one on the street or in the park would admit to having seen him."

"I'm sorry you had to be present at such a horrific event," Whitney said. "But then, in your new situation, perhaps you've grown used to close encounters with all types of malfeasance." It was as close to criticizing her as he would allow himself to come. And he softened it with a benevolent smile.

"We're usually called in after the crime has been committed," Prudence remarked.

"Does that mean you and Geoffrey Hunter are working the case?"

"We'd rather not have it generally known."

"I won't give you away. But I *would* like to tell Flora. She's

intrigued by what you young ladies want to do nowadays."
Shocked would have been a better word to describe his wife's
opinion.

"It's Lord Peng's son who needs our help," Prudence said.
"As well as Lady Peng and her two daughters."

"Is that where I come in?" Whitney asked. "I'm much too
practical to think you've gone to the trouble of taking me aside
purely to renew the family acquaintance."

"Johnny Peng studied at the Royal Naval College in Portsmouth," Prudence began.

"He would have done better to apprentice aboard ship, unless he was at the college to learn engineering," Whitney said. "I
seem to remember that a number of young Chinese men attended classes there at one time, but that was years ago."

"Until recently you were President Cleveland's Secretary of
the Navy," Prudence said.

"That doesn't make me a sailor. And a term or two at Portsmouth doesn't make Lord Peng's son a midshipman."

This wasn't going in the direction Prudence had intended.

"The Chinese government wants the Peng family to return
to China."

"That doesn't sound unusual, under the circumstances."

"Johnny has reason to believe that Lord Peng was about to
be recalled, and that he would have been stripped of wealth and
rank by Peking. Almost certainly executed." Prudence paused.
"In Chinese custom, if the father cannot be prosecuted, the son
takes his place." She lowered her voice to a near whisper. "Lady
Peng fears her son will be beheaded."

"It's the policy of the United States not to interfere with the
internal workings of another country," Whitney said, dismissing the personal side of the Peng dilemma. The eyes behind the
rimless pince-nez iced over.

"Not even to save a life?" Prudence asked. "What I'm suggesting is just that you have a word with the new Secretary of
the Navy, and that a way be found to allow the Pengs to be ex-

ceptions to the laws directed at restricting access of Chinese to the United States."

"Because this Johnny Peng is an educated man?"

"Exactly. And because to send him back to China is to condemn him to death. He's done nothing to deserve it. In America we don't hold a man responsible for the sins of his parents."

"Your Mr. Peng isn't an American citizen."

"President Harrison voted against the Chinese Exclusion Act when he was a senator. Surely, if the current Secretary of the Navy were to bring this case before him, he'd be inclined to issue an extradition waiver in the Pengs' favor."

"Two points, young lawyer Prudence. Harrison wants to be reelected two years from now. He'll lose the western states if he shows himself weak on the Chinese question, especially now that so many border crossings are being made through Canada. This president upholds the law, whether he personally agrees with it or not."

Prudence could feel the heat of the candles and smell the sweat of the dancers. The loss of what she'd confidently hoped for was weakening her at the knees and making the room swim before her eyes.

"The second point, dear lady, is that it would not be in my own best interests to sponsor the Peng family. I don't know them personally and I have no wish to increase the number of Celestials seeking permanent residence in our country. Their labor was necessary in the goldfields and to build the transcontinental railroad, but the goldfields have played out and the last spike was driven into the transcontinental rails more than twenty years ago. We don't need the Chinese anymore. The problem is that they don't seem to realize it. They won't go back where they came from."

She could feel his eyes boring into her own. Implacable, unyielding, perhaps a trifle amused that the daughter of an old friend should think to ask such a preposterous favor.

Whitney reached for two glasses of champagne from a passing waiter. He pressed one chilled crystal flute into Prudence's trembling fingers.

"You've overreached yourself on this one, Prudence. Stick to crime, if you must, but stay away from politics. And never, never mix the two."

Bowing politely, the handsome, urbane, charming gentleman who had so easily and completely rebuffed her withdrew from the alcove and disappeared into the crowd ringing the dance floor.

Prudence sipped the sparkling wine, then drank it down as though it were water. Aunt Gillian always said that bitter medicine was best taken at a gulp.

"I'm building a kingdom here," Wei Fu Jian said as unemotionally as though he were announcing the weather. "Elder Brother stole everything from me. My ancestral family, my future, my name, the life I was born to live. You. He had me kidnapped, smuggled aboard a steamer, sold into contract labor that was supposed to be a death sentence. He made it so I could never return to China, never name him as my tormentor. But I survived."

"I knew nothing of that," Lady Peng said.

They were walking in the small walled garden behind Wei's brick building, a private, narrow space made into a tunnel of greenery by overarching trees and tightly woven vines. A hidden door opened onto a flight of steps leading to the cellar where an underground passage led to a building several streets away. Wei had vowed never to be trapped again, never to leave himself without a means to escape hired stalkers.

"He was very clever, my older brother. Coldhearted, greedy, predatory, politically ambitious. Your marriage was essential to the path he'd staked out for himself."

"Not the marriage," Lady Peng corrected, "the link to an ancient lineage that my family provided. I was never important to him except as a tool to be used and discarded when it was no longer needed." She had hidden her feelings for so many years that speaking the truth was as comforting as the warmth of an amah's embrace. Lady Peng had never known the consolation of a mother's love or a father's pride. A husband's true affection. She had been born an object to be traded, of value only for what she represented.

"You cannot go back."

"They will track us down."

"Not here. Not in my kingdom."

Not for anything would she deny him his dream, but Lady Peng had spent much of her adult life outside China. She knew what it was like to live in a white man's world. Even in the rarified atmosphere of diplomatic credentials there had been slights, whispers, looks. Victoria's empire stretched around the globe, but its only privileged citizens were born in the home country. To be English was to claim superiority over every other race and creed. It was as natural as breathing though it choked half the world to death.

She didn't expect America to be any different.

"New York City's Chinatown will learn from what's been done in San Francisco," Wei said. "The community strengthens itself through unity and mutual support, by establishing societies that a man can count on to help him when he needs a place to live, a job, food to sustain his body, and the knowledge of who he is to nourish his soul. The societies have grown strong in San Francisco. Soon one or more of them will send a representative east to organize us, but he'll arrive to find that he's too late. We won't be a finger on someone else's hand."

"That's what you meant when you said you were building a kingdom," Lady Peng said.

"It's nearly complete," Wei said. "The structure is in place, my soldiers recruited. It only remains to convince a few remaining shopkeepers and day laborers that their future lies under the umbrella of my protection."

"And if a man chooses not to join with you?"

"He will find it to his advantage to be a member of my tong." Wei raised a hand, smiled at the outstretched fingers, and made a slow, grasping fist.

Lady Peng looked at the man she had loved as a young woman, the man she had declared she wanted to marry, and saw traces in him of the older brother whose wife she had been forced to become.

CHAPTER 15

Geoffrey took the champagne flute from Prudence's hand.

"I'm not finished," she protested.

He smiled as though they were discussing nothing more disconcerting than the flowers that were beginning to wilt in the heat generated by banks of candles.

"Yes, you are," he murmured. "I think you've drunk enough."

"William Whitney as good as called me a bluestocking idiot."

"More fool he."

"Senator Hiscock was worse. I barely made my argument when he cut me off and said the Chinese question had been settled once and for all by legislation that would remain law for the foreseeable future. He called me *little lady,* as though I were twelve years old and should still be upstairs in the nursery." She looked around for a waiter with a tray of full glasses.

"I think it's time we left." Geoffrey took her firmly by one gloved elbow, steering her through the crowd that paid them little attention now that the debutantes had taken their places on the floor for the first of the elaborate quadrilles they'd been rehearsing for days.

"I'd like to give Mr. Whitney and Senator Hiscock a piece of my mind," Prudence said as they made their way toward Delmonico's Fifth Avenue entrance. "I was too taken aback to be anything but polite, but now I realize my father would never have let them have the last word."

"You're not your father, Prudence. Men like Whitney and Hiscock don't listen to what women have to say. They rarely consider anything that isn't financially rewarding. They and others like them own the country. When you own something, you'll move heaven and earth to keep anyone from taking it away from you."

It was such an astonishing thing for Geoffrey to say that it stopped her in her tracks. His family in North Carolina still owned vast tracts of land if not the laborers who worked the fields. He was as much a part of the moneyed elite of the country as she was.

They climbed into Prudence's carriage in silence.

"There's no hurry," she told Kincaid, settling back against the tufted velvet cushioned interior.

James Kincaid had been the family's coachman since Prudence was a girl. He knew that when he was told there was *no hurry* it meant there was a conversation going on below him that required privacy and time. It was a beautiful late winter night, stars twinkling in a clear black sky. The snowstorm that was blanketing Albany had spared New York City. For now, at least. He kept the pair of matched bays to a sedate walk and hunched his shoulders into the thick woolen coat that would keep him warm for as long as Miss Prudence needed her confidential time.

"I tackled Senator Hiscock after Whitney turned me down," she told Geoffrey, still angry and embarrassed at how cavalierly her father's old friend had treated her. "I don't think he listened to half what I had to say. As soon as he heard the word *Chinese,* he tuned me out. I could tell by the vacant expression in his eyes."

"I'm sorry you had to put up with that, Prudence," Geoffrey

said. "I really thought you had a chance of success, more so with Whitney than Hiscock, but still . . ."

"I knew it was a long shot," she said, "but I thought that if I told them about Johnny's education and the threat to his life, one or the other of them would see him as a person, not a faceless alien trying to crash his unwelcome way into their country. I badly misjudged the extent of the prejudice that exists against the Chinese."

"That's to your credit. I've never known you to assess character by skin color, nationality, or economic status. It's a rare quality, Prudence, one of which you should be proud."

The cold night air was clearing her head of champagne fog. She nestled a gloved hand into the warmth of Geoffrey's crooked arm, letting her head rest for a moment against his shoulder. He could sometimes be so understanding that she wondered why she kept putting him off when she knew, she sensed, that he very much wanted something more to grow between them than what they already shared. At a moment like this, she wanted it, also.

"Do we still have a client?" Geoffrey asked, jolting her back to the reality of a case that might not even be theirs anymore.

"We did yesterday. I spoke to Johnny and to Lady Peng while I was under house arrest at Wei Fu Jian's. Neither of them had fired us."

"*House arrest?*"

"That's what it felt like. A very comfortable, very luxurious detention, but with absolutely no chance of leaving. There were guards in the stairwell and at every doorway. Very competent looking. Armed, of course. And looking like fighters about to launch themselves onto an attacker if necessary."

"Wei probably has them trained in martial arts. Silent and deadly assassins, very unlike the noisy Irish and Italian gangs we're more used to."

"Do you think that's what he is, the head of a criminal gang?" Prudence asked.

"It makes sense. When an entire people find themselves locked out of opportunity and the professions, the logical step is to turn to crime. Our finest titans of industry all have incidents in their backgrounds that won't bear close inspection, and they don't have the excuse of being stymied in their ambitions by bigotry and intolerance."

"I still can't find the link to Lord Peng. His murder doesn't seem connected to anything we've learned about the family or the diplomatic situation. Granted he may have been in his government's disfavor, but I can't see an assassin being dispatched to kill him on foreign ground. What if the executioner hadn't managed to get away? What if he'd been captured and then implicated the Chinese government in the murder? Can you imagine the headlines?"

"They may not care," Geoffrey said.

"I thought saving face was one of the most important aspects of their culture," Prudence said. She'd tried to familiarize herself with Chinese history and customs after the invitation to the exhibition opening had arrived.

"I think the answers to our questions lie in the Peng family history," Geoffrey mused. "No professional killer would have struck in a room crowded with onlookers and museum guards. Not with a knife that could have been snatched from his hand or lost in the excitement of the attack. This was a highly personal homicide, fueled by an almost insane anger or thirst for revenge."

"How coincidental is it that Lord Peng's younger brother is a powerful resident of New York City's Chinatown? Mei Sha told me the children had never heard of this uncle until Lady Peng told them of the plan to disappear from the hotel."

"The first question is whether Lord Peng knew of his brother's whereabouts when he agreed to open the exhibition instead of going straight to Washington. Or Lady Peng. Did she know?"

"And when did Wei Fu Jian learn the name of the new cultural attaché? Shouldn't his family name also be Peng?"

"Unless he entered this country under a false identity," Geoffrey said.

"I need to go back to Chinatown," Prudence decided.

"Maybe both of us," Geoffrey said. "Warren Lowry gave me the name of a police officer at the Sixth Precinct who owes him a favor. We're more likely to get accurate information about Wei from him than anyone else."

"Not if he's on the take," Prudence argued. "Haven't I heard you say you could count the honest cops in the city on the fingers of one hand?"

"I may have exaggerated slightly."

"We can't go to the precinct house without everyone in the building knowing who we are and what we want. That could be dangerous if Warren's friend is bucking the system."

"We'll figure something out," Geoffrey said, settling farther back into the carriage seat, clasping the hand Prudence had nestled into the crook of his arm. This was where she sometimes turned skittish, drawing away from him, changing the subject of whatever they were discussing.

But tonight she allowed herself to remain pressed against him. When he leaned down to catch a glimpse of her face in the flickering light from the gas streetlamps, she turned and smiled, raising her lips to his.

Shen Woon poured a cup of fragrant jasmine tea for his guest from Washington. Both men were tired. Shen Woon from the parade of countrymen paying their New Year's respects, Huang Ma Tu from trying to figure out how the Peng affair had so quickly and inexplicably gone wrong.

The widow and her children, who should have been preparing to board the train that would take them across this benighted country to San Francisco and the ship waiting to

transport them back to China, had instead disappeared some-
time during the dark night hours of late Saturday and early
Sunday. Vanished into thin air like puffs of smoke from the
firecrackers that had been noisily exploding in the Chinatown
streets.

"Where could they have gone?" Huang asked, sipping the
scalding hot beverage that eased the painful knots in his stomach.
"The amah has also left the hotel. The bodyguard doesn't know
exactly when, but it has to have been to rejoin the family."

"She was the one who put a sleeping potion in the wine the
servants were given?"

"The bodyguard remembers that she brought him wine
when he was on duty in the hallway outside the suite. *A very
nice old lady*, was how he described her. Hardworking, devoted
to the daughters, always smiling and bowing politely."

"If she came to Chinatown, someone will have noticed her.
There are very few of our women here, and no elderly amahs
that I'm aware of."

"The ambassador is concerned. He wants to know if you
have trustworthy men you can send out to search for the Pengs."

Shen Woon spread his hands in the gesture of helplessness
no one could mistake. "They didn't disappear by themselves,"
he said. "Someone spirited them away from the hotel without
their being seen or followed. That takes planning."

"Are you suggesting that the scheme was concocted before
Lord Peng left London?"

The consul shrugged. "It seems likely."

"Lord Peng was very well thought of at Victoria's court,"
Huang said, mulling this new wrinkle he would have to explain
to the ambassador.

"Then I would look into the possibility that someone in her
majesty's government has seen to it that Lord Peng's family is
safely ensconced in a British colony."

"Canada?"

"It's a very large country. Dominion, to be strictly accurate."

"But why?"

"He was a wealthy man, afraid for his life if he suspected that the premier had turned against him. Put yourself in his place."

"He didn't foresee that a madman in blue workingman's jacket and trousers would come out of nowhere wielding a knife."

"No. That he did not anticipate."

"Which makes me think it wasn't a political killing."

"I doubt we'll ever know." Shen Woon poured more tea.

"If not Canada, then where?" Huang asked.

"The Bahamas." Wei Fu Jian had whispered the words into Shen Woon's ear as he pressed a heavy purse into the consul's hand. "The voyage to New York was to confuse pursuers."

"The ambassador has been granted a meeting with the American Secretary of State," Huang said. "To express the premier's wish that the Peng family not be granted resident status in the United States."

"Easily done," Shen Woon predicted. "But I doubt they're still on American soil."

"There remains the matter of Lord Peng's son. The premier will not be satisfied until Peng Fa Cho has answered for his father's indiscretions. Honor must be served."

Shen Woon's eyebrows climbed slowly up his forehead.

"I don't know the details," Huang confessed. "I don't think the ambassador does, either."

"Lord Peng was not Manchu," Shen Woon reminded him. "If I'm not mistaken, the family is Han, from one of the southern provinces. They came into imperial favor when many of the southern Manchu governors were replaced by Han." He didn't mention the widespread corruption that had weakened and threatened Manchu rule and the Qing dynasty itself. It was never prudent to reveal one's personal opinions and allegiances.

"The empress dowager doesn't look favorably on officials

who have allowed themselves to become too westernized. She doesn't oppose reform, but she insists that it be neither rapid nor extensive. Nothing can be advocated without her express permission." Huang's western attire and facility in the English language were sometimes worrisome to the ambassador, who had warned his assistant more than once to be more discreet, less obviously affected by American culture. Until now, Huang had paid little attention to the cautions.

"Perhaps Lord Peng became too British. He sent his son to the Royal Naval College after the empress had decreed that no more Chinese students were to be educated abroad."

"I've met him," Huang said. "Did you know that he calls himself *Johnny* Peng? That's apparently a name his English friends chose for him."

"Male friends, I hope."

It was such an outrageous complication that Huang wanted to refuse to consider it.

"It wouldn't be the first time a western female has become intrigued by an exotic alien," the consul said, using terms often found in newspaper articles about his fellow countrymen. "When the attraction results in a misalliance, it's usually because the woman is from a missionary family and persuades the man to enter into a Christian marriage." Shen Woon scowled.

"Lord Peng would never have been appointed to Washington if his son had been consorting with an Englishwoman."

"Johnny Peng would have been discreet," Shen Woon said.

"No one keeps secrets from the empress dowager," Huang reminded him. It was one of the most frightening things about Empress Dowager Cixi. She no longer acted as regent for the Guangxu Emperor, but her hand was in every political pot and her opinion ruled every government policy and decision.

"I only mention the possibility because we are no closer to understanding why Lord Peng had to die than we were at the moment it happened," the consul said. He had no idea why

Wei Fu Jian wanted Washington to believe Lord Peng's family had fled to the Bahamas. The size of the purse he had received silenced any questions he might have asked.

"I suppose it's conceivable," Huang said. He refrained from mentioning the latest telegram from Washington that had hinted at his own return to China if the Peng situation were not swiftly resolved. Espousing the idea of a retreat to the Bahamas arranged by the late Lord Peng himself would place the burden of responsibility squarely on the shoulders of the empress's agents in London. There was still the matter of the death to deal with, but Huang thought it might be dropped if the empress believed the Pengs had removed themselves from the political scene. Agents would be dispatched eventually to the Bahamas, but probably not immediately. Disappearing into a British colony was not an unknown way to escape a government's wrath. One could also consider that Empress Dowager Cixi was midway through her sixth decade of life. Who knew how much longer she would influence the emperor?

"If Johnny Peng is as westernized as you believe, he might well have turned away from the honor he owes his father to avenge his death," Shen Woon said, offering an acceptable explanation for why the Peng heir was no longer in America.

"And if Lord Peng had made arrangements in the Bahamas, it would have been a considerable expenditure."

"One the family would be loath to lose," the consul agreed.

"We still don't know who did the killing or why," Huang said, deciding that the idea of an escape from Peking's wrath to the Bahamas solved at least one of his problems.

"Does it matter?" Shen Woon asked. "If the murder was for a personal reason, and if Johnny Peng sees fit to abdicate his responsibility to avenge the family name, then why should Peking concern itself with the death of a man destined for execution anyway?"

"Why indeed?" Huang said, sipping at his tea, running over

in his head how he would rephrase Shen Woon's line of reasoning.

Most of diplomacy was finding an acceptable excuse for dismissing an unsolvable problem. Huang thought the consul might have hit upon a very neat response that the ambassador and Peking would endorse. Which meant Huang's head sat a bit more securely on his shoulders.

For the time being.

CHAPTER 16

Alfred Hanrahan met Prudence and Geoffrey at an empty storefront on Doyers Street south of Pell.

"Rumor has it some Presbyterians are interested in the property," Hanrahan told them as he unlocked the front door and ushered them inside. "Anyone who notices us will assume you're from the church board come to take another look at the place before finalizing an offer."

"Are there multiple bidders?" Geoffrey asked, looking around at the dim, dusty space. The wood floor was splintery, with nails protruding just high enough to catch a boot heel. The only daylight in the single large room filtered its way through two dirt-streaked display windows. A narrow door gave onto what he supposed would be the alleyway behind the building.

"What would they do with it?" Prudence shook dust from the hem of her skirt and kept one gloved hand ready to brush away cobwebs.

"They're proposing a mission on the first floor, Bible study rooms on the second, and quarters for the minister and his wife above that." Hanrahan turned to Geoffrey. "The Presbyterians will find themselves out in the cold when push comes to shove. They have the funds to offer a decent price for the building, but an organization calling itself the Eastern Benevolent Association has a much bigger purse. The department would like to see a Christian mission go in, but that's not going to happen. Chinatown is organizing itself, the way San Francisco's Chinese population has. It'll happen soon."

"Somebody has to be masterminding the effort," Prudence said.

"We hear Wei Fu Jian's name more than any other," Hanrahan said. "That's why I agreed to meet with you when Lowry contacted me. He said the case you were working on was confidential, but that you had questions about Wei that needed answers. And that you might be able to provide information I'm not likely to pick up on the streets."

"We think Wei Fu Jian isn't his real name," Geoffrey began.

Hanrahan shrugged. "That's not unusual in Chinatown. The only name that matters is the one on the papers that got a man through immigration."

"We've heard about the smuggling and the paper sons," Prudence said. "Do you have any idea when Wei came to America?"

"Probably at least twenty or twenty-five years ago, given the age he claims to be now. He had to have been young and strong enough to work on the railroads because by then the California goldfields were played out. I'd lay odds he pounded track for the Canadians until he could get himself across the border into New York State. Smugglers run illegals into the city from up around Niagara and all along the canal area."

"So time spent working the Canadian transcontinental railroad, then a run across the border and down to the city," Geoffrey said.

"That would be my best guess," Hanrahan agreed. "We began noticing him about eight years ago, when the West Coast population of Chinese started flooding east. The new arrivals needed money, and Wei lent it to them. Nobody knows where he got his stake, but right from the beginning he had deep pockets."

"The building he owns is impressive," Prudence said.

"You've been there?" Hanrahan asked.

"Just briefly." She'd made a mistake revealing even that much, though she and Geoffrey had agreed that Lowry's contact at the Sixth Precinct had to suspect they were working the Peng murder case. Why else would two uptown private inquiry agents be asking questions in Chinatown?

"Loan sharks have always trolled the gambling houses and opium parlors," Hanrahan said. "But Wei did things differently. Still does. He lent money at a healthy but not exorbitant interest rate, and if a man was late with his payment, he didn't have him beaten senseless. Gave him more time to repay the debt and often as not found him a job. Sometimes working for him. That builds loyalty. We think he's probably the richest man in Chinatown now. And likely to become the most powerful if he succeeds in building his own tong before the San Francisco gangs move in and take over. He skirts the law, but we've yet to catch him breaking it."

How to find out if Wei's deep pockets fattened the Sixth Precinct salary envelopes? Hanrahan nodded and then shrugged his shoulders as if the question had been asked aloud. Precincts all over the city had their collective hands out. Why should it be any different at the station house on Elizabeth Street?

Something about Alfred Hanrahan was niggling at Prudence, but she couldn't put her finger on exactly what it was. Lowry had told them that he was one of the few officers who had requested the Sixth Precinct, which included Five Points as well as Chinatown. Some of the meanest streets and hardest duty in the city. Immigrant gangs, crushing poverty, alleyway prostitution, and bodies left to rot where they fell until a city morgue wagon picked them up. Knifings, beatings, alcohol poisoning, and tuberculosis were the most common causes of death among adults; children died from being born.

"Nobody down here will help you find the man you're looking for," Hanrahan said as he escorted Prudence and Geoffrey out of the storefront, locking the door behind them. "If Lord Peng was a contract killing, the assassin who carried it out is either already dead or halfway across the country. There's no reason to think Wei Fu Jian ordered it, but he might have agreed to arrange the escape. I assume that's why you're asking about him."

Neither Prudence nor Geoffrey contradicted him.

Nor did they tell him that Wei Fu Jian was the murdered man's younger brother.

Mei Sha's world had shrunk to a few rooms in a brick building secured by armed guards whose orders were not to allow any of their employer's guests to venture out onto the street or spend too much time at the windows. No one was to know they were there, which was itself an almost impossible feat to pull off in the crowded streets of Chinatown.

She'd played endless games of *xiangqi* with Johnny, embroidered bright red peonies onto black silk slippers at Lady Peng's direction, and brushed An Bao's long hair until it shone like polished ebony. Amah clucked over her restlessness and embellished the tale of the escape from the hotel so many times that Mei Sha was reduced to blinking her eyes and staring fixedly into space to keep from yawning. She'd almost given up asking, but finally Amah agreed that yes, Mei Sha could walk in the walled garden, but only if she did not enter it alone.

Wei had closeted himself with Johnny on men's business, An Bao never walked if she could help it, and Amah had promised to assist Lady Peng with a bath.

"One of the guards can take me down and watch from the doorway," Mei Sha said. "I won't stay long."

Mei Sha had seldom been able to sit still ever since she had learned to walk. Privately, Amah thought Mei should have been born a boy, but it wasn't a notion she could share with anyone.

"It's cold. You'll need a warm coat." Amah helped her youngest charge into a quilted jacket that reached to her knees, made sure she had a pair of gloves, and wound a thick scarf around her neck.

The guard outside the living quarters could not leave his post, but he watched her progress from above as Mei navigated two flights of stairs to the building's ground floor. Another guard opened the door to the walled garden, stepping outside for a moment to inspect the private space where Mei had seen her mother deep in conversation with the man she sometimes addressed as Younger Brother. Lady Peng had turned a deaf ear to her children's inquiries, as though her mind had abandoned the problems of the present and gone wandering in a far distant past. Remembering and weighing events that had happened long before any of them were born.

Not having her questions answered was to Mei Sha like a hand running the wrong way along a cat's back. She missed London and she yearned for the challenges of the exceptionally modern curriculum at the exclusive girls' boarding school that had been modeled on Eton. Though the idea had originated with Queen Victoria, it was Johnny who had convinced her parents that she and they both would benefit from placing her in close proximity to the daughters of some of Great Britain's noblest houses. For that Mei Sha would always be grateful to her brother. She never bothered to reveal that the girls themselves referred to their presence at the school as having been *dumped* or *gotten out of the way.* Unless she looked in a mirror, Mei Sha—calling herself May—could believe she was really one of them.

Wei Fu Jian's beautiful rooms were stifling, pushing her further back into a culture she had hoped to escape. The embroidered silks weighed her down, the gold blinded her, the incense lulled her into inaction. She couldn't think, couldn't plan, couldn't envision where she would go or how she would get there. Very soon after meeting Bettina Lowry, she'd realized that her new friend would never have the courage to help her into a new life. And where would the money come from? May had received a weekly stipend at school; it was part of the modern course of study to learn how to budget one's spending in preparation for overseeing the running of an elaborate household. It was through learning how little the coins bought that she discovered the need for more.

Perhaps her dream of living on her own was just that—a fantasy with which to occupy idle hours and appease an unsettled spirit. But then she thought of Prudence MacKenzie, as independent a woman as she'd ever met. Wealthy, a part of society but entering it only on her terms. A lawyer. An inquiry agent. Partners with a man to whom she wasn't married.

As Mei paced the brick path beneath the bare tree limbs and hanging vines, she pictured herself dressed as she had seen Miss MacKenzie—fashionably slim and elegant, but free of the fussy frills and furbelows that made grown women look like tasseled pillows.

Perhaps this flight into Chinatown could be turned to her advantage. If Uncle Fu Jian wasn't the autocrat her father had been. If Miss MacKenzie could devise a legal maneuver that would allow the family to evade the ship waiting for them in San Francisco harbor.

If ... if ... if ...

She gave a little skip, the first moment of lightheartedness she had known since she had seen her father's blood spilled and wondered why anyone believed that the color red brought luck and good fortune.

The brick wall of Wei Fu Jian's private garden was eight feet tall, topped by shards of broken glass embedded in cement. No one, looking up at the formidable obstacle in front of him, had ever been known to scale it. Over the years, Wei and his guards had grown to think of the garden as a safe place in an insecure world. A mistake they should not have made.

Glass could pierce through canvas, but less dangerously so when the canvas was reinforced with a sheet of the vulcanized rubber that was beginning to be used aboard ships to protect cargo. A rope thrown around a tree limb on a moonless night, the canvas pitched across the top of the wall, agile feet and strong arms scrabbling upward. The man who broke into Wei's fortress had brought rice cakes in his pockets and water in a flask. He would wait as long as he had to for one of his chosen victims to stroll toward the spot where he lay hidden atop the folded canvas and the coiled rope.

The padded coat Amah had insisted she wear was too heavy. Too bulky. Mei's arms protruded from her sides like the unbendable appendages of a wooden doll. Bits of wool from the scarf stuck to her lips, and the gloves on her hands made her fingers itch. It was a cold, clear day, but the high garden walls blocked the wind that siphoned down Chinatown's narrow streets and the pale sun overhead gave an illusion of warmth.

She stuffed the gloves into the pockets of her coat, then fumbled at the frog closures with fingers colder and clumsier than she had thought they would be. Everything seemed to be going wrong today. She wanted to stamp her feet and scream in frustration, but then she remembered the guard behind the door. The last thing in the world Mei needed was to become a joke among Uncle Fu Jian's men.

She glanced behind her, but no one seemed to be watching. The guard who had let her out must be sheltering behind the door, which, she noticed, stood open an inch or two. It reminded her of boarding school days, when teachers and senior girls lurked around every corner, eagerly alert to the mistakes and foibles of the younger pupils. Mei had avoided trouble only by being hypervigilant and fast on her feet, necessary skills she'd developed over the years to avoid Amah's reprimands and her father's censures.

The last of the frog closures gave way, and the coat flopped open. Did she dare slide it down her arms, at least for a few minutes? The windows above her were empty. Her mother must have summoned Amah to fill the cumbersome zinc bathing tub.

The heavy padded garment hung from her shoulders as she squirmed her way free from its weight and breathed the fresh air with the first feeling of freedom she'd had since coming to Chinatown. The next thing she would do, she decided, was convince her mother that it would be a good thing to acquire some western clothing in case they had to disappear again. Trunks of beautiful apparel remained at the Fifth Avenue Hotel, but she'd never be able to wear any of it. The world had to believe the Peng family was so far away as to be unreachable.

Mei heard the whisper of soft leather on brick before she saw anything. The slip slip of someone stealthily approaching. It had to be Johnny, getting back at her for all the games of *xiangqi* at which she'd beaten him. Johnny had never been good at competitions; she'd often wondered how and why he'd chosen to study engineering if he couldn't visualize his pieces three moves ahead of an opponent on the *xiangqi* board. She wouldn't give him the satisfaction of shouting and leaping out at her.

Mei stepped behind a pair of dwarf cynoki cypresses, their evergreen foliage wide and dense. Once, at boarding school, she and another girl had ambushed a particularly tattletale prefect, throwing a blanket over the informer, and then dousing it with icy water.

Next to the cypresses was a small bench from which she could envelop Johnny in the heavy padded coat. Amah might scold and tell them they were too old for games, but Johnny and Mei had teased and played jokes on one another since early childhood. She was coiled tighter than a mattress spring. If she didn't do something wild and slightly crazy, she'd explode.

She didn't expect to see a man dressed in dark blue trousers, jacket, and round hat, a black silk scarf hiding the bottom half of his face. Didn't expect the queue that reached midway down his back. Uncle Fu Jian's men didn't wear the queue. The man was carrying something concealed in his wide sleeve, something that shone brightly when he turned, crouched, and listened. Someone rolling a can outside the wall, down the alley. Mei shrank back as far as she could into the spreading branches of the cypress trees, afraid to breathe too loudly. She was sure she'd seen a knife, sure the intruder was the man from the museum.

"Come out, little girl," he whispered. "I know you're there."

But he didn't. He was looking in the wrong direction, and when he rose from the crouch his back was to her. An arm's length away, in front of the bench.

She didn't give herself time to think. One foot leaped onto the stone seat, the other a fraction of a second later, steadying her as she brought the thickly padded coat down over the head of the man whose full face she still hadn't seen.

Then she screamed, as loudly as she could. Over and over, as she ran toward the door that burst open, men pouring out of it like hungry rats from a burrow.

CHAPTER 17

"You don't look like a minister's wife," Geoffrey told Prudence as they strolled down Mott Street toward Pell.

"What does that mean?"

"Alfred Hanrahan was fooling himself if he thought anyone in Chinatown would mistake us for Christian missionaries."

"He's hiding something, Geoffrey."

"Nothing and no one in this case is straightforward."

"It's something personal."

"What makes you assume that?"

Prudence stopped for a moment to peer into the interior of a narrow shop whose walls were lined with labeled wooden drawers and shelves holding clear glass jars filled with dried herbs. Barrels of twisted ginger roots, dark red pepper pods, and salted seahorses were lined up along the counter. The smell was rich, earthy, and pungent.

"Doesn't it strike you as odd that he requested the Sixth Precinct?" she asked, smiling and bowing toward the dim figure at the rear of the shop as she backed away from the door.

"Hanrahan is an Irish name. Maybe he has family ties in the area around Five Points."

"The entire New York Police Department is Irish and Catholic," Prudence reminded him. "Respectable immigrants move out of the tenements as soon as they can afford to live somewhere else. It's not that."

"All Lowry said was that Hanrahan owed him a favor. He didn't specify why or what it was."

"He's dark for an Irishman."

"Black Irish," Geoffrey said. "Mostly from the western counties. Supposedly the offspring of generations of Spanish traders working the Atlantic coast. Or so I've read."

"It's something else," Prudence argued.

"You're seeing complications where there aren't any. We have hurdles enough to overcome without looking for more."

"I don't feel as though we're in control," she continued. "Maybe that's why I'm so jumpy." She stopped in front of another shop. "I think I'll buy a small buddha for Josiah to put on his desk."

"He won't thank you for it."

"That's the point."

They made the turn onto Pell, intending to stroll past Wei Fu Jian's building without stopping. Keeping their distance on the other side of the street. One of Wei's men would recognize Prudence and report her presence. If Wei or Johnny had information to pass on, someone would come to the shop door and beckon them in. If not, they'd continue on to Bowery where Danny Dennis was waiting for them.

It wasn't until they were almost opposite Wei's Chinese Imports and Antiquities that they realized the small crowd of men idly smoking and talking on the sidewalk was too concentrated to be coincidental.

"Take my arm, Prudence," Geoffrey urged. "Something's wrong over there."

A moment later the shop door opened to the tinkle of high-pitched chimes.

"Let's go."

He stepped off the curb and guided Prudence across the street. The men parted to let them through, then closed behind them. Johnny Peng stood in the shadows of the dimly lit space, beckoning them in.

"What is it?" Prudence asked.

"Not here," Johnny said. "Outside. In the garden."

He hurried them along the aisles of the import-export business, through a door opening onto the stairway to the upper floors, out a ground-floor entrance at the back of the building. A grim-faced armed guard waved them through, and another led them on a brick path toward where they could hear voices raised in fierce argument.

"It happened just a few minutes ago," Johnny said. "She's all right. Mei Sha wasn't hurt."

"Stop, Johnny," Prudence said, catching hold of his sleeve. "You'd better explain this."

"May was walking in the garden. Alone. A guard was supposed to keep her in sight, but he'd stepped in out of the cold. Fortunately, he left the door open."

"What happened?" Geoffrey asked, thinking he could make a good guess. It had to be the man who had engineered a killing at the Met and attempted to murder Johnny Peng when no one was supposed to know the family had left the Fifth Avenue Hotel. "Was she attacked?"

"She would have been, but she heard something and thought I was creeping up on her to play a joke, so she hid. When she realized what was really going on she jumped on him, threw her padded coat over his head, and ran like the devil was after her. Screaming at the top of her lungs."

"Did they catch him? Did your uncle's men grab him before he could get away?" Prudence didn't see how anyone could clamber over the eight-foot wall enclosing the garden.

"He's gone. We can't figure out how he did it. My uncle is

furious. He's mad at Mei for going out alone, mad at Amah for allowing it, and really angry with the guards who were supposed to prevent something like this from happening."

Johnny spoke in Chinese to the armed man waiting for them. "My uncle sent me out to get you. He's waiting."

"We were meeting with Alfred Hanrahan, Warren Lowry's contact at the Sixth Precinct," Prudence explained, lifting her skirts with one hand so they wouldn't drag on the uneven brick pathway.

"You didn't tell him where we were?"

"Of course not. But the station house can be a good source of information about newcomers." It didn't sound very logical, even to her. Hanrahan had said that most of Chinatown's inhabitants kept as far away from the police as possible. Even if they were familiar with English, they pretended not to understand if an officer spoke to them on the street.

"And was it? A good source of information?"

"Nothing. But part of running an investigation is following every lead as far as it goes, even when you're not sure it's going to pan out."

"My uncle has forbidden me to inform the police about what happened."

"That's to be expected," Geoffrey murmured to Prudence.

Wei Fu Jian couldn't afford to have it known in Chinatown that an enemy had breached his defenses. Power depended on being believed to be invincible. If he couldn't protect himself, how could he be expected to protect others?

Figures could be seen in the shrubbery, armed men with eyes fixed on the ground searching for signs of the intruder's presence, for any clue as to how he scaled the wall, how he managed to disappear when Mei Sha's screams alerted Wei's men to a danger they had not anticipated.

Lady Peng stood beside her daughter, face raised as if searching for answers in the cloudy winter sky. Prudence had never seen emotion twist those pale, beautiful features, but today she read something akin to despair and tightly reined in terror on them. It was the first intimation that Lord Peng's widow, the incarnation of cold self-control, might be crumbling beneath attacks she neither understood nor could withstand. Wei Fu Jian had fallen silent, but no one could mistake his stillness for anything but grim determination.

A black silk scarf dangled from one of Mei Sha's clenched fists.

"My men are searching every inch of the garden," Wei said, as Prudence and Geoffrey approached. "I assume Fa Cho has told you what happened here?"

"How did he get over the wall?" Geoffrey asked. It was the single most important puzzle to solve if the Peng family were to be kept safe.

"We don't know yet."

"But you're sure it was the same assassin who struck down Lord Peng?"

"He had his face covered with this," Mei Sha said, holding out the black silk scarf. "I must have pulled it off when I threw the coat over him. I don't remember doing it, but one of the guards found the scarf on the ground. He thought it might be mine, but it isn't."

Lady Peng reached out as though to silence her daughter, but Wei Fu Jian shook his head. Mei Sha's stubborn courage and quick thinking had saved her life, perhaps the lives of others had the killer managed to get inside the building. Women acting as warriors were not unknown in Chinese myth and legend; they were creatures to be admired though not imitated. Wei had begun to formulate plans for his nephew. Now he wondered if the slender young girl who had so dangerously defied the restrictions placed on her could also figure in the future he was crafting.

Prudence took the scarf from Mei, pinching it between two

fingers. She held it briefly to her face, inhaling the scent of sweat despite the cold, the acrid residue of vinegary wine, the slight greasiness of skin oil. She turned to Geoffrey, eyebrows raised in query. "Danny takes Flower out on the cab most days," she said quietly. "To train her. He says she has as good a nose as Blossom."

"My father started his hunters following scent trails when they were eight-week-old pups." Geoffrey did not mention that casting after humans was as much a part of their instruction as learning to track down game. It was a part of his past he'd chosen to forget whenever possible.

"Flower is nearly six months."

"It's worth a try."

Mr. Washington was too easily recognizable for Danny to park his hansom cab in front of Wei Fu Jian's building. "Anyone who sees him will trace the two of us back to Hunter and MacKenzie," he told Geoffrey. "That's a chance I think you'd rather not take. We're already taking a risk by me driving along Bowery. It's not where I usually pick up or deliver passengers."

"Take the cab up to Cooper Square," Geoffrey instructed. "We'll meet you there in about an hour."

Danny handed down the almost six-month-old puppy named Flower, already nearly as big as a full-grown average size dog. Like her mother, Blossom, her thick coat was somewhere between gold and red, and her tail was a long, feathery plume. She licked Geoffrey's face on the way to the sidewalk, greeting one of her favorite humans with the animal equivalent of an ecstatic smile.

"You'll need this," Danny said, pulling out a brown leather leash from beneath his seat. "She's not fully trained yet, and with all the new smells around, she's likely to take off running. You won't be able to catch her if she does, and I can't guarantee she'll come back when you call. Eventually, but not right away.

Blossom always had a mind of her own, and this dog takes after her mother in more ways than one."

Geoffrey clipped on the leash while Flower and Mr. Washington touched noses.

"Let's go, girl," he said, setting off along Pell Street at a pace that kept Flower from stopping every few feet to investigate yet another scent. By the time they reached the Wei building, Flower seemed to have realized that she was on her way to work. Head cocked high, tail held out stiffly behind her, she paced along at Geoffrey's side as though she knew exactly where they were going and what she would be asked to do when they got there.

The crowd of men parted to let them through, hands reaching out to quickly stroke the beautiful fur as Flower passed among them. Danny had trained her not to react to an admiring touch, but once or twice her upper lip curled back and a hand was quickly withdrawn.

She sat and cocked her head to one side when Geoffrey paused at the entrance to the garden, then thumped her tail enthusiastically as soon as she heard Prudence's voice. Another of her favorite humans, this one often slipped her bits of food she carried in a little sack that dangled from her wrist. Flower knew not to nip at the delicious-smelling bag, but she did occasionally nudge it. And was almost always rewarded.

Prudence went down on one knee when Geoffrey unsnapped the leash and the beautiful pup that looked so much like her mother bounded down the brick path. Flower didn't jump, but her whole body wriggled in delight as Prudence petted and cooed and kissed her nose. If there hadn't been an unmistakable attraction between Danny's huge white horse and the red-gold puppy, Prudence would have kept her at the house on Fifth Avenue. But in the end, she knew Flower would be happier in the hay-strewn horse stable with Mr. Washington and Danny's crew of street urchins than in a lady's parlor.

"Are you sure about this?" Johnny asked. "She looks awfully young to be able to track a scent."

"You went fox hunting in England, didn't you?" Prudence asked.

"Of course."

"They start training those hounds as soon as they're weaned." Prudence wasn't sure of her facts, but she'd listened to her aunt Gillian, the dowager Viscountess Rotherton, deliver a spirited diatribe on the subject while a guest at a country estate in Essex. It seemed logical, and she smiled as she caught Johnny looking at Flower with more curiosity than doubt.

The men searching the garden for the second time gradually stilled. Wei Fu Jian had given orders that once the visitors' dog arrived, they were to stand down and let the animal work.

Few could afford to feed a dog in the new world to which they had emigrated, but they'd brought with them stories and legends of dogs that protected against ghosts and evil spirits and the memory of lion-dog statues guarding Buddhist temples and city gates. Flower was the most beautiful canine they had ever seen, wholly unlike the caged dogs sold for food in Chinese markets. She was foreign, but something about her reminded them of the myths that were always better to contemplate than real life.

Prudence held out the black silk scarf as the others fell silent and watched.

Flower inhaled the scent, every inch of her concentrated on what she was breathing. She seemed not to notice the humans watching as she lowered her head to the ground and began searching. Back and forth she went, intent on finding the trail left by footsteps, crushed grass stems, and broken bits of foliage. When she found it, she paused, glancing behind her at Prudence and Geoffrey to alert them that the hunt was about to begin. Then she set off at a steady pace, nose inches above the February damp of the earth, retracing the route the intruder had followed.

She pointed at the spot where he'd scaled the wall. Once she'd found it for them, Wei's men searched until they plucked shreds of canvas from the barrier of broken glass and identified the scuff marks made by climbing feet in soft-soled shoes. Then she tracked his movements around the garden, paused where he had stood assessing his killing ground, recreated the scuffle with Mei Sha, inhaling again the strong scent that clung to the coat she had thrown over him. It lay on the brick walk where he had fought his way out of it, every movement shedding more of his distinctive odor.

From the crumpled heap of the coat, Flower left the brick path for a corner of the garden where a screen of red-berried holly had been cultivated to soften the stark lines of the wall. The dark green leaves shone as if they'd been waxed, the blood-red berries bright in the dull winter light. She nosed through the bushes, one paw occasionally scrabbling at the dirt. Then, abruptly, she stopped. Sat. Stared at the ground. Waited.

Geoffrey was the first to reach her. He praised her and clipped the leash he'd been carrying to her collar. Then he, too, studied the ground. Other than what appeared to be the tracks of Wei's men who had combed this and every other inch of the garden for clues, there didn't appear to be anything to see. But he held out an arm to keep Wei Fu Jian and others from crowding too close to where Flower continued to sit, immobile, eyes and snout fixed on what she and no one else knew was in front of her.

"What is it, Geoffrey?" Prudence asked.

"I don't know yet. She's obviously tracked him this far with the strong scents from the scarf and the coat, but I don't know why she's stopped. It's as if he's disappeared into thin air." He looked around and above him, searching for a tree branch that might bear the marks of desperate climbing. There was nothing close enough.

Blossom had never lost a scent when she'd worked the New York City streets with the boy who had been her first and most

beloved master. It was unthinkable that her puppy had not inherited that formidable skill.

Geoffrey dropped to his knees beside Flower, took off his
gloves, and began running his hands over the ground at which
the dog was concentrating, moving forward a few inches, then
to one side and deeper into the hedge of prickly holly.

Flower whined softly, as if to encourage him, a series of
barely audible noises slowly increasing in pitch and volume as
he crept closer to what she'd brought him to find.

When Geoffrey got to his feet, his hands were filthy with
damp earth, but his eyes gleamed with satisfaction. "It's a tunnel," he said, beating back branches with one booted foot. "The
trapdoor is small, barely large enough for a man to squeeze
through, but the dirt around it has been disturbed recently.
This is how he made his escape, and why you couldn't find
him. He went down, not up and over."

"One of my guards is missing," Wei Fu Jian said, nodding
toward the semi-circle of men who had begun to close in
around him. Two of them broke away and returned a few moments later carrying shovels, rakes, and pruning shears. At a
nod from Wei, they cut back the concealing holly branches and
raked dirt from around the outlines of a hinged wood plank.

Geoffrey gave Flower permission to release, and Wei nodded to the man closest to the trapdoor.

It rose easily in his hand, freshly oiled hinges gleaming as the
light poured down into darkness. Narrow wooden slats had
been anchored into the sides of the tunnel to act as a ladder and
support the earth walls where the vertical shaft disappeared
into the horizontal tunnel. Something lay in a crumpled heap at
the bottom.

The man who had climbed down shouted up a name. Words
that brought grim tightness to the lips of those who understood
them.

"The guard," Wei pronounced. "His throat has been cut."
He snapped orders in Chinese.

"That could have been me," Mei Sha whispered.

"Brave girl," Prudence murmured, slipping a comforting arm around Mei's waist.

Flower slid her cold, wet nose into the nest of Mei Sha's trembling fingers.

Wei Fu Jian beckoned to Johnny. The two men left the garden.

"He's going to war," Geoffrey predicted. "Taking Johnny with him."

"This is not what I wanted," Lady Peng said as Younger Brother's men closed in around her. "Another prison."

Chapter 18

W ei Fu Jian greeted them in the scarlet-and-gold parlor whose windows fronted on Pell Street. The curtains had been drawn, lamps and incense sticks lit, tea served on lacquered trays.

"I regret you've been drawn into this," he told Prudence and Geoffrey as they seated themselves and a servant took Flower out of the room on her leash. "I had planned to relieve you of the burden of my brother's death, but Lady Peng will not hear of it. Nor will Fa Cho. That's a very westernized attitude to display toward the head of a Chinese family." He smiled at his nephew and his brother's widow, but there was an edge of frustration in Wei's look that was close to barely repressed anger.

"The essence of diplomacy is learning to accept and engineer compromises," Lady Peng said. "The Empress Dowager Cixi is a model to many of us." By which she meant women of rank who were not content to leave all the reins of power in the hands of husbands, sons, and other male relatives.

If Johnny and Mei Sha had seen an independent side to their mother during the London years, they had never discussed it, content with occasionally invoking her assistance when seeking a favor from their father. It hadn't occurred to either of them that Lady Peng was successful because she had learned to move behind the scenes with such quiet and circuitous skill that not even her husband suspected her of devious behavior.

Prudence, however, recognized the maneuvering for what it was and silently applauded another woman who was masterfully making her way through a man's world. Lady Peng might not have chosen to confront her social milieu as bluntly as Prudence, but she hadn't surrendered to it either.

"We had hoped to enlist the help of some powerful political figures who could arrange special residence visas for you," Geoffrey began, firmly believing that bad news should be delivered before the good news that mitigated its effect. "That hasn't happened. Neither of the two men we approached was willing to go against the prevalent anti-Chinese bias in Washington."

"Did you really expect to succeed?" Wei asked.

"There was the possibility of a favorable outcome. The Pengs wouldn't have had to remain in hiding and it was a way of bypassing the court system, which we'd been advised would almost certainly rule against them." Following Lady Peng's lead, Prudence kept her intonation conciliatory, her cadence measured.

"Will the men whose help you solicited contact the police to arrest us?" Johnny asked.

"I don't think so," Prudence said. "Both of them were friends of my late father. I believe they'll prefer to forget we ever had a conversation about Lord Peng's family." She paused. "I think they were embarrassed that the daughter of an old acquaintance had had the temerity to broach so unladylike and political a subject. They'll pretend it never happened."

"Chinatown is changing," Wei Fu Jian said. "Ten years ago there were only about a thousand of us living in a city of over a million and a half people. That's an estimate; no one really knows for sure. But I can tell you that the population has at least doubled since then. More and more of our countrymen are leaving California for the greater freedom of New York."

"But not returning to China?" Geoffrey asked.

"That's a dream most have abandoned," Wei said. "They'll make provisions for their bones to be sent back, but their lives will end here."

"I want my husband's killer found," Lady Peng broke in. "I will not rest until that's been done, and neither will my son." She turned to the two daughters who sat together on a red brocade couch. "An Bao and Mei Sha will make the same vow. None of us will seek our own happiness until the murderer has been caught and justice been done."

It was a clever stratagem, Prudence thought. No one could argue with the rightness of the widow's declaration, but she'd also decided her future and the lives of her children before control could be taken away from her. An oath in any culture was a sacred obligation. Johnny, his sisters, and their mother were effectively frozen in place and time, their primary purpose in life to avenge Lord Peng's death. Nothing could be allowed to interfere with that resolve. Lady Peng might appear to accede to Wei's male and familial authority, but she had tied him as tightly as the others to her demand for retribution. It was obvious, from the expression on Younger Brother's face, that he understood what she'd done.

"Matthew Lam is your man in Chinatown?" Wei asked. He already knew the answer, but it was important to set boundaries and establish systems of control.

"He is," Geoffrey confirmed.

"Who else?"

"We've spoken with Alfred Hanrahan at the Sixth Precinct," Prudence contributed. Deliberately, she left his agency connection vague.

Wei nodded, slotting Hanrahan into his mental list of useful contacts to be bribed, threatened, or eliminated. He did not mention that he had already seen to it that the Chinese ambassador in Washington would be informed that the Peng family had likely fled to the Bahamas where, presumably, the empress dowager would be content to let them disappear into the colonial landscape.

"We've also interrogated the Delmonico's staff," Geoffrey said. "One of them confirmed a description of the man we believe wielded the knife. In his late twenties or early thirties, thin, wearing workingman's clothes and a queue. Good-looking, he thought. Chinese. He was allowed to enter the museum through the kitchen because the Delmonico's people believed he was part of Lord Peng's entourage. No one questioned or stopped him."

"Will the New York City Police Department pursue the matter?"

"The detective in charge of the investigation has a reputation for never leaving a case unsolved," Prudence said. "His name is Steven Phelan. His partner is Pat Corcoran. We've dealt with both of them before."

"So for Detective Phelan, it's a question of protecting his reputation?" Wei asked, cutting to the heart of the matter.

"He won't walk away," Geoffrey confirmed.

"Unless ordered to do so," Wei said. "A man who obeys orders saves face even when he must swallow his pride."

"True."

The police were as warped as the gangs. Did Wei already have a hand in Thomas Byrnes's pocket? The head of the detective department had a formidable reputation for efficient cruelty and unscrupulous methods but had managed to remain untouched by charges of personal corruption. So far. Geoffrey thought Wei might be letting them know in his typically ambiguous way that they were not to worry about interference from the New York City Police Department.

"I have a proposition to offer you," Wei said, raising a hand for more tea. "One which I believe will benefit all of us." He looked pointedly at his nephew and at Geoffrey.

"We're listening." Prudence refused to allow herself to be sidelined from the conversation. She caught Lady Peng's eye and saw there a glimmer of collaboration.

"The building you were looking at with Officer Hanrahan already belongs to me, though the Presbyterians have not been notified that their offer will be rejected," Wei said. "I propose that since you've laid the groundwork for deception, we carry through. Announce that a Congregationalist minister and his wife will be moving into the premises and that thanks to the generosity of the merchants of Chinatown, the property is being made ready for their arrival. I can arrange to have the necessary work completed in two or three days. No one expects missionary establishments to be graced with anything but the basic necessities."

"Go on." Geoffrey had a broad smile on his face. He'd loved nothing more than undercover work during his Pinkerton career.

"That will give you a base in Chinatown and an entrée into the population that no one will question. We're used to Christian ministers pushing their way into our lives and trying to convert us. You'll be able to ask any questions you want. You might not always get useful answers, but the men you talk to will simply think you're typically impolite and uncouth foreigners."

"No one will mistake us for church people," Prudence protested, remembering that as they strolled down Mott Street Geoffrey had said she didn't look much like a minister's wife.

"You haven't seen me in my black clergyman's suit and hat," her partner said. "Cheap, baggy, shiny with age. A threadbare white shirt and string tie. And you'll look the part in high-necked black bombazine with a cameo brooch at the base of the collar."

"Hanrahan said no one in Chinatown would help us find the man we're looking for." Prudence ignored Geoffrey's remarks, speaking directly to Wei. "The police aren't to be trusted, and we won't be either, especially by immigrants whose paperwork isn't in order."

"There'll be cooperation if I let it be known that you have my backing," Wei said. "I made inquiries."

"Inquiries?"

"The consul has contacts in city government. He assures me that your firm has acquired a very good reputation in just a few years. Like that policeman you talked about, Hunter and MacKenzie doesn't walk away from cases and never fails to solve them." He glanced at Lady Peng and Johnny, who were hanging on his every word. "I'm guaranteeing protection for my brother's family, but the solving of the crime of murder will lie with you. A wise but unskilled man does not attempt to perform a task that another has mastered."

Lady Peng lightly clapped her hands as though Wei had said something immensely profound.

"But I have conditions," Wei continued.

Of course he had conditions, Prudence thought. *He's holding all the winning cards.*

Hanrahan had said that Wei Fu Jian was the wealthiest man in Chinatown and that his name was associated with rumors of a nascent organization that would rival the Italian and Irish gangs for power over their immigrant countrymen. That meant graft, gambling, prostitution. Liquor. Opium dens. Protection.

"The Eastern Benevolent Association has to become reality before one of the San Francisco tongs decides to establish itself here. Time is running out. I have to move quickly."

Wei didn't concede that his brother's death had upset the timetable of his carefully planned schemes, but Prudence understood what he meant. And she suddenly thought that Wei might not hold all the winning cards after all. She and Geoffrey might be just as necessary to him as he was to them.

She wondered whether Josiah would fit into a storefront Congregationalist ministry. For a moment, she lost the thread of the conversation.

"A man has to eat," Wei was saying. "Restaurant owners read the faces of their customers. They can tell at a glance if someone can pay for his supper or if he'll turn out empty pockets at the end of a meal."

What was that supposed to mean?

"Sooner or later the man who killed Elder Brother and invaded my garden will tire of cold rice balls and tepid tea off a pushcart. He'll want a cooked meal and warm *huangjiu* to wash it down. The owner of the restaurant where he surfaces will alert us to the presence of a stranger. Your Matthew Lam will be dispatched to follow him. All the waiters in Chinatown wear black pants, white shirts, and bow ties. Our quarry won't be able to distinguish Lam from the regular staff at whichever restaurant he's chosen to frequent. When you deem the moment appropriate, he will be apprehended and brought here."

"Do we have that much time?" Prudence asked.

"Will he come after me again?" Mei Sha's voice was firm, but the hands she hid inside her sleeves trembled against the embroidered silk.

"We won't allow that to happen," Johnny said. He turned to his uncle for reassurance.

"The man whose throat was slit paid for a moment of negligence with his life. The death will serve as a warning to the other guards. None of them will relax their vigilance from now on." Wei reached out to stroke the slight movement of his niece's sleeve. "You're safe now, Mei Sha."

"What about the tunnel, Uncle?"

"It joins a network of underground passages running beneath many of the buildings in Chinatown, some of them excavated by the Irish and German gangs before they moved into the Five Points. I won't order it destroyed, but I've given instructions that a heavy door is to be installed where the vertical shaft joins the horizontal. There will be a lock and an iron bolt on our side."

"Is there another tunnel? From inside the shop?" Geoffrey asked. He couldn't imagine someone like Wei Fu Jian not providing himself with a secret escape route.

"I made sure it was reinforced with new timbers soon after I bought the property," Wei said, not volunteering either the tunnel's location or its direction. "And that it couldn't be breached from one of the other tunnels. It was careless of me not to have suspected that there would be a second shaft in the garden."

"We all make the occasional miscalculation," Prudence said.

"Not if we want to stay alive," Wei Fu Jian said.

"We need to explore the tunnel system." Prudence stared down at the open shaft from which she could hear the sound of hammers striking against metal. In less than an hour's time the ladder embedded in the dirt wall had been reinforced, rotting rungs replaced with new wood, and the door Wei had spoken of installed.

"I asked," Geoffrey said. "He won't allow it. His men have orders to stop us if we try."

"That's ridiculous. How are we to operate in Chinatown if we're ignorant of what is obviously well known to everyone else?"

"The building on Doyers Street will have a tunnel," Geoffrey said. "My guess is that we'll find the entrance somewhere in the basement. Concealed behind a shelf or the coal chute. We'll find it."

"I still don't understand what we'll accomplish by disguising ourselves as missionaries." Prudence was rapidly running out of patience.

"It's actually not a bad idea," Geoffrey said. "Think about it. Christian missionaries are expected to push their way in wherever they're not wanted, hand out leaflets and bibles, ask personal questions no one else would dare even hint at. They stand on street corners, accost passersby, generally make nuisances of themselves. Eventually, because no one pays them any attention, people forget they're there. It's a wonderful way to gather information."

"If we spoke Chinese." But Prudence smiled as she said it.

"I agree that the language barrier is a problem. Not insurmountable, because everyone speaks at least enough English to look for work and get by."

"I had a mental image of the two of us standing all alone in that filthy storefront waiting for potential converts to come through the door. And no one did."

"Some of the population will have had contact with missionaries back in China," Geoffrey said. "They may even have been baptized."

"What about Matthew Lam?" Prudence asked. "Wouldn't he be of more use working for us at the mission than in that noodle restaurant? He could be our interpreter."

"I'll check with Wei," Geoffrey said.

"Matthew is *our* employee," Prudence argued. "We shouldn't have to have Younger Brother's permission." Calling him Younger Brother soothed her annoyance with the situation. Slightly.

"I have a feeling that nothing happens in Chinatown without Wei Fu Jian's tacit consent," Geoffrey said. "And that it's going to be even more so once he gets the Eastern Benevolent Association up and running."

"We need to let Josiah know what's happened," Prudence said. "Do you think you can persuade him to wear a baggy black suit with shiny knees, and no waistcoat?"

CHAPTER 19

"I think we ought to wear what's called the Geneva gown," Josiah said, holding up a catalog opened to a full-page illustration of appropriate clerical attire. "You can wear the white preaching bands all the time or just in the pulpit."

"I won't be preaching," Geoffrey said. The only time he had set foot inside a church in recent years was to attend a wedding or funeral.

"What do you know about Congregationalists?" Prudence asked.

"I know Harvard and Yale were at one time divinity schools that educated and trained Congregationalist clergy," Geoffrey said. "And that they sent missionaries all over the world. They're considered liberals in the religion wars."

"As a deacon, I'm eligible to wear both the Geneva robe and the full preaching bands," Josiah remarked apropos of nothing. If he had to give up his bespoke black suits and brilliantly embroidered vests, he was determined to trade them for something eye-catching and at least moderately exotic.

"I think if we concentrate on establishing something along the lines of a community center, we should be able to avoid any deep discussions of religion," Prudence said. "I don't imagine many of the men in Chinatown are interested in converting."

"Rice Christians," Geoffrey said. "That's what the missionaries in China called the people who accepted baptism in exchange for free meals or jobs around the mission compound.

"We can put Christian symbols on the storefront walls, throw a cloth over a table to make it look like an altar, and scatter Bibles everywhere. That should do it."

"Some of these models have covered buttons from neck to hem," Josiah continued. "Wide sleeves, pleats all down the front, and I think we could add a white silk stole with gold fringe and gold embroidered crosses."

"No gowns, no stoles, and no preaching bands," Geoffrey said, plucking the catalog from Josiah's hands. "Where did you get this?"

"I borrowed it from a friend."

"You have a friend who's a clergyman?" Prudence asked.

"My friend was in the wardrobe department at the Academy of Music for years until he began designing costumes for society balls. Mrs. Vanderbilt's 1883 costume ball to celebrate her new Fifth Avenue mansion? My friend was responsible for some of the more extravagant successes that night. You probably read about them in the papers."

"We won't be needing him," Geoffrey said. "We're going to be poor Congregationalists, not a pretentious bone in our bodies or an extra nickel in our pockets."

"Nobody wants to become part of an organization that has to beg pennies for its livelihood," Josiah said. "The most important churches in New York City are also the richest. That's the way of the world."

He didn't contradict his employers very often, but he was sure he was right about this. Poverty didn't attract followers. Everyone who woke up cold and hungry in a crowded tenement had dreamed at least once of being as wealthy as the Vanderbilts.

"The man we're looking for is hiding in plain sight by pretending to be like everyone else in Chinatown," Prudence said. "Most of them—the lucky ones—work for daily wages and barely get by. He won't be any different. We'll only find him if we can appear to be so unimportant that people disregard us. Forget we're there. And if he makes a mistake."

"The other side to the coin is that he may be a hired killer," Geoffrey said. "The attack at the museum didn't appear to be the work of a professional, but the attempts on Johnny and Mei Sha were carefully planned and meticulously carried out. He's cut the throats of three of Wei Fu Jian's men. The only thing that saved Johnny was Danny's whip, and with Mei Sha it was her own quick wits."

"And bravery," Prudence added. "Lord Peng's assassination might have seemed like a symbolic act against the Chinese government at first, but no longer. Whoever killed him or hired the killer is bent on eradicating the entire family. That's a personal vendetta. There's a reason behind what's happening. We just don't know what it is."

"Lord Peng is the key. He was the primary target, so the rationale for the other attacks lies in his past. Perhaps in London. Perhaps as long ago and far away as China, before his first diplomatic posting." Geoffrey paged through the clerical catalog as though it held the secret he was seeking, pausing briefly at a white pulpit robe with red panels running down the front. Shook his head. Closed the catalog and laid it on his desk.

"I don't think either Johnny or Mei Sha have any idea why their father was killed," Prudence said. "An Bao probably remembers their life in China better than the other two. She's not the eldest child, but that's where her feet were bound. Pain isn't something you forget."

"Do we know how old they were when the family left for London?" Geoffrey asked.

"No, except for Mei Sha, who was almost three, but that shouldn't be difficult to find out." Prudence could feel the thrust of the investigation changing direction. Their goal was still to find Lord Peng's killer, but in order to do so they would have to probe the family's past. "I have a feeling An Bao could tell us at least some of what we need to know. She reminds me of one of those young women who stands silently at the back of a room and observes, but rarely speaks."

"We shouldn't forget the amah," Geoffrey said. "She was probably born in the servants' quarters of the Peng compound." Generations of slaves had spent their entire lives on his family's North Carolina plantations, their births, deaths, and sales recorded in the ledgers meticulously kept by their masters. The woman he had called Mammy had known everything there was to know about the Hunter family. She was dead now, but he often wondered what she had really felt for the people who had owned her. He passed a hand over his eyes to force away the memory.

"I've got articles about the Chinese New Year celebrations in the *Times,* the *Sun*, and the *Herald,*" Josiah said, bringing a stack of that week's newspapers to Geoffrey's desk and retrieving the clerical catalog.

"We were there," Prudence said.

"Each paper comes at the story from a different angle," Josiah continued, "but what's interesting to me is the slant."

"The slant?"

Josiah had Geoffrey's attention now. Chinatown was such a closed culture that he'd mostly unsuccessfully racked his brain trying to come up with a way to penetrate its secrets. Matthew Lam and the policeman Alfred Hanrahan had seemed the best solutions, but it was frustrating to have to admit that posing as Congregationalists was as close as he and Prudence would get to undercover work on this case.

"Look at this article in the *Times,*" Josiah said, folding the paper into quarters and handing it to Prudence. "It's the one you were reading and left on your desk when Lady Peng sent a messenger to invite you for that ride in Central Park."

"I remember," Prudence. "I don't think I ever finished it."

"You didn't," Josiah said. "But it's important. According to this reporter, hundreds of men from all over New York and New Jersey poured into Mott Street a week early because of a misleading story in another paper. Then he goes on to explain the Chinese calendar."

"He calls it *lunacy*," Prudence said, scanning the article and passing the folded newspaper to Geoffrey. "Look at the words he uses to describe what the few white residents of the neighborhood think of Chinese New Year. *Diabolical, debauchery.* Why am I surprised at the contradiction? The cream of New York society gathers at the Metropolitan Museum of Art to pay homage to centuries of Chinese art and culture while at the same time deriding the mass of people on whose backs that heritage was created."

"*John Chinaman,*" Geoffrey said, scribbling notes to himself as he scanned the article. The slaves freed at the end of the war had been called far worse names. And still were. But it was an effective way to disparage an entire ethnic or racial population.

"The *Sun* calls their imaginary Chinatown inhabitant Lee Fong. From the way the article is written, I would assume the reporter has created a character meant to represent what he wants his readers to consider typical. He describes him as *a little Chinese aristocrat*," Josiah said.

"That's a not-so-subtle mockery," Prudence said. "But here at the end of the story he seems to be using real names. Someone called Wong Fue Shing, who appears to be the leader of the Chung Wah Kung Saw Society at Sixteen Mott Street. This can't be the group Wei Fu Jian was talking about organizing."

"It's not." Alfred Hanrahan stood at Geoffrey's office door, an apologetic grin on his face. "I don't mean to intrude, but there wasn't anyone at the front desk."

"That's all right," Geoffrey said, waving a red-faced Josiah back into his chair. "We could use some help."

"We're in over our heads," Prudence said, "and that's not an easy thing to admit."

"Chinatown isn't your typical New York City neighborhood," Hanrahan said. He took the *Sun* article Prudence held out and skimmed it. "There's no byline but I think I know the reporter who wrote this. He usually gets his facts right, but sometimes he lets his imagination run away with him. And he's got a habit of paying for information, which means he gets what he wants to hear."

"What do you know about the society he mentions?" Geoffrey asked.

"It's an offshoot of an organization in San Francisco called the Chinese Consolidated Benevolent Association, probably better known as the Chinese Six Companies. They act as an umbrella group for the family and district clubs that sprang up during the gold rush days. Basically, they're an unrecognized government that levies a fee from everyone who lives in San Francisco's Chinatown. The New York City branch came into being about seven or eight years ago. It's remained a presence but hasn't evolved into a power yet."

"How does Wei Fu Jian fit into the picture?" Prudence asked.

"There's a lot more money to be made in gambling, opium, prostitution, smuggling, and protection than in lending money to pushcart vendors and small businesses like grocery stores and restaurants," Hanrahan said. "Every city ward has its gangs, and every immigrant group finds itself ruled by its worst elements. It starts with extortion, but that's only the tip of the iceberg. Wei Fu Jian is establishing a tong, and that's a very different setup than one of the so-called benevolent societies."

"An organization that pledges its members to secrecy and exacts brutal punishments for those who oppose, it" Josiah said.

"Wei knows that it's only a matter of time until the San

Francisco tongs decide to move east," Hanrahan said, nodding appreciatively at Josiah.

"He said much the same thing to us," Prudence said. "But I don't recall him using the word *tong*."

"He probably prefers *benevolent association*," Hanrahan agreed. "It's much less threatening. But that's not what I came to see you about." He set down the newspaper he was still holding. "Rumors have started to spread that Wei is entertaining guests in the building on Pell Street where he has his apartment on the top floor. There's also a story I find hard to believe, that one of his visitors was attacked in the garden by an assailant who escaped into the tunnels after slitting the throat of a guard."

Geoffrey said nothing. Prudence stared at her fingers.

"And there's speculation that a Congregationalist minister and his wife will be moving into that storefront I showed you."

"With their deacon," Josiah said.

"I hope you know what you're doing." Hanrahan fingered the badge on his uniform coat. "I may not be able to give you the kind of help you might need."

"The man we're after will bring a lot of newspaper attention to Chinatown when he's caught," Geoffrey said. "We don't think anybody wants that. Murder has a way of putting off tourists."

"Or it attracts them once the killer is hanged," Hanrahan said.

"Everything else suffers when the public and the do-gooders demand reform. Brothels get raided, gambling parlors are shut down, opium dens find that their customers are afraid to be caught on the premises."

"For a while, maybe," Hanrahan agreed. "But they all come back eventually. Sometimes they reopen the day after a raid if enough money changes hands. I've seen it happen."

"Whose side are you on?" Prudence demanded.

"I'm just letting you know what to expect." Hanrahan straightened his uniform coat and moved toward the door. "When Warren Lowry got in touch with me, he mentioned that he and his sister had met the Peng family aboard ship, and that Bettina and one of the Peng daughters had struck up a friendship. He hinted that he had a vested interest in the investigation, so to speak, even though he's realizing that he can't leave Bettina alone right now."

Hand on the doorknob, he turned back for a moment. "There's something else you should be aware of. The papers haven't picked up on it yet, but there's a detective from Mulberry Street Headquarters whose badge might be in danger. Seems some important figures in a case he's working have disappeared. No one knows exactly when. Or how. But word in the ranks is that Byrnes is fit to be tied. And you don't want to get on the wrong side of the head of the Detective Bureau. It's not a good place to be."

"He knows," Prudence said after Hanrahan had closed the outside office door behind him and they'd listened to his footsteps retreat down the hall.

"From what he said, it sounds as though most of Chinatown knows. Or suspects," Geoffrey added.

"I suppose it's better to be under the wing of someone who sells protection rather than someone who needs it." Prudence smiled uncertainly. "Wei doesn't seem very dangerous."

"He's a snake," Geoffrey said. "Smooth, hidden, but unlikely to attack unless you provoke him."

"Then we'll have to be very careful not to make him angry," Prudence said.

"I think he has something in mind for Johnny that will throw everything off balance," Geoffrey said.

Prudence waited.

"Every lord needs an heir. Why not the son of the woman you once wanted to be your wife?"

"She'd never permit it. Not if what Hanrahan told us is accurate. Her only son the second-in-command of a criminal gang? Not Lady Peng."

"She may not have a choice," Geoffrey said. "Johnny can lose his head or whatever ethics he's managed to cultivate. It's not much of a decision to make, especially since the latter comes with power, money, prestige, and probably a long and comfortable life for every member of the family."

"Would you, Geoffrey?" Prudence asked.

"In a heartbeat. I've always said that the only thing more exciting than being the stalker is being the prey."

Sometimes she couldn't tell when he was serious or teasing. Not until she caught the glint of laughter in his dark eyes and knew Geoffrey was once more having her on.

"Should we all go armed?" Josiah asked. He had one of the nickel-finished Colt New Army and Navy double-action revolvers with an ivory grip. Bought on a whim and only taken out of its box in the privacy of his apartment.

"We're Congregationalists," Geoffrey said. "Not cowboys."

CHAPTER 20

It took Wei Fu Jian's men only a day and a half to clean and furnish the storefront on Doyers Street. Above it hung a sign proclaiming in English and Chinese that this was the site of the Chinatown Congregational Mission Church.

"It looks authentic," Geoffrey said, stepping into the narrow, cobblestoned street to get a better look at the newly washed windows and repainted door.

"So do you." Prudence brushed dust from her shabby black bombazine skirt and wondered if she'd get used to the feel of a cotton chemise under her corset. Josiah had argued in favor of authenticity for all of them, and enlisted Prudence's maid to persuade her mistress that only the upper classes enjoyed silk and lace undergarments.

Geoffrey looked very much the part he was playing, having sent Josiah and his costumer friend to purchase secondhand suits, white shirts with frayed cuffs, threadbare vests, and nearly shapeless hats. The only concession he'd made was to order them to thoroughly dust the used clothing with insect-repelling crushed mothballs. Despite hanging outside in Prudence's stable yard overnight, they still reeked of camphor.

He'd vetoed the idea of a stage beard and mutton chops.

"Every clergyman I've ever met has impressive hair on his face." Josiah's assertion had been backed up by the supposedly authentic models in the clerical garb catalog. "Dark as your hair is, you could have the beginnings of a decent beard in less than a month."

Geoffrey had no intention of staying in Chinatown long enough to grow a missionary beard. If all went well, and their plans bore fruit, within a week or two he and Prudence should have a good lead on the man they were seeking. They'd talked about turning him over to the New York City Police Department, but even Hanrahan had been skeptical. Sometimes justice was better served when officialdom was bypassed.

The storefront had been dusted, swept, and furnished with rows of wooden chairs and benches along the walls. A large cross hung in plain sight opposite the door, and a long table had been covered with a purple velvet cloth and white linen napkin. A pair of metal candlesticks flanked a large bible, open to the Old Testament Book of Isaiah. Prudence wondered why that reading had been chosen and decided it was probably random.

"'Hear the word of the Lord, ye rulers of Sodom; give ear unto the law of our God, ye people of Gomorrah,'" she read aloud. "That's certainly very threatening."

"Missionaries have voices of thunder," Josiah said. "The only way to recruit new Christians is to scare them into belief. You have to make them too frightened of hell to question the doctrine you're pounding into them."

"Maybe I'll have you write my sermons," Geoffrey said. He'd had no idea Josiah knew anything about religion.

"I found a book." Josiah opened the briefcase he carried everywhere. "Here you are. *Sermons on the Christian Life of Faith and Duty.* I bought it off a pushcart. The binding had to be reglued, but it should hold together for a while."

"Just what I need." Geoffrey tucked the small brown volume into one of the capacious pockets of his baggy jacket. "Let's see what's been done to the upper floors."

"We don't want anyone coming in before we're ready for them," Prudence said. She locked the street door and pulled down the shade. Someone had hung a sign in the window reading OPEN on one side and CLOSED on the other.

Then she took off the bonnet that hid her hair, tightly coiled into an unflattering bun resting against the nape of her neck, and rubbed vigorously where the scratchy felt of the hat had irritated her scalp. She stirred the few hot coals in the potbellied stove that heated the entire building, and gingerly fed sticks of firewood into the firebox. "I'm not sure I know what I'm doing," she muttered as Geoffrey and Josiah watched. "But at least we won't freeze to death."

"I think you'd make an excellent housewife," Geoffrey teased. "Accomplished in all things domestic, and definitely a step above parlor maid status."

"I'm not listening to you," Prudence declared, sweeping past him to the narrow, uncarpeted stairway that was barely wide enough to accommodate two people passing one another.

Geoffrey grinned and Josiah tried not to smile.

Each of the second and third floors boasted two rooms, just large enough to hold a single narrow bed and a washstand. Well-worn sheets and a thin blanket lay folded on each bed. Except for a Christian cross, the walls were bare. Only the front-facing room on each floor had a window, and there was no indoor plumbing. The attic servants' rooms in Prudence's Fifth Avenue mansion were opulent compared to where she, Geoffrey, and Josiah would be spending their nights for who knew how long. She'd braced herself for the stark simplicity of the Quaker Refuge for the Sick Poor where she volunteered, but this was worse than she had imagined. She wondered where and how soon she could get a cat; there were bound to be bugs and rodents everywhere.

The rooms on the fourth and fifth floors were locked.

"Do we have keys?" Prudence asked Geoffrey.

"Just to the front and back doors."

"What's out back?" Prudence jiggled the doorknobs.

"A narrow, filthy alleyway," Geoffrey said. "Not wide enough to get more than a single wagon down it at a time. I suggest we keep that door locked permanently. I'll put the key on a nail beside it in case we have to make a quick exit."

"I wonder what's behind these doors."

"Things Wei would rather we didn't see," Geoffrey said. "Or nothing. Do you have your picklocks?" He knew Prudence always carried them in her reticule.

"I may look like a Congregationalist minister's wife, but I don't think like one," she said, handing over the tools Geoffrey had asked for and pulling out the small gold watch pinned to her bodice. "You're out of practice. I'll time you."

"Not a record, but not bad," he said a few moments later, reading the face of the watch she held out to him.

Josiah was the first to enter the fourth-floor rooms, two narrow chambers joined by a connecting door. Stacks of wooden boxes were packed tightly against the walls, all of them marked with Chinese characters it was beyond his ability to translate. He pried open a slightly loose-looking lid and extracted a square package of sailcloth.

"Opium," Geoffrey said, touching the tip of his finger to the white powder and then to his tongue. "A very high grade. From the quantity, I'd say Wei is supplying most of the parlors in Chinatown. It's not illegal, but now that opium and morphine are both subject to taxation, smuggling has become an even bigger business than it was before Congress decided that the government should make money off the trade."

"That's very scathing of you," Prudence said.

"It's as close to the truth as either of us is likely to get. The object isn't really to regulate the importation of opium; it's to arouse more anti-Chinese sentiment, to make sure there's popular support to extend the Chinese Exclusion Act when it expires next year."

"What's it doing here?" Josiah asked. "There aren't even any guards in this building."

"If you can find a clean window overlooking the alley, I think you'll find we're far from alone here," Geoffrey said. "Doyers is the shortest, most twisted street in Chinatown. Easy to defend, easy for someone to get trapped at the bend. Wei knows exactly what he's doing."

"What's in these larger crates?" Josiah asked, tugging at slats that were nailed too tightly to budge.

"Use this as a pry bar," Geoffrey said, handing over his sword cane. He'd removed the intricate scrollwork along the shaft so that now it looked like an ordinary cheap walking stick.

"I don't want to snap the blade," Josiah protested.

"You can't," Geoffrey said.

"Rolls of silk," Josiah breathed as the first of the slats gave way and he could use his hands instead of the custom-made sword cane to pull off the others. "I imagine the rest of these contain the items he sells in his emporium. Lamps, vases, carved ivory, furniture."

"Some of the meanest-looking knives I've ever seen," Prudence said. She'd taken the cane from Josiah and gone to work on a long box that she'd thought might contain rifles. "Swords, too. But mainly knives."

"Wei's men are silent killers," Geoffrey said. "But I imagine we'll find guns if we keep looking."

"Is there any point?" Prudence asked. "Hanrahan told us what Wei is up to, what he's planning. Nothing less than to take over the running of Chinatown. Every man on every street will pay him a fee and owe him allegiance. It'll be like ruling a small, independent country at the lower end of Manhattan."

"Fireworks over here," Josiah called, pointing to a box he'd just opened. "I smelled what I thought was gunpowder."

"Saltpeter and sulphur," Geoffrey said. "Let's close these up. Wei may suspect we've invaded his private storage spaces, but we don't have to leave him proof of it."

"Whose side are we on?" Prudence asked when they'd descended the stairway to the ground floor, and she'd stirred up the fire again.

"There's no stopping what Wei intends to accomplish, if that's what you mean," Geoffrey said. "He's planned it too well. The only thing I think we can say with any certainty that he didn't anticipate was Lord Peng's arrival in New York City."

"Someone else didn't foresee it either," Josiah said. "Unless . . . Are you certain Wei isn't behind the killing?"

"No, I'm not," Geoffrey said. "It's too early to rule out anyone."

"Except Lady Peng and her children," Prudence said.

"Not even them," Geoffrey insisted. "Perhaps not Johnny and his sisters, but Lady Peng is certainly capable of engineering the attack we saw. All it would take is one man to do her bidding. Either through blind devotion or hard cash."

"I hadn't considered her a suspect," Prudence said.

"The amah could have acted as intermediary," Geoffrey continued.

"What would killing Lord Peng gain for her?" Prudence asked. "We always ask *cui bono?* Who profits?"

"I think it could depend on whether she planned on returning to China as a widow."

"She didn't know Wei Fu Jian was here in America," Prudence said. "I'm as sure of that as I am of anything else about this case. She believed he was dead."

Josiah mumbled something too softly for either Geoffrey or Prudence to make out what he'd said, then he flipped the sign on the front door to OPEN and turned the key in the lock.

Matthew Lam, dressed in wide-legged dark trousers and frogged jacket, stood on the threshold.

"Wei Fu Jian sent me," he said, surveying the storefront's churchly furnishings. "He thinks I'll be of more value as your interpreter than as a waiter in the Golden Dragon Noodle Palace."

"He has other waiters who will report a newcomer or anyone acting suspiciously," Geoffrey said.

"Language skills are harder to come by than serving a plate of food, is what he said." Lam shrugged.

"He's right," Prudence agreed. "One of the things we've talked about is not always waiting here for people to come to us. Geoffrey and I need to go out into the community, stand on street corners, hand out bible tracts, offer to help with whatever problems people with limited English can't solve by themselves. The intent is to gain their trust so when we ask the important questions, they'll give us honest answers."

"They'll be more likely to tell me the truth but then ask that I not repeat it to the foreign devils," Lam said.

"You're part foreign devil," Prudence said.

"Is that why you took the job?" Geoffrey asked. "So the foreign devil part of you could better understand who your father was and what that makes you?"

Josiah faded into the shadows in the corner where the potbellied stove stood. He took out the notebook no one else could read because it was kept in Pitman shorthand and waited. He'd sensed a secret about Matthew Lam from the moment the young man had first walked into the Hunter and MacKenzie office.

"We never heard from him again after he returned to China," Lam said. "He had all the paperwork needed to get back into the country, but apparently, he didn't even try. He abandoned us, my mother and me. It broke her heart. She was never the same, always waiting for a letter to arrive, looking out the window for him to walk up the lane, listening for the sound of his voice calling her name. When I was at Yale, I made some inquiries through missionaries I met there at the Divinity School. If the name I gave them was really his, he already had a wife when he met and married my mother. The impression I got was that he flirted with Christianity for a few years and when it didn't suit him anymore, he walked away from it. By suited, I mean that Christianity didn't bring him the wealth and prestige he thought it would. That's who he was, and that's who I am. At least half of me is."

"The information you were given might not be accurate," Geoffrey said.

"It was hearsay, but I'm inclined to believe it."

"You never told her?" Prudence said.

"And I never will. But I've always wondered what it would be like to live among his people as one of them, what I would learn about myself if I did."

The flames in the potbellied stove crackled and Josiah's pencil whispered across the pages of his stenographer's notebook.

Hardly anyone passing by the premises of the Chinatown Congregational Mission Church did more than glance at the newly painted sign and keep walking. Work was the most important thing in their lives, work from dawn to dark so that infinitesimally small sums of money could be earned, saved, and sent back to China for the families left behind. Most of the men knew that the days of visiting and returning to America were over. If you left now, odds were you would never be allowed to return. Filial piety obliged them to see to the welfare of aging parents, so to ensure that the line would continue, they married and planted the seed of at least one child before boarding the boat that took them across the Pacific Ocean to the Beautiful Country. The Manchus had decreed that a man who cut off his queue was subject to beheading, so to cut it off was to acknowledge permanent exile. Most newcomers continued to wear it. For some, it was that symbol and the futile hope of rejoining their ancestors that kept them going.

Alfred Hanrahan stood in the storefront's recessed doorway and watched the procession of laborers hurry along Doyers Street to the businesses on Pell and Mott Streets. Doyers was dark and cramped, as full of twists and turns as a snake, the least prosperous and most dangerous street in Chinatown. He wondered why Wei Fu Jian had chosen this spot to purchase a small building and install the detectives Lady Peng and her son had hired. Hanrahan had known where the Pengs were hiding within hours of the nighttime arrival of the carriage that brought them there. The murders of the two guards had never been reported to the police and no one inquired about the missing men. He assumed Wei had seen to their burials. To do otherwise would have stirred up anger and resentment among their fellows for whom the rituals of death were as important as the daily routines of life.

Hanrahan was an orderly man who liked his mind to be as rigidly organized as the rented room in which he lived. He lined up the players in the Peng case the way he laid out his hair and clothes brushes, his combs, toothpowder and toothbrush. Straight as soldiers on parade. Each to the role fate had assigned him to play. Only one place lay empty, that of Lord Peng's killer. From time to time Hanrahan laid a suspect into the ghostly outline, but no one fitted in well enough to remain. Lack of motive was the problem he hadn't been able to resolve. He didn't know *why* Lord Peng had been killed, and he didn't think anyone else did, either.

He had enormous respect for the Pinkerton National Detective Agency, for the way they trained their operatives and the impressive results they achieved. It stood to reason that ex-Pink Geoffrey Hunter had a better chance of ferreting out the killer—if he was hiding in Chinatown—than either the police or Wei Fu Jian. The police were only marginally interested in solving crimes and Wei was on the cusp of becoming the un-crowned ruler of a burgeoning kingdom that could only grow bigger and more influential as the years passed.

It was interesting to Hanrahan that Hunter had chosen to add a half-Chinese recruit to his team. Even though he himself had had only one Chinese grandparent and to the undiscerning eye was racially white, he had always been haunted by a sup-pressed curiosity about the ancestor whose name had been obliterated from the family history. It was why he had volun-teered for the Sixth Precinct, an assignment virtually no one else considered anything but punishment. Matthew Lam could not hide his Chinese ancestry, and perhaps he'd made his peace with the two worlds from which he came. It was something Hanrahan would have liked to talk to him about. But couldn't. Wouldn't.

Lam was inside with the pseudo-Congregationalists. Han-rahan could see all of them through the recently washed win-dows. Miss MacKenzie unaware that no amount of worn bombazine could disguise her upbringing, the secretary too neat and tidy to be mistaken for an impoverished deacon, Hunter the most convincing of the three despite the aura of menace that was as much a part of him as the dark eyes that im-mobilized you as securely as a pinned insect.

Hanrahan opened the door, pausing for a moment to let the tinkle of the bell fastened above it announce his arrival. He hadn't made up his mind yet just how he would play this out. Time would tell.

One of the passersby took note of the latest Christian incur-sion and slipped into the alleyway at the first opportunity. Too narrow for most carts, the dirt passage had been cleared of most debris to eliminate any mounds behind which to hide. Trash cans stood by back doors, but their lids were firmly secured.

Halfway down the alley he spotted the first of Wei Fu Jian's men, lounging against a wall, smoking a cigarette, affecting an air of indifference to everything going on around him. A broad-brimmed black hat shaded his face, but his eyes followed every movement in the alley and his ears assessed every sound.

Once the passerby had identified the first guard, he quickly located the others.

He would have to make his way into the Chinatown Congregationalist Mission Church through the front door. He wondered if this building, like so many others, was connected to the web of underground tunnels he'd spent hours exploring until he was as comfortable in their darkness as he was in the streets above.

It was always best to have two entrances to a place. Two exits. It was why he had scaled the wall around Wei Fu Jian's garden, leaving the dirt and the bushes above the tunnel undisturbed until he needed to make a quick escape. Gardens were tricky places. You could never tell when someone might choose to prune a plant or replace it with something different. An alleyway at night could present problems if it was guarded. Which this one was. But nobody expected a burglar to walk boldly through a front door.

Tonight, he would sharpen the knife that lay hidden in his mattress.

CHAPTER 21

The waiter from the Golden Dragon Noodle Palace was the handsomest Chinese man Mei Sha had ever seen, including her brother, Johnny.

She'd met very few of her own countrymen in England, and the only social life she'd known had been infrequent introductions to the older brothers of her boarding school acquaintances. None of them had done more than extend the very briefest of obligatory courtesies. She might be the daughter of a high-ranking Chinese diplomat, but she was definitely outside the marriage market pale. Like mated with like. Fortunes, titles, and lineage were rarely entirely ignored, even by the most impetuous members of the British aristocracy. Not when it came to the serious business of contracting a lifetime alliance.

But a handsome young man was a handsome young man, no matter who his parents were. A girl could and did dream. Late at night, giggling under the covers, they'd all confessed to impossible attractions, to wondering how exactly one went about kissing, and that other thing, of course. What you did after marriage that no one ever talked about, but everyone knew produced the necessary heir and a spare. Freedom was what

they all longed for, but no one knew exactly what it was. Or
how to attain it. Except through marriage. Which meant you
no longer had to do what your mother ordered you to do. Of
course, there was that bit about obeying one's husband. Still . . .

Mei Sha was restless. She had no one to talk to, and the plan
to meet and marry a wealthy American she'd daydreamed
aboard ship now seemed more impossible than ever. And foolish. What had she been thinking? She had no money of her
own, no clothes unless the trunks left behind at the Fifth Avenue Hotel could be claimed, and no entrée into what she had
been forced to admit was a society as tightly closed against her
as the British. Bettina was far too fragile to be a co-conspirator,
and the wonderfully independent Miss MacKenzie was too responsible and steady an adult to be a party to Mei Sha's wild
imaginings. And now she was in hiding, her life in mortal danger. It just wasn't fair!

The garden was no longer an escape. Whenever Mei Sha
stepped through the door to the outside, one of her uncle's guards
materialized. They all knew she'd single-handedly fought off a
knife-wielding intruder, so there was always a glint of admiration in their eyes, but none of them dared let her out of their
sight. Wei Fu Jian had made it clear that if the security of his
building was breached again, the punishment would rival anything imposed by a savage warlord in a homeland not known
for mercy.

Johnny was less than useless. The easy camaraderie that had
developed between sister and brother as both of them became
more English than anyone else in the family, had dried up, so
that when they met in the dining room now, they had nothing
to say. Uncle Fu Jian presided over every meal, cementing his
role as head of the family, his dark eyes sweeping with a palpa-
ble intensity over his nieces' robes and his nephew's attitude.
An Bao was invariably impeccably correct; Mei Sha knew that
something was always wanting in her appearance. A lock of

hair come loose and trailing along her cheek, a fold of silk not precisely creased, eyes not downcast demurely. When the more adventuresome girls at boarding school wanted to show how little they cared for rules, they used swear words they'd overheard their brothers say. Mei Sha had never repeated them aloud, but she ran them through her mind like a string of pebbles thrown angrily into still water. It helped, but not enough.

She'd learned the waiter's name by accident. Miss MacKenzie had been talking about him, suggesting that he might better contribute to solving the case if he acted as the translator she and Mr. Hunter needed. Then she pushed it. Mei Sha had waited for an explosion when Miss MacKenzie told Uncle Fu Jian that Matthew Lam was her employee, and although she did not mind his performing an occasional task for him, she reserved the right to decide where Matthew Lam should chiefly direct his talents and his time. Did Mr. Wei not agree?

She hadn't heard the answer because the lovely English syllables had drowned out everything else. Matthew, Matthew, Matthew Lam. May and Matthew. Matthew and May. The way their names fit together was an omen, a sign, a portent of auspicious things to come. Except that confined to the upper floors of Wei's Chinese Imports and Antiquities as she was, Mei Sha despaired of ever seeing handsome Matthew again.

When she absentmindedly sewed an upside-down green leaf on the slipper she was embroidering, her mother asked if she was ill. *Not ill, no, not ill. But very tired, not sleeping well.* Girls at boarding school who claimed not to be able to sleep were often sent to the infirmary where rules were lax, and a rare bit of privacy enjoyed. Lady Peng ordered fragrant jasmine tea and suggested that her daughter set aside her sewing for the time being lest she prick a finger.

It wasn't much, but Mei Sha had learned at school that wars are won one small battle at a time. She drank her jasmine tea and excused herself from the parlor to lie down. On the way to her room, she detoured into Johnny's armoire where several sets of dark cotton pants and frogged jackets were piled beside his shoes. Like the ones worn by her uncle's guards and the household servants. She didn't stop to try to figure out why clothes like that were in her brother's room; she folded a pair of trousers, a jacket, and a round hat into a bundle small enough to slip beneath her robe and then concealed them under her mattress. That night, by candlelight, she hemmed the trousers and the jacket sleeves, taking tucks wherever she could. Nothing was a perfect fit, but no one expected a workingman's clothes to be anything but utilitarian.

The compromise Wei Fu Jian had agreed to was that Matthew Lam would work as Prudence and Geoffrey's translator by day, but that as soon as the dinner hour approached, he would return to the Golden Dragon Noodle Palace to resume his waiter's duties.

"That doesn't really make sense," Prudence complained to Geoffrey. "I doubt he'll overhear anything useful in a restaurant known to be patronized by the most powerful man in Chinatown."

"Wei is saving face. You have a claim on Matthew's services, which he acknowledges, but he tempers that with a small show of power over both of you. Actually, it's masterfully done, and without a raised voice or the suggestion of a threat."

"All this dancing about to save face is what a society woman does every afternoon when she pays calls and every evening when she dresses in diamonds and sallies forth to overshadow all her supposed friends. I don't have much patience with it," Prudence said.

"I can tell by the sound of your voice." Geoffrey offered her a pamphlet from a bundle Josiah had had printed that morning. "What do you think of this?"

"It's not very eye-catching."

"It's supposed to be a serious examination of the state of soul that can land you in hell."

"Sin?"

"All kinds of sin. Euphemisms for what can't be printed, and lurid descriptions of the fiery pits where devils stab the damned with pitchforks."

"Where did you get it?"

"Josiah found several of them on one of those pushcarts he favors. He had a printer duplicate the most sensational bits and pieces."

"It's in English, Geoffrey. Don't we need what we're handing out to have at least a headline in Chinese? How will anyone know what this is?"

"It doesn't matter. They'll end up in privies, anyway. It's just window dressing."

"Has Matthew seen it?"

"I don't think so. Josiah didn't pick them up until after Matthew had left."

"The mission doesn't officially open until tomorrow," Prudence reminded him. "I've seen a few men slow down and peer through the windows as they walked by. What do we do if we end up with a crowd of people wanting to be converted?"

"Tomorrow's Friday. Everyone will be working. We'll station ourselves on the corners of Mott Street where the heaviest traffic is. How are you at ringing a bell?" Geoffrey handed her a heavy brass bell whose clapper made a loud clanging sound.

"I'm not carrying that thing," Prudence protested.

"You can shout out the good news of salvation or ring the bell. Your choice," Geoffrey offered.

"This may be the most ridiculous thing we've ever done."

"We're undercover, remember? And someday we'll tell the story and laugh about it."

"I'll be the bell ringer," Prudence decided, giving a tentative shake that produced an unmelodious bong. "But I think I'll put cotton in my ears before we set out."

*   *   *

Workingmen got up in the dark, drank their tea, and ate cold rice sitting on the edge of their narrow bunks. They were out on the street as the sun came up.

Wei Fu Jian dressed for the day to the murmurs of his guards relieving one another at their posts and the soft slap of servants' shoes against the floor and in the stairwells. He listened for a moment, alert to any unexpected sound, but heard nothing that was not as much a part of the daily ritual as the tea he liked to drink so hot it burned his tongue.

He would put the final organizational touches to the Eastern Benevolent Association this morning so that by noon, New York City's first tong would be up and running. He liked that expression that Johnny had said was used in England at the start of a horse race. Wei was certain that the San Francisco tongs were jockeying for position, each planning to outdo the other in the unclaimed Chinese settlements of the East Coast of America. So it would indeed be a race whose winner would outrun every challenger. *Crossing the finish line* was another phrase Johnny had used. Wei intended to be the only contestant to achieve that goal. For a few years, at least, until the West Coast tongs established and consolidated their presence outside California, the Eastern Benevolent Association would be the *only* tong. Being first in any field meant being strongest. Wei intended to reign over his Chinatown until the day he could no longer put two feet outside his bed. Then Johnny would take over.

Mei Sha crept from the Wei's Chinese Imports and Antiquities building while the downstairs guards were conferring beneath the stairwell, sneaking the quick cigarettes they were forbidden to smoke while on duty. Nothing suspicious had been observed during the night, but Wei Fu Jian had let it be known that something momentous would be happening today. It was hardly a secret, but to curry their employer's favor they would pretend surprise when he announced the inauguration of the Eastern Benevolent Association. The chuckle of their subdued laughter hid the quiet snick of the street door opening.

Mei Sha had never been anywhere without someone watching her. Her amah most of the time, but in England Lord Peng and the British government had assigned at least one professional bodyguard even while she was at boarding school. She wasn't supposed to be aware of his presence, but she'd sometimes glimpse a dark-coated figure standing beneath a tree and know that eyes were upon her.

Here, in a narrow street of New York City's Chinatown, she was one of many slender figures scurrying along to work, eyes darting from shop to sidewalk, cobbled street to horse-drawn cart. Shopkeepers were opening their stores, setting out the day's produce, leaning against doorways to shout encouragement to potential customers. Everyone in Chinatown seemed to know everyone else, and perhaps that was because so many of them came from the same southeastern provinces of China that they nearly all belonged to the enormous family clans that had lived there for centuries. Mei Sha felt no curious eyes following her, no hand grasp her arm to haul her back to her uncle, not so much as a stray dog sniff at her shoes. She was, miraculously, anonymous in the crowd.

The Chinatown Congregationalist Mission Church on Doyers Street was her destination. And Matthew Lam. She had remembered that Mr. Hunter and Miss MacKenzie would begin their missionary careers this morning, and that Matthew was to accompany them as they made their way from street corner to street corner. Mei Sha didn't know what to expect when she revealed herself to them, but it shouldn't matter. Matthew would see her and she him. A flame would erupt between them. That's what happened in the novels she read. Love once acknowledged could never be denied.

As she made the turn from Pell onto Doyers, a flash of something bright caught her eye. She turned her head to glance behind her. Nothing but the scattered mass of men on their way to work, a few stragglers stopping at the carts selling rice balls and steamed buns.

The night smells were giving way to the daytime odors of frying food, fresh horse droppings, and human sweat. Mei Sha felt alive, as she had the few times she'd persuaded Amah to walk in one of the London parks or buy violets from a flower girl. So many of Mei Sha's waking hours were spent imitating life that when the real thing came along, she was stunned by how hungry she was to embrace it.

Doyers was narrower than she'd expected it to be, emptier than Pell. Darker even though the morning was brightening. Two blocks down it seemed to dead end, until she realized that what she'd mistaken for a cul-de-sac was a sharp bend. Mei Sha breathed a sigh of relief. She hadn't missed the storefront mission after all. It was just that the strangeness of the street had confused her.

Now that she really looked, she realized that Doyers sported the same small shops and eating places as Mott and Pell Streets, just not as prosperous looking. Why had Uncle Fu Jian chosen this street for Miss MacKenzie and Mr. Hunter? Chinatown's secrets would surely lie where there were more people out and about. Doyers had a menacing feel about it. She walked faster and couldn't resist glancing nervously behind her. No one. Of course she wasn't being followed. She'd been too clever for Uncle Fu Jian's guards, just as she'd sometimes successfully broken the boarding school rules.

Another flash of light caught her eye. This time, when she looked behind her, she saw a slender young man whose right hand seemed to be pulling and pushing at something half concealed by his jacket. Something that when the bottom edge of the jacket caught on it, shone bright and sharp and dangerous.

Mei Sha didn't hesitate. She ran—as fast and furiously as her unbound feet would carry her.

The breath caught in her throat as her arms swung like pendulums propelling her down the length of Doyers Street.

Almost to the bend.

Around the bend.

And there, stepping out from a storefront, came Miss Prudence MacKenzie, carrying what looked like a heavy brass bell. Behind her, cane over his arm, Mr. Hunter turned to lock the door behind a man she didn't know wearing a shabby black suit and . . . Matthew!

Who yelled something at her, then sprinted in her direction, passed Mei Sha like the wind, and disappeared from sight around the bend.

CHAPTER 22

"I lost him in the crowd on Mott Street," Matthew Lam reported. Despite the early-morning February chill, sweat poured down his face and he breathed out bellows of vapor that hung in the air like fog. "I had him in sight for a while on Pell, but with everyone wearing the same kind of clothes he disappeared. Once he stopped running there was no distinguishing him from every other man hurrying to work. I stopped by the precinct house and told Hanrahan what happened."

He'd spoken directly to Geoffrey. Now he turned to Mei Sha, huddled by the potbellied stove where Prudence was doing her best to stoke a small fire.

"Are you all right? He didn't hurt you, did he?"

The big brown eyes Mei Sha turned to him were full of tears. She hadn't meant to bring danger to the people who were looking for her father's killer, hadn't realized that having once been a target herself, it was more than likely she would remain so until the knife she'd seen flashing beneath a frogged coat was plunged into her back.

Prudence had tongue lashed her as efficiently as a boarding school mistress, then sent Josiah to advise Wei Fu Jian of his niece's whereabouts. Instead of being hailed as an adventurous heroine, Mei Sha had heard stark truths about herself that no one else had dared voice. Spoiled. Irresponsible. Recklessly impetuous. Careless of the safety of others. She'd tuned out the tirade when she felt the first drops on her cheeks and knew she was sliding into uncontrollable weeping. The only thing holding her together now was pride.

"Mei Sha? Are you all right?" Matthew knelt before her and clasped her cold hands in his. "What you did was foolish, but you're safe now. You made it through."

His kindness broke her. She choked on her own sobs.

Prudence caught Geoffrey's eye and shook her head. It wasn't time yet to offer comfort. Mei Sha was a long way from truly understanding the folly of what she'd done. Despite what had happened in Wei's garden, she seemed still to believe it was all an incomprehensibly thrilling game they were playing. The fact that her father was dead had hardly touched her. Nor, Prudence reminded Geoffrey in a hissed whisper, had it made much of an impression on his wife, his son, and his other daughter. Lord Peng was gone forever, but no one seemed to care.

Josiah's trip to Wei's Chinese Imports and Antiquities was rapid and uneventful. No one paid attention to the older gentleman dressed in a shabby black American suit. But it was his first extended solo excursion into the streets of Chinatown, and he was enthralled by the fragrant piles of sweet, steamed custard and coconut buns hawked from food carts, the chestnut odor of red bean paste, and the burned sugar smell of fried pancakes. It was all he could do not to stop and buy a bagful, but in his disguise of impoverished Congregationalist deacon, he'd emptied his pockets of all but a few coins. Later, he promised himself, perhaps on the way back he'd stop for one, just one of the sesame-seed-encrusted dough balls that he had read were a special dessert of the Chinese New Year.

It took some persuading to penetrate the cordon of men who guarded Wei Fu Jian's private quarters, but once assured of who he was and who he worked for, Josiah was escorted to Lady Peng.

"Wei Fu Jian and Johnny left together several hours ago," she told him. "I'm sorry you missed them."

"Miss Mei Sha came to the storefront mission this morning." Josiah hadn't figured out a gracious way to tell this formidable lady what her youngest daughter had done, so he opted for the bald truth. "Miss MacKenzie and Mr. Hunter sent me to assure you she's safe."

Lady Peng seemed not to understand what he'd said.

"There was an incident, but she wasn't injured in any way."

Still no reaction from Lady Peng, who sat as motionless as a statue. Finally, when Josiah was about to stutter out another assurance of Mei Sha's safety, she raised one elegant hand. A maid appeared out of nowhere, bowed to the instructions given her in rapid-fire Chinese, and scuttled out of the parlor. Moments later she was back, this time bending close over her mistress to whisper in her ear.

"It seems my youngest child is not in her room where I presumed her to be," Lady Peng said. "So I think you should tell me the whole story, Mr. Gregory. Please start at the beginning and leave nothing out."

"We were leaving the mission," he began, wishing he'd stopped for one of those sesame balls after all. His stomach had made an embarrassing noise. "I think Miss Prudence saw her first, coming toward us down Doyers Street, but I don't think any of us recognized her to begin with. She was dressed in men's trousers and jacket, so if she hadn't been running, we probably wouldn't have noticed her at all."

"Why was my daughter running, Mr. Gregory?"

"Matthew Lam didn't wait to find out. He took off like a fireworks rocket, and when he did, the man who had been chasing Miss Mei Sha gave up the pursuit and raced in the opposite direction. Matthew went after him, but he got away." Josiah paused, waiting for Lady Peng to question him further. She didn't. "He had a knife. Miss Mei Sha swears he was pulling it in and out of a sheath attached to his belt. She saw it flash in the sunlight."

"It seems I owe the lives of two of my children to your Mr. Lam's swift intervention," Lady Peng said. "Please tell Miss MacKenzie and Mr. Hunter that they are to keep Mei Sha at the storefront until someone comes for her. I don't know when that will be. I'll send word to Wei Fu Jian, but this is a very important day for him. It may be a while before Mei Sha can be brought back here. In the meantime, convey my thanks to Mr. Lam."

Lady Peng stood and nodded gracefully in Josiah's general direction.

One of the guards from the stairwell appeared at his side, leading him out and down to the street entrance without comment.

On the way back to the mission, Josiah bought a sesame roll and one each of the steamed cream and coconut buns. They were as delicious as they looked.

"Did you see his face?" Hanrahan asked Mei Sha. He was trying very hard to conceal his annoyance at the stupidity of this cosseted young girl whose impetuosity had nearly cost her her life. Again.

"He never got close enough."

"But you're sure it was the same man who assaulted you in Wei Fu Jian's garden?"

"Who else could it have been?" She'd worked through the tears to something akin to righteous indignation at being so rudely questioned. First Miss MacKenzie had scolded her, then she'd been turned over to this police officer while everyone else gathered together to plan what to do next. Shutting her out. Ig-noring her. Matthew, who'd been so kind—who'd saved her life—was acting now as if she didn't exist.

"Miss Peng, can you tell me why you're dressed the way you are? And why you left Wei Fu Jian's building without telling anyone where you were going?"

Mei Sha opened and then shut her mouth. She clicked her teeth together stubbornly. What right did this man have to ask her such personal questions? It wasn't any of his business what she chose to wear and where she chose to go. Her mother's ex-asperated voice echoed in her mind. Mei Sha had disappeared into the green vastness of Hyde Park once, simply because she couldn't stand the staid silence of the diplomatic compound anymore. For that outing she'd stolen—borrowed—a maid's uniform from the basement laundry line.

She looked down at the dark blue cotton trousers with the neatly stitched hems, her feet in black silk shoes peeping out. She'd had to wear her own footwear, and really, it was a good thing because she'd never have been able to run fast enough to stay ahead of the man with the knife if she'd worn her brother's shoes stuffed with crumpled paper or handkerchiefs.

"There are hardly any women in Chinatown," Mei Sha said, raising her head and squaring her shoulders. "I didn't want to attract attention. And I didn't tell anyone where I was going because I knew they'd try to stop me." There. She'd told the truth. Everything she'd said made good sense. There was no reason for Officer Hanrahan to continue questioning her. She stood up.

"I'm not finished," Hanrahan said.

"I have nothing more to tell you." Mei Sha looked toward Prudence for help.

"You don't know when something you don't think signifi-cant may prove to be important," Hanrahan said. He stood as Prudence spoke quietly to Geoffrey and then walked across the room.

She placed a hand lightly on Mei Sha's shoulder, keeping it there until the girl sat down. Then she pulled a chair close and placed a sweet-smelling paper package on the girl's lap. "Dragon's Beard candy. My secretary has a legendary sweet tooth. He bought this for you at one of the street carts."

The lines of stubbornness around Mei Sha's mouth eased. She seemed suddenly younger, uncertain of what to do next. "My amah used to make it for us when we were little."

"I tasted a piece. It's very sweet and nutty," Prudence said.

Mei Sha unfolded the paper and smiled down at the thin strands of spun sugar that resembled a delicate bird's nest. The candy melted on her tongue.

"Do you think you would recognize the man who followed you if you saw him again?" Hanrahan asked, risking a quick nod of thanks in Prudence's direction.

"I saw a flash of light." Mei Sha wiped a sticky finger over her lips. "Twice. The second time is when I knew it was a knife. But I never saw his face. Not today and not in the garden."

"When did you first notice him? Was he standing in front of a store? At a pushcart? Walking along the street? Where?"

"It was when I turned onto Doyers from Pell," Mei Sha said. She closed her eyes as if to picture the moment, then opened them again and shook her head. "I saw a gleam of something I thought was sunlight reflecting off a store window, I guess, but it didn't register that it might be a person. Not until the second flash. And by then I'd started down Doyers and he was already behind me. I don't know when or where he started following."

"Could he have been waiting outside Wei Fu Jian's emporium?" Prudence asked.

"He could," Hanrahan agreed.

"Is it me he's after?" Mei Sha whispered. "Or does he just want to kill another Peng? Any Peng."

And now the reaction finally set in. Mei's lips trembled, her eyes grew large and frightened, and when Prudence put an arm around her shoulders she burrowed into its comfort and warmth.

"I've made some tea." Josiah set down a tray on which rested a squat green teapot and a cluster of small, handleless cups. "And I brought you the rest of the Dragon's Beard candy." The rich scent of boiled, spun sugar filled the air as he unwrapped a package of glossy white paper. "I was told that it's best eaten right after it's made," he said. "And this couldn't be fresher."

"Shall I be mother?" Prudence asked, thinking that the English tea phrase would be reassuring to Mei Sha, who, she realized, was lonelier than anyone in her family suspected.

Mei Sha nodded and held out a cup for Prudence to fill.

"Thank you," she murmured. "For everything. I'm sorry."

Hanrahan left Mei Sha to Prudence's matter-of-fact support, not quite as exasperated by the young woman as he had been during the first few minutes of the questioning. Youth excused a lot, but he wasn't entirely ready to ignore her responsibility for the latest close call. She should have stayed in the safe haven provided her, and she definitely shouldn't have gone prancing along Chinatown's streets disguised as a workingman. It was only unbelievably good luck that had saved her.

Matthew Lam had withdrawn as soon as Hanrahan began interviewing Mei Sha, retreating across the room to talk to Geoffrey Hunter and Josiah Gregory in a low, urgent voice. The success or failure of the undercover operation depended largely on these three men, only one of whom had both exhaustive training and years of experience.

Putting away his policeman's narrow notebook, Hanrahan pulled a piece of paper from his pocket as he joined them. "I have a list," he said. "It cost a pretty penny, but it contains the names of all the most recent arrivals in Chinatown, their ages, work experience as far as could be determined, and what my informant thinks is reasonably accurate information about where they came from and how they got here."

He handed the list to Geoffrey. "Not many names because I eliminated anyone who didn't seem to be in the right age range from the description you provided. The most relevant piece was the comment by the Delmonico's waiter that if he hadn't been Chinese, the man he saw entering the museum kitchen would have been handsome. So that removed anyone with facial scarring or features that a casual observer would term ugly."

"Eleven?" Geoffrey said, passing the list to Josiah, who shared it with Matthew Lam.

"Those are the most likely," Hanrahan confirmed. "Young, agile, strong but slender, good-looking, arriving in Chinatown around the time the announcement was made in the newspapers that Lord Peng had been named to the diplomatic mission in Washington and would be traveling through New York City. His role in opening the exhibit at the Met was hardly a secret. General di Cesnola is a past master at generating publicity. Nobody who read a paper in the past few weeks could have missed one of the stories he planted."

"Planted?" Josiah asked.

"Reporters don't make big salaries," Hanrahan said. "Like cops, they're open to bribes. I'd say they expect and depend on them."

"This will work if our killer was hired and sent here for this specific job. What's got us puzzled now is the continued attacks on the family," Geoffrey said.

It was no secret that he and Prudence were leaning toward a personal rather than a political motive for the killing. Hanrahan, out on the Chinatown streets every day, favored a paid assassination for reasons yet unknown.

"I can find out where these men eat when they don't gulp down soup and rice balls from a pushcart vendor," Lam said, copying the names onto a page torn from Josiah's notebook. "With any luck, at least a few of them will show up at the Golden Dragon. The other waiters may be able to provide us with more facts. Maybe even additional names."

"I'll leave you then," Hanrahan said, glancing one more time at Mei Sha. "See if you can keep her from getting herself killed.

Right now, the Pengs' presence in Chinatown is supposed to be a secret. I'm not sure how much longer that will last, but it will definitely make the papers if the murdered Lord Peng's daughter is found with a knife in her back."

As if she'd heard him, Mei Sha looked up from her Dragon's Beard candy and tea. Ignoring Hanrahan, she smiled at Matthew Lam. A sweet, tremulous curve of the lips that spoke volumes.

Matthew smiled back.

CHAPTER 23

"Mei Sha is to stay with us until someone comes to pick her up." Josiah looked over at Lord Peng's younger daughter, following the movement of her fingers as she picked crushed bits of peanuts and sesame seeds from the sugary residue on the oiled paper in which the Dragon's Beard candy had been wrapped.

"That means we can't go out onto the street corners today," Prudence said. She'd sat by Mei Sha until the girl quieted down and seemed ready to be left alone, then she'd drifted to the other side of the room where Matthew Lam was rearranging the names on Hanrahan's list. "That's fine with me. I wasn't looking forward to clanging the bell." The smell of all that sugar had made her slightly dizzy.

Matthew glanced up at Prudence, who was squinting down at the wrinkled paper and the mess he'd made of it. He'd grouped names together, circled addresses, added numbers.

"Some of these men live in the same boardinghouses," he explained. "For a few coins I should be able to learn more about them than Hanrahan's informant was able to tell us."

"You don't want to go it alone," Geoffrey said, coming to

stand alongside Prudence, looking over Matthew's shoulder as the list continued to change shape. "And especially not at night."

"If Wei or Lady Peng sends someone to take Mei Sha back to the emporium, we could visit most of these places this afternoon. Josiah and Miss Prudence can stay here in case a stray believer wanders by."

Neither man wanted to say aloud that Prudence might not be safe on the streets with only Josiah to protect her.

"I have my derringer," Prudence said. The tiny gun had gotten her out of more than one dangerous situation.

"You might need more than that," Geoffrey said. "The alleys are dark and narrow. You wouldn't see an attacker until he was right on you. And then it's too late."

Prudence muttered something unprintable, picked up the brass bell, and stalked outside, slamming the storefront door behind her. The clang of the vigorously swinging bell was loud and unmelodious.

"Where did you get that thing?" Geoffrey asked. "It sounds like it's cracked."

"Pushcart," Josiah said, shrugging his shoulders and raising his eyebrows. "It was a bargain."

Both men watched as Prudence paced up and down on the sidewalk.

"I hope it wasn't something I said," Josiah commented.

"Not you. Me," Geoffrey assured him. "I've never learned the art of warning her to be careful. It always comes out as though I don't trust her to be able to take care of herself."

It was on the tip of Josiah's tongue to say that Miss Prudence too often got in trouble not to need a warning, but he choked off the observation. He didn't want to take the chance of it getting back to her. Miss Prudence in a temper was a formidable sight.

"I wouldn't believe it if I weren't seeing it with my own eyes," Geoffrey said, as the clamor faded, and the street door opened. "She's snagged someone."

Josiah scurried over to Mei Sha, whispering frantically at her when she refused to get out of her chair and come away with him. He glanced desperately at Geoffrey, who shook his head. Better to sit quietly together rather than attract attention. Josiah picked up the hat Mei Sha had taken off and jammed it down on her head, pulling it as low over her forehead as he could.

The man who trailed politely behind Prudence was perhaps in his early thirties, dressed in the same dark wide-legged trousers and frogged jacket that was practically a uniform in Chinatown. His queue reached nearly to his waist, the shaved part of his head covered by a round black hat that was almost a cap. He was immaculately clean, as though just out of his New Year's bath. Not a speck of workingman's dust or grime on him.

He bowed to everyone in general and then to individuals, smiled, and introduced himself. In fluent English.

"My name is Gao Fong," he said, bowing again. "I welcome you on behalf of those of us who had the honor to be taught by your illustrious missionaries."

Prudence set the annoying bell on the makeshift altar. She had a look on her face that could only be described as triumphant.

One by one, emulating Gao Feng's courteous bows, they introduced themselves. Except for Mei Sha, who bowed, but said nothing. Kept her head slightly inclined so the hat brim hid most of her face. From a distance, nothing gave away the fact that she was female.

"Are you a baptized Christian then?" Geoffrey asked. He remembered traveling preachers in the old South asking that question as often as they remarked on the heat of the day. Religion was as much a part of your identity as your surname or the color of your skin. He hoped the Chinese converts had grown accustomed to the peculiar clerical custom.

"I am not," Gao Fong said. "There were no Christians in our family, but my father valued some of the other things taught by your people. Chiefly, the English language. He believed it would prove of great value, and so it has."

Prudence was desperately trying to find a way to ask this well-mannered man when and how he had come to America, but to do so without causing offense. He might not be a convert, but he was the next best thing. And so far, the only resident of Chinatown to step over the threshold.

"I spent some years in San Francisco before coming to New York. Learning my craft. There are many skilled bone scrapers on the West Coast, but the need recently became more pressing here. I am employed by the Sang Chao Funeral Home on Mott Street. We can accommodate all wishes for the honor of the deceased."

Prudence thought he sounded like a not very well written advertisement of the type to be found in the back pages of weekend newspapers. "Bone scraper?"

"Perhaps you haven't been told of the custom of returning our bones to lie with those of our ancestors?"

The Chinese ambassador's envoy had mentioned intentionally shallow graves when discussing Lord Peng's burial, but in Geoffrey's experience, feigning ignorance of a topic was one of the better ways of acquiring information. "Perhaps you might explain?" he asked.

"Our country is sometimes called the Celestial Empire by westerners," Gao began. "We do not consider ourselves complete unless in death we lie with our ancestors. To die is to pass into another life. The dead intercede for the living; the tie between them must never be broken. It is almost impossible to send a man's body across an ocean; even in China, where distances can be insurmountable, the scraping and cleaning of bones is not unknown."

Mei Sha hadn't raised her head, but there was an awareness

about the way she held herself that told Prudence she was listening closely.

"After seven years in his grave, we remove what remains attached to a man's bones. The cleaning that we do is a sacred ritual, one not to be hurried or accomplished without due reverence. The purified bones are identified, placed into a tin box or an urn, and then into a wooden box which is also marked with his name. The box is returned to the family, to the home village, to be placed with the bones of his ancestors. This is a filial duty, but it is also one that is often carried out by the overseas societies that represent families or provinces."

"You said you worked for a funeral home," Geoffrey said. "What does that have to do with repatriating bones?"

"We keep good records of everyone who has passed through our establishment," Gao said. "We know where an individual is buried and how long he's been in the ground."

"My father was killed a week ago today." Mei Sha lifted her head and pushed back the hat that was shielding her face. "No one has told me whether he's been properly buried yet. Whenever I inquire, I'm told not to ask questions about something that doesn't concern me. How can the death of a father not be the business of his daughter?"

"I believe I had the privilege of preparing Lord Peng for his interment," Gao said, seemingly not at all surprised to be addressed by a young woman disguising herself as a man. She hadn't identified herself, yet he knew who she was. "The arrangements were made by the consul and someone from the embassy in Washington."

"Was there a cortege?" Prudence asked. "I was under the impression that Chinese funerals were formal and elaborate, to honor the deceased and his family."

"The consul explained that, under the circumstances, it had been decided that while Lord Peng was to receive all due individual honors, the funeral itself was to be conducted without pomp and ceremony."

"No one was to know the place or the time," Prudence concluded. She'd been excited to escort Gao Fong into the storefront mission, but something about the glib way he was answering the questions put to him ruffled her feathers. It was as if he had taken charge of the conversation instead of being its chief subject. He was entirely too self-possessed for her liking. Then she immediately chided herself for drawing conclusions before all the facts were in, something Geoffrey reminded her about far too often.

"I can assure you that your father was accorded the dignity of his rank," Gao said. He sketched a brief bow toward Mei Sha but didn't move in her direction or address her by name.

"Perhaps you could come back at another time," Prudence said. "We are not quite ready to receive visitors." She took two quick steps to place herself between Gao Feng and Mei Sha.

"You were ringing the bell," he said quietly.

It wasn't exactly menace in his voice, but something firm and cold that sent an unwelcome shiver up Prudence's spine. A moment later Geoffrey joined her.

Gao Fong took a step back, then smiled, bowed, and moved toward the door. Before he disappeared out onto the street, he turned the OPEN sign to CLOSED.

"Why didn't they tell me he was already buried?" Mei Sha asked. "I'm not a child anymore. They don't have to hide things." She pulled off the concealing hat and hurled it to the floor.

"You wouldn't have been allowed to attend," Prudence soothed. "None of the family can be seen in public. You've all disappeared. No one is supposed to know where."

"That man recognized me. He knew who I was even before I pulled up my hat," Mei Sha fumed. "He never said my name, but I'm sure he could have."

"How is that possible?" Prudence asked, looking from Geoffrey to Josiah and then to Matthew Lam. "We've been scrupulously careful, and I can't imagine an informant among Wei Fu Jian's men."

"Did you see the knife hanging from his belt?" Lam asked.

"It was long and thin enough to be a boning knife," Geoffrey said. "The kind butchers use."

"Knives aren't used to prepare the human bones for shipment," Lam said. "They're not allowed, although I don't know why. The cleaners use scrapers instead."

"Are you sure?" Prudence asked.

"I did some research at Yale, talking to the old hands at the Divinity School. All of them could describe customs I'd never heard of. They might not know why something had to be done in a certain way, but they could certainly recall what they'd seen and been told."

"Why would a funeral home worker need to carry a boning knife?" Prudence asked.

"He wouldn't," Geoffrey said.

"I wonder if the bodies of the three guards that were killed were taken to the Sang Chao Funeral Home," Josiah said.

"Why do you ask?" Lam folded Hanrahan's list and put it into his trouser pocket.

"No reason." Josiah had had a sudden disturbing vision of the man who had slit their throats washing their bodies, stitching up the mortal wounds, dressing them in their finest clothes, combing their hair, and applying skin-colored powder to cover the marks of violence. It seemed very far-fetched, but not beyond the horror stories that ran daily in some of the city's newspapers. He decided not to mention it.

"If Gao Fong knows that Lord Peng's family is hiding in Chinatown, there must be others who suspect as much," Prudence said.

"Funeral parlor owners and workers cultivate confidentiality," Geoffrey said. "Families have to trust them. A corpse has no secrets from the person who washes it."

"Could Lord Peng's burial have taken place at night?" Prudence asked.

"We won't get any information from the Sang Chao Funeral Home," Geoffrey said. "They've undoubtedly been well paid for their silence. Gao Fong shouldn't have told us what he did."

"He had a reason," Lam said. "It was too smoothly done not to have been deliberate."

"I had a feeling he was toying with us," Prudence said slowly.

Mei Sha stood at the front door, looking out, trying to see the street in both directions without stepping onto the sidewalk. "I don't see where he's gone," she said. "Do you suppose Officer Hanrahan could tell us something about him?"

"Such as?" Prudence was puzzled by Mei Sha's query. The girl's attentiveness seemed scattered, as though she lost interest in a person or a topic almost as soon as she became curious. One or two questions and she was off on another tangent. Gao Fong was certainly good-looking, in the way that many young men reaching their thirties were. Past the awkwardness of youth, well-muscled, facial features fully defined. A certain air of confidence and a quality of enticing sexuality that could be as heavy as scent. Except for the coincidence of Mei Sha's presence in the storefront when Prudence rang her bell, they would never have met. A bone scraper did not raise his eyes to gaze on the daughter of an important family.

"I suppose it doesn't matter," Mei Sha said. "He's not on Hanrahan's list, so he's not a newcomer to Chinatown." Lady Peng and her amah would both be shocked beyond words if she voiced an interest in someone as far below her as Gao Fong.

"Would you like me to walk you back to Wei's Chinese Imports?" Matthew Lam asked. "I think whoever was chasing you has long since disappeared. He wouldn't stay nearby and risk your recognizing him."

"Lady Peng was very definite," Josiah protested. "Mei Sha wasn't to leave until an escort was sent."

"I may not be as well armed as Wei Fu Jian's bodyguards," Lam said. "But I was on the track and wrestling teams at Yale. Mei Sha will be safe with me."

"I'll come with you," Geoffrey said. "I have questions to ask Lady Peng." He didn't give Prudence or Josiah time to protest. "It's just possible that Gao Fong will come back. I wouldn't put it past him, especially since we turned him out rather rudely. If he does return, I'm counting on the two of you to wring whatever information you can get from him. Especially where Lord Peng is buried."

"Why that?" Prudence asked.

"If we're dealing with a personal vendetta, we might also have to face desecration of the grave. Think about it for a moment. When a culture places as much importance on honoring its dead as the Chinese do, the ultimate insult would be to defile someone's final resting place."

"That's a horrible thought," Prudence said. "I don't even want to consider it."

"We have to."

"Is that what you want to talk to Lady Peng about?"

"I may suggest that she ask Wei to post a guard for a while. Especially at night."

Geoffrey had taken a moment to speak quietly to Matthew while Mei Sha stared out onto the street trying to figure out which way Gao Fong had walked. The plan they'd hurriedly sketched out was simple, but there was just enough of an element of danger so there was no question of taking Prudence along.

They'd deliver the girl to the mercies of her mother, then start working on Hanrahan's list. It was broad daylight; there were two of them, both armed, and Geoffrey had a bag of coins to sweeten the questioning. If they hurried, they could get to all

of the boardinghouses on the list before the occupants returned
from work.

He thought Prudence might be suspicious; it wasn't really
very likely that Gao Fong would show up at the mission twice
in one day. But she let them go with a smile and a wave, waiting
until they were out of sight before locking the mission door
and reaching for her shawl.

"We'll follow them," she told Josiah. "I have questions to
ask Lady Peng myself. And I'm not sure they're the kind she
would answer if a man asked them."

CHAPTER 24

Prudence and Josiah watched from down the street as Geoffrey and Matthew escorted Mei Sha into the private entrance of the apartment floors above Wei Fu Jian's Chinese Imports and Antiquities.

"Now what?" Josiah asked.

"We wait," Prudence answered. She ducked into the recessed doorway of a grocery store. A strong odor of salt fish and dried seaweed drifted through the opened door as a customer carrying a bundle of months' old eggs and dried sharks' fins squeezed past her. "Delicacies," she commented, smiling broadly at Josiah, whose palate favored sweets and heavily sauced meats.

"It may be a while. Mr. Hunter said he had questions to ask Lady Peng."

"I don't believe that for a moment," Prudence said. "He and Matthew will check out the boardinghouses on Hanrahan's list. They're not places frequented by ladies or gentlemen of fastidious tastes. Meaning you and me."

Josiah sniffed in suppressed indignation but decided not to

pursue the topic. He wasn't an avid investigator, but there were times when exclusion from dangerous or indecorous investigations felt like an insult.

"Here they come now," Prudence announced. "They've turned toward Mott Street."

"That didn't take long." Josiah consulted his gold pocket watch. "Less than ten minutes."

"I doubt they did more than escort Mei Sha to the upstairs parlor and turn her over to Lady Peng's tender care," Prudence said.

"We won't see her again for a while," Josiah predicted.

"She's impulsive. I don't think she knows who she wants to be—the proper daughter of an important Chinese family or an adventuresome runaway. It doesn't bode well for the future."

"What prospects do they have?" Josiah asked. "The Pengs, I mean."

"The murder opened up Pandora's box," Prudence said. "If I'm remembering the myth correctly, the only thing left inside before Pandora managed to close it again was hope."

"In this case, I'd say that hope goes by the name of Wei Fu Jian."

Josiah surprised her sometimes, Prudence thought as they crossed the street after Geoffrey and Matthew had disappeared from sight. He'd pierced right to the heart of the dilemma facing the woman they were going to see. Lady Peng and Wei Fu Jian. What exactly was the relationship between the widow and her brother-in-law? What had it been back in China? It was going to be an awkward conversation, but this time, Prudence decided, she wouldn't yield to the constraints of polite inquiry.

"Technically, this is a rooming house," Geoffrey said as he and Matthew neared the first of the addresses on Hanrahan's revised list. "A boardinghouse serves meals and is supposed to pride itself on cultivating a family atmosphere. What we've got here in Chinatown are buildings converted into tiny bedrooms or dormitories fitted out with as many rows of bunk beds as the proprietor can squeeze in. There's no privacy, no cooking facilities, and probably no running water."

"I share a room above the Golden Dragon Noodle Palace with another waiter," Matthew said.

"Consider yourself lucky. Some of these places rent a bed to two people at a time. One man works a day shift, the other a night job."

The street door creaked open and slammed against an inner wall.

"Bad hinges," Geoffrey muttered. He glanced down at the floor. "Watch where you step."

A broom and dustpan stood in a dim corner, apparently waiting for whoever was in charge of sweeping. Perhaps in return for a lowering of his rent? As Geoffrey and Matthew let their eyes adjust to the lack of light, either natural or artificial, an elderly man appeared at the end of the hallway, waving his arms and calling out.

Matthew bowed, greeted him politely, and translated.

"He wants to know what we're doing here. I told him we're church people, looking for three of his roomers who came to us seeking help. He doesn't like it, but I think he'll cooperate. For the right kind of persuasion."

Geoffrey bowed, drew a small purse from his pocket, and hefted it on the palm of his hand. The clink of coins caught the old man's attention, but when he extended a wrinkled, crabbed hand, the purse disappeared. Geoffrey shook his head and gestured in Matthew's direction.

The dialogue that followed was garrulous and high pitched. To Geoffrey's ears, it sounded argumentative. At one point, the elderly landlord, if that was who he was, turned abruptly and shuffled off in the direction from which he'd come. Matthew called out something that stopped and turned him around.

"I hope you can afford this," Matthew muttered in English. "I've had to double the original offer."

"It won't break us," Geoffrey said. "Whatever it costs, we need either to eliminate the men on this list or at least narrow down the number of suspects."

"The first man is twenty-eight," Matthew began, translating as fast as he could while Geoffrey took down pertinent details in his narrow detective's notebook. Now that the price was right, the old man was a river of information. "He works in a laundry two blocks from here and speaks the best English of all the roomers because he came to America when he was sixteen. He was working last Friday morning. The old man caught him before he left and gave him a pile of dirty clothes. He brought them back clean and folded that night." Matthew paused to take a breath. "Are you getting it all down?"

"Keep going," Geoffrey said.

This kind of investigating was painstakingly slow, but it got results. Eventually.

Mei Sha was nowhere in sight.

"My daughter has been confined to her room," Lady Peng explained. "I've told Amah that she is not to let her out. And all the guards will be warned that if she gets past them, Wei Fu Jian will be informed of their negligence. She won't be bothering you again, Miss MacKenzie."

"I didn't really mind," Prudence said. "She's bright and full of energy." For a moment she hesitated over what else she had to tell Lady Peng, but there was no concealing it and no point putting it off. "I wonder if Josiah told you the details of Mei Sha's adventure this morning."

"Some of them, perhaps not all. He said she showed up at your storefront mission dressed in clothing I now know she took from her brother's armoire. She had been chased by a man wielding a knife, but she was safe. He didn't elaborate much more than that."

"We didn't want to alarm you unduly."

"You'll find I'm not easily unnerved," Lady Peng said.

Josiah had politely declined her offer to be seated and stationed himself at the wall of windows overlooking Pell Street. A crack in the drawn curtains allowed him to see the bustle of the busy sidewalk below. It was a welcome distraction.

"Mei Sha was followed," Prudence began. "We don't know where her pursuer picked her up because Mei didn't spot him until she turned onto Doyers Street. She caught the flash of sun on a knife, for the second time since leaving here. When she looked behind her and realized what was happening, she ran. Fortunately, we saw her as she came around the bend. As Josiah explained to you, the man pursuing her was armed, Lady Peng. We're certain of that, if not much else. Matthew Lam chased him off, whoever he was."

"I am aware that it's the second time I have to thank him for saving one of my children," Lady Peng said. "Wei Fu Jian must be told."

"Of course," Prudence agreed. "But that's not enough."

"He'll set more guards. I'll warn Johnny and An Bao."

"I need information that you may not want to give me." Prudence turned to Josiah. "Perhaps you'd wait in the garden?" she suggested.

Lady Peng gestured to the maid who seemed always to be waiting in her mistress's shadow. Josiah followed her from the parlor. "She will tell the guards to let him through. They'll make sure he's safe."

They sat for a few moments in silence, listening to the sound of footsteps descending the stairs. The same maid who had escorted Josiah out returned with a tray of tea and pale almond cookies.

"I've lived in the West long enough to know that even in England, people can be blunt when needs be. I imagine Americans are even more to the point when it suits them," Lady Peng said. She poured the tea and offered the almond cookies.

"Directness can be a useful tool when time is of the essence," Prudence said.

"Well put. I assume you're beating around the bush for a purpose."

"I'm not often at a loss for words, but I don't want to offend you."

"My husband has been murdered, my son was almost killed, and my youngest daughter's life has been imperiled twice. Could anything you have to say be worse to bear than knowing I may yet lose one of my children?" Lady Peng's posture was ramrod straight and her voice steady.

"Did your husband have a second wife?" Prudence blurted out. She felt heat flood upward from her neck and knew her ears had flushed a bright red beneath the hair pulled over them into an unfashionable bun.

"It's against the law for a man to have two wives," Lady Peng said.

"I meant back in China."

"So did I."

"I thought wealthy Chinese men were allowed more than one wife," Prudence said.

"One wife only," Lady Peng corrected. "But he is allowed to have as many concubines as he can afford to keep. Or as his wife permits him to bring into the house without disturbing its harmony."

"I thought I understood what I was talking about, but you've thoroughly confused me," Prudence said.

"Westerners, especially western missionaries, have never grasped the finer points of Chinese culture," Lady Peng said. "A man of wealth and position may buy a concubine, as one buys a slave. If the proper procedures are followed, her children are acknowledged as his legitimate offspring though their birth does not improve the legal status of the mother. One of a concubine's most important functions is obedience to her master's wife, but she will never attain that rank herself."

"Did Lord Peng . . . ?"

"Yes. He had two concubines. One remains in China, in the family's ancestral home. When we left for London, she was charged with caring for Lord Peng's parents and for the other members of the family should Lord Peng or Johnny not return to take up those responsibilities. The other concubine is dead, as is the child she carried."

This was the thread that had woken Prudence from a deep sleep and propelled her upright in her bed. *What if . . . ?*

"How did they die?" she asked, almost afraid to hear the answer.

Lady Peng gestured to her maid, whispered a few words in her ear, and dismissed her from the room. She sipped at her tea and nibbled an almond cookie until the girl returned, placing a thick piece of folded paper in her mistress's hand. Lady Peng toyed for a moment with the broken red wax seal, then passed the paper to Prudence. "It's a letter I found in my husband's papers some time ago. He gave orders that it be destroyed, but I was able to take it from a stack of communications his secretary hadn't yet burned. He never knew I had it. Never knew I'd read it."

"I can't decipher this," Prudence said, staring down at columns of Chinese characters inked blackly with a fine brush.

"I wanted you to see how the information was transmitted to him, and that what I am about to translate is as real and substantial as either one of us."

"I'll have to take your word, Lady Peng," Prudence said. "I can't verify for myself something I cannot read."

Lady Peng nodded. "I understand. Perhaps there is a way to authenticate this letter that will satisfy you, but until then . . ."

It was obvious to Prudence that this woman had never had her word questioned or her will crossed. "It's a necessity of the profession, needing to authenticate what one is told. How else can an inquiry agent get at the truth?"

"The letter is signed by the man my late husband appointed

to be the Peng family household steward," Lady Peng began.
"This is his signature and the family seal." She pointed to characters at the bottom of the letter and to the broken red wax in-
signia.

Other than to admire the beauty of the calligraphy, Prudence made no response. This was Lady Peng's hand to play.

"I'll skip over the formal greetings," Lady Peng began, running a finger along the lines as if Prudence could read them
with her. "Here is where he begins the account of the concubine's death. Her name was Chu Hua, which means chrysan-
themum in English. The flower symbolizes life and happiness.
Lord Peng had renamed her. He wanted more sons, which we
both knew neither I nor his other concubine could give him."

"When did she join the household?" Prudence asked, hoping
she'd phrased the question correctly. *Mistress* was what a New
York City banker's kept woman was usually called, but that
didn't seem equivalent to a concubine as Lady Peng had described the role.

"Before we left for England. There was time for her to conceive, which was what she was expected to do, but my husband's hopes were not realized. He returned from time to time,
when he was summoned by Empress Dowager Cixi, but the
girl never quickened." Lady Peng paused. "Until a few years
ago, when it was impossible that the child she was carrying
could be her master's. The steward confirms that she tried to
run away, that she was caught and brought back to the house,
and that a midwife examined her. She was fed opium, as was the
gardener with whom she had coupled. Five grains each, more
than enough to cause death. He writes that the bodies were dis-
posed of, but he gives no details of what was done with them.
That alone is a terrible punishment."

Prudence wasn't sure what she had expected, but it wasn't
murder. Three murders if you counted the concubine's unborn
child. "Were they forced to swallow the opium?" she asked.

"A slave is the possession of its owner," Lady Peng said. "So is a concubine. She has rights and privileges, but she cannot be unfaithful to her master without severe punishment. The man who joins her in betrayal is also guilty. They may have been offered a choice: opium or a far more painful death by drowning or a rope. Which would you have chosen, Miss MacKenzie?"

"In a case like that, does anything happen to the family that sold her?"

"They are shamed."

"Nothing else?"

"Not unless they have been complicit. If the concubine met her lover with their knowledge, for example, or in a property they owned. Chu Hua's family was poor; a beautiful daughter was the only wealth they had. But the steward says that the loss of face was more than they could bear. Mother and father both ended their lives. He doesn't say how."

"Did they have other children?"

Lady Peng turned a sharp eye on Prudence, as if she'd said something entirely new and vitally important. She held up one finger to demand uninterrupted silence, then quickly scanned the letter again. "He does not mention any brothers or sisters. That *is* what you were asking?"

"A brother, yes."

"Give me a moment." Lady Peng's eyes closed, her head dipped. The single upraised finger requested that she not be disturbed.

Prudence dunked an almond cookie in her tea so it wouldn't crunch when she bit down on it.

"There was a son," Lady Peng said slowly. "Younger than his sister. I remember that he was considered proof the girl could bear a male child. A daughter's fertility is often measured by her mother's."

"But the steward doesn't say what happened to him after his sister and his parents died?"

"No."

"How old would he have been at that time?"

"Sixteen perhaps."

"Old enough to understand the punishment his sister suffered. Is it possible the parents were also offered opium?"

"Five lives to erase the stigma of disloyalty?"

"Perhaps six." Prudence's dream rushed back with all the force of truth. "Lady Peng, suppose the boy was also marked to die, but because he was young and strong, the men sent to carry out the punishment sold him as contract labor bound for America or Canada? If what I've read about the practice is true, it was a brisk trade. And very profitable. They would have pocketed the finder's fee and not told the steward what they'd done."

"So the brother did not die, but he might as well have," Lady Peng speculated.

"He might have worked on the transcontinental Canadian railroad, as did so many others," Prudence said. "At some point he made it across the border and down into New York City. He may have been here for years before . . ."

"Before he read in one of your newspapers that Peng Tha Mah was opening an exhibition of Chinese art and artifacts at the Metropolitan Museum of Art," Lady Peng completed the sentence. "Lord Peng had ordered his sister and the child she carried executed. Perhaps also the man's father and mother. It would be an act of filial duty to avenge their deaths."

"Did you ever see him, the concubine's brother, when you were still in China?"

"No. Nor did I know his name. Not even hers, before it was changed. Lord Peng cut all blood ties when he bought her. The parents signed a contract."

"One death wasn't enough to satisfy him," Prudence said.

"I have three children. Johnny, An Bao, and Mei Sha."

"The concubine, the babe she carried, and the lover who

sired the child." Prudence ticked them off on her fingers. "He will consider your life payment for his mother. Lord Peng gave the orders."

It seemed too simple to be true, but the expression on Lady Peng's face betrayed neither surprise nor disbelief.

"He wants us all dead," Lady Peng said. "He considers it his filial obligation to end our lives."

"Then it becomes our job to see that it doesn't happen," Prudence said. "Filial obligation be damned!"

CHAPTER 25

"Mr. Hunter isn't going to buy it," Josiah said quietly. "The whole thing sounds too much like the plot of a cheap novel."

"I've been wondering about that." Prudence placed the annoying bell in plain sight on the makeshift altar. She'd tripped over it coming into the mission from Wei's Chinese Imports. Josiah had caught her arm before she fell, saving her from what could have been a bad fall, but causing a nasty wrench. "We need corroborating evidence."

"I doubt we'll find it."

"Maybe not evidence as such," Prudence said, rubbing her sore shoulder. "But at least the testimony of someone other than Lady Peng who might have been aware of Lord Peng's peculiar situation."

"Two concubines, you mean? I doubt anyone in China would find it odd or in any way remarkable. He was a very wealthy man from an important family."

"If the concubines were brought into the house before the family left for London, perhaps Johnny would remember something about them," Prudence mused. "He's Lady Peng's eldest."

"Which means you'd be asking him about two women who shared his father's bed for the sole purpose of bearing him sons, but who could never attain the rank of wife."

"It doesn't seem to make much difference," Prudence remarked. "As long as proper protocols are followed and there's a signed contract, it might as well be a marriage as far as any children are concerned. That's if I've understood what Lady Peng was explaining."

"What about raising the question with Wei Fu Jian?" Josiah asked. "Lord Peng was his brother."

"And apparently a rival for Lady Peng." Prudence absently rubbed the shoulder again. It was getting stiffer by the minute. "What about the amah? She had the courage to escape from the hotel suite when Lady Peng left her behind, and I know she's been with the family ever since the children were born. An amah is a Chinese nanny, but more like a regular servant than the English version."

"She shoved her way into Mr. Hunter's suite and handed me a bottle of chloral hydrate," Josiah said. "Then she nearly attacked him with his own cane."

"Perfect!" Prudence exclaimed. "She won't be afraid to tell us what we need to hear if she thinks her beloved charges are in danger. They may be adults now, but she'll always consider them her children."

"Will you tell Mr. Hunter what we learned from Lady Peng?" Josiah prodded. He held back from giving his opinion, but just barely.

"Not yet," Prudence decided. She rubbed her shoulder again. "We're not very enthusiastic missionaries, hiding out in here instead of ringing that blasted bell and distributing leaflets."

"I never did understand the reasoning behind this charade," Josiah said. Wearing dusty black clothes that didn't fit properly hadn't been what he'd had in mind when he'd first looked at the clerical catalog.

"It gives us a cover and a place where we can retreat without having to go uptown every evening and come back every morning. Tourists and missionaries are the only outsiders who bother to come to Chinatown."

"I wonder if we're being spied upon."

"What makes you think that?" Prudence asked.

"If I were an illegal hiding out and terrified every single day that I'd be discovered, I'd want to find out everything I could about the nosy strangers who suddenly appeared and took an interest in me."

"It's not that bad, Josiah. There have been missionaries in China for a very long time. They may not make many converts, but people are used to them."

"Do you really think Lord Peng ordered his pregnant concubine killed?"

"It's very possible," Prudence said. "Actually, the more I consider it, the more I believe it's probably true. There are places in this world where life doesn't have much value and where a powerful man can murder with impunity."

"We're not so very different," Josiah said. "Perhaps less open about it." Some of the cases on which he'd worked had revealed truly appalling sides of human nature.

He got up to stir the fire in the stove and fill the kettle. "There's a bottle of Minard's King of Pain Liniment in my bag, Miss Prudence. A friend of mine brought some back from Canada. Everybody up there uses it."

"What does it smell like?"

"Camphor and turpentine."

"Delightful."

"What smells like camphor and turpentine?" Geoffrey asked, locking the outside door behind him and checking to be sure the sign was turned to CLOSED. "Matthew will be sending over food from the Golden Noodle later on. I told him I wasn't sure it was appropriate for missionaries to be seen eating in one of Chinatown's best restaurants."

"Miss Prudence has a bad shoulder," Josiah explained. "I brought some liniment with me."

"Nothing serious. I tripped over the bell and would have hit the floor if Josiah hadn't caught me. You're back late."

Neither Prudence nor Josiah would confess to having watched Geoffrey and Matthew leave Wei's Antiquities for the rooming houses clustered on Mott Street.

"Matthew and I decided to check some of the names on Hanrahan's list after we returned Wei Sha to her mother," Geoffrey said, as if that hadn't been the plan all along. "I wasn't able to speak with Lady Peng."

The kettle whistled. "Chinese or English?" Josiah asked. He was already pouring milk into a small pitcher and reaching for saucers, teacups, and the sugar bowl. He'd packed a box of butter cookies along with the liniment, which was still upstairs.

"Definitely English," Prudence said. "Aunt Gillian claims it cures everything from head pain to heartache."

"We've eliminated all but two of Hanrahan's suspicious characters," Geoffrey said, setting the much-wrinkled and written-over piece of paper on the table.

"What were they like, the rooming houses?" Prudence asked. The hot tea really was loosening her tight shoulder.

"I'm not sure I can describe them adequately. Tiny rooms crammed with tiered bunk beds. Narrow, thin mattresses, a single blanket, not always a pillow. The smell was overwhelming male body odor. Fusty and damp. But the premises were usually clean. That was surprising, given some of the slums I've been in over the years."

"Surely all the men were out working."

"Not all. They can save more money to send back to China if two men share the cost of a bed. One works nights, the other works days."

"Dear God," Josiah breathed. The idea of sharing a room with someone was bad enough, but climbing into a bed still warm with another man's fug was inconceivable.

Prudence picked up Hanrahan's list.

"Turn it over," Geoffrey instructed.

"Ye Da," she read aloud. "Yan He."

"As luck would have it, they were in the last rooming house on the list, so we didn't find them until mid-afternoon. They'd paid for a small, shared room instead of the common area, and they arrived two weeks ago."

"About the time Lord Peng and his family left London," Prudence said.

"Exactly. My guess is they took a ship that sailed to a Canadian port, then were transported down to New York by a very highly paid smuggler who brought them in alone instead of as part of a larger group."

"Are they still there?" Josiah asked.

"We think so. The room is paid through next week."

"Which means arrangements are already in place to get them out," Prudence said.

"Everything about the way they're operating indicates they're professionals," Geoffrey continued.

"But they haven't succeeded," Prudence reminded him.

"That's the nut I haven't cracked. Lord Peng's killing was done and over with before people knew what was happening. We only have a description of one of them, but the other was probably somewhere in the vicinity. They both made a clean getaway. So why stay around? Why make that nighttime attempt on Johnny? Why penetrate the garden and wait there for Mei Sha? Or more likely whichever member of the family happened to walk out first? If they're hired killers and Lord Peng was the only target, they should have been back over the Canadian border the next day."

Prudence glanced at Josiah. Maybe now *was* the time to tell Geoffrey about Lord Peng's dead concubine. It would certainly buoy up a working theory of personal revenge. She slipped the list under the edge of the bell.

The door handle rattled, followed by a determined banging. Someone was ignoring the CLOSED sign.

"I'll go," Josiah said.

He thought he'd go upstairs to get that bottle of liniment as soon as he got rid of the unwelcome visitor. Miss Prudence probably didn't realize how often she was rubbing the sore muscle in her shoulder.

"We're closed," Josiah said, pointing to the sign. Without thinking, he turned the door key.

The elaborately gowned man who pushed past him headed straight for Geoffrey, bowing politely but urgently as soon as he reached him.

"Honored *Mù Shī*," he said, "I am Sang Chao, proprietor of the Sang Chao Funeral Home on Mott Street." He paused for a moment, letting his name and establishment sink in. "One of my miserable employees disturbed your tranquility earlier today. Gao Fong, the bone scraper."

Prudence's head snapped up.

"The man is very skilled at what he does best, but he has much to learn about the privacy great families demand when one of their number requires our services."

Dies, Prudence translated.

"Regrettably, he sometimes has the brain of a goat," Sang Chao said.

"*Mù shī* means pastor," Josiah whispered as he bent over Geoffrey to remove his tea things. Matthew Lam had told him that as the senior minister of the group, Geoffrey could expect to be called by a number of honorifics.

Sang Chao's brightly colored embroidered jacket and long

skirt lit up the dim interior of the storefront, the silk glistening in reflected light from the kerosene lanterns. It was cold even with the potbellied stove burning, but their visitor's face shone with beads of nervous sweat.

"I must know exactly what my dolt of a hireling said to you if I am to phrase an expression of regret that the Honorable Wei Fu Jian will accept." He unfurled a fan and snapped it nervously.

"Gao Fong spoke of the Chinese embassy in Washington and the consul here in New York," Geoffrey said, modulating his voice into what he remembered the preachers of his youth sounded like when they weren't ranting from the pulpit. *Unctuous* was how his father had described them.

Sang Chao waited.

"That's information that could probably be found in any of the newspapers covering the death at the museum last week, but if the bone scraper is in possession of more sensitive knowledge, you would be wise to ensure he reveals nothing. Wei Fu Jian will not be pleased in any case, if he hasn't heard already." It had taken some circumlocution, but Geoffrey had managed an answer without ever uttering Lord Peng's name or mentioning Mei Sha's presence.

"Three of Wei Fu Jian's men also passed through our parlor."

"Gao Fong has perhaps more secrets to keep than he can manage."

"He has been warned."

"Then perhaps it is wiser to drop the matter than to pursue it," Geoffrey said.

"I cannot afford to incur Wei Fu Jian's wrath," Sang Chao said. "I have worked hard for too many years to lose everything now."

"Perhaps you'd better explain."

"A man prospers more when he has the support of other men than he does if he works alone."

"I can't argue with that," Geoffrey said.

"Earlier today I signed a document that makes me a member of the Eastern Benevolent Association. Do you know what that is?"

"We've heard of it," Prudence said, forgetting for a moment that she was a woman and a minister's wife, two good reasons not to interrupt when men were speaking.

"We can only survive in this country if we band together for protection," Sang Chao said. "You are missionaries. You know our culture. Perhaps you even know our country. In San Francisco men have formed associations based on the villages from which they came or the family name—the real family name—they bear. If a man falls ill and cannot pay what he owes, the benevolent association will step in to help. If a pushcart vendor wishes to open a grocery store or a restaurant, he finds the money he needs in the association to which he belongs. We've long known that organizers from San Francisco would come to New York, but Wei Fu Jian has today—this very day—established a benevolent association that does not owe allegiance to men who live thousands of miles away."

"You must demonstrate loyalty," Geoffrey said.

"A man who does not fulfill his pledge is expelled. No other member of the association will frequent his business. He is shunned."

"And you want me—you want us—to help you explain to Wei Fu Jian that his secrets are safe and that the mouth of the foolish man with the brain of a goat has been sealed."

"Everyone in Chinatown knows that this building was bought and lent to your mission by Wei Fu Jian. He favors you, though we don't know why. He's not a Christian."

"How is something like this done?" Geoffrey asked. "I don't want to risk offending him."

"I will send a message asking permission to call upon him," Sang Chao explained. "You will come with me, Honorable *Mù Shī*, to show that I appear before him in good faith and with the approval of a man of respect."

"I haven't been in Chinatown long enough to have earned anyone's respect," Geoffrey protested, though he had already decided to accede to Sang Chao's request.

"It is possible that Wei Fu Jian will require Gao Fong also to appear so as to prostrate himself and beg for pardon," Sang Chao mused.

"That seems a bit exaggerated," Prudence said quietly to Josiah.

"Will you accommodate me in this, honored sir?"

Geoffrey hesitated, then nodded.

"I will make the arrangements." Sang Chao bowed to each of them in turn, then walked backward halfway across the room before turning and disappearing onto the street.

"That's the most extraordinary thing I've ever heard," Prudence said. "Imagine having to kneel down to beg someone's pardon."

"And touch your forehead to the floor," Geoffrey added. "Three times is customary in some cultures, as many as nine head knocks elsewhere." His black eyes sparked in a very un-ministerial way as Josiah came down the second-floor stairs carrying the Minard's King of Pain Liniment.

"I'm quite capable of applying this myself," Prudence snapped, uncapping the bottle and releasing the noxious smell of camphor and turpentine into the room. "Are you sure it works?"

"My friend swears by it," Josiah said.

"I think I'll wait until I go to bed." Prudence stowed the bottle on the altar next to the bell. "This is starting to look and smell like witchcraft," she said, pinching her nose. She picked up the barely legible list and turned it over. "When will you question Ye Da and Yan He?"

"Hanrahan and a couple of other officers from the Sixth Precinct will pick them up at the rooming house early tomorrow morning."

"On what charge?" Josiah asked. He liked things to be legal and proper.

Geoffrey shrugged. "They don't need a charge to bring them in for questioning. At least not down here."

"Will you be there?" Prudence asked.

"Not officially."

"What does that mean?"

"I'll be at the back of the interrogation room, so I'll see and hear everything, but I'll let Hanrahan ask the questions. They use translators, by the way."

"Don't any of the police speak Chinese? Never mind, of course they don't. That was a ridiculous question."

The front doorknob rattled again, followed by a flurry of loud knocks.

"I don't want to talk to him if that's Sang Chao back with another request," Geoffrey said, getting up to stretch as Josiah hurried to answer the rapping.

"Dinner," he called out, carrying a cardboard box toward the table that was masquerading as an altar. "Did Matthew say he would bring it himself or send someone?"

"Send someone," Geoffrey answered. "Matthew's waiting on the important tables at the restaurant tonight. Apparently, Wei Fu Jian is giving a special dinner for the men he's recruited to be officers of the Eastern Benevolent Association."

"I'm starving," Prudence said. "I never know which pushcarts to trust."

"Stick with the buns," Josiah advised, unpacking bowls, plates, serving dishes, spoons, and chopsticks. "They're fried, so the hot grease kills anything that will make you sick. That's what I've been told, anyway. It's worked so far." He lifted out two teapots and a nest of small cups. "I hope this is jasmine." He raised the lids and sniffed. "One jasmine, one oolong."

"No more interruptions," Prudence said, scooping steamed white rice onto a plate.

"It's already dark out." Geoffrey handled his chopsticks as though he'd been born using them. "I don't think we'll be disturbed any more tonight."

He wasn't quite right, but none of them would know it. Not for sure.

CHAPTER 26

The dishes Matthew had chosen and sent from the Golden Dragon Noodle Palace were part of the banquet Wei Fu Jian had ordered prepared for the newly appointed officers of the Eastern Benevolent Association. Shark fin soup, prawn longevity noodles, suckling pig, roasted duck, fried rice and vegetables, almond jelly and red bean cakes. Culinary creations Geoffrey, Prudence, and Josiah gamely tried but couldn't always identify, some of them so drenched in peppery sauces they had to be washed down with cup after cup of fragrant tea and warm rice wine.

It wasn't until she was holding a sweet red bean cake in her hand, wondering how it had gotten there, that Prudence realized she was tipsy. She felt hot all over, as though someone had opened the potbellied stove door, and as she looked over at Geoffrey and Josiah, their faces began to blur and then swim off into the distance.

"I think something's wrong," she whispered, her voice pounding in her ears as her fingers let loose of the bean cake and her head descended toward her empty plate.

Josiah crumpled, then slid from the chair in which he was sitting, sprawled on the floor with limbs flung in all directions.

Geoffrey was the last to go down. He fought it the hardest, trying to reach into his throat to make himself gag before whatever he'd ingested knocked him out. The final thing he saw before he, too, lost consciousness, was the blue-and-white patterned teapot from which he'd poured his jasmine tea.

He didn't wait long before picking the lock of the Chinatown Congregational Mission Church.

The tea had been liberally but not overwhelmingly dosed. Depending on how much they drank, which would be influenced by how much red pepper sauce they consumed, the missionaries he suspected weren't really church people might be out for only an hour or so. Time enough to search their pockets and the upstairs rooms if he was quick about it. The one to watch out for was the pastor. He was much bigger than his wife, taller and broader than the assistant. He might swim his way back to consciousness in as little as thirty minutes, by which time there must be no sign that anyone had intruded on their privacy.

The head preacher's coat and pockets were examined first, but they yielded nothing except a few folded bits of paper, some coins, and an almost empty wallet. Very disappointing. The deacon carried even less on him, though one of his pockets was lined with crumbs. The woman had placed her reticule on the altar, drawstrings slightly undone. A handkerchief, a few coins, and a beautifully scrolled derringer. He doubted that minister's wives went about their daily chores armed.

Upstairs, he discovered that the missionaries, even the husband and wife, slept in separate rooms. And under the deacon's mattress he discovered why. He slipped one of the HUNTER AND MACKENZIE, INVESTIGATIVE LAW business cards into the pocket of his indigo-dyed cotton trousers, carefully replacing exactly as he had found them the folders he glanced at. It took only a few minutes to be certain that they had so far discovered nothing that would link him to Lord Peng or the murder at the museum.

The last thing he did was to empty the dregs of the pot of jasmine tea onto the splintery floorboards, wrapping the leaves in a piece of paper he would take away with him. He dropped a pinch of fresh tea leaves into the pot and wet them well with steaming water from the kettle on the stove.

He'd taken the precaution of coming to the mission unarmed, but as he stood in the lamplight looking around for any telltale sign of his presence, his fingers twitched. What was missing from the scene was blood, red blood flowing from cut throats, rippling through the debris of plates and serving dishes, dripping onto the floor, scenting the air with the richness of meat.

He sighed regretfully.

And then he left.

Josiah was the first to stir. He'd created a small pile of red pepper flakes on the edge of his plate, artfully concealed beneath a layer of unidentified vegetables. So he'd drunk less of the jasmine tea than Prudence and Geoffrey. And he'd mitigated the effect of the drink with several of the sweet red bean cakes.

He was groggy, his head ached, and he was lying on the floor, splayed out in a most undignified fashion. It took considerable effort to get to a sitting position, to wobble to his knees, and then to haul himself to his feet by crawling up the back of a chair. The stove gave off a steady heat, the lanterns burned brightly, and when he turned to check, he saw that the door was still firmly closed. Everything looked exactly as it had in those last few seconds before Josiah passed out.

Except that Prudence's head lay on her empty plate and

Geoffrey's upper body was sprawled across the table, as though he'd been reaching for something.

Josiah's mouth was dry, his lips stiff and near to cracking when he tried to speak. He closed his eyes to fight off a wave of nausea, and when he opened them again Prudence was stirring, and Geoffrey had lit one of the evil-smelling dark cigars he ordered by the box from the Black Patch area of western Kentucky. The harsh, acrid smoke acted like women's smelling salts, jolting him back to consciousness.

"Are you all right?" he asked Josiah, who was vaguely aware that he'd collapsed a second time.

Prudence had pushed aside the plate on which her cheek had rested and was wiping off sauce from the roasted duck. She looked perplexed and angry, too, as if uncertain what had happened to her but in no doubt that it had been an attack of some sort. "Water," she croaked, pushing herself to her feet. "We need water."

A bucket stood beside the stove, ready to replenish the kettle whenever tea was made. She carried it to the table, filled the communal dipper and passed it to her companions. "Drink as much as you can," she instructed them. "Whatever we were given has to be washed out of our systems."

"Is there any one of these dishes that we all ate?" Geoffrey asked, using chopsticks to stir what remained on the serving platters.

Nobody could remember. Josiah uncovered his cache of red pepper flakes, but he'd eaten the sauce they'd floated in. From what they could see of each other's plates, so had the others.

Prudence lifted the lids of the teapots. "The oolong is all gone, but there's some jasmine tea left." She wiped out one of the soup bowls with a wet napkin, then poured the tea into it and carried the bowl to a far corner. "Mice," she said. "They're everywhere."

"You think they'll drink plain jasmine tea?" Josiah asked.

He crumbled half of a sweet red bean cake into his napkin. "Put some of this in the bowl."

"Why?" Geoffrey asked.

"Josiah said something earlier this afternoon." Prudence sprinkled the cake crumbs into the tea. "Do you remember?"

"What was it?" Geoffrey had a high regard for Josiah's intuition. It might not solve a mystery, but it sometimes cut through the fog of obfuscation.

"I wondered if we were being watched," he said.

"Spied upon," Prudence corrected. "You said if you were hiding out and had no papers, you'd want to learn everything you could about nosy strangers who suddenly appeared and started asking questions about you."

"Ye Da and Yan He," Geoffrey said.

"So soon?" Prudence asked.

"The landlord must have told them Matthew and I had come around and were asking questions about recent arrivals." He checked his watch and then looked outside. "It gets dark early in February. If the landlord told them about us as soon as they got in from work, there was plenty of time to hatch a plan."

"But the food came from the Golden Dragon Noodle Palace," Josiah protested. "Matthew Lam sent it."

"It may have been prepared at the restaurant and given to one of the potboys to deliver, but if Ye Da and Yan He were watching us, they could easily have intercepted the order."

"Chloral hydrate in the tea?" Prudence suggested.

"Why not? Lady Peng's amah used it at the hotel, and women of the night slip a drop into a man's drink when they want to lift his wallet. It's cheap, available everywhere, and effective."

"We're proof of that," Josiah said mournfully.

"I think I heard something," Prudence said, turning toward the corner where she'd left the bowl of tea and cake crumbs. She picked up one of the lanterns and swung it in that direction. A skinny gray mouse scampered away into the darkness.

"Well at least we know what it wasn't," Josiah said. "That's a relief. Jasmine tea is one of my favorites."

He found the evidence later that night, just before he crawled into bed, exhausted but uncertain he'd be able to fall asleep. He'd made it a practice to write a short report at the end of every day, the notes tucked into a folder that was stored beneath his mattress. Safe, Josiah thought, because who would bother to ransack his room, bare and dreary as it was. A precise man, he liked corners to align and pencils to be sharp. Always.

The sheet of paper on which he was recording his daily observations was only slightly off-kilter, but Josiah tapped the folder sharply every time he closed it, lining up the contents precisely. It always looked exactly the same when he opened it to make his next entry. But not tonight. Off by just a fraction of an inch, but visibly crooked. At least to his critical eye.

There'd been some discussion of whether they had well and truly been fed chloral hydrate after the gray mouse had eaten the tea-soaked bean cake crumbs and scurried away, apparently unaffected. But there could be no doubt now that their lives had been tampered with.

"I make most of my notes in Pitman shorthand," Josiah told Prudence and Geoffrey, holding the folder as though it had been contaminated. Which, to his way of thinking, it had. "So whoever broke in couldn't have made sense of some of what he saw. But that doesn't change the fact that we were burgled."

Prudence had never seen Josiah in anything but a suit, white shirt, waistcoat, and tie. He looked smaller and more vulnerable in the long nightgown he'd been too distressed to realize was all he was wearing. Standing on the splintery hall floor in just a pair of socks. She didn't ask if he was certain that someone had searched beneath his mattress; Josiah never made mistakes about how he'd organized things.

"Was anything else meddled with?" Geoffrey asked. He'd

remained downstairs, lanterns extinguished, after sending Prudence and Josiah off to bed, prowling the lower floor like a night hunting panther. Listening to footsteps passing by, to cat yowls and the slithering of rats. Waiting, in case the intruder returned. Or one of Wei Fu Jian's guards took up a position across the street. When Josiah knocked on his bedroom door, Geoffrey had just come up. He'd still been fully dressed.

"Not as far as I can tell. There wasn't anything else of interest. A clean shirt and some folded smallclothes in the armoire." It was the first time Josiah had gone anywhere overnight without a neatly packed trunk to see him through the experience.

"Prudence?"

The three of them trooped into her narrow room, the men backing awkwardly out again to make space for a search. Brisk and brief. Like Geoffrey and Josiah, she was playing a role that didn't allow for personal luxuries. A change of stockings and chemise, a hand-knitted shawl borrowed from her maid, and the nightgown she was wearing was all Prudence had brought with her. Except for the wool robe she hastily put on as soon as she opened the armoire, saw it hanging there, and realized she was as scantily clothed as Josiah, who was still too upset to register the impropriety of it.

"If he was here, he left no trace of himself behind," she said. "And there was nothing to find even if he looked."

It was the same in Geoffrey's room. "He was cautious, thorough, and not in a hurry. Whoever he was."

"I'm not going to be able to sleep in that room," Josiah said, "knowing that a burglar rifled through my bed."

"We'll move you to the room next to that one," Prudence said.

"What about the sheets and blanket?" Josiah's voice was growing steadier as anger replaced fear and nerves.

"We can't do anything tonight except give them a good shake. That will have to do," Prudence said reassuringly. She was half-asleep on her feet, but visibly trembling. Tiny shivers of apprehension. And cold.

"I'll stay up for a while," Geoffrey promised. He closed Prudence's bedroom door, then shepherded Josiah up the stairs to his new room and freshly shaken bedding.

When he came back down, he brewed a pot of Louisiana chicory coffee, relit the Black Patch cigar he'd used to jolt himself out of the drug stupor, and sat in the dark, staring out at the street through the uncurtained, unshaded storefront windows. Motionless. Silent. The glow of the cigar warning whoever was out there that someone inside was waiting for him.

The delivery boy who was carrying the missionaries' dinner to the storefront on Doyers Street only made it as far as the bend before someone whose face he could not see in the dark slipped a knife between his ribs and caught the carton of food as it fell toward the sidewalk.

The body was hauled into an alley and propped against a building, one hand holding a bottle. Anyone glancing down the passageway would assume another drunk or opium smoker had decided to pass the night in the company of the rats scampering through the garbage.

The jasmine tea was swiftly doctored, the food laid in front of the mission door. A swift, loud knock, footsteps running up Doyers and around the bend.

Where he waited. Out of sight.

Until enough time had passed for the drops to do their work.

Later, after he'd searched the bedrooms, wet fresh jasmine tea leaves with water from the kettle on the potbellied stove, and locked the mission door behind him, he loaded the body into a two-wheel cart and moved it closer to Five Points. Emptied the pockets.

The dishwasher who doubled as delivery boy would be found, but bodies were commonplace early-morning discoveries around Five Points. Once hauled off to the city morgue, and with no family to report him gone, the next stop was a pauper's grave on Hart Island. It was even possible that the inquiry agent disguised as a minister would never learn the full truth of what had happened. The restaurant would hire someone else, and within days, no one would remember the missing dish-washer's name.

It was time to claim his next victims.

CHAPTER 27

The beat cops working the dangerous blocks around Five Points usually patrolled in pairs, especially after dark. By the early hours post-midnight, billy clubs swinging at their sides, they'd drunk enough free pints to ignore most of what was going on around them, rationalizing that even the worst street ruffians usually coshed marks who were asking for it. The sidewalks gradually emptied, the ladies of the evening eventually deciding to end the working day. Except for the occasional echo of an out of tune caterwaul the hours from four A.M. until dawn could be as quiet as a weekday church.

It was a dog who first caught Patrolman Joseph Walsh's attention as he and his partner passed an alleyway a few blocks from the intersection of the streets that had given Five Points its name. The animal trotted into a pool of gaslight carrying something in its mouth that looked like a human hand. It growled and dropped whatever it was when Walsh blew his whistle and twirled his billy club through the air. He turned tail and ran when the policeman charged in his direction.

"What is it?" Peter Gallagher asked, not quite as steady on his feet as he'd need to be when he clocked out at the station house in a few hours. Joe Walsh had a better head for the drink than he did.

"What does it look like?"

"Sausages tied together with a bit of string?"

"I'll make a check of the alley," Walsh said, leaving Gallagher standing beneath the gaslight that had been turned down low when the crowds thinned out. He was bored and not as soused as he would have liked to be.

The body had been rolled behind a couple of barrels, then flattened against the wall of a building. Rats had been at it. They stood their ground as Walsh approached, and only fled when the policeman threw pieces of broken brick at them, squealing when a sharp edge pierced their fur. The dog who'd bitten off the hand had been a skinny mongrel with pus crusting around its eyes and bite marks on its hide, desperate enough for food to dare a pack of the city's most vicious scavengers.

Walsh pulled away the barrels, then nudged the body with his boot. He held his bullseye lantern close to the unblinking eyes, swept it over the body until he found where the knife had gone between the ribs. It was a neat killing. Professional. The victim probably never knew what was happening until it was too late.

"Chinaman," Walsh announced when he'd rejoined his partner out on the street. "Looks familiar, too. I'd swear he's delivered food to the station house from the Golden Dragon."

"They all look alike to me." Gallagher reached out a hand to balance himself against the lamppost.

"You're sure about that?" Hanrahan asked when he overheard Joe Walsh making his report. "The dead man worked at the Golden Dragon?"

Coffee cup in hand, he'd been standing by the precinct intake desk, waiting for Geoffrey Hunter to arrive before beginning the Ye Da and Yan He interrogations.

It was a poorly kept secret that over the years, the Chinatown officers had developed a liking for chop suey, and that it was in a restaurant's best interests to keep them supplied. Sometimes the desk sergeant paid, sometimes he didn't. It all worked out in the end.

"I took a gander at his face before the death cart came," Walsh said. "It's him, all right. The wagon's still outside if you want to have a look-see."

"I'll handle this one, Sergeant," Hanrahan said, reaching for the paperwork. He set down his coffee cup, skimmed the hastily scribbled report. "Don't go anywhere, Joe."

Walsh's shift was ending, and he was eager to sign out and be on his way, not at all happy when Hanrahan ordered him to retrieve the body, and have it carried into the cellars of the Sixth Precinct station house, where it was cold enough not to need to be iced down. "Not the Bellevue morgue?" he objected.

"Just do what I told you, and then report back. I've got questions that need answers," Hanrahan said. He tore a piece of paper out of his notebook and handed it to the desk sergeant. "Have a messenger take this to the Golden Dragon right away. They won't be open, so he'll have to pound on the door until someone answers."

"What's going on?" Geoffrey Hunter stepped aside as two burly policemen carried what looked like a canvas-wrapped body across the waiting room and down a flight of stairs.

For a few moments, everyone turned and watched in silence as the dead man passed. It wasn't every day a corpse took up residence in the basement.

"I'll explain as we go," Hanrahan said. "I want you to take a look at him, see if he seems familiar. I've sent for Matthew Lam, too. The beat cop who found him claims he worked at the Golden Dragon. Says he recognized him because he used to make deliveries here."

A shudder ran down Geoffrey's back as he followed Hanrahan down the stairs.

By the time the corpse had been laid out on a stained wooden table as far away from the coal-burning furnace as they could place it, he'd told Hanrahan about the storefront intruder and the effect of whatever he'd put in the delivery from the Golden Dragon. "I'm guessing it was chloral hydrate because it had to have been fast acting, and none of us suffered any ill effects except for aching heads. Our rooms were searched, too."

"How did he get in?"

Geoffrey shrugged. "Picked the lock. Or Josiah may not have fastened the bolt when he brought in the food. I asked him, but aside from being highly insulted, he couldn't be sure. If Matthew can corroborate your patrolman's identification and confirm that this is the man who was sent from the restaurant to the mission, we'll have a better idea of where Ye Da and Yan He stand in all this."

"I had them picked up last night around nine o'clock," Hanrahan said. "I was afraid they'd skip if we waited until morning. They've been in the cells since they were brought in." He rolled the canvas back from the dead man's face. "Familiar?"

Geoffrey took his time, but he knew from the first glance that he'd never seen this person before. "Whoever set the food down outside our door knocked and then ran. None of us got a look at him."

"Poor bastard," Hanrahan said.

"His name is Dong Gen." Matthew Lam had slipped down the stairs so quietly they hadn't heard him. He wore a workingman's outfit of indigo-dyed trousers and frogged jacket that looked like it had been picked up off the floor and needed laundering. His hair was uncombed, and his face had the crumpled look of someone newly roused from sleep. "I came as soon as I got your note."

"Is this the man who was supposed to deliver our dinner last night?" Geoffrey asked. For the record and because you never accepted one witness's word as gospel.

"I sent him out myself," Matthew said. "He's a dishwasher, but he can earn tips whenever we need someone to carry food to a customer. Zhu Ling doesn't like to make a regular practice of it, but he allows for exceptions." He whispered something under his breath that sounded like a Christian prayer and made a small sign of the cross on the dead man's forehead. "What happened?"

"A knife between the ribs," Hanrahan said. "Someone else delivered the meal. Laced with chloral hydrate."

"Good God!"

"We're all right. Disturbed and angry, but unharmed."

"What did he want?"

"We wondered about that. Prudence and I both think someone didn't buy our cover stories and decided to find out for himself who we were. He found his answer under Josiah's mattress."

"I think it's time we cross-examined our pair of reluctant guests," Hanrahan suggested, leading the way toward the stairs. "We brought in the two men you and Hunter located yesterday."

"I'd like to listen in," Matthew said. "And take a look at them in case they're familiar."

"Unofficially," Hanrahan said.

"Unofficially, of course. How would that work?"

"You and Geoffrey can lean against the wall of the interrogation room as though you belong there. Don't speak and don't look surprised at anything I say or do."

"The third degree?" Matthew had read in the papers about the new way of getting information out of suspects. Most people seemed to think there was nothing wrong with beating answers out of men who'd been arrested.

"Not my style," Hanrahan said.

Ye Da and Yan He had been picked up by the police with the grease of their pushcart dinner still on their fingers.

Like many of the bachelor residents of Chinatown's rooming houses, they ate most of their meals from barrows or in cheap restaurants that catered to customers with little money to spend and less time to indulge in the necessary business of eating. A man who didn't have the extra coin to spend on an opium pipe or a visit to one of the gambling parlors might linger in the streets until darkness fell and he was almost too tired to climb the stairs to his narrow bed.

Ye Da and Yan He, possessors of expensively forged documents, had come along to the Sixth Precinct without argument.

They hadn't expected to be detained overnight.

The translator from the consul's office told them to look blank, confused, and frightened. The Irish cops who made up almost the entirety of the New York Police Department didn't take kindly to detainees who challenged their authority or refused to cooperate. None of them spoke Chinese, so it was always best to pretend not to understand more than a few words of English. They'd gotten their papers from a good source; there was nothing to worry about on that score. All they had to do was come up with an alibi for the few hours last night between when they'd gotten off work and when they were hauled in. They could do that, couldn't they?

So they waited, speaking Chinese, but keeping their voices low as they talked. The door to the interrogation room fit poorly into its frame. No telling who might be standing in the hallway. Listening. Perhaps with another translator by his side.

Officer Hanrahan escorted Geoffrey and Matthew into the room but made no introductions. He seated himself at the table, flipped quickly through the intake material, and spoke directly to Ye Da and Yan He, as if confident they could understand him.

"It will go best for you if you answer my questions truthfully and without attempting to hold back anything. Is that understood?"

Both men nodded a moment or two before the translator finished speaking.

Hanrahan smiled.

"I want to know when you arrived in Chinatown, how you

got here, where you've found work, and whether someone can vouch for where you were and what you were doing last night."

Hanrahan sat back in his chair as the translator did his job. He gave the three of them enough time to answer his questions and come up with a decent story. No policeman expected a suspect to tell the truth the first time out, but since Police Commissioner Byrnes had introduced and publicized the tactics of the third degree, fewer lies were being told and men who hoped to escape a bad beating skated a little closer to the facts of the matter under investigation.

There was hardly any point contesting the papers Hanrahan was certain weren't authentic. They looked good, and it wasn't the police department's job to chase down illegals. They had their hands full arresting pickpockets, drunks, burglars, street corner prostitutes, and gang members who hadn't the common sense to post lookouts when they beat the hell out of each other and endangered innocent bystanders. Men committed rapes, husbands beat their wives senseless, various types of assault were too commonplace to be remarked, and everyone enjoyed reading about murders over breakfast. In addition to fighting brutal crime, each station house had a couple of men assigned to collect the payoffs every policeman expected. No one wearing the uniform had the time or the inclination to drown himself in the paperwork it took to get rid of another new arrival who hadn't bothered to learn English yet.

"Are you ready?" Hanrahan asked, opening his notebook, wetting the lead tip of his pencil.

"Ye Da and Yan He came to New York from San Francisco several weeks ago," the translator began. "They don't remember the exact date."

"By way of Canada?"

"By train."

"Don't you mean they were smuggled into the United States from a Canadian port where they were admitted into that country using forged identity papers?" It was an educated guess at best, but Hanrahan thought he detected a faint nervous flutter of the eyelids and entirely too much comprehension of English. "Did you warn them that things will go badly if they don't tell the truth?"

Yan He started to say something in Chinese, but the translator laid a hand on his arm and nodded toward where Matthew Lam and Geoffrey seemed to be propping up the wall and not paying much attention to what was being said. After that, except for a few words of clarification now and then, he and Ye Da stayed silent.

"They worked at the Heavenly Pure Laundry until seven o'clock. The owner will vouch for them. Then they walked to the rooming house on Mott Street, stopping only to buy food from one of the pushcarts. That vendor will confirm their purchases and how long they remained nearby eating and talking. The old man who cleans the rooming house will tell you that they went up to the room they share at approximately eight-thirty. As you know, they had already removed their clothing and prepared for bed when your officers rousted them. You may ask as many questions as you like, Officer, but they have nothing more to say."

The translator leaned back in his chair.

Ye Da and Yan He fixed unblinking stares on Hanrahan, hands concealed in the wide sleeves of their jackets. If they were nervous, they were hiding it well.

"I'll be back in a few minutes," Hanrahan said, taking the papers and notebook with him as he left the room. Geoffrey and Matthew followed.

This first round of questioning had been a delaying tactic, an opportunity for Matthew to listen in on the conversation between suspects and translator. Perhaps identify them as having bought a meal at the Golden Dragon.

"Well?" asked Hanrahan.

"They're being very careful," Matthew said. "The translator warned them about me."

"I saw that."

"I couldn't make out what they were saying before we went in. They were speaking too softly. But once you'd asked your questions, it was pretty straightforward. Something is off, but I couldn't tell you what it is. Just a feeling I have that they aren't who they're pretending to be. I've never seen them before, but these are educated men, not illiterate workers."

"You're sure?"

"As much as I can be. We might know more after we've checked their alibis."

"That's already been done," Hanrahan said. "Someone at the rooming house told us where they work and gave us the name of the pushcart vendor they usually buy food from."

"So the stories hold up?" Geoffrey asked.

"Tight as a drum," Hanrahan said.

"Pastor Hunter isn't here," Prudence said. "I don't recall that he was expecting you this early."

Sang Chao had told Geoffrey he would send word as soon as he'd made the arrangements with Wei Fu Jian, but no such message had been delivered before her partner had left for the Sixth Precinct.

Sang Chao's face fell, then tightened. He turned to the man standing behind him, peppering him with a volley of staccato Chinese that needed no translation. He was furious, and he was taking it out on the person whose careless mouth had caused this embarrassing and perhaps costly situation in the first place.

Gao Fong bowed his head and slumped his shoulders, the picture of dejection and remorse. He was wearing a heavily embroidered robe that didn't quite fit, obviously borrowed from or forced upon him by his employer. Nothing about him looked normal today; it was as though he'd been given a role to play and told exactly what to do. Threatened with who knew what punishment if he didn't succeed in appeasing the wrath of the honorable master of the Eastern Benevolent Association. He looked up once, and although he didn't say anything, his pleading eyes met Prudence's.

"We don't need Mr. Hunter to stand beside you during your audience with Wei Fu Jian," Prudence said. *Audience?* Why on earth had she used that preposterous word for a simple conversation that shouldn't take more than five minutes from start to finish? "I'll take you to him myself."

Sang Chao shook his head vigorously, obviously appalled that a woman should suggest such an arrangement. This was a matter to be settled with all due respect for the individual honor of the parties involved. A woman could play no part in it.

"I have business at Wei's Antiquities," Prudence continued, skirting around mention of Lady Peng. "While I'm there, I can spare a few minutes to explain what happened. It's no trouble, I assure you."

Sang Chao continued shaking his head, but Gao Fong had gone very still, eyes darting back and forth from Prudence to the owner of the funeral parlor where he worked. He opened his mouth as if to say something, then closed it. But he seemed to stretch toward Sang Chao, as if by sending energy in that direction he could influence the man to accept the missionary woman's suggestion.

"I thought this was important to you," Prudence said. She'd finally gotten the point that it was *she* Sang Chao was resisting, not the idea of going to Wei's Antiquities on his own. "You may find when you get there that Wei Fu Jian has decided he can't see you after all. He's a very busy man, as I'm sure you realize all too well. You'll need my help." It annoyed her to be rebuffed like this by someone who ought to have been grateful for her aid. As a woman, she'd had to get used to it. But that didn't mean she liked it. Or that she had to accept it.

"It's entirely up to you," she said airily, reaching for her hat and reticule. "Josiah, would you like to come along?"

He wouldn't have missed her meeting with the amah for the world.

Without another word, she breezed out of the storefront, waiting on the sidewalk for Sang Chao and Gao Fong to sidle past her. She locked the door, dropped the key into her reticule, then turned and began to walk toward the Doyers Street bend.

"They're coming along right behind us," Josiah murmured.

"I knew they would," Prudence said. "I didn't give them any choice."

CHAPTER 28

The second floor of Wei's Chinese Imports and Antiquities had been transformed into the official headquarters of the Eastern Benevolent Association, an organization that by the restrained elegance of its premises promised much to the men who had each paid ten dollars for membership.

The color red predominated, reminding everyone that luck and prosperity would enrich the lives of those who remained faithful to the group and to one another. Intricately carved furniture—tables and chairs for playing *xiangqi* and mahjong, beds for sleeping until a man could buy a spot in a rooming house—had been constructed from the red pines growing in the Adirondack forests, far cheaper than pieces imported from China. One of the basic goals of the association was to encourage and support new Chinese businesses; a small furniture workshop employed five men already. Wei envisioned ten times that number in a few years.

"I had no idea that what he was talking about would be this impressive," Prudence said to Josiah.

"We knew he was wealthy. And an important figure in Chinatown."

"There's nothing like this in most of the Irish and Italian immigrant communities."

"The Catholic Church is what unites them," Josiah said. "That's what I've been told, at any rate. That and a penchant for criminal gangs."

"The Chinese associations are built around common ancestry—the same family name—or living in the same area of the country. That's how Wei explained them to me, and how the San Francisco groups are structured."

"He's doing something different here. It feels more like some of the gang headquarters Mr. Hunter's ex-Pinks have told us about."

"The Black Hand?" Prudence asked.

"And others. Menacing, ostentatious, and arrogant—all at the same time. They emerge wherever there's a population that can be exploited and preyed upon."

"Do you think that's what he's really doing? Laying the foundation for his own criminal kingdom?"

"I don't know, Miss Prudence. I haven't been able to figure out this case from the first step we took into Chinatown. It's a different world." Josiah nodded toward where Sang Chao and Gao Fong stood waiting for Wei to appear and invite them deeper into the large common room that Prudence and Josiah hadn't hesitated to explore without anyone's permission. "He's not here. That's part of the setup. You make someone mark time to prove your superiority over him."

"Is that what Wei is doing?"

Josiah shrugged.

"I think we should get on with what we came for," Prudence said.

She'd done what she could for Sang Chao and his loose-lipped employee, but they were a distraction on which she'd already spent enough time. The disposition of Lord Peng's body and the eventual repatriation of his bones to his homeland were issues neither she nor Geoffrey could set to rights.

The thrust of the investigation they'd been hired to pursue had to be the continuing threat to the Peng family, which could only be resolved when the killer was identified and apprehended. The thread Prudence was pursuing seemed promising, though she wasn't sure enough of its validity to have shared it with her partner. Not a good place to be. She definitely needed more evidence if it was going to become strong enough to act upon.

"I don't know how long you'll have to wait," she told Sang Chao when it became obvious that the appointment he thought he'd arranged was no longer certain.

"No matter." He'd spoken briefly to the clerk who had ushered them into the meeting hall. "Wei Fu Jian has been called away unexpectedly, but he left word that he would return as soon as possible. We have been offered tea."

That seemed to do it. Sang Chao and Gao Fong would settle themselves into tea and *xiangqi* until they were summoned into the great man's presence. However long that took.

Lady Peng wasn't in the living quarters either.

"She and my uncle went out together this morning after breakfast." Mei Sha was wearing an odd combination of western and traditional Chinese clothing that suited her divided personality better than either style alone. She'd greeted both Prudence and Josiah warmly, but without referring to their most recent awkward encounter. "It was supposed to be very hush-hush and Mummy was heavily veiled, but they're up to something. I can feel it in the air."

"You don't know what it is?" Prudence asked.

"Other than arranging for a more permanent hiding place for us, I can't imagine what it could be."

"Did Johnny go with them?"

"He's not the head of the family. He takes orders from my father's brother, which means he's working for this new benevolent association. You wouldn't recognize him, Miss Prudence.

He doesn't look like Lord Peng's English educated son anymore. I suppose that's the point. I never thought I'd say it, but he blends in. He disappears. We used to speak English together all the time. Not now." Mei Sha was clearly perplexed.

"Is your amah here?" Prudence asked.

"Amah? She's getting ready to see to An Bao's feet," Mei Sha blurted out, ducking her head in embarrassment when she realized that Josiah had heard her. "Amah massages, washes, and dries them every day," she murmured.

"Surely they're not still bound?" Prudence had read everything she could find on the custom of creating golden lotus feet.

"They have to be kept very clean, especially where the toes were broken and bent under."

It was difficult to tell whether Mei Sha was defending the loathsome practice or trying to reassure Prudence that her sister did not suffer because of the tradition from which Mei had been spared.

"I want to ask her some questions," Prudence said.

"An Bao?"

"Your amah."

"What could she tell you that I couldn't?"

"Questions about your family's life in China, before Empress Dowager Cixi sent your father abroad as a diplomat."

"I was a baby," Mei Sha said. "My first memories are of London."

"Precisely. I wouldn't ask if it weren't important," Prudence insisted. "I've already spoken to your mother. Now I need to hear the stories *behind* what she told me."

"I don't understand."

"Servants know things about their masters and mistresses that no one else does."

"But if you've already talked to my mother . . ."

"This is important, Mei Sha."

"I want to hear what she has to say. And the questions you'll ask."

"She's cared for and protected you since you were born."

"She was my wet nurse."

"Then you'll understand why she may not want you to know what I have to find out if we're ever to discover your father's killer."

"Is *he* staying?" Mei Sha nodded toward Josiah.

"I'll talk to her alone," Prudence said.

"Her English isn't very good."

"I think it's probably better than you imagine."

Mei Sha's lips tightened. Her teeth clicked together. She shook her head.

"Is there somewhere we could conceal ourselves?" Josiah asked. He got up and walked to the archway leading to an adjoining room. Heavy draperies had been pulled back on either side, fastened to the wall by tasseled gold cords. "What about this?" He untied the cords, then stood back as the draperies filled the empty passage. He stepped through, disappearing from sight. "Can you hear me?" His voice was muffled, but otherwise easily understood.

Mei Sha's face cleared. She grinned like the mischievous child she was, sliding through the red velvet drapes so smoothly they hardly swayed. "There are screens here we could move," she called out.

Josiah must have argued with her because a few moments later she flounced back into the parlor, clearly furious about something.

"Are you sure you want to do this?" Prudence asked, attempting to smooth over whatever Josiah and Mei Sha had disagreed about. "You may not like what you hear. And you'll have to remain silent, no matter what your amah says." She didn't like the elaborate deception Mei Sha was orchestrating, but if this was the only way to get the answers she needed, so be it.

"She's not the easiest of clients to deal with," Josiah said when Mei Sha had left the room.

"Technically, she isn't a client. Johnny signed the contract."

"We may not have much time if Wei Fu Jian and Lady Peng are expected back soon." Josiah picked up an ivory elephant with gold-tipped tusks, examined it critically, put it down, moved on to another of the small tables on which miniature statues and porcelain bowls were displayed.

"I'm not going to waste time beating around the bush," Prudence said. "If Amah is as shrewd as I think she must be, she's worried. Perhaps frightened. Ghosts from the past have a way of catching up with us, and the Chinese are particularly sensitive to threats from beyond the grave."

"You call her Amah?"

"It's like the British calling their children's nurse Nanny when it's also what she does. She's a nanny."

"I'm not sure I'd like my name canceled by what's essentially the title of my job," Josiah said. "It does away with personhood."

"But in this instance it may work to our advantage," Prudence said. She raised a finger to her lips, then stood up as Josiah scuttled past her and through the red velvet drapes.

An Bao, tall, slender, the youthful reincarnation of her mother's beauty, bowed politely, then ushered forward the short, stocky woman who had dosed the rest of the family servants with chloral hydrate and fled to Geoffrey Hunter's suite when Lady Peng left her behind.

"I will translate for Amah," An Bao said. "My sister has explained what you want, and although I do not understand why this is necessary, I give my consent." She motioned toward a footstool, murmuring permission in Chinese for Amah to seat herself. "Mei Sha will leave us," she continued in English. "She has said that you do not believe what we will discuss is suitable for young ears."

An Bao waited until only she, Amah, and the American detective lady remained in the room. "Please begin, Miss MacKenzie."

"I spoke with Lady Peng yesterday at some length. She showed me a letter that had come from China to Lord Peng and explained what it said." A low hum accompanied Prudence as she spoke, An Bao translating her every word into Chinese. Accurately, she hoped. Without embellishment. By the time she had finished recounting the concubine's story, An Bao's voice had begun to tremble, and Amah's eyes had teared over.

"Do you remember Chu Hua?" Prudence asked An Bao.

An Bao nodded. "She was very young when she came to our house. Very beautiful and very kind. She held me in her arms when the foot binding began. The pain was excruciating as the bones were broken. Every time the bandages were removed for washing, I begged them not to put new ones on."

She glanced down at the elaborately embroidered slippers on her tiny feet. "As you can see, Miss MacKenzie, none of my crying and pleading did any good. Mei Sha was fortunate. She was a baby when the empress dowager ordered my father abroad. It was too late for me."

"No man of noble family would have married a woman with large feet," Amah said. Her English was heavily accented, but fluent. It was obvious that the old woman had hidden that proficiency from Lady Peng and her daughters. If the family had spoken English to hide secrets from her, the stratagem hadn't worked.

"Tell us what you recall about Chu Hua," Prudence urged.

An Bao reached for one of her amah's hands, clasping it gently in her own. "The truth cannot hurt as badly as a hidden lie," she said. "The longer a lie remains uncovered, the more rotten it grows. Until finally, the stench becomes unbearable, and it bursts of its own accord. Like an abscess that eats away at the bone. And kills."

Amah sat in silence, tears running down her cheeks. When she finally raised her head, it was to smile at An Bao and nod.

"Lord Peng bought Chu Hua after Mei Sha was born. Lady Peng had almost died. The doctor who attended the birth said another child *would* take her life. So, unless your father added another concubine to the household, there would be no more sons. He wanted sons.

"I think he would have brought Chu Hua with us to Europe, but counselors to the empress dowager advised against it. Victoria would not have accepted Lord Peng's credentials if he'd arrived in England with what would have been considered two wives. So he left Chu Hua behind. She had not given him the son he'd demanded of her, but it wasn't for lack of trying. He used her often and sometimes mercilessly. The sound of her weeping and cries of pain would echo into the courtyard from behind the doors of her quarters. There was blood when there shouldn't have been. Bruises everywhere on her body."

"Did my mother know what was going on?" An Bao asked.

"She was ill after Mei Sha was born. The empress dowager summoned her to the Forbidden City to be treated by her own doctors."

"I never knew that," An Bao said.

"The empress could read and write," Amah said. "So could Lady Peng. Her father was a scholar of great renown, but never the parent of a son. So he taught the most intelligent of his daughters. The empress and Lady Peng became fast friends during the time your mother spent at the dowager's side. It is said that words are a tighter bond than silken cords."

"Was that why my father was chosen to go to Queen Victoria's court?"

Amah shrugged. "Perhaps. The empress sees to the prosperity of those she favors and ensures the downfall of those she doesn't."

"We've heard a rumor that Lord Peng's death might have been an execution," Prudence said.

"It was the empress dowager who suggested that Lady Peng's husband satisfy his wish for more sons with a concubine. She did it to save her friend from an accidental pregnancy. The Empress Dowager Cixi herself had been a concubine who gained power by giving birth to an heir. What neither of them predicted was Lord Peng's anger when the woman chosen by the empress did not conceive."

"Chosen by the empress?" Prudence repeated.

"Approved by the empress," Amah corrected herself. "In China it isn't uncommon for poor farm tenants to provide generations of servants to their overlords. Certain families become known for being hardworking, loyal, and occasionally siring extraordinarily beautiful women. The empress's agents would have had no difficulty finding a suitable candidate. She may even have suggested several names."

"If Lord Peng did order Chu Hua's death, would that have been a slight against the empress dowager? A challenge to her authority since he had the concubine killed without consulting her?" Prudence asked. "Is it possible that Chu Hua came from a family that had fallen on hard times but had blood ties to the empress dowager? And that their poverty was why they agreed to sell their daughter to Lord Peng?" The more she allowed herself to sink into a culture she had never experienced until slightly more than a week ago, the easier it became to accept the logic of their reasoning.

"If the empress dowager had a hand in choosing Chu Hua, my father would have had to seek the empress's permission to have her killed," An Bao said. "He would have had to prove that his concubine had betrayed him."

"The letter your mother read to me mentioned neither of those conditions."

"There was some doubt," Amah began.

"What do you mean?" Prudence asked.

"Lord Peng returned several times to China during the years he was attached to the embassy in London. Each time he received private instructions from the empress and then spent several weeks at the Peng family compound to honor his parents and to try to leave a son behind to care for them in their old age. Johnny was in school in England. The empress had plans for him."

"You're saying that it's possible the child Chu Hua was carrying was Lord Peng's?"

"Possible." Amah removed her hand from An Bao's clasp. "There would have been no way to prove it until the child grew old enough to show a resemblance to the man who fathered him. Lord Peng could not take that chance. The steward who carried out his orders assured him there was no other choice."

"I thought he was desperate for sons," An Bao said bitterly.

"The concubine wasn't the only one he ordered killed," Prudence said. She spoke softly and directly to An Bao, who was proving to be much more like her fatalistic mother than she had thought possible. "According to what the steward wrote, the gardener was given opium at the same time as Chu Hua. Then later, I presume not long after the first deaths, Chu Hua's parents were eliminated. Her brother, too. But Lady Peng and I have speculated that perhaps the men sent to kill the brother saw an opportunity for profit. Suppose instead of forcing him to ingest a fatal dose of opium, they sold him as a contract laborer, shipped him out to the United States or Canada, pocketed the bounty, and told the steward he was dead?"

"Filial honor," An Bao whispered.

"Lord Peng might have been targeted for execution by agents of the empress for reasons we don't know, but before they could act, Chu Hua's brother moved to avenge the deaths of his sister, her child, his mother, and his father," Prudence summed up.

"And he isn't finished yet," Mei Sha said.

No one had noticed the slight ripple of the crimson curtains as the youngest Peng child slipped through them and stood as still as a statue to hear her father pronounced a murderer and the cause of the attempts on hers and Johnny's lives.

Josiah, shocked to the core to hear his and Miss Prudence's suspicions reinforced, stood at Mei Sha's side.

The amah lowered her face into her hands, rounded her back, and sobbed without a sound.

Chapter 29

Lady Peng had accepted that neither she nor any of her children would return to China.

She and Empress Dowager Cixi had been close friends once, years ago, the only two ladies in the Forbidden City who could read and write with ease and fluency. They had worked together in the quiet afternoons when other ladies slept, stretching their minds, honing their calligraphy skills, exchanging knowledge with the thirst of young scholars, creating a bond between them they expected to last a lifetime.

Then Lord Peng ordered his concubine killed.

When a woman married, she left her birth family and became part of her husband's family. She would serve *his* parents in their old age, owe allegiance to *his* family's honor, give birth to children who would ensure the continuation of *his* line. By the same logic, Lady Peng shared the blame of her husband's insult to the empress dowager; his death did not relieve her of the burden of his disgrace. The two widows who had found friendship as young women would have enriched each other's older days. But it could not be.

Lady Peng suspected that the empress dowager might have

dispatched agents to eliminate Lord Peng while he was between diplomatic missions. It would have been very like her to arrange that an obstacle be removed while still away from the shadow of the court. If, as Prudence MacKenzie suspected, the concubine's brother had gotten to Lord Peng first, the nightmare wasn't over. The empress dowager's professional executioners were probably not to be feared, but the brother had already proved that his concept of filial piety required that Lord Peng's children share their father's fate. Not until he was found would any of them be safe.

Even if it was uncertain whether the empress was a threat to her son, Lady Peng's future must be lived here, in this new country, under the protection of the man she had once hoped to marry and who was now offering her a second chance at happiness. They had talked long into the night, planning what must happen next, building a destiny that did not include a return to China. The Eastern Benevolent Association would expand Wei Fu Jian's already considerable power in Chinatown, but he and Lady Peng both agreed that the association needed more than cooperation, goodwill, and loyal, hardworking members to ensure its success and their authority. It required a strong arm of enforcement.

His name was Liang Hu, a fierce young man who had gathered others of his ilk around him in a gang that quickly coalesced into a tong. His first business venture was to offer protection to the beleaguered madams of houses of prostitution whose bouncers could not always control viciously drunk clients. A damaged or dead whore cut deeply into profits, and madams who refused the offer of protection found their premises overwhelmed. Next to fall under Liang Hu's protection were gambling parlors and opium dens. The men he dispatched to restore and maintain order were called soldiers. *Boo how doy.* They pinned up their queues in advance of a skirmish—highbinders—and hung their favorite weapons around their waists. Knives and hatchets so sharp they could slice off a man's hand with a single stroke.

His portion of the Chinatown pie was small, but Liang Hu was a man to watch. The police knew it and so did Wei Fu Jian. He had sent one of his bodyguards to Liang with a tale of discontent that was just precise enough to be believable. The informant kept Wei apprised of the tong's growth, Liang's leadership, and the opportune moment for Wei to make his move. That time was now.

The three of them met without witnesses in a room large enough to swallow up the sounds of their voices should anyone be foolish enough to attempt to listen at the door. It was earlier in the morning than important business was usually conducted, but that was on purpose. Lady Peng had been thickly veiled, but the fewer men who saw her enter and descend from Wei's carriage the better. Too little time had elapsed since Lord Peng's murder for people to forget that his widow had disappeared into the night. She hadn't surfaced in Washington, D.C., nor San Francisco. One newspaper had reported that an unnamed source placed her and her three children in the Bahamas.

It hadn't been difficult for Wei Fu Jian to trace Liang Hu's family lines. He'd entered the United States under his own name and with papers that were authentic. He was a fourth son, with no hope of satisfying his ambitions unless his three older brothers died. All of them were healthy and had fathered multiple sons, making Liang Hu's prospects even less promising. He emigrated to the United States with money in his pocket and ties to funds in China from which he could draw whatever he needed. The future in his new country looked bright. Then the explosion of anti-Chinese prejudice and the Chinese Exclusion Law changed everything.

When he surfaced in New York City after too many miserable years in San Francisco, it was with a grim determination never to have to kowtow to anyone again as long as he lived.

He wouldn't bow and scrape before a white man, wouldn't run like a thief in the night to escape a murderous crowd, wouldn't know hunger pains so fierce they stole his sleep. And most important, he would found his own dynasty in America despite the dearth of Chinese women. His wife, when he chose her, would be of good blood, like his. Not a peasant, not a woman of easy virtue, not a cowed convert of the Christian missionaries. Power and wealth first, then the wife and sons. As it should be.

"I won't insult your intelligence by pretending you don't know why I asked for this meeting," Wei Fu Jian began.

"Congratulations are to be extended on the establishment of the Eastern Benevolent Association," Liang said. He thought he knew the identity of the woman who had accompanied Wei, but until she spoke or lifted her veil, he would not address her. Would act as though she were not there at all. "Such an organization has long been needed here."

"So I have been told by every man who has paid his membership dues."

"The only reason a man would not subscribe would be if he didn't have the money to do so."

"In which case the association would lend it to him," Wei said.

"On very lenient terms," Liang suggested.

"Our purpose is to assist our members as they carve out businesses that will earn them a living in this unwelcoming country."

"A charitable organization."

"Not entirely. Charity and profit need not be enemies."

"Protection and enforcement," Liang Hu said. "That is what I sell and how I acquire the assets that will someday make me as wealthy and powerful a man as you, Honorable Wei." He bowed, then lapsed into silence. The next move was not his to make.

"I have a daughter," Lady Peng said, lifting the veil that had hidden her face until now. "You do not have a wife to provide you with sons and grace the fine rooms you will furnish."

"The American government has seen fit to exclude Chinese women from its country."

"My daughter will not return to China. Her name will be changed, and papers will be drawn up that will satisfy any inquiry made by the American authorities."

"The Eastern Benevolent Association needs a shadow operation," Wei explained. "It is to be expected that many criminal types will want to prey on Chinatown's inhabitants as they become prosperous. That cannot be allowed to happen. Protection must be organized, must not be permitted to beggar the very men whose coins contribute to its power."

"The scorpion must not sting itself."

They were reasoned, hardheaded men who knew that neither of them alone would be as strong as the two of them together. Chinatown would grow. In time, their people would be accepted, would move into positions of power just as the Irish had taken over the New York City Police Department and created their own version of city politics through Tammany Hall. In time, anti-Chinese legislation would be ignored or rescinded. The key was to be ready when that moment came. Foundations had to be laid, cadres of loyal followers recruited, solid financial institutions secured. Patience. A vision for the years to come, and patience for the long journey to attain it.

The bargain was struck.

An Bao's future was sealed though no one in the room where the compact was agreed upon had mentioned her name.

In the end, Hanrahan decided to release Ye Da and Yan He.

"We haven't enough evidence to hold them," he told Geoffrey and Matthew. "I doubt their alibis can be broken, and the lawyer who showed up to represent them this morning was sent by the Chinese consul."

"Is that usual?" Geoffrey asked. "Do consuls customarily become involved in the lives of ordinary citizens?"

"Only if an incident looks as though it could boil over into an international dispute," Hanrahan said. "With the Chinese it's typically been questions of residency or citizenship that they've chosen to take to court. This is a criminal case. Picking up two laundry workers to question them about their whereabouts shouldn't have triggered this kind of high-powered response. We'll let them go, but we'll keep an eye on them."

"They were the only two on the list who looked promising." Matthew positioned himself to be able to hear what was said inside the interrogation room when Hanrahan announced his decision. "The lawyer has told them to go back to the rooming house and stay there," he told Geoffrey. "Shall we follow?"

"They're educated men, you said?"

"Definitely. It's in the way they express themselves. I've met enough Chinese students at the divinity schools to be able to tell the difference between the speech of a man who's been to school and one who hasn't. These two have tried to hide it, but I don't think they expected to meet up with someone working for the police who understood Chinese and could distinguish between dialects."

"We'll give them enough time to believe no one is trailing them," Geoffrey decided. "We know where the rooming house is."

"And the laundry where they're working," Matthew added.

"I'll send a patrolman into the area to keep track of their comings and goings," Hanrahan promised.

"We shouldn't expect them to stay longer than a day or two. If they're professionals, that is. They'll clear out in the middle of the night, and they won't leave anything behind." Geoffrey smiled, a grim twisting of the lips that fooled no one. "That's what I would do."

*　　*　　*

Wei Fu Jian hadn't forgotten that the proprietor of the Sang Chao Funeral Home had requested an appointment and that he'd agreed. He knew the reason Sang Chao was seeking him out, and considered it proof that the Eastern Benevolent Association had already extended its influence throughout Chinatown.

Wei had spent months speaking to small business owners before putting forth the idea that a formal organization along the lines of what already existed in San Francisco was what was needed in New York City. He hadn't pushed, not even when he reached into his own pocket and supplied a workingman with a loan that carried little interest and no pressure to repay. When the moment came to formalize the association's structure, determine the amount of the membership dues, and draft a list of services to be provided, it had been a foregone conclusion that he and he alone would lead it.

Sang Chao was the first to worry that he had offended Wei Fu Jian and that his affiliation with the association would suffer because of it, but over time, others would follow. The primary of many patterns was being established, the roles of suppliant and master defined, and the foundation laid for their ongoing relationship. If all went as planned, Sang Chao would sing Wei's praises and applaud his generosity of spirit. It was always best to wrap a steel bar in layers of padded silk.

Sang Chao had rehearsed his apology for Gao Fong's loose tongue until well into the night, polishing every phrase until even one of the empress dowager's own court officials could have found no fault with it. Not once did Wei interrupt. He listened, holding the features of his face in masklike stillness, only his eyes shifting occasionally from Sang Chao to the man standing slightly behind him.

Lord Peng's private obsequies had been reported in only a few of the city's newspapers. Two paragraphs. Shen Woon had used every bit of his consular power to kill the story, and when he added that it was believed the late diplomat's family had sought refuge under British protection in an unnamed colony, interest paled. Wei had thought he could keep the family's presence in Chinatown secret, but the incident on the night of their arrival had quickly disabused him of that. The infiltration of his garden and Mei's narrow escape on a crowded street had erased any lingering doubt. So while Sang Chao trembled at his employee's abuse of the privacy of the dead, Wei knew that there were others in Chinatown who had also divined the identity of his hidden guests. One in particular. Or a pair of killers.

He forgave Gao Fong his carelessness and assured Sang Chao that it would not be held against him or his well-respected business. Wei Fu Jian had other things on his mind, one of them the task of telling his niece that he had found her a husband.

A package was delivered to the rooming house where Ye Da and Yan He were arguing about how much longer to wait before making their escape.

"I was told to make sure it was placed in your hands and no one else's." The old man who swept the hallways and emptied the chamber pots did not mention the silver dollar he'd been handed to perform that service. Nor that the individual who gave him his instructions was dressed finer than any of the building's tenants. The old man thought he had seen him once or twice before, at a distance. During a street celebration when the consul had put in a brief appearance? His eyesight and his memory weren't the best, but sometimes he saw something or someone not easy to forget.

Inside several layers of brown paper wrapping lay a packet of American money, identity papers that looked real, and two tickets on a steamship bound for China.

"The consul?" Ye Da guessed.

"Probably forwarded on from Washington," Yan He said.

They were experienced operatives, neither of them good-looking enough to remember. Ordinary. Easily lost in a crowd.

Trained in martial arts, knifework, and disappearing. Professional assassins whose quarry had been taken down by someone else.

"What are the odds?" Ye Da asked.

"Not good."

"We're shark bait." Failing to kill a man of Lord Peng's stature when that's what you'd been hired to do was tantamount to suicide. You were a loose end, a string that could be traced back to the puppeteer who had bought you. He hadn't discussed it with Yan He, but Ye Da knew his partner would agree.

"We can't use these," Yan He struck a match, waited for Ye Da's nod, then set fire to the identity papers. He examined the American currency for identifying marks, set the bundle aside when he found none.

"We can sell the tickets," Ye Da said.

"I'm not risking San Francisco."

"Where do we go then?"

"We stay right here. Liang Hu is recruiting." Yan He coiled his queue atop his head, then secured it with bamboo picks and a round silk cap. "In a few years, this Chinatown will have made a name for itself. Liang Hu will pay well for veteran soldiers. No one will come after his *boo how doy.*"

The waiting was over. Time to vanish.

CHAPTER 30

An Bao didn't protest, didn't argue when Lady Peng informed her that a husband had been found for her and a marriage arranged. It wouldn't have done any good. Her three-inch-long golden lotus feet were visible proof that she was a Chinese woman whose sole purpose in life was to obey. Lord Peng was dead, but his brother was not. The man who called himself Wei Fu Jian had taken control of her life. Positioned beside him, agreeing with every decision he made, stood her mother.

It wasn't that An Bao didn't understand that there were women in the world who did not kowtow to men. She had visited Queen Victoria's court and seen for herself the incredible spectacle of a female who ruled in her own right. Mei Sha had brought strange ideas back from boarding school, sharing them eagerly with her sister, never taunting her for the broken, deformed toes and arches concealed in tiny, embroidered shoes. It was only an accident of fate that had spared the younger girl the agonizing years required to achieve the absurdity of that concept of beauty.

An Bao had never possessed the type of volatile personality that would have made Mei Sha's life a living hell had her father not taken the family with him on his diplomatic posting to London. The notion of sending the younger daughter to a British boarding school had come from Queen Victoria herself, a casual suggestion that the Chinese legation eventually decided it could not ignore, especially after Johnny Peng vigorously supported the idea. Victoria had a penchant for taking an interest in the girl children of some of the tribal rulers of her far-flung empire, although once she handed them over to an army or naval officer to raise, she seldom thought of them again. She had found An Bao an exceptionally beautiful young woman, but the small feet that the queen was told had to be bathed, oiled, and rewrapped every day ruled out the notion of a British playing field or a school with several stories of stairs to climb.

So An Bao had remained in the isolation of her family's home when Johnny and Mei Sha went out into the world. But a governess was hired to teach her English so that if she was summoned to court again, she would be able to converse with Victoria. The woman was a bluestocking, of impeccable lineage, but determined to yield neither her body nor her mind to a husband not of her own choosing. Never to surrender whatever hard-won independence she could wrest from a society determined to keep her docile and leashed. She taught An Bao English, but she also instilled in her the germ of the dangerous, odious, thoroughly reprehensible belief that a woman could be a man's equal. It was only a tiny seed, hidden away in darkness, but Lady Peng's announcement had set it sprouting.

"I won't do it," An Bao announced to Amah when her mother had assured her that arrangements were being made and her only role in them was to bathe and perfume her body.

"I'll help you," Mei Sha offered impulsively, throwing her arms around the sister who had never been anything but kind and loving. She had no idea how, and only a vague notion that the brave and unconventional Miss Prudence MacKenzie would somehow provide the answer to their dilemma. Hadn't she rescued them from the Fifth Avenue Hotel? Weren't she and her partner, the handsome Geoffrey Hunter, working to find the assassin who had killed Lord Peng, attacked Johnny, and twice tried to assault Mei Sha herself?

Amah clucked sympathetically, shaking her head in commiseration because these offspring of Lord and Lady Peng were the only children she would ever be given to nourish and care for. She would offer up her life for them, but she was also a practical woman of such low social standing that she reckoned An Bao's only hope of survival was to obey with seeming good grace. Later on, when her docility had earned her a measure of privacy, the girl could embrace the fleeting, momentary illusions of freedom that were all wives of her rank could expect from marriage. Lady Peng had said that sumptuous silk wedding robes and headdress would be delivered later in the day. In the meantime, there was the bath to prepare.

The two sisters whispered together as their amah bustled about the private quarters above Wei's Chinese Imports and Antiquities and the new offices of the Eastern Benevolent Association. Mei Sha shook her head vehemently as An Bao made the preposterous threat that centuries of Chinese concubines had embraced when every other recourse failed them.

"All I want is to see him," An Bao said, stopping Amah cold with the impossibility of her demand. Husbands and wives met at their wedding, not before. "I know my mother and my uncle will not change their minds, but I won't blindly agree to spend the rest of my life with a man who is a complete stranger to me. Even the English allow some contact when parents arrange marriages. Mei Sha knows that from the girls she met at school, don't you?" she asked her sister.

"Some of them already knew who they would marry," Mei Sha agreed. "The contracts had been drawn up while they were still children. But yes, they were permitted to meet and talk and even dance with their future husbands. Under strict supervision, of course. It was said that the queen herself chose Prince Albert over his older brother when the two of them were invited to present themselves at the English court as matrimonial possibilities."

Amah cultivated a quiet, cowed façade of deference in Lady Peng's presence, but the two girls she had nursed from infancy often saw a different side of her. "That school was never a good place for you," she said fiercely, waving a work-worn hand at Mei Sha. "An Bao will fulfill the obligations of a dutiful daughter, and she will do so without complaint."

An Bao took a small brown bottle from where she had hidden it in her sleeve. She unscrewed the metal cap and held it inches from her lips. The chloral hydrate Lady Peng had brought with her from London to America and that Amah had used to such devastating effect at the Fifth Avenue Hotel. A few drops induced sleep. More than that brought death.

"You'll help us," she said as Amah's eyes fixed on the bottle held in her charge's slender fingers. "Or I'll drink this. All of it." Her voice was calm and determined. Suicide was the surest weapon in a Chinese woman's arsenal. She wasn't afraid to use it. "All I want is to see him," she repeated stubbornly. She didn't add that if what she saw of her future husband boded ill for her future, she might still drain the bottle. Death by chloral hydrate was a long sleep, painless and darkly comforting.

Amah didn't hesitate. She was used to maneuvering within the confines of her shackled life. An Bao would marry, but if Amah could figure out a way to grant the girl's wish, the three of them would remember the great adventure for the rest of their lives. And chuckle over it, the way women did when they accomplished something forbidden by the men who ruled them.

"His name is Liang Hu," Mei Sha contributed. Listening at closed doors was another skill she had mastered in her English boarding school. "He is the leader of an organization with headquarters on lower Doyers Street." She frowned, not sure about the veracity of her next bit of information. "I think he's agreed to join forces with the Eastern Benevolent Association."

"I was the price our uncle paid for that alliance," An Bao said. It made sense, and if a marriage had been arranged for her in China, it would have been a practical and productive affiliation between two important families. No one ever considered the feelings of the bride and groom. They were incidental figures in the larger scheme of dynastic expansion.

"Neither of you can be seen on the street," Amah said. "Not dressed like that. We'll disguise you in workingmen's blue trousers and jackets."

"I can't walk far," An Bao reminded them.

"Anyone who sees her will know she's a woman with bound feet," Mei Sha said. "No one else sways like that."

"In the countryside, some women with bound feet work the fields." Amah stared down at Mei Sha's embroidered slippers. "They stuff cotton rags into regular size shoes. You did it when we sneaked out of the Fifth Avenue Hotel."

"The carriage was parked just around the corner from the hotel. Will it work if I have to walk for more than several blocks?" An Bao asked skeptically. Her feet were exceptionally well cared for and no longer pained her, but she knew her limitations.

"It will," Amah promised. She was already planning where to obtain the trousers, jackets, broad-brimmed hats, and leather-soled shoes the girls would need. Correction. An Bao would need. Amah had disobeyed Lady Peng's orders to burn the garments her younger daughter had stolen from Johnny's room. Washed and neatly folded, they lay concealed beneath Amah's mattress.

"When?" Mei Sha demanded. She could feel the thrill of a risky escapade making its way up her spine, setting the blood coursing rapidly through her veins.

"An hour," Amah said. "I'll have everything ready in an

hour." Best not to wait and give Lady Peng time to consider that An Bao might balk.

"No one must know," An Bao insisted.

"Not even Miss Prudence?" Mei Sha asked.

"No one." An Bao was firm. Though few people suspected it, she could be as determined about some things as her redoubtable mother.

"This won't be comfortable, and you'll have to balance on the heels of your feet," Amah reminded An Bao as she stuffed cotton handkerchiefs in the toes of a pair of plain black street shoes. "Your walk will look odd, but at least it won't be the gait of a woman with bound feet. We can hope that anyone who notices will think you've suffered an injury of some sort."

Mei Sha had fashioned two narrow queues out of braided horsehair taken from a decorative fly whisk and sewn them to the inner bands of the hats she and An Bao planned to wear. They wouldn't survive close examination, but their own hair was too thick and lustrous to pass for the thin, greasy locks of a man. People moved quickly along the crowded streets. With luck they'd blend in enough to escape notice. Amah had decided not to attempt to disguise herself. A very few Chinese women had settled in Chinatown before the passage of the Page Act in 1875 restricted female immigration. She was old enough to pretend to be one of the early arrivals.

"You follow close behind me," she instructed her two charges. "Don't look around, don't catch anyone's eye, don't talk. Your voices are too high-pitched to be anything but female. Liang Hu's headquarters are at the Bowery end of Doyers Street."

"How do you know that?" Mei Sha asked.

"One of the guards. There's already a rumor going around that Liang and Wei Fu Jian are planning to merge their organizations. Men gossip as much as women."

With the formal announcement of the creation of the Eastern

Benevolent Association, traffic had increased substantially at the building that housed Wei's Chinese Imports and Antiquities. Guards had been pulled from the upper stairway leading to the private quarters and reassigned to the two lower floors where the association had opened its new offices and members demonstrated their loyalty by spending whatever they could spare on items many of them could ill afford. It made the exit onto Pell Street easier to manage, something Amah had been counting on. The Peng women had never appeared in anything but embroidered silk robes. No one spared more than a passing glance at two more workingmen and an old lady.

Hands hidden in the sleeves of their jackets, faces concealed beneath their hat brims, An Bao and Mei Sha followed closely behind Amah. "Pretend to be in a hurry. Act distracted, as if you're late to work and you're worried about what your employer will say to you," she had told them. "If you believe it yourself, so will others." It was one of the ways she'd managed to live a much better life all these years than had she remained in the village where she'd been born. A harried servant gave the impression of putting all her energy into the job she was supposed to be doing. Servants who appeared nonchalant and at their ease usually did not last long in wealthy households.

An Bao walked as closely to the front of the buildings they passed as she dared, knowing that there would be moments when she would have to reach out to keep herself from falling. Mei Sha positioned herself where a quick step would bring her to her sister's side. As long as An Bao stayed on her feet, there was a good chance they would remain unremarked. If she fell, if her hat came off, if she cried out, the deception would be over. From what Amah had been able to learn, both Wei Fu Jian and Liang Hu had eyes on every street in Chinatown.

They made it to the intersection of Pell and Doyers without incident. An Bao was breathing heavily from the effort of trying to appear to be walking normally. Her face was flushed with the effort and her heart beat so loudly with the daring of what they were doing that she was sure everyone around her could hear it. But so far no one had spared them more than a quick glance. Amah had been right, as she usually was. Staying alive meant working long, hard hours. Leaving little time or inclination to dawdle or stare at strangers.

Doyers Street, narrow and with the distinctive bend that made it impossible to see the entire length of the street at a single glance, was also less crowded, its shops smaller, dingier, less prosperous than the ones on Pell and Mott Streets. It made An Bao wonder why her future husband had chosen it for the headquarters of the gang Amah had learned he was supposed to have modeled on the tongs of San Francisco. Until she realized that the bend could conceal an ambush as well as an approaching attack.

A man slouching in the doorway of a small restaurant followed their progress, eyes dropping to their feet, head turning as they passed. He straightened, then seemed to decide there was nothing threatening about the elderly woman and two young men. He leaned against the doorframe again, dismissed them from his mind. An Bao understood that they had successfully passed the first of Liang Hu's defenses as they left the bend behind them. She flashed a smile at Mei Sha, who nodded in triumph. This was so much more exciting that anything either of them had done in London.

Prudence might have missed them if she'd been out on the street ringing her blasted bell and handing out religious tracts. She was dressed as a minister's wife, but she'd had trouble settling into the role. It was too restrictive. The drab black dress, devoid of ornamentation and decidedly unfashionable, was also ill-fitting. She'd covered her upper body with a shawl against the February chill, but there was nothing she could do to disguise the restlessness that had driven her to pace back and forth across the storefront's empty front room. Geoffrey was off at the police station, Josiah had retreated upstairs to fuss over his folders and write yet another page of notes, and not a single would-be convert had opened the mission's door. It was as if everyone in Chinatown knew that a farce was being enacted on Doyers Street and had chosen to stay away.

Except for that odd fellow who had identified himself as a bone scraper. And sought them out. She shuddered, imagining what it must be like to remove shreds of decomposed flesh from bones that had lain in the ground for five to seven years. Why would anyone care where his bones rested after he was dead? What was this compulsion to rebury them in a country thousands of miles away? She supposed it had to do with the veneration of their ancestors that she had read about and only dimly identified with. Except for her late parents and perhaps Geoffrey, she couldn't think of anyone at whose side she cared to spend eternity. Especially not if it meant being dug up and having her bones scraped clean.

She looked out the storefront window just as Amah and her charges were passing. A woman bowed with age, followed by two young men, one of them walking with a peculiar heel-balancing gait and touching building fronts as if to steady himself. Prudence was deep in the large room's shadows; she hadn't bothered to light a lamp. So when Mei Sha absentmindedly turned her face toward the apparently empty mission and a shaft of winter sunlight lit up her features, she was easily recognizable. But unaware that Prudence had seen her.

There wasn't time to run upstairs and tell Josiah where she was going. He would have tried to stop her anyway. Prudence had done it before, rushed impulsively into what looked like opportunity before it turned into mortal danger, and she'd always come out all right. A bit the worse for the harangues with which Geoffrey bombarded her, but as successful as an inquiry agent could hope to be. Where were they going, Mei Sha, An Bao, and their amah? It had to be the three of them. No one else. Disguised and moving as fast as An Bao's bound feet would allow. Prudence had seen Mei Sha run, and she guessed that even Amah, despite her age, could scurry along fast enough to avoid most dangers, but An Bao was as much a prisoner of her beauty as if she had iron chains fastened around her ankles.

Raising her shawl over her head and pulling it forward, Prudence stepped out of the mission storefront and waited in the recessed doorway for the trio to move far enough down the street not to hear her footsteps behind them. She had a moment of uncertainty when she considered what Geoffrey would have to say if he ever found out what she'd done, but she dismissed it with a quick shake of her head and a tighter grip on the shawl. All she intended to do was follow Lady Peng's daughters to wherever it was they were going, wait for them to conduct their business, and see them on their way back to where they were supposed to be hiding. They had gotten restless, especially Mei Sha, and somehow talked their amah into accompanying them on an adventure. Nothing would happen and they'd have a story to share and laugh over for years to come. It was something with which any well brought up young lady could sympathize, even though she'd have to pretend to be shocked.

An Bao, Mei Sha, and Amah had come to a halt before a shop whose signage in Chinese characters Prudence couldn't decipher. They seemed to be considering what to do next.

A cluster of young men, most of them smoking and all of them suddenly alert, lounged on the sidewalk at the end of the street. They reminded Prudence of the knots of armed guards who passed themselves off as casual loiterers in front of Wei Fu Jian's establishment. From a distance the display windows looked bare, but there were lamps lit inside the storefront. Shadows moved. The front door opened, closed again.

Prudence continued walking until her elbow brushed Mei Sha's side. The girl turned; their eyes met. Prudence shook her head, a warning to say nothing. Mei Sha tugged at An Bao's sleeve. Amah hissed and reached for something hidden beneath her clothing, changed her mind, shrugged, and flashed a conspiratorial smile at the woman who had interrogated her only a few hours ago.

Prudence, taller than Lady Peng's daughters, bent forward until her shawl concealed that Mei Sha was whispering furiously at her. When she straightened, it was with a gleam of intrigue in her eyes and a half smile on her lips. No one should be forced to meet a husband for the first time at the moment the ceremony began. What if he were deformed in some way? Ugly beyond belief? Thirty or forty years of a shared life lay ahead, unless blessed widowhood freed the wife. An Bao, breathing more steadily now after the long, difficult walk, stared at the crowd of dangerous-looking young men, fixing her eyes on the door through which she would have to pass in order to catch a glimpse of the man her mother and uncle had chosen for her to marry. If he frightened her, if he was ugly beyond bearing, she was determined to disappear or drink the chloral hydrate. She didn't think of either choice as anything but escape.

Prudence saw her briefly clasp Mei Sha's arm, then start to move forward, head held high, but the wide brim of her hat still shielding her beautiful face. Mei Sha appeared as thrilled as she was determined. Amah looked merely resigned.

They had crowded together in the doorway of what Prudence now realized was another of the medicinal and spice shops that were almost as common as restaurants in Chinatown. Before An Bao cleared the recess and stepped out onto the open sidewalk again, a force like the wind of a sudden storm thrust them backward, the door opened behind them, and they tumbled into the narrow space in front of the counters.

A knife flashed.

Amah pushed her way in front of An Bao and Mei Sha, shoving Prudence to one side, pulling from her waistband a blade nearly as large as the one Gao Fong held. She hissed, but this time it was with all the menace of a venomous snake. There was no mistaking her intent. She would die to save her precious charges, but only after plunging her knife into the heart of the man who crouched before her.

"Down on the floor," Gao Fong shouted at the spice dealer.

Older than Amah, thin to the point of emaciation, the man collapsed out of sight behind his counter.

It was a standoff.

CHAPTER 31

Liang Hu recognized Ye Da and Yan He for the professionals they were. He needed men who did not lose their composure when everything went haywire, who could take a life without a second thought, who were not addicted to opium, and who prided themselves on mastery of traditional Chinese martial arts. Disciplined soldiers whose ambition did not extend to deposing the man who had recruited them. He'd been aware of their presence in Chinatown since shortly after their arrival, but none of his informers had been able to learn why they had come and who had sent them. Then Lord Peng was knifed at the Metropolitan Museum. Liang assumed one or the other of the newcomers had done it and that they had retreated to the rooming house on Mott Street to await a safe extraction.

Then had come the nighttime attack on Johnny Peng, the infiltration of Wei Fu Jian's garden, and the attempted killing of one of his guests. Liang no longer believed either Ye Da or Yan He could be credited with those failures; professionals rarely allowed poor planning or carelessness to defeat them. He suspected before almost anyone else that an amateur had taken out Lord Peng, a rogue murderer consumed by rage and the need for vengeance. A bungler, to judge by his results so far, a dabbler in violence whose efforts ranged from inept to occasionally gifted with a stroke of genius and unbelievable luck. The use of the tunnels to penetrate Wei's garden had cost a guard's life and come uncomfortably close to dispatching a young woman.

Liang's informer inside Wei's organization had confirmed what everyone in Chinatown suspected—the Peng family had taken refuge in the brick building on Pell Street that housed Wei's Chinese Imports and Antiquities. Interesting information at the time, but of much greater import now that Liang was to marry the elder daughter. The informer said she was a beauty and most importantly, possessed of the three-inch golden lotus feet that would contribute significantly to her husband's prestige. The younger girl, the one who had stymied a murderer by throwing her coat over his head, was nearly valueless on the marriage market; her feet had not been bound. She was courageous, daring, adventuresome, and utterly unafraid. Qualities no husband wanted in a wife.

Liang would not insult Ye Da and Yan He by demanding that they tell him the name of the individual who had hired them and the identity of the person they had been sent to New York City to eliminate. Professionals did not disclose problematic information, and nothing could be more damning than revealing the details of a contracted execution. He hired them at a decent salary—with the promise of increases should they prove worthy—then sent them out to mingle with some of the other *boo how doy* while he conferred with his inner circle of counselors. What had begun as a small gang of streetwise minor criminals was rapidly evolving into a tong that would have done justice to the San Francisco models.

Ye Da and Yan He congratulated themselves as they moved among the other soldiers whiling away time on the sidewalk outside the storefront that was serving as headquarters and gathering place. They smoked and threw dice, eyes darting in every direction, alert to sounds, shapes, movement. Liang would order the door opened when he was ready, but not until he had finished whatever discussions he was having and dispensed the day's orders. There was talk of acquiring a larger building, especially now that Liang was joining forces with Wei Fu Jian, but nothing official had been announced.

Doyers Street was remarkably empty for what should have been a busy time of day. Sometimes, when Liang's men gathered outside the storefront, cautious shoppers turned and made their way back to Pell and Mott Streets.

Ye Da saw what looked like an old woman and two young men walking slowly down the street from around the bend. Behind them suddenly appeared the American woman who had moved into the Chinatown Congregational Mission Church with her pastor husband and his deacon. She had a shawl pulled over her head and seemed intent on following without being recognized. He motioned to Yan He, whispered in his ear. The pastor had shown up at the police station and witnessed their interrogation. Not something most missionaries did.

They moved away from the loose knot of Liang's men and walked out into the street for an unobstructed view of the sidewalk. Another figure had emerged from behind the bend, a man who was keeping his distance from the American woman but was so focused on her and the three people she was following that an intensity of purpose hung over him like the vibration of a temple bell.

Liang stepped out of the doorway, inviting the *boo how doy* inside where tea was steeping and small tables had been set up for *xiangqi*, mahjong, and Liar's Dice. He was in a generous, expansive mood, looking forward to a few days of celebration. Two goals accomplished now. The street gang had taken on the power and dignity of a tong, and he'd been offered a woman worthy of his ambitions.

The newest members of the tong caught his eye when they heard the door open, then immediately turned back to watching something on the street. In the direction of the bend. Where

Liang always stationed a lookout so no one could approach around that turn without being seen.

It happened so quickly that it might have been a flickering scene from a magic lantern show. One moment the group of three and the American woman in black were standing in front of a spice shop, the next instant they were gone. Liang blinked and looked again. He'd taken his eye off them just long enough to frown at Ye Da and Yan He, about to call out to them to join the rest of the *boo how doy*.

"The bone scraper from Sang Chao's Funeral Home," Yan He said, winding his queue tightly beneath his cap, tapping lightly on the two leather pouches that held his knife and hatchet. He wouldn't engage without Liang's permission now that he'd pledged loyalty to the tong's leader, but he was readying himself.

"He came up behind them," Ye Da explained. "Pushed the tall woman and the other three through the door of that shop and slammed it behind them."

"An old woman," Yan He said. "A younger man, maybe only a boy, and another who is dressed as a man, but isn't."

"Explain," Liang demanded.

"In the village where I come from, women with bound feet stuff rags into men's shoes so they can climb the mountainside and work the fields." Yan He held out a hand to demonstrate their gait. "They balance on their heels, like this." He took a few awkward steps. "People often think that women with bound feet are helpless, but that isn't true."

"There are no women with bound feet in Chinatown," Liang said. And then suddenly remembered that there were at least two. Lady Peng and her elder daughter. The one whose name was An Bao. His future bride.

"One of us will inform the pastor at the Congregational Mission Church of what has happened," Ye Da said.

"He's not a real minister," Yan He said. "He was at the police station with a waiter from the Golden Dragon Noodle Palace and the detective who had us arrested. He never took his eyes off us while we were being questioned."

"He speaks Chinese?" Liang asked.

"I don't think so, but he has a look about him of someone who recognizes a lie even though he doesn't understand what is being said. He's a policeman of some sort."

"Wei Fu Jian provided him with the storefront mission," Liang said.

"Then he also hired him to find Lord Peng's killer," Ye Da said. "We were his first targets, but he knows by now that the dead man met his fate at other hands."

"Go," Liang urged. "Find this minister in disguise and also inform Wei Fu Jian of what's happened."

Ye Da took off at a run.

To the man who poked his head out the door to see what was keeping him, Liang Hu gave rapid instructions.

"Come with me," he said to Yan He. "I trust your knife is sharp and your hatchet ready to be thrown?"

"I never miss," Yan He said.

"Chu Hua was your sister," Prudence said, edging to one side of where Mei Sha and An Bao stood behind their amah.

"She never betrayed him."

The knife with which Gao Fong was threatening them was wider and longer than the weapon Amah was using to hold him off. Now he pulled another knife from his belt, thinner, both edges of the blade honed to slice flesh.

The old lady continued her strange hissing, crouched like a wrestler, shifting her weight from one foot to the other.

It would all be over in a few seconds, Prudence thought, once Gao Fong made his move. Brave though she was, Amah wouldn't stand a chance against him. Mei Sha and An Bao would fall to the floor, their throats slit, crimson blood spewing down the front of their bodies as they twitched into death. Then it would be her turn.

"Lord Peng is dead," she said. "He's paid the price for what he ordered be done. Lady Peng's children are innocent. You have no quarrel with them." If she could stall him, distract him, there might be a way to reach the derringer strapped to her ankle. In close quarters the tiny gun could be as deadly as the larger guns carried by men.

"I remember Chu Hua," An Bao said, her voice pitched low. Sympathetic. Soothing. "I was just a child, but she was always kind to me. A second mother. She held me in her arms when my feet were first bound and I cried with the pain of it. If she had been allowed to birth her child, he would have been my half brother."

"He forced my parents to swallow opium," Gao Fong said. "They were old and defenseless against him. Filial piety demands that a son avenge the killing of his father. I am fulfilling my duty and upholding his honor."

"Then it's over," Prudence said. "The debt is paid. If you take the lives of the guiltless, you become the man who wronged you. Your filial piety turns into cruel murder for which you will never be forgiven, not in this life or the next."

"My esteemed parents, my sister, the child she carried, and the man I would have been," Gao Fong said. "Lord Peng must answer for all of these. He destroyed the line that would have honored my family's ancestors. His line, too, must end."

The old man who had crouched behind his spice counter inched his head above its surface. One bony hand crept toward a collection of glass bottles filled with medicinal dried herbs, shriveled animal organs, and withered roots. Mei Sha shifted just enough to draw Gao Fong's attention away from that side of the store. Prudence shook her head quickly, as though to dash frightened tears from her eyes. She knew what the spice merchant was doing, but the knives holding them at bay would deliver mortal wounds if they tried to rush the bone scraper. She needed time, precious seconds to get to the weapon whose two bullets could bring him down.

The shop was dim, but it darkened even more as four of Liang's men crowded into the recessed doorway, blocking daylight from passing through the glass. Mei Sha reached for An Bao's hand as the sisters realized what was happening. Prudence tried to read Gao Fong's body language, half expecting him to fling himself past Amah's knife and onto the bodies of Lord Peng's daughters. Would he flail and stab without concern for his own life in order to take theirs as his last living act?

A man's voice rang out, speaking in Chinese.

"He's telling Gao Fong that no harm will come to him if he releases us," Mei Sha translated. "His grievance will be heard, and fair judgment rendered."

"Cover me," Prudence whispered, bending over as Mei Sha and An Bao huddled together, their padded trousers and jackets shielding her as she fumbled beneath her long skirt for the derringer strapped just above her ankle. She'd rushed out of the mission without her reticule, so instead of two small revolvers, she had only the one. An ivory-handled over-and-under. Two bullets she could fire at point-blank range. No second chance if either of them missed.

Geoffrey wasted no time asking for extraneous details or wondering why Ye Da, who had needed a translator at the police station, now spoke fluent English. He didn't ask the man if he was sure of his facts. A professional did not make mistakes.

He strapped his deadly accurate Colt into a concealed shoulder holster and shoved extra bullets into his pockets. An armed Josiah following on his heels, Geoffrey set off down Doyers Street at a run, stopping only when Yan He blocked his way.

"They're inside the spice shop," he said. "Gao Fong has two knives on them, but he wasn't counting on the amah." His English was as fluent and colloquial as Ye Da's.

"Another knife?"

"From the way she's crouched in front of him, she knows how to use it."

"I've come up against her before," Geoffrey said. "She's buying us time."

"They won't try to break in until Liang Hu gives the order." Yan He gestured toward the men on the sidewalk and in the street. All of them had coiled their queues beneath their hats. It was what they did before a street brawl, second nature when confrontation threatened.

"Liang Hu is their leader." Alfred Hanrahan, breathing hard after pelting down Doyers Street in Geoffrey's wake, nodded in the direction of a handsome Chinese man who appeared to be in his early thirties. Taller than average, muscular across his shoulders, but lithe and panther graceful in his movements, he paced back and forth in front of the spice shop, as if contemplating how best to effect access without endangering the captives within.

There was no time to stand on ceremony.

"This is Geoffrey Hunter. He's been working Lord Peng's case for Wei Fu Jian," Hanrahan said, opting for speed rather than the customary drawn-out phrases of a proper introduction. "I'm Alfred Hanrahan, Sixth Precinct."

Liang nodded, as though nothing he'd heard was new to him.

"Does the shop connect to the underground tunnels?" Geoffrey asked.

Liang beckoned to one of his men, snapped questions at him in Chinese.

"All of the shops along Doyers were connected by the tunnels at one time. Some of them have been closed off. My tunnel man thinks the spice shop has an entrance from its basement that's still accessible."

"How do we get down there?"

"Follow me." Liang fired orders at the *boo how doy* he'd called his tunnel man. He nodded at Ye Da, summoned six others by name, and led the way toward the building that had become the tong's temporary headquarters. As he strode along, he hefted a loaded gun in one hand, a wickedly sharp throwing hatchet in the other. They passed through the doorway and crossed the large central room where Geoffrey saw gaming tables and steaming pots of tea. Liang paused just long enough for someone to unfasten the elaborate coat he wore, replacing it with a dark blue jacket that would make him nearly invisible in the dim tunnels.

They descended into the lower floor by a wooden staircase that shuddered under the weight of the swiftly moving men and made their way through piles of discarded furniture to a narrow door just wide enough for one man to pass through at a time. A *boo how doy* lifted the iron bar that secured it and lit two torches that hung in brackets on the damp tunnel walls. He said something Geoffrey did not understand, then strode forward over the rough ground, breaking into a trot when they joined the main tunnel paralleling the street above them. The only sounds were the crackling whoosh of the torches, the shuffle of feet on dirt, and the regular, controlled breathing of the men. Orders had been given. Each soldier knew his assigned task. It was, Geoffrey thought, as precise a maneuver as anything well-trained military could execute.

The silence that fell over them when they reached the smaller tunnel leading to the spice shop was leaden. The men moved as stealthily as though tracking game in a forest, not a brush of shoe against ground or a whispered question giving away their presence. If the setup here was like the one at the tong headquarters, they would pass into a basement storage room where stairs of who knew what strength or condition would lead up to the shop. Every man there wondered if the door would be barred, and what Liang would order them to do if it was.

It wasn't. The doorknob turned noiselessly in Liang's hand, the door itself so well-oiled that its hinges didn't make a sound as it swung open. The shopkeeper's lunch sat on a teakwood tray atop a crate, the smell of the food permeating the basement's dank air. Other crates were stacked against the walls, locked into grilled cages to safeguard them from predators.

Opium and morphine, Geoffrey guessed, imported Chinese medical nostrums worth their weight in gold. The basement was immaculately clean and neat, swept free of dust and debris, lit by a lantern hanging above the healer's meal. Someone had used the tunnels to deliver his food. A woman probably, because it wasn't considered safe for a female to be on the streets alone. That explained the unlocked door. An hour earlier, and they might have found it securely closed against them.

They heard nothing above them. Not a sound.

CHAPTER 32

Nothing was going as he'd planned.

This morning, when he'd hidden himself across the street from Wei's Chinese Imports and Antiquities, Gao Fong had resolved to end it all before another day had passed. The longer he failed to achieve what he had promised the shade of his dead father, the stronger grew the security around Lady Peng and her children.

Last night, unable to sleep, he'd tossed and turned until his eyes burned. He'd almost given up when he suddenly realized that Sang Chao had unknowingly provided him with the perfect excuse to request a meeting with Lord Peng's widow. What grieving relative didn't want to be reassured that a beloved deceased had been accorded all the gentle ministrations a dedicated funeral staff could provide? In Lord Peng's case, that included the washing and stitching up of the knife wounds that had taken his life.

The diplomat, on orders from the embassy in Washington, relayed by the consul, had been buried without fanfare, without a parade, without the mountains of flowers that would have decorated the carriages carrying him and his family to his final resting place. For a man of his rank, it had been a shockingly simple burial. Incense and joss paper had been ceremonially burned, but the only witnesses to the burial had been Sang Chao's staff. A sudden illness had prevented the consul from attending.

Gao Fong wasn't unknown to the guards. He would remind them that he and Sang Chao had been welcomed into the benevolent association, had been served tea while they played *xiangqi* and waited for their appointment with Wei Fu Jian. Regrettably, Lady Peng had been indisposed, so the consolation of assuring her that her late husband's funerary rites had been conducted with decorum had not been possible. He had returned to assure the lady that all was well and to answer any questions she might have.

The plan had been foolproof.

Then the two daughters and their nurse had stepped out onto the sidewalk, disguised as workingmen. But he recognized the younger one right away. Hadn't he seen her face clearly at the mission? Hadn't he spoken directly to her? He didn't stop to think when they set off toward Mott Street. He'd followed behind, never showing himself until he'd rushed forward, pushed and shoved them into the spice shop, and drawn his knife.

Now he was trapped. He would kill the female children of the man who had stolen so much from him, stab the amah and the American woman, too, if they got in his way. But the son, the precious son, the Peng heir, had escaped him.

He howled, a long doleful wail of anguish. Raised both his arms. Gloried for a moment at the sight of the sharpened blades. Grunted at the amah to stand aside. Readied himself to fulfill his filial duty.

The stairs leading from the spice shop's basement to the street level were old but well maintained. The first creak coincided with Gao Fong's howl of desolate frustration. He didn't hear the telltale noise of footsteps, but Prudence did.

She inched An Bao and Mei Sha to one side and stepped forward, standing between the counter and Amah, bending quickly to wrestle again with the derringer that seemed stuck in its ankle holster. A wave of pain shot through her sore shoulder and hurtled down to her fingers, numbing them. She felt the derringer loosen, but for a moment she dared not pull it from its holster, afraid she would drop it. Another stairstep creak and she rose from her crouched position with a womanly wail of despair, the gun hidden in the curved palm of her hand. Two bullets. A wound in arm or leg wouldn't stop Gao Fong, might only goad him on to greater slashing fury. She concentrated on willing away the throbbing ache in her shoulder. Each shot had to be fired with fatal aim.

Amah too had heard the faint groan of a dried-out wooden board. Years of listening in the night for the movements of a restless child had sharpened her hearing and fine-tuned her senses. She could distinguish between the rustle of a sheet and the smoother glide of a blanket, the touch of bare feet on the floor, and the fall of a toy or small pillow. She recognized the footstep of a man and intuited what was happening. Hadn't Wei's supposedly safe garden been invaded through the network of tunnels running below Chinatown's streets?

She didn't dare take her eyes off Gao Fong, not even for the few seconds it would take to glance at Prudence in the hope of communicating her discovery. When she felt the American woman beside her crouch down, fumble at her ankle, then rise sobbing to her feet, she knew the other was aware that a rescue effort was only minutes away.

But would it be in time?

Much as he wanted to lead the file of men across the basement floor and up the staircase to where the women were being held, Geoffrey knew he shouldn't. He didn't speak Chinese, and in the crucial first few seconds through the door, whoever shouted commands at Gao Fong had to do so in his native tongue. He spoke excellent English, but in those moments of potential catastrophe, it might desert him. Might confuse him. Might spur him on to a frenzied, knife-wielding leap onto his victims.

Liang Hu took his place at the head of his men, handsome face taut with determination. Gun in one hand, throwing ax in the other, he nodded to the man immediately behind him to open the door. None of them knew whether it would take them into the storefront itself or a curtained-off storage area, but there wasn't time to examine the possibilities. They'd heard Gao Fong's cry and Prudence MacKenzie's odd, strangled gasping noises. Only Geoffrey realized that she'd sensed they were coming and had tried to cover whatever faint sounds they were making.

The door opened onto a storage room, but the curtain had been left half-drawn, and through the opening Liang Hu and then Geoffrey saw Amah crouched like a wrestler, hissing like a cobra, waving a knife before her. Prudence was so close to Amah's side their upper arms touched, and Geoffrey saw that she had somehow managed to retrieve the derringer he insisted she always wear strapped to her ankle. *Good girl,* he congratulated her wordlessly, and then realized that if she was forced to fire, it would be out of desperation because Gao Fong had moved to attack.

Mei Sha spotted them first. Survival instincts honed by her boarding school years, she kept her gaze resolutely forward, but nudged her sister. An Bao's eyes met Liang Hu's. In that eleventh hour moment she recognized the man she had never seen before, the unknown future husband she had been intent on getting at least a glimpse of before she was constrained to become his wife. He was young, he was handsome. He had come to rescue and claim her, wielding one of the traditional weapons of their culture. She wouldn't give away his presence but even as her eyes quickly turned away, she felt a surge of warm security. He would save her. He would save them all.

Amah sensed it before the others, the faint tremors of muscles bunching to move quickly, the indrawn breath that would be expelled as a bellow when Gao Fong sprang.

She didn't wait.

She aimed her knife for his stomach, but he batted it aside with ease. The blade sliced an arm, but not deeply enough to make him drop his weapon. He would have swept one of his knives across her throat, but a bullet from Prudence MacKenzie's derringer struck him in the upper chest. She'd aimed for the heart and missed it.

For the next few moments no one knew exactly what was happening in the small spice shop. Bodies thumped, blood spurted, women screamed. The old man behind the counter emerged brandishing the stone pestle he used to crush herbs into powder.

Prudence fired her second shot, but it went wild as Geoffrey pushed her to the floor and covered her body with his. Mei Sha picked up the knife Amah had dropped and assumed the wrestler's stance, arms outstretched to safeguard the nurse who had always protected her.

Gao Fong hadn't stood a chance against Liang Hu's men, but before he went down, he wounded the most vulnerable woman in the shop. An Bao. Blood streamed across her fingers from just below her elbow. She swayed, reached out. And was caught by Liang Hu. He tore the sleeve from her jacket, ripped it into bandage wide strips, and wrapped them around the wound. The blood flow stopped.

"Whose idea was this?" Geoffrey said as he sat up, Prudence in his arms, her hair tumbling out of its minister's wife bun. He looked around them at the *boo how doy* still hefting their knives and hatchets, the bled-out body of the man who had terrorized them, Mei Sha laughing hysterically, the shop owner no doubt wondering how long it would take him to set things to rights.

Geoffrey grinned, the way he always did when a case that could have ended badly instead finished well. "Whose idea was this?" he repeated.

No one answered.

For once, Prudence knew it hadn't been hers.

Lady Peng shared Lord Peng's story with Liang Hu.

"The bone scraper did what filial piety required," Liang said, looking around him discreetly. Wei Fu Jian's private apartments were luxuriously furnished. An Bao would expect no less, but his own living quarters were no match. Not yet. He made a mental note to hire the most expensive decorator in Chinatown to remedy the situation.

"He carried it too far," Prudence argued. "If I understand what you mean, it should have ended with the taking of Lord Peng's life. He was the one who gave the order that Chu Hua be made to swallow opium."

"It's complicated," Wei explained. "The concubine's parents and brother were not responsible for her crime, if crime she committed, yet the dishonor of one member reflects on everyone in the family. It isn't unknown for relatives of men who are guilty of treason to be executed or exiled. An offense against filial piety is one of the ten abominations, so Gao Fong was honor fated to avenge his father's death."

"He was haunted," Prudence said.

Lady Peng shrugged. "We are every one of us haunted by our pasts."

Of all the Peng women, she seemed the most inclined to cling to tradition when it suited her and flout it when she pleased. Yet she was also the most conventionally beautiful of the women, from her three-inch golden lotus feet to the perfectly styled gleaming black hair with not a single thread of white. Mei Sha would never be a beauty, would never put up with what the creation and preservation of feminine allure demanded. An Bao resembled her mother in everything but Lady Peng's steely determination. Gentleness showed on the daughter's face, strength on the mother's.

"Sang Chao will see to Gao Fong's burial," Johnny announced. It had been his duty to arrange for the disposal of the remains of the man who had killed his father out of a sense of filial piety. "In time, the bones will be sent back to China. We have seen to that, also." He had glided effortlessly into the position of second-in-command under Wei while maintaining silence on their relationship.

"Under his real name?" Mei Sha asked.

"No. That would tempt fate. His story will be allowed to recede into the darkness where it belongs. Our father's also," Johnny added.

"There is one more consideration," Lady Peng said. "A widow who remarries is scorned in China. Her destiny is to remain with her husband's family, to serve them all the days of her life. Such is not the case in western countries."

"Some of my boarding school friends had stepmothers and stepfathers," Mei Sha piped up. "One girl had had two stepfathers, each one with a better title and more fortune than his predecessor."

"Your mother and I intend to marry," Wei Fu Jian said. He bowed in Lady Peng's direction, then beamed a very western smile. "My elder brother could not bear that she might love me more than him. Like Gao Fong, I too was taken to a ship against my will and brought to America, with no hope of ever returning to her."

It was like one of the tragic love stories that had entertained the Chinese for hundreds of years, Prudence thought. Josiah had brought her a beautifully illustrated book found on one of his pushcart forays. One of them, *The Butterfly Lovers,* had nearly brought her to tears, until she decided that to fling your-self into your dead lover's grave only to emerge—with him—as a pair of butterflies, was taking things a bit too far.

"I hope you'll honor us with an invitation to the wedding," Geoffrey said. He turned to Liang Hu. "And to yours, also."

Prudence stared at him. Geoffrey had said more than once that he preferred to avoid sumptuous events like society wed-dings. But then she realized that both of these nuptials would be celebrated richly, but quietly. The Chinese consul had con-tinued to spread the fiction that Lady Peng and An Bao were hiding out in the Bahamas.

"Prudence?" Geoffrey asked. His black eyes sparkled with mischief.

"Yes, of course," she answered. What was the matter with him? Of course she'd attend Lady Peng's and An Bao's mar-riages. "I would be greatly honored to be included."

"That's not exactly what I was asking," he said. "But it will do for now."

EPILOGUE

"You could still attend the John Jacob Astor wedding in Philadelphia," Josiah said helpfully, making notes in the appointments book he kept with scrupulous accuracy.

Prudence had taken the engraved card from the parade of other invitations marching across her mantelpiece and brought it into the office because it required being out of town for at least two or three days. "Don't we have other cases waiting?" she asked hopefully. Once upon a time she'd enjoyed attending the occasional society function, but eagle-eyed matrons had lately begun to focus meaningful looks on her bare engagement ring finger and stare demandingly at Geoffrey. Who was never intimidated by anyone.

"There's no rush about any of them," Josiah declared. No dead bodies lying about on the floor, no missing debutantes, no pressing demands from Lady Rotherton across the Atlantic. Money was always being embezzled, spouses suspected of cheating, and potential partners needing to be investigated. The bread-and-butter work of any inquiry agency, but nothing to awaken the imagination and start the heart thudding.

"I suppose we could go. Geoffrey, what do you think?" Prudence asked not very enthusiastically. "I RSVP'd that we'd be attending, just in case."

"Is the Peng file closed?" he asked Josiah.

"Except for any final notes and follow-up." Pen poised in midair, Josiah prepared to take down his employer's dictation.

"I think it was one of the most unusual investigations we've done," Prudence said, glad to steer the conversation away from the Astor-Willing wedding and the private train the Astor family had arranged to run from New York City to Philadelphia for the convenience of their most important guests.

"Not all our clients intentionally disappear," Geoffrey agreed.

"Arrangements are being made for the younger daughter, Mei Sha, to work with a governess," Josiah said, referring to notes he'd already inscribed in the file. "A recent graduate of Smith College in Northampton, Massachusetts. Apparently, the college was established by a bequest from a woman who believed young women should have the opportunity to experience the same academic training as young men." He sniffed disapprovingly.

"It would be too dangerous for her to surface on a college campus," Prudence commented. "Reporters are always on the lookout for a good story, and what could be better than the discovery of a fugitive daughter of a murdered diplomat? I assume that's how the government would classify her."

"She'll have forged papers and a new name, as will all the Pengs. But it's best not to stir the waters," Geoffrey said. "I doubt we'll hear from any of them again."

"The weddings?" Prudence asked.

"Won't even make a ripple in Chinatown," Geoffrey predicted. "We'll receive very politely phrased announcements in the mail, with perhaps a personal note expressing regret but assuming we'll understand that the appearance at the nuptials of two of New York City's increasingly well-known inquiry agents would not have been well-advised."

"No communications from the Chinese government?" Prudence asked.

"Nothing," Josiah confirmed. "The empress is reported to have gone silent on the subject of one of her favorite former diplomats. Speculation is that he fell from favor but avoided disgrace by the expediency of being murdered while still abroad. One of our sources on the *Times* international desk passed along that nugget of information."

"One more thing," Prudence said. "Warren and Bettina Lowry sailed for Europe three days ago. He sent a brief note. No explanation other than Bettina's condition had deteriorated." She didn't offer to share the note.

"That's it then," Geoffrey said, signing off on the file's cover sheet.

He fingered the small square Tiffany box he'd been carrying around for too long. "What about the wedding in Philadelphia, Prudence?"

AUTHOR'S NOTE

One of the great pleasures of writing historical fiction is the author's commitment to recreate a past era through meticulous research. The present fades away and history comes alive through newspapers, letters, biographies, memoirs, and cold facts unearthed by academic historians. I've taken Prudence MacKenzie and Geoffrey Hunter from the ballrooms of Gilded Age high society to New York City's brothels and its most dangerous slums, to an island off the coast of Georgia, and to the burgeoning hydroelectric and tourist mecca of Niagara Falls. And I've gone along with them every step of the way.

When I set out to write the series, I had a list of social issues and historical events into which I wanted to plunge my protagonists. The setting for each book would become another character. It is my belief that almost no one lives a life uninfluenced by his environment, by the people with whom he comes in contact, and the global or local events that dictate what he can and cannot do. So it is in a novel. Characters are constrained by the world the author creates for them. Which brings Prudence and Geoffrey to New York City's Chinatown in early February 1891.

Why Chinatown? Because on May 6, 1882, President Chester A. Arthur signed into law the Chinese Exclusion Act, the only piece of federal legislation ever enacted that banned the whole of a specific national, racial, or ethnic population from entering the United States. For a period of ten years, the Act would exclude ordinary Chinese from the country where thousands of their countrymen had been recruited to work in the California goldfields and build the transcontinental railroad.

The Gold Rush was long played out, and the ceremonial Golden Spike of the nearly two-thousand-mile railroad line had been driven on May 10, 1869. Much of the hard, dangerous, dirty, ill-paying work of building the country was done. Chinese laborers were no longer needed. Chinese women had been barred from the United States by the Page Act of 1875. Now it was time to bar the gates to all Chinese and lock them out once and for all.

Many Chinese residents of the Pacific coast fled east to escape the virulent anti-Chinese sentiment that infected California politics. The 1890 census records slightly more than two thousand foreign-born Chinese in New York City, the vast majority of them squeezed into crowded quarters on Mott, Pell, and Doyers Streets—christened Chinatown by the press. For Prudence and Geoffrey, it was a world they had never visited, a culture of which they were ignorant. For the writer, it was the chance to step back with them in time to a period of openly voiced discrimination and fiercely scurrilous newspaper editorials and articles. To a world where daily battles had to be fought against rejection, bigotry, inequity, and outright racism. Life in the new country was far from easy for any of them.

Prudence and Geoffrey must solve a murder, but as with all their cases, they learn as much about themselves and the society in which they live as they do about the criminals they bring to justice.

ACKNOWLEDGMENTS

As always, sincere thanks to John Scognamiglio, who edits with a sure, deft touch. Never too much, never too little.

And to Jessica Faust and BookEnds Literary Agency, where writers find a home and a warm welcome whenever they need it.

And to Pearl Saban, who checks every fact and every comma.

And to my husband, who has to live with a writer during all the throes of creation.